White City Blue

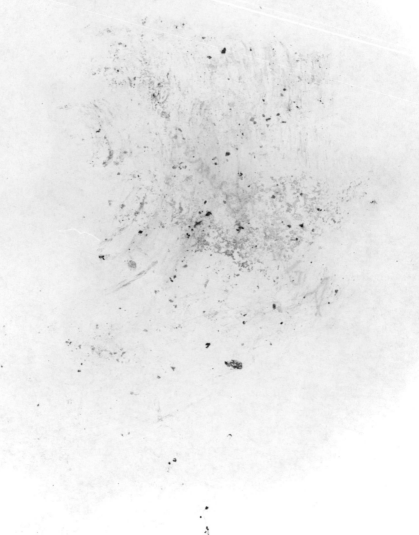

CHAPTER 1

FLAKES, MINCERS AND VRONKY TREE

The one and only thing you could have predicted about my meeting the woman who changed my life was that it would happen while I was trying to sell her something. It's how I get to know all my women. It's one of the many perks of the job.

It must have been all of six months ago now, yet somehow I remember it well. Two beds, en suite bathroom to second bed, small roof terrace, gch, kitchen/diner, nr all amenities of King Street, Hammersmith. It was badly overpriced, a fleece job. Yet she'd have gone for it, if I hadn't stopped her. She'd have signed the papers just like that.

Selling is what I do for a living. I unload houses, bijou apartments, charming maisonettes, large garden flats in need of some redecoration. In short, and truth to tell, I'm an estate agent.

It wasn't a great ambition of mine to be an agent. I say that not by way of apology – I don't feel ashamed of what I do. It isn't all inbred Ruperts

1

and pearl-eyed Amandas with Alice bands. In fact, I have a degree in Politics and Philosophy from the University of West Middlesex, or if you prefer its original nomenclature – my friend Nodge always *insists* on it – Staines Technical College.

You might well ask what an estate agent was doing at university. It's not as if they do courses in it. 'Meaning and Semantics in Finagling, Advanced Huckstering and Partial Reality – An Introductory Module'. No. You can't *learn* what I know. It's more in the nature of an art. Like doing a symphony or something.

Anyway. I was never much committed to studying. I've never really committed myself to anything, I suppose. I do what I can get away with for as long as I can get away with it. No. I expect I went to university for all the conventional reasons. A wish to put off work for three more years after school – and I'd heard that this course, despite its fancy title, was a soft option. The offer of a place had been made and, since I found my A-levels simple (I'm smart, certainly smart enough to conceal the fact that I'm smart), I assumed a degree would be more of the same process of textbook upchuck and good exam technique. Also, my girlfriend at the time lived close by and we were going to be together for ever. Also, I thought if I had a degree, I wouldn't feel so much that I was an ignorant nobody from Shepherd's Bush. And also, I thought it would help get me a decent job.

Some of the more common illusions, then, of

childhood. Me and my girlfriend split up and I was left on a diet of hand-gallops for the next six months. The degree wasn't nearly as easy as I thought it was going to be – on quite a few occasions my head hurt from so much *thinking*. It's a funny business thinking, I can tell you. All those invisible clouds floating above your head. All that stuff to think *about*.

I still felt like an ignorant nobody from Shepherd's Bush, but now I felt like one with pretensions. A degree from Staines Tech – especially a 2:2 – doesn't exactly buy you a ticket into any of the professions, and what's more it directly excludes you from many of the skilled and semi-skilled manual trades. Bricklayers, plumbers, electricians and so forth can *smell* education like so much gone-off aftershave. And they hate it. (Unless it's for their children. It's great for children, *essenshul*. They just hate it in adults.)

So I spent six months after university unemployed, getting less and less capable of supporting myself both materially and psychologically, until a distant uncle of mine told me how a friend of his was looking for someone to help out in a local estate agent.

Farley, Ratchett & Gwynne were a small agency with big ambitions. They were prepared to cut corners in order to get commissions and so was I. This was the mid- to late 1980s and the property market was in the last days of going ballistic. I didn't have anything better to do, so I thought

I'd give it a go. Since then I haven't looked back. I can't get *outside* of it enough to look back. It's a habit I've fallen into. I know now that life is habit, more or less. You do something, then you do it again, then again, and before you know it, that's what you are, and that's who you are, and you can't imagine being anything or anyone else.

Habit, or choice, or something in between, it's been good to me, the property business. Although sometimes it seems a little – well, empty. Unsatisfying.

From one perspective, I suppose there's something obscene about it. Crawling around on the inside of other people's lives. Showing off their personal, interior space like it was watches on a stall in Oxford Street, flogging off their walls, their air, their sense of decoration. It's like you're an intruder all the time, never in your own place. You're always the misfit, although you have to come across as the opposite – confident, unflinching, positive. But it pays well. I've done all right. Compared with Nodge anyway.

Not that it's a competition. How could it be, when it's all a matter of habit, habit and luck? Your life. The way things turn out.

Yet at the same time, there's a part of me for which it seems to make a kind of sense. I have come to see that now that I am thirty, now that I have ended up so firmly, and confirmed and completely, as an estate agent, a seller of space, of emptiness, of reinvention. Sometimes perhaps there *is* a hidden

4

pattern to these things, as Veronica always claims. Like Nodge ending up as a taxi driver when what he wanted to do all through school was travel the world, and like Tony ending up a hairdresser when his chief interest in life is examining himself in mirrors, and Colin spending his life in front of a computer screen interacting with machinery, the non-living.

Me, I wanted another, bigger, wider, shinier life. That's probably the deeper reason – if such things exist – why I went to university. Like I could give a shit for Politics or Philosophy. No. A bigger, shinier life. It's almost certainly why I ended up an estate agent – all those windows into other people's worlds, that limitless menu of apparent possibilities, day after day after day. It's research – research for passing myself off as somebody else, and then, eventually, becoming them. Just by habit.

Something else, too. I've always wanted to be liked. Everyone does, I suppose. I'm just prepared to admit it. It's kind of more of a naked need than a desire with me. I hate it if someone doesn't like me. And so a job which seemed to turn so much on making people like you, on making them trust you, appealed to me. And you don't have all the effort afterwards of maintaining a friendship. If you sell their flat at a good price, or find them a nice one, they love you. I get kissed, hugged, praised, thanked. It's terrific for self-esteem. Then it's goodbye, and on to the next person to woo.

5

After a while, of course – the 1980s being the 1980s – I managed to make enough money for some kind of new, fresh version of my Shepherd's Bush self. Like the Bush itself, I was tarted up, I was an up-and-coming area. But it became apparent to me that it wasn't enough. The cash was good – you could get the suits, the cars, the gear, the little mews house in W6, well on the ladder to W11 and then, finally, W8. But they still always found me out somehow, those people I wanted to be, with their secret codes, and pampered voices and hidden assumptions, and knowledge of wine and opera, and the people they knew. It became clear to me that if I really wanted to get out of Shepherd's Bush, I needed more than a big bank balance. After all, now the 1990s have come and nearly gone, along with my twenties, I needed someone to teach me escapology, fast. And I needed a symbol to show that I wasn't who people kept insisting I was.

I didn't know when I first saw Veronica that she was my ticket out of there. That is to say, that I was going to fall in love with her. At first I thought she was just another mark, another sucker punter.

We'd arranged to meet at the flat, which was in a large mansion block in West Kensington – exorbitant service charges and a truly old-style rapacious freeholder I had to keep off the agenda somehow. I was all Prada'd up on my last month's commission, plus a full-on tan that I'd got from two weeks in Koh Samui, and I had the Beemer outside. I could actually feel the money on me like the touch of some strange, fragrant oil. I felt like I could get exactly what I wanted, what money demanded. Because money isn't paper and metal and plastic and bank statements. It's a feeling, like everything else.

The buzzer buzzed and I let her into the flat, which was small and grubby and badly overpriced. This was not something only I could see; I knew she would see it too. David Blunkett would be able to see it, on a dark night. That's the point. She's not meant to buy *this* one – this is part of the psychological softening up that one has to undergo, as a punter. It's about lowering expectations. So that when we finally show anything half or even quarter decent, it'll look like the bargain of a lifetime. On such matters as the psychology of need and diminishment of self, we could advise Mossad.

She was class, I could see that from the moment she walked in the room. Manolo Blahnik shoes, a little black and white Bardot dress which I would guess was Agnès B, short-cut Peter Pan hair, shocking red. Five five, slightly shorter than me, not bad-looking but more Zoe Ball than Eva Herzigova. A kind of stretched face, as if the bones were trying to get out, with soft cottony skin. I liked her nose particularly, kind of fleshy, as if God had thrown a lump of dough at the centre of her face instead of designing one just for a bit of a giggle, or perhaps because he was bored. A

7

fat nose then, but cute. The eyes were slightly mismatched – one larger than the other – but they had those lazy, heavy eyelids that always hinted at a powerful libido. Very slim too, with long, terrific legs. Flat-chested, but I'm very liberated about such matters. Looked her age, but not older than. She was certainly in her late twenties, possibly early thirties.

Posh, but not too much so – maybe two rungs above me, but not three. Three is too many to jump. I'm realistic about these things. I'm an estate agent – you learn to be realistic. You learn the value of things, you learn about people with an inflated idea of themselves. They come in the office every day, flakes we call them, or mincers, asking to look at places they can't afford, salivating over fixtures and fittings that cost more than their entire credit rating, drooling at the prospect of something somewhere in the future that will make them feel like they're in a television ad or a copy of *Vogue Decor*. It's not realistic. There's a ceiling.

Now Veronica was right there, at the ceiling. Touchable if you balanced on tiptoe. She spoke well, but not cut-glass or anything. You definitely can't jump too far in terms of class. You get young and old together, black and white, ugly and handsome, rich and poor. But it's still practically unheard of, in England, for the classes to cross the great divide – at least in my experience. Me and Veronica were definitely pushing the limits, but it was just about on the cards.

So. She was attractive, not beautiful. On the turn, a bit of a retread, probably just broken up a long-term relationship and getting very slightly worried about her prospects. I checked her watch: Raymond Weil, mid-range, too new to be inherited.

From the flat she was looking at, I could infer that she was well heeled, but not stinking rich. I guessed she was educated from the book she was carrying with her when she came in – something by Virginia Woolf. I could also tell from the fact that it was dog-eared in three places in the first ten pages that she was reading it out of a sense of duty rather than enjoyment, which was fine with me. That meant she was a woman who understood that appearances matter.

I did the obvious – asked whether it was for her and her boyfriend (no, they'd just split up), whether she'd be living alone (yes, but no archness in the reply, no flirt). She told me her name was Vronky, which I thought I had misheard, until she explained it was short for Veronica, Veronica Tree.

We're distantly related to the Beerbohm Trees, don't you know? she murmured, saying the last three words mock-posh, ultra-posh, as if it was a joke, but underneath I could tell she was proud of it. And although I didn't have the faintest idea who the Bare Bumtrees were, I was impressed.

She hummed and hawed her way round the flat, and I could tell she wasn't keen, which established

9

a ground-floor intelligence. But then, Vinnie Jones with a head injury . . .

I told her what she already knew, that she didn't want this flat, that we get a lot better than this for the same price, that the freeholder was an old villain and that she shouldn't touch it with a bargepole. Again, part of the softening-up process. Get them to trust you. Get them to like you. If they're a woman, get them into bed if possible, but only *after* you've closed the deal. I'm a closer, me. I always close.

She seemed grateful, but duly surprised, that I should have filled her in on the true status of the drum. She even flicked her eyebrows a bit, flared that tubby nose and wondered why I'd been so honest, to which I said, of course, that she was too classy for a place like this and that, anyway, I liked her. Then I looked very slowly at my Rolex, so that she could see I was money, and I said I had to be somewhere now and would she like a lift?

She said yes, and so she got a look at the Beemer, which was also important. I was on form that day, made her laugh once or twice about Dirty Bob, who ran the block that I so astutely turned her away from – how he used to regularly come in to break the main services so that he could charge the lease-holders to get them repaired. I didn't mention, of course, that Dirty Bob was one of our very best customers and that if my boss knew that I was disrespecting him, I would get the tin-tack there and then.

She hesitated when I stopped to let her off at Kensington High Street, as if waiting for something, but it was too soon to make a play. I told her I'd call her if anything more suitable came on. You have to take it slow, selling flats, selling yourself. Above all, don't let them see need. Buyers and sellers both understand this, but for sellers it's more of a live issue.

There was one more softener – a slightly better, but still pretty dreadful drum around the back of Olympia that I again apologized for, told her my boss had insisted on it. Again, there was never any intention of selling it. It was just the stage for the play. *Shitheaps first*. As the F, R&G motto goes.

This was the following Thursday, five days after the first meeting, just enough to make her feel that finding a flat wasn't going to be easy, not so long as to make her think I wasn't trying. I could tell that she trusted me now, even liked me. And I felt I had her number too – a television researcher; on the cusp of becoming an assistant producer, but who wanted to be a director. But who never would be. Salary, about 25–30K, but trust fund there somewhere. One dead grandmother, another on hold. Five to ten years before maturity, i.e. demise of said granny. All in all, a good prospect for, minimum, a bunk-up, maximum a short 'relationship', i.e. one to five bunk-ups. (More than five confers girlfriend status. I try to make a point of stopping at four.)

Whatever. She was a stone-cold cert for shifting a flat on to, anyway. So there we were in the

Olympia flat. It smelt bad, the paintwork was terrible, but it had one or two features that put it above the first place. It wasn't in a basement and apart from the mucus-green carpet and 1970s Habitat lampshades, there was quite a good feel to it – high ceilings, big windows. Again it was badly overpriced; I knew Veronica wasn't going to go for it. What she *was* going to go for was the place behind Bush Green I had lined up. Dirty Bob was also the freeholder, through one of his anonymous holding companies, but it was probably best not to mention that.

This one in Bush Green was a sellable flat. Not a bargain – there's no such thing, unless you're on the inside track, like me, or a cash buyer – not a palace, but sellable, a quarter to a half decent. Still had a list of faults as long as Tony's bazooka, but I guessed that Veronica wanted to move fast – on all fronts – trusted me, and was prepared to take my word on it. As I chatted to her, I realized with a certain amount of surprise that I actually *did* like her – not only her looks, but the way she kept herself apart from herself. There was – how can I put this? – a *decent gap* between when she thought and when she spoke, there was *consideration*. It was a mark of self-possession, something I find greatly attractive for some reason. Perhaps because it's the quality I've always lacked. Events sweep me up, clean my clock, leave me gasping.

Anyway, I was determined not to let it get in the way of making the sale. We chatted this way and that, flirting a little now, laughing even. I prefer woman buyers – they're more romantic in their approach, which makes them an easier mark, and they don't do pointless things like knock on partition walls and lift up the carpets to look at the floorboards.

I'd done my bit to create a sense of urgency – explained that there was very little on the market, that most of the decent stuff was going to cash buyers very quickly. I agreed with whatever she said – you always agree with a purchaser, however dumb, and Veronica, it was beginning to emerge, wasn't even remotely dumb. Then I made my play.

Vronky, I can see this isn't your cup of tea. And to be honest with you, I think you probably can do better. But it's a tough market at the moment. You're going to have to be patient. I mean, we occasionally get . . .

I stopped in my tracks for a moment, held the position, as if some Jove-like thought had just penetrated my bonce.

Wait a minute. Something's just occurred to me. Let me try something. It's a long shot, but I suppose there's no harm. Let me just call the office.

I took out my mobile, my six-gun, my Bowie knife, my mojo, and dialled. My home answering machine did its thing: *Hi, this is Frankie. You know what to do, so do it and fuck off.*

Giles? Hi, it's Frankie Blue. Yes. No, I'm down at Olympia now with Ms Tree. Is Rupert there? He is? OK, I'll hold.

13

I turned to Veronica, who was caught up in the drama now. Stories. It's how you capture people. I knew that she was hooked, that I had mastered her. It gave me a hard-on right there and then. I hoped she wouldn't look at my groin. Unlike Tony's, my knob isn't up to much, so it was unlikely that she would notice. I gave a little shimmy anyway, to rearrange things down there. Then I gave her my best encouraging smile, and she smiled right back. Her teeth were a little bit crooked at the front, so I marked her down one tenth of a point.

Rupert, hi. I presume that little maisonette behind Bush Green has gone by now? Uh-huh. Uh-huh. Oh. That's a bit of luck. Who's got the keys? Good. No. Pretend they're lost. Just hold them off. I'll drop by in . . . hold on just a minute –

I turned to Veronica and held my palm over the mouthpiece of the mobile, which was still dutifully recording each precise syllable of bull-shit.

Listen, Vronky. We might have struck it lucky here. There's this property that came on just this morning, that we got as part of a multiples deal. Farquarsons, and Braxton-Halliday are marketing it too. The vendors are desperate to sell, but I know that Farquarsons had a cash buyer lined up. They've rung twice for the keys. There's just a chance that we may be able to beat them to it. But I think we'd have to go over there right now.

Veronica shook her head, bit her lip, wrung her hands a little.

14

I – I can't. I've got to be back at work in half an hour.

I let that sit there for a few long seconds. Then I uncovered the mobile again.

*Rupert, hold on a minute. No, please. Listen, I'll be right with you. No. **Don't** let them have them.*

I pointed to the phone in the flat. I said in a voice that made it clear there was no room for dissent – no, let me put it plainly, I *ordered* her. It was fucking beautiful.

Give your office a ring. Say that you've got a headache.

She considered for a moment, for a mere moment. Then she gave one firm nod. I gave her a full closer's smile, radiant like the sun, and went back to the mobile.

We'll drop round and pick up the keys in a minute. Don't let them out of your sight. Excellent. Thanks, Rupe. You're a mensch.

I laughed into the phone, a dirty kind of laugh that when I am laughing spontaneously I do not possess. My answering machine emitted a high-pitched whine.

Noooo. It's not that at all. She's just a very nice young woman. Yes, that too, if you must know. Mmm-hmm. Yeah, well, believe it or not even I have a heart sometimes.

I punched the off button of the cellphone and returned it to my pocket, where it met the cluster of keys that would open the Bush Green maisonette. I would have to make a mock drop-off to the office

15

– perhaps keep Rupert and Giles up to speed, perhaps grab a coffee.

What was that about? said Veronica, a little bit coyly.

What?

That last bit. 'It's not that at all.'

Oh, that. That was just Rupert winding me up.

How?

Now you're going to embarrass me.

I don't mind.

Well, he said I must fancy you to go to this much effort.

She summoned a slight blush. A tiny droop in those heavy, heavy lids. Good. Some innocence left then, after all those lapsed love affairs, those tiffs, those misunderstandings and let-downs, those laddered tights and sad, wet handkerchiefs, those secret diaries and midnight chats with sympathetic girlfriends.

We took off together for the maisonette at Shepherd's Bush. I stopped off at the office to pretend to pick up the keys. Giles and I had a good laugh at the way it was going. God, the power and beauty of scamming, of scammery, of the big scamola. I drove her towards Shepherd's Bush Green, from the office in Holland Park Avenue. I scratched about for a little bit more intimacy. Now I decided to find if I was right about the television job. I covered my bets; she could also be in a small, quality PR company, or at a push junior rights manager for a book publisher. But I was still laying three to one on that it was television. A lot of the one- and two-bedders around here go to BBC staffers, because of the proximity.

So why are you looking in this area? Handy for work, is it?

Yes. That's right.

I thought as much. Don't tell me. You make fly-on-the-wall documentaries.

She laughed. A good laugh, low and disrespectful.

What?

Don't tell me. You've got a hidden camera in your brooch. You're doing something on estate agents.

Oh, I see. You think I work for the BBC.

I would guess a director, or perhaps an editor.

She gave a little private smile, then said, *I'm afraid you're way off the mark. Although I do work in a cutting room of sorts.*

I shrugged, turned into the street where the flat was.

Ah . . . here we are. It's a great patch this. Recession-proof area. Tennis club at the end of the road. I don't suppose you play?

Not really.

No. Pity. A sushi bar has just opened around the corner, by the way. Look, there's our board.

Sure enough, a weather-beaten, paint-flaked wooden board with *Farley, Ratchett & Gwynne* inscribed on it was swaying in the slight breeze. It looked like it had been up there for ages, but it couldn't have been up for more than two months.

You got that up pretty fast.

Hmmh?

If it only came on the market this morning.

It's a cutthroat business. And property, particularly one- and two-bedders, is very in demand around here, particularly if you work at the BBC.

But I just said, I don't.

Of course, that's right. Sorry. Aagh . . . look. A space. Hold on. What is it you do then? Watch this. I can get this baby into a vacuum.

I started to reverse. Let go of the rational mind, sense the space behind me. *The force is with me, Lord Kenobi. I must let go . . . be at one with the universe.*

I'm a pathologist.

I smacked into the beaten-up Escort that was behind. There was a faint tinkle of breaking glass.

Oh dear. That doesn't sound too healthy, said Veronica sweetly.

I was slightly panicking by now. There was an old man watching me from the pavement and I hate people watching me while I'm trying to park. It reminds me of the way teachers used to stand over you at school. It puts me right off my dinner. He was enjoying this, having nothing more urgent in his diary than further decay. I tried to make the gap again. The old man started to make gestures, to try and guide me in. It took me four more tries until I took the car in perfectly. I leapt out to examine the damage.

You want to be a bit more careful, said Grandad, and I forced my teeth to grin.

Faking grins is my stock in trade, but I find this particularly difficult because I hate old people. They remind me of death. I hate thinking about death, which is why Veronica gave me the willies somewhat when she mentioned her job. Assuming she wasn't winding me up. She was out of the car too now, clicking her tongue sympathetically.

It's just your taillight. You're covered by insurance presumably.

Let's not worry about it. You've got to get back to work, obviously.

My clients aren't going anywhere.

I laughed uneasily and started manoeuvring towards the front door: 1930s style, stained glass. I felt on the defensive somehow, partly because of smashing the light, partly because of Veronica's professed occupation. She'd been saving it up, hadn't she? No, it wasn't possible. I asked her, she answered my question. So easy to deny the amount of accident in the world.

This is a lovely feature, isn't it? Not many of these old doors left.

They're a nightmare to keep clean.

No, you're absolutely right, Vronky. Still, it's what's inside that counts.

I opened the door. There was a nasty smell inside, like someone hadn't flushed the toilet. Bad start. We walked up a short flight of stairs to the first floor. The flat was empty of furniture

19

and the carpets had been torn out, which gave it a decent feeling of space. There was plenty of light, and good high ceilings.

Nice feeling of space.

Difficult to heat.

You're absolutely right. It's good heating, though. Just installed.

I found myself momentarily confused as to why it was that we hadn't shifted it yet. Then, on the wall by the stairs leading up to the second floor, I noticed a thin snaking line crawling across the newly painted and plastered wall. I had been wondering why of all the walls in the flat this one looked immaculate. Then I recalled – one of Dirty Bob's old tricks. The flat had subsidence, and the hope was to price it low and force through a quick sale without a proper survey. I must have spent too long having this thought, because Veronica noticed where I was staring.

Those look a bit worrying.

I shouldn't bother about it. London's built on clay. If you want something that doesn't have a bit of movement, you're in the wrong city.

But –

We've had a few dry summers. It hasn't fallen down yet and it's a hundred years old.

All the usual smokescreen. It wasn't a healthy subject to stay on. I tried to get her up the stairs.

There's a lovely little shower room up here and a kind of box room which would do very well as a study, if you bring much work home with you . . .

I blinked. I was losing the plot fast. Furthermore, Veronica's dress was riding up her hips on the way up the stairs. They really were brilliant legs.

Sorry. Obviously you won't be . . .

That's all right. I do a lot of paperwork at home. Of course, none of the actual . . . you know. Cutting. That's all at the hospital.

She gave a slight smile. I got the idea that she was enjoying making me uncomfortable. She was arranged against the window now, staring out at the dismal terrace below. The top floor had a lower ceiling, but it still had a good feel. I suddenly sensed that she was keen on the flat. I felt I could hook her, if I wanted. But something held me back.

*What exactly is it . . . is it that you **do** then?*

Now she turned from the window and straightened up to me. She looked me right in the eyes, held my gaze, so that I had to turn away. There was something in that gaze, something that frightened me and excited me at the same time. I think it might have been – this sounds stupid, I know – I think it might have been *honesty*. Whatever it was, it put the wind up me.

I dissect people. I look inside them. To find damage, she said, as if she was making me some kind of a challenge. And I think she was, she was challenging me, for in the next instant she changed her tone, went all businesslike, and ran her finger along the ledge of the windowsill.

21

I like it. I think it has good feng shui. Do you believe in feng shui?

This is one of the wild cards about women, particularly when they're unaccompanied. They often claim to have vibrations about a place, which sometimes can be very frustrating, especially when everything else seems to be going well. On the other hand, these superstitions can be very handy, as on this occasion.

Now she looked at me again. This time, I held her gaze.

Absolutely, I said.

What do you think then? she said.

I answered right away.

I think you should pitch an offer. What have you got to lose? Not too low under the asking, maybe a few K short. It's a very good buy. But you'll have to move fast.

No, I mean about the feng shui.

Oh. The feng shui . . .

I pronounced it correctly: fang shway. I screwed up my face in the best Jackie Chan kung-fu wiseguy style.

The feng shui is good, I think. As I'm sure you know, every house has nine areas, each relating to a different aspect of life. I can feel that there's a lot of positive energy in all of these areas. Particularly relationships.

I say this with only the slightest hint of suggestiveness.

I would need to know a lot more about you to give a proper reading of whether this was the right place for you. Birth date, the state of your life and energy and so forth. But crudely, this place isn't too bad. I don't like the fact that this corridor leads straight from the front door to the back. And the fact that the toilet faces the front door is not good. That can lead wealth energy to drain. But in every other sense, I would say this place was pretty sound. Nothing that couldn't be fixed with a few strategically placed mirrors, plants. Or water elements, of course.

As you can see, I always do my homework. A working knowledge of the magical imaginations of women can be worth several K a year in commissions.

Then Veronica said, *Of course.*

She was clearly impressed. But she obviously wasn't a total flake, because then she said, *What about a survey?*

Fine. A survey's good. But don't forget, there's a cash buyer after this, and I can only pretend to have lost the keys so long. A lot of people don't bother nowadays, anyway.

She held my gaze a bit longer, then let it go, as if she had asked a question – a different question – and it had been answered. I seemed to feel some slight disappointment from her. She turned back again, as if wanting to make sure that she'd heard the answer correctly.

So you think I should go for it?

I don't know what did it. Perhaps because it was at that moment I noticed that there was a hole in the calf of her tights. This called forward an extraordinary emotion in me: both sympathy and a kind of animal, dirty-dog excitement. I almost wanted to kiss her there and then, but above and beyond this, I wanted to protect her. Which was ridiculous, as she seemed not at all in need of protecting from anyone, apart from, of course, me and all the people like me. Of which there are millions.

Just then I knew it was going to happen. My body, my tongue and the air in my throat betrayed me. Still, there was a long, long pause before I said, *I don't know.*

Honesty will often come as easily to me as lies – they don't cancel each other out, they're just different ways of expressing yourself and achieving your ends – but in this case, I felt that a kind of genuine struggle was taking place. I felt faintly surprised. I half-waited for some syrupy feeling of virtue to start working outwards, but I knew from experience that this only happened in old books, Dickens and all those cunts with whiskers.

I don't think so.

Veronica's eyes rounded slightly, but otherwise she gave no sign of surprise. She stood in front of me, quite still, other than a pointless opening and closing of the catch on her handbag. I could sense her looking at me, but I was looking past her and out of the window. In truth, I was feeling embarrassed at having told the truth. I remembered from my early experiments with it, how uncomfortable and unrewarding it could feel. A good lie – well

and imaginatively executed, undetected, effective –
is that much more satisfying. The truth is so *lazy*.

Why not?

Now I felt myself unfreeze a bit and focus
approximately on her face. I felt ridiculous, weak.
Yet it was as if some channel had opened up inside
me which I could not negotiate an exit from. There
was no proper way back to my starting position, so
I decided to continue.

*Well, Dirty Bob's the freeholder for one thing.
Also, it has subsidence. Those little baby cracks in
the stairwell have big brothers and sisters and uncles
and cousins just underneath.*

I paused, as if listening to myself. I was beginning
to enjoy the effect.

*There's a chance, actually, that it may not be
subsidence. Because the bloke next door has a sound
system that takes up most of a double bedroom. Tends
to vibrate the walls a bit. He's on holiday for a month.
He's quite a nice bloke, but a little stubborn, a little bit,
how should I say? What's the word? Psychopathic. Oh,
and there's dry rot starting in one corner of the roof.
Dirty Bob's leaving it to ripen for a while then you're
liable to quite a significant service charge. So, on the
whole then, I think it's probably not the best you could
do, given your resources, lifestyle parameters and other
such requirements.*

There was another long pause. Veronica tried to
tug at a few strands of her hair, but it was really
too short to get hold of. She was extraordinarily
thin, but not unattractively so somehow. I liked

25

thin women. Nothing against fatties, mind you. Tony loves 'em. Fair play for the chubby chasers. But I felt slightness, smallness made them more different from me. When you held them. I loved that difference.

I tried to work out whether her hair was dyed or not. There were no roots showing, but that wasn't proof of anything. Then, without the glimmer of a smile, but with a tiny drop in those heavy, sexy eyelids and a small series of understanding nods, she said, *The feng shui is good, though?*

I shook my head.

No. That's fucked too.

At this point she immediately let out a laugh, a high chuckle, or peal, quite different from the guttural, slightly saucy job she'd performed before. The stretched face stretched further, the fat little nose jiggled, the skin tone began to approach the chilli-pepper red of her hair. That nose just crucified me. I found myself laughing too, at first politely, then in gusts. We duetted; then it died down into a stillness. I could hear the Central Line train from the Shepherd's Bush underground rumbling. That was another thing, but still . . .

Would you like to have dinner with me? she said, just like that.

Where? I said, quite taken aback by the question.

Where? I don't know. Maybe the new sushi bar.

I shook my head again.

There's no sushi bar?

She laughed again, caught me up in it once more. Still laughing, I drove her back to her work. We went out for the first time that Friday night.

That was six months and two weeks ago. Of course, at that time I didn't have the faintest idea of what was going to happen. I often manage to blag women while showing them flats – it's something of the reflected glamour of the surroundings, something of the power it gives me, as if I actually owned all the places myself. But I did feel that she was special in some way. Not only in herself, but in her timing. Everything, and everyone, has a time; a person has to fit yours. So she was the right-enough woman, at the right-enough time. I vaguely sensed though never quite acknowledged then that I was getting weary of Colin, and Nodge, and Tony, and football, and the next kind of ethnic restaurant, and five-a-side, and pints and E and chop and drinking games and pulling and carrying on pretending that it was the best thing there was or could ever be, and that anything else was a lame compromise. I was weary of *myself*.

Not that it hadn't been great sometimes, and sometimes even now was. But more and more it felt like history that hadn't yet found its way into the past. Stuck right there in the present, gumming everything up. You could tell, because history is what our meetings – Colin, Tony, Nodge and me – are getting to be *about*. Not that great spontaneous rap, that impro, of irony

27

and sub-irony and sub-sub-irony, and dry wind-up and piss-take, that you can do when you've tapped the vein that runs between you, that can have you doubling up with laughter and the joy of having mates – the illicitness of it, the crudeness of it, the wonderful little-boy playfulness of it. No, not that, but, like I say, history, the immediate and distant past. What have you done? Where have you been? What have you seen? How was X when you saw her? How was that match you went to? Do you remember when? Too much of that now. Too much.

After all, I was thirty years old – and there was a sense of this life fraying at the edges, smelling just slightly of decay, on the turn. She seemed ideal to . . . renew my world, so to speak, or to help me remake it into something not necessarily better, but different. Something with its own special tortures and irritations and boredoms and ringing, mocking laughters.

I decided what I was going to do – to resolve the situation as it were – also, funnily enough, as a direct consequence of the showing of a property. A house in this case on the Shepherd's Bush/Hammersmith border. It was probably a month after meeting Veronica, three weeks since we started 'going out', i.e. shagging each other. Perhaps – as Vronky would doubtless have it – there was synchronicity going on. I have to admit it was weird. But coincidence can be like that sometimes.

The house was an end terrace on one of the streets near Brook Green. It was a nice little place actually, and no more ridiculously overpriced than any other property in that street. This time, the potential buyers had come to the office. They were ancient – in their sixties at least. One man, one woman, both of them well wrinkled up like a brace of Shar Pei. They drove behind me in the Beemer in some kind of joke crate – a Morris Minor, I think it was. I glanced up at the mirror and saw that one of them had their head back and was laughing fit to bust, while the other smiled and twinkled all over the place. That alone was unusual. Most of the ancients in my experience spent their time moaning and bitching at each other or sitting in dazed, indifferent silence.

When we got there, the Morris pulled up slowly behind me. Then the man got out, walked round the car and opened the door for the woman, standing politely to one side as she got out. That was sweet, I thought. You don't often see that nowadays. Oldies can be cute like that.

I took them inside and gave them the basic spiel – lots of light, blah, nice and convenient for shops, blah, plenty of space, blah, good decorative order, blah blah blah. They didn't seem to be listening, just very quietly walking around the house side by side, talking quietly to each other, one or the other chuckling gently from time to time. Their faces were unremarkable, though they both looked pretty fit I suppose, and lacked that faint accusatory air of pathos that so many nearlydeads had. The other odd thing was that they touched each other a lot – brushed against each other's clothes, touched each other's hands. It was sort of weird. I'd seen the same kind of thing at school in teenagers, but never among geris.

I looked at my notes. Harry Butson and Maud Louise Coldstream. Anything around 300K. So what was with the Morris? Were they flakes, mincers? Were they even married? No. I was sure, somehow, that they were serious punters. Although their clothes were old and worn, they seemed somehow dignified and self-contained. And some of the jewellery that old Maud was wearing, although not at all flashy, somehow smelt of green. I can't really explain it. When you're an agent, you just learn to tell these things.

Anyway, at one point I had to retreat upstairs for a pony in what I still often forgot to call a loo rather than a toilet, so I was gone for quite a long time, what with the Dhansak I'd had the previous night. When I came out something very weird was going on. I had to rub my eyes in order to get it straight.

They were in the master bedroom – good proportions, 18 x 14, new carpet, fitted wardrobes – and, get this, they were stretched out on the bed kissing each other, which in itself is disturbing, but in this case it was *with tongues*. It sounds repulsive, I know, but in actual fact it was strangely touching. These ugly, old withered things behaving like . . . ordinary people, like the unafflicted.

The man, who was lean and well spoken without seeming at all hoity-toity, noticed me come into the room. He smiled calmly in acknowledgement but didn't seem remotely embarrassed. The woman – I swear, when I think of it, she was pushing seventy – then got up and started bouncing up and down on the bed.

This should be able to take it, eh, Harry? she said, and winked at me.

Maud is insatiable, said Harry, and the woman gave a big throaty giggle, then let herself fall backwards on to the mattress again.

I actually felt myself blush, and Maud noticed and said kindly, *Don't worry about him, young man. He's always pulling someone's leg. Anyway, even if it were true, he's not up to it any more, poor old dog. I sometimes think I shall have to start looking elsewhere for my entertainment.*

With this she shot me a look of such naked sauciness that I blushed still deeper. This time it was Harry who was laughing.

They tottered up from the bed and Maud nearly seemed to fall. Harry immediately reached out for her and held her firmly by the arm until she'd straightened up again. The look of concern that suddenly replaced the look of merriment was . . . I don't know. Touching, I suppose.

They fidgeted around the house a bit more and then put an offer in, adding, however, that they wouldn't be able to take possession for three months because they were going on a camping tour in the Far East. I assumed this was a joke, but it emerged that they were perfectly serious. Harry had just cashed in some big pension scheme on turning sixty-five and they were going to blow it all on 'the pleasures of the Orient', as Maud put it, with a wink.

Somehow watching them put me in an altogether happier frame of mind than I had been in. When I thought of old people, I thought of my parents, or Diamond Tony's or Colin's, or Nodge's – all of them indifferent to, or even contemptuous of each other. Then it suddenly occurred to me, perhaps it was one of those Autumn Romances you read about in *Women's Journal* or whatever crap it was that my mum bought. Perhaps they'd got off with each other at the Darby and Joan club last week or something, and had had a bunk-up for the first time in thirty years.

So as they were heading back to the Morris, I just had to ask. I was shaking Harry's hand, firm and confident just like Uncle Billy taught me, and I said, *I hope you don't mind me asking, but have you two been together long?*

Harry smiled.

No, not really.

I nodded, thinking, *I knew it.*

Maud gave him a pinch on the shoulder.

Not unless you consider thirty-five years a long time. We don't, do we, Harry?

Seems like a bloody long time. But he laughed as he said it.

Then he did something extraordinary. He turned to me and put his arm round my shoulder. Not like he was a poof, but as if he had known me all my life or something. And oddly, it didn't feel bad, or embarrassing. It felt like . . . like I'd always wished my dad would have felt like when he was alive. Had he ever put his hand on my shoulder, that is. Which he hadn't.

Then Harry said, quite clearly, but under his breath, *A man should sign up, son, with the right woman. It's the best life has to give. Don't wait about like these silly sods nowadays. Get down to it.*

He squeezed my shoulder with his hand. It felt surprisingly strong.

Is there anyone special for you, son?

Well, maybe. There's someone I'm thinking of.

Is it serious?

It's a possibility, I suppose.

I was surprised to hear myself say this.

Well, don't muck about. That's the beginning and end of it.

And then he was off in that silly, frog-faced Morris. Yet for some reason, his words floated around my head, came back to me in my dreams. Thinking how nice it would be, to be like old Harry and Maud, about a hundred and fifty years hence.

CHAPTER 2

THE FRIENDS OF FRANK THE FIB

So now it's just another Tuesday night on the Goldhawk Road. I'm on my fifth bottle of Staropramen, trying to get well and truly binnered, but my mind feels absolutely unfogged. It's not a matter of wanting. I *need* to be drunk. Tonight I've got to tell them that I'm leaving them, that it's over, that it hasn't worked out, that I'm selling them down the river.

Diamond Tony, Nodge and Colin are all with me, inside the Bush Ranger, watching the Rangers game on the satellite screen. A hundred other faces are upturned also, mostly male. They have scorched faces from Spanish tans, greased French crops, white lager-foam moustaches, M A 1 nylon jackets. Stone-washed jeans, white Reeboks, gold earrings, fake Ralphs from the Bush Market. It's all sports casual, surf-wear and over-designed running shoes, Nike Air Maxes up against the Reebok DMX 2000 series. The whole place has an odour of Fosters Ice and Lynx Aftershave. I like it. It smells like home.

Of the four of us – I like to think – only Colin looks typical, a genuine pitch potato. It isn't just the clothes – the baggies, the Rangers/Wasps official sweatshirt, the little rash of old adolescent spots around the mouth, the beer-stained windcheater – but the expression on his face. Rapt, astonished, praying. Caring far too much, for someone thirty years old.

Colin, more than any of us, lives for this, for these moments, in a crowd in front of a green rectangle, destinies being juggled. I see his face shining with tension. Yet, for a moment, he looks five years old as Kevin Gallen strikes at an open goal and manages to send it elegantly dundering fifteen feet past the left-hand post. Colin's small face crumples in bitterness and betrayal, as if some personal unkindess has been deliberately done to him.

He still has QPR posters covering the walls of his bedroom from floor to ceiling, and goes to every match that he can, just as he has since he was fifteen years old. Although normally the quiet and affable one, when he's worked up his emotions get entirely out of control. Sometimes he cries, although he will always hide himself first. Colin has never quite managed to master the public indifference that the rest of us present as our emotional lives.

Right now he is nodding his head back and forth in a kind of fit of disappointment. On one level, Colin, I sometimes think, is a little backward – still living with his mother, never having any girlfriends.

But what emotions he does have he invests in the world he limits himself to – his horror videos, his computer, his friends, his football. I think for a moment he's going to cry right now, but to my relief he turns instead and rummages glumly in his packet of crisps. Walkers Double Crunch Chilli.

I can't get lost in the game. I can't care. I've been thinking about Veronica all day. No, I've been thinking about *myself* all day and wondering about the effect of what I am going to have to say to *them*. I feel I'm in a pocket of air, watching the whole heaving scene from within a bubble. I catch Tony's face in close-up, as it distorts in profile, rising to meet the screen.

Tony – Anthony Diamonte, otherwise known as Diamond Tony or DT – is laughing loudly. Tony always laughs loudest of the four of us, but this time his determination to compete with the rest of the heaving room has upped the volume. Tony always wants to win everything, even when there's no game being played. He's half out of his chair, giving the *wanker* sign to Gallen, who has fallen on his knees and is covering his eyes with his hands. The floodlights give Gallen four shadows. Tony's laughter, at this moment, is contemptuous, without humour.

In the reflected light of the screen, his cream-coloured Jil Sander rollneck looks the colour of a pistachio nut. He must be steaming hot in that thing, but he looks absolutely cool and undisturbed by the raging heat. The fact that he is *money* is apparent even in the smoky half-light. The Mulberry Black Cavalry Twill coat draped over his quarterback shoulders, the bespoke suit, the Patrick Cox shoes, the Oris Big Crown Commander watch. Even his face is money, that Eurotrash look, all olive skin and floppy black hair, big gleaming teeth in a perfect smile. You wouldn't think he was just a barber – sorry, *hairstylist* – from Shepherd's Bush; you would think he was a matador, or a glamorous extra in an Italian arthouse movie.

Women love Tony. They don't care it's all a fake – the tan, the style, the smile. He's handsome, I suppose. I have to admit that. However much I lie to others – and I do, I do – I try to be honest with myself. It's hard, though I don't know why.

Tony looks very sophisticated, even though he's just a yob, same as the rest of us. More of a yob, actually, because I'm not a yob at all, come to think of it, and neither is Nodge or Colin. Most soccer fans around here stopped being yobs years ago. They read Irvine Welsh and listen to Classic FM, then clock in for work at the print shop or the carpet warehouse. Nothing fits the world any more. Me with my degree, Tony with his thousand pound suits, Nodge and his unreadable books. A cab driver with his nose in Rohinton Mistry, for fuck's sake. It's all hybrid, atomized.

But Tony, for all his cash, is – and don't get me wrong, he's a mate, I love him – Tony is . . .

The word that springs to mind is *cruel*.

No, cruel isn't right. That implies someone who gets a pleasure out of hurting other people, and Tony isn't like that. He just doesn't *mind* hurting people, if they're in his way. It's nothing personal. He just thinks there are more important things than never hurting anyone's feelings. It's very un-English, I suppose. But then Tony isn't English. He's Sicilian, or at least his parents are. He hates to be reminded of this. Around his neck, the hand and the horns to ward of evil spirits. Solid gold.

Anyway, when you get to know him you realize that it's all an act and that in fact, underneath, he's all right. I suppose he must be, because otherwise he wouldn't be my mate.

And he is my mate, my best mate. He's a laugh. He makes things *happen*. He's a cyclone. And he's always been there. Not nearly as long as Colin, but as long as Nodge. Fifteen years now, it must be.

I turn to Nodge. The Staropramen is beginning to work now, pulling me apart from the crowd instead of drawing me in. Nodge has stuck out his lips in a sort of sour, lemony way, but otherwise has not moved an inch. He has this economy of movement. Never shifts if he doesn't have to. Like he was planted. Like he had a perpetual right to the exact space he has occupied and no one was going to say otherwise.

His face gives the same impression. Running to fat, doughy, all gathered together in the centre, slightly convex, like someone punched him in the face once and it collapsed inwards, leaving a big soft rim at the edges. It looks like it is protected by its perimeter, a buffer zone of pinkness and hair and chin. It's a face that is immovable, that will stand its ground. A stubborn face, not easily roused. Running low, half-way across it, like a large, sleeping caterpillar, is a Liam Gallagher unibrow, an unbroken line of thick hair above his eyes.

The expression is familiar, that of judgement and condemnation. It suggests that he will personally *never* forgive Gallen this transgression, that he's given him enough chances in the past. He takes football very personally, Nodge, almost morally. Like Gallen hasn't simply made a mistake but done something *bad*. Nevertheless, Nodge likes to pretend that it doesn't matter very much to him, that he's too grown up for that sort of thing. It's not as serious for him as Colin, but he cares, make no mistake.

He reaches down and hitches up his Next black canvas trousers an inch, a nervous habit that he developed from a lifetime of his mother turning up his trousers too long. Nodge always wears either black, grey or, for joyous occasions, chocolate brown. He thinks of himself as down to earth. It's all Timberland, Gap Essentials, Stone Island, CAT logger boots and puffa jackets with Nodge.

He utters two words, at a regular volume, punctuating each one with a pointed finger at the figure of a collapsed Gallen on the giant screen.

Not. Acceptable.

That's good. It could be Nodge's motto. He should have it carved above his door.

There's two minutes left to play and Rangers are 1–0 down. It's important, I suppose, that we win, or at least draw, and yet I find myself suddenly having a strange and disturbing thought: *why?* I've been having a lot of odd thoughts lately – perhaps it's an early mid-life crisis, though thirty is a bit young, I suppose. It's like my life doesn't fit any more.

Doesn't fit *what?* Maybe the drink is affecting me more than I think.

Yet, I mean, it's not as if any of the team come from Shepherd's Bush, the same as we do, or once did. The ground is there, true enough. But the players are mercenaries, soldiers of fortune. So why is it that our emotions are somehow knitted into these eleven flailing losers? And as I think of myself thinking the forbidden thought, I also begin to think – it *doesn't* matter. In fact, I couldn't really care less.

I go back to watching the football. Nigel Quashie lofts a hopeful ball into the box. Gallen picks it up, muffs it, but manages to fumble it back to Quashie again. He catches it on the inside of his foot, punts it up in the air. The referee is looking at his watch. Gallen then steps forward, hovers under the ball. In a single movement, he throws himself up into space, inverts himself, connects with the ball with his head on the ground and his feet in the air, and with a perfect overhead, smacks it past the goalie into the corner of the net from ten yards.

The Bush Ranger erupts. Nodge has his arms round me, Tony gives me a kiss, Colin is dancing ecstatically. All the faces in the pub have lit up and for that one brief second, for that tremendous moment, we all love each other with a sodium-burning intensity. At these rare and wonderful times, to be a mate, to have your mates – there's nothing better. Lager spills on the floor, overturned in the ecstasy. Up on screen, they're doing the same, five teams members in blue and white shirts hugging and kissing in perfect joy.

A thin tone sounds from the speaker at the side of the screen, the final whistle. We're about to celebrate some more when a ripple runs through the pub. Although it's the final whistle play seems to be continuing. Gallen is throwing his arms up in fury. The Rangers players are surrounding the referee. It slowly dawns that the whistle was for offside, not for full time. A pall of disbelief falls over the room. The energies of love and conquest ebb out into the cold street. A low moan sets up. The replay shows that Gallen was a good five yards offside.

Play continues. Ten seconds later, the real full-time whistle. Now we're all standing five feet apart, smoky air separating us like a crash barrier. Colin seems to show a slight crumpling, does not speak. Tony aims a beer nut at the screen, poises it between his index finger and thumb and lets rip.

41

It bounces off the surface and on to the oatmeal carpet. Nodge hasn't forgiven Gallen and crushes his empty beer can in his hand. He is muttering repetitively as if something has stalled inside.

Hopeless. Gallen. Hopeless. Gallen.

I'm determined to tell them all tonight. It's just a question of finding the right moment. The picture diminishes, disappears. In the room, a post-mortem has got under way.

Same old story. They just can't close the deal.

The defence is a fucking shambles. Steve Morrow, what a cunt. The opposition should have had two or three more away. We don't clear, we fumble. We muff. We're faffers.

We should sell Gallen like, like a hot potato.

Drop him, you mean.

What?

You drop hot potatoes.

Fuck off.

*Who's going to buy **Gallen**?*

This continues for several minutes, then Tony downs his drink and says in a tone that suggests it's all settled, *Anyone up for a curry?*

I don't know.

I'm a bit –

I want something with a bit of MSG. Has the Happy Garden reopened?

Don't know. No.

There's this new place –

That new trendy Indian?

Yeah. The God of Small Things.

*It's not called **that**.*

It is. It's a kind of Indian tapas bar. All bits and pieces.

Pathetic.

I'd prefer a Chinese.

Let's get out of here anyway, I say.

I've had enough of the heaving mass of disappointment. How far can Rangers fall? Down, down the divisions. Tony and me go to walk out, and Colin and Nodge follow on, Nodge hesitating, worried that he's been streamrollered over the curry but deciding that it's not worth the aggravation.

Let's go in the cab, eh, Nodge? says Tony. *It's a bit of a way.*

Nodge shakes his head. He says he's had one drink too many, but really it's his private protest. He's got the egg on. Nodge still wants a Chinese, so he's not going to give us all a trip in his taxi, which is parked just outside the Bush Ranger, black and shining under the streetlight. Nodge always keeps it nice and clean. A Metrocab, the newest model.

Two young black men are leaning against it. They have pulled-down hoods, sullen stares, trainers like hovercrafts. There's a full pint of lager on the bonnet of Nodge's cab. Nodge moves towards it, but Tony gets there first. Tony picks up the pint and pours it down the drain, then, with a mocking smile, hands the glass back to one of the black guys. The man looks back blankly, then turns away. After a minute, they both consult and walk quietly, quickly past us. One of them drops a piece of paper and I bend to pick it up.

Tony turns back to us with a clearly audible snort of derision, then walks off, down the Goldhawk Road. I hold the piece of paper in my hand and glance back at the cab. Two Rangers supporters – big, tattooed – have walked over now and are staring perplexedly at the spot where the glass had been. Nodge sees this and walks off quickly, a pace behind Tony, talking through slightly clenched teeth. Me and Colin follow on, also hastily.

It wasn't his fucking drink.

Tony doesn't say anything.

I mean, it's not as if there was any damage done anyway.

Nodge's voice rises a decibel or two.

It's a bit bloody childish.

Tony still doesn't say anything, but slows down to let Nodge catch up.

You could just have asked them to move.

Tony nearly stops, and for a moment I think he's going to apologize. That would be a first, not only for DT but for all of us. We never apologize, not to each other anyway. Don't ask me why. It's a kind of custom.

Stop going on, Nodge, will you, for fuck's sake? They were up to no good anyway. Having a night out mugging punters. Let's just have a curry and forget it. This new place is meant to be the dog's bollocks, says Tony.

He doesn't even look back when he says it, just

44

carries right on. The voice is modulated so as not to be challenging but neutral, pulling off most of the thorns from the words. It's what passes for apology in our system of communication. Nodge seems to think about it, then lets it pass. He bites his lip. Nodge has the most bitten lip in history. It's more like a puppy's rubber bone than a lip. No one has ever seen Nodge lose his temper. He designates self-control as vital, a mark of having grown up.

Colin looks nervous. He hates discord, and it's difficult to agree with both of them when two people are having an argument. I'm still in my bubble, watching the Bush go by. Irish theme pubs advertising Wexford vs. Tipperary. One not to miss. The Fab Fish Bar, the Shepherd's Bush Market sign in a crescent above an arch, showing bananas, carnival streamers, chilli peppers, pineapples, a teapot, cats. It's going rusty at the edge, like the fake sheet-metal sheep that decorate the subways at Bush Green. The letters SBM announce the market in a semicircle in the air.

I feel the piece of paper that the black guy dropped and glance at it. It is a badly produced leaflet with the headline 'Where Are We All Going?' It is illustrated with a picture of a source of light. I've seen these before, pushed through my door. They're Jehovah's Witness pamphlets. Typical Tony then. Scattershot firing, innocents caught.

We're walking fast now, down the Goldhawk Road, waiting for the tension to be neutralized by the passage of time. I'm trying to keep my mind off Veronica. We stop to cross the road; a poster is stuck on a fence: 'Hang Rapists and Paedophiles'. Next to it, 'The Third Position. No G in Jesus. No K in Christ. Respect wickedness, not evil. No devil.'

Colin has stopped at the Universal Jeans centre and is looking in the window. Calvin Klein, Boss, YSL, Moschino, DKNY, Armani. You'd think from the labels you were in South Molton Street, but the clothes are horrible. One pair of jeans in particular is devastatingly shit – stone-washed, baggy, extremely nasty.

Large, says Colin, transfixed.

Colin. Not a clue. Tony barely glances. He's walking with Nodge now, side by side.

Now we're walking, fast, in a formation of four, past boarded-up shops, Halal butchers, pizza joints, balti houses, Coin-ops, scrap-metal dealers. One shop has nothing but posters of Mecca inside and a big sign saying, 'Welcome to the Wonderful World of Islam'.

Allah Akbar! shouts Tony.

Kill the infidel whoreson dog Rushdie, says Nodge, trying to be Arabic but instead sounding like Peter Sellers doing his coolie thing.

Colin looks blank, then says, *Fuck the Pope*.

Colin doesn't know who Rushdie is. Tony knows who he is, but hates him and thus is a strong supporter of the fatwa. Tony likes Andy McNab, or, when he's feeling intellectual, anything by James

Ellroy, the sicker the better. *The Black Dahlia* is his favourite. I know who Rushdie is, even started one of his books, but gave it up on page twelve. It's bollocks. Nodge claims to have finished *Satanic Verses* and even to have liked it. Sitting in that cab by himself all day gives him all sorts of funny ideas. Nodge would like more than anything to be clever, but he isn't. I *am* clever, but I do my best to disguise it. It's a bit of an embarrassment in Shepherd's Bush.

We walk past a Polish deli, a Lebanese take-away, a Turkish kebab shop, a Caribbean restaurant and a Dominoes Pizza. To our left, the gentrified cottages of W6.

A Wine Warehouse stands as herald to the shift in economic geography. Baskets of flowers are hanging from lampposts now. Here the restaurants get half trendy – the Brackenbury, the Anglesea, some vegetarian hole. Visible half a mile to the right, the White City Estate, where Colin still lives with his mum. On the borders of White City, but in a privatized, upwardly mobile zone of red-brick terraces and brass door-knockers, my place. A nice whitewashed two-up two-down, courtesy of Farley, Ratchett & Gwynne.

Tony and Nodge, still in the lead, stop outside what looks like a brand-new restaurant. It's minimalist, cuboid, with smoked glass and plain concrete walls. Inside it's three-quarters full of identikit BBC researchers talking wall-to-wall tosh.

This is it, says Tony.

47

Looks a bit of a wankhole, says Nodge.

Let's give it a go, I say.

Colin nods. Colin's always nodding. He's the man from Del Monte, he say yes. Agreement is part of his basic mode of expression. It's virtually a speech impediment.

We all walk in and are shown to a table by the window. Fat butterflies pirouette in my gut. The menus are brought, not the good old-fashioned red-vinyl ones featuring Chicken Curry, Murgh Aloo and Bhindi Bhaji at knock-down prices, but something that looks like parchment with delicate copperplate writing on it.

We remove our coats, hang them on the back of the chairs and start inspecting. Nodge is revving up for a good moan already. Nodge complains, Tony provokes, Colin agrees. That's the basic pattern. I'm an all-rounder. If I have a speciality at all, it's lying, I suppose. I'm rather good at it.

Nodge is getting sorely pissed off. I can see it in the way his lips tighten as his eyes first scan the dishes. They go white when he sees the prices. Cabbies don't make what you would think, and it's hard to imagine that Nodge, with his somewhat rarefied, that is to say non-existent, charm, does a big trade in tips.

This is a big bucket of toss, he says, loud enough for the passing waiter, suited up in a four-button, no-collar, jet-black, chrome-buttoned sheath, to curl a lip.

I stare at the menu and I see what he means.

Lobster caressed in a light cumin sauce reclining on a bed of lentils. Tony sits opposite me, his face lit up. He loves this place.

I fancy the Reshmi Kebab, he says.

Nodge reads out loud in his best gravedigger's voice. He's very dry, is Nodge.

Like the satin they are named after, these kebabs of minced chicken feel luxurious on your palate. He pauses for effect, then repeats, *What a great big bucket of toss.*

Tony takes no notice. He has stiffened slightly, out of respect for the formality of the environment. Just like Nodge wants to be clever, Tony wants to be accepted and smart and fashionable. We all want to fit in, in our particular way. Perhaps that's why I'm frightened of telling them about Veronica. Because *they're* where I fit. They help hold me up, they're my history.

In other words, there's no getting rid of them. Not that I want to. Or not that the bit of me that *thinks* wants to. But of course, I have other bits. Bits that push me around without words.

It nearly happened last week. I nearly killed them all. Nearly stabbed them all to death. I'm not kidding. It was Veronica. She made me do it. Made me *want* to do it anyway.

CHAPTER 3

THE BLUE CHIP UNTOUCHABLES

It was last Thursday evening. We were at my house on the White City borders. It's still a bit of a mixed area – one or two flat-cappers, one or two roll-up puffers, bitter drinkers, war moaners, leftover from the 1950s and 1960s – but mainly it's young couples with Volvos, Beemers and Peugeot 205s. I like it unmixed. It makes me feel more secure in my achieved place in the world.

Veronica came home, or what would soon become her home, after a long day chopping up goners. I sometimes think I can smell it on her, the death. Strangely, it's erotic. It makes me struggle harder in bed to deny that thing, that unsellable, unbargainable fact. No offers, absolutely asking price only.

But our minds, as yet, had not turned in that direction. We were just vegging out. It's one of your basic traditional qualities of having a girlfriend – not having to talk, not having to impress, not having to do anything particular at all. You just share the same space. You can't do that with men only, with mates. You have to do something to establish yourself as amusing or interesting. Too much silence itches. In relationships, silence is allowed. And that's what we were doing. Silence. I like it.

Not so long ago, me and Veronica would only see each other at weekends – that's Friday, Saturday and Sunday night – and one other night in the week; a ratio of freedom to commitment of 3:4. That's reasonable, I think. Slightly beyond the normal girlfriend ratio (usually 4:3), well short of a full relationship (0:7). But as the marriage approaches, the F:C ratio is slipping badly. She's round here most nights now, and the ratio is moving towards more like 2:5 or even 1:6. I don't mind, I suppose. Processes like these aren't really stoppable anyway. It's organic, inevitable. Nobody decides, nobody really wants it to happen. But it happens anyway. I go out with my mates a few nights a week, she goes out with hers, but somehow or other, without any particular arrangement having been made, we both usually end up here.

And that's the feeling of freedom being eroded; the absorption of space into one person from another. It isn't to do with mathematical time. Veronica's very presence, although not permanent yet, is changing the way I feel inside, and I don't mean in a mulchy, marshmallow lovey way. I feel that, that I'm breathing in a different manner; quicker, more urgent, as if oxygen is in short supply. It's part of the transformation. You get used to it, I suppose.

The house I bought back in '91, when property was suffering. I had been waiting for that moment, for the market to drop and drop and drop, until it could drop no further, until it would choke once, twice, then begin turn around. I picked it up for 120K and immediately the price started rising. It's worth twice that now. When I'm lonely, or sad, or just lying in the bath, I reassure myself with that. I take the figure of 120 and rotate it in my head, invisibly in the air just above, and watch it morph and stretch until it takes on the shape of a new number: 250. Then I convert it into words: A quarter of a million. The word million gives me a shudder, makes me want to play with myself. Mmmillion. Mmmmmmmmmillion. Mmmmmm.

Only three more of those fourths, and I'd be a millionaire. Then I know I'd be happy. Then I'd know that I'd won.

So long as Tony hadn't made two million.

The cottage itself is nothing very extraordinary, either in structure or in decor. Before I had it knocked through downstairs, it was simply a two-up two-down, with a kitchen at the back with doors leading out into a small patio and an even smaller lawn. Now the downstairs is a single large room, with the stairs freestanding, running from the east wall up to the first, and only, floor. It's reasonably light and spacious, big wooden sash windows, structurally sound. I've kept the decoration simple – bare floorboards, white walls, that kind of thing, a few prints. Veronica says it's anonymous, corporate, but I know from experience that it's a mistake to leave too large an imprint of your personality on your property, because, chances are, the purchaser isn't going to like your personality. So I'm playing it safe. I don't want anything that could lead to rejection. Anyway, I won't be here much longer; marriage is an opportunity to trade up.

I suppose there's only one wall of the house that directly expresses something about me or my life, and this is transportable, removable, erasable. It's a huge collage – and I mean huge, about 5 x 5 – of snapshots. I had a frame built for it and then I meticulously stuck in every picture I had in old photo albums and in the bottom of drawers and in boxes in attics. Within the twenty-five-square-feet space, there are hundreds of photographs, some black and white, mostly colour. I made it in a frenzy one night about a week after my father died. That was last year. It reassured me that I was still connected, that I would not float away.

I noticed that Veronica was staring at the board. She often does this, even though she has no idea who most of the people in the photographs are. And it's true that there is something compulsive and hypnotic about this sea of faces and bodies, of preserved milliseconds. Every time I look at it, I see something new, some lost friend I had forgotten, some distant moment I had lost. Living is all forgetting, forgetting and remembering. This board had the power to draw out of you the invisible, the missing, the irretrievably broken. It was all in bits, but it made up a whole. And the bits were bits of me, every single one of them.

Shoeless, I went and stood behind her. I did not know if she was aware of me or not, so absorbed was she. I reckon all new relationships involve trying to steal the past of the other, to get some ownership of it. This is what gaping at old photographs is all about, I suppose. But it's the place you can never get into in the end. Previous boyfriends and girlfriends are displayed with embarrassment or pride. Old holidays in cheap Mediterranean villas are anecdotalized. Fashion mistakes are acknowledged and laughed at. It is something of a game, something of a cabaret, but it's crucial.

I let my eye fall anywhere. It found a small, rectangular photograph with rounded corners. Something in me recoiled when I looked at it. It was Joe, my father, with his arm round me on the settee, I mean sofa, back at Rockley Road, W12, just to the west of where the shopping centre is now. Only, if you look closely, you'll see that it isn't actually around me at all. Like a nervous boy on his first date, his arm has crept around the back of my head – I am about seven or eight, I suppose, and wearing the QPR kit that I lived in at that age – but it doesn't actually touch. It looks like it's about to, but I can tell you from direct memory that it doesn't.

I can remember that moment on my sofa so clearly. Mum standing in front of us, telling us to get closer together, Dad getting more and more bluff and irritated. You can see it there in his face, in the already-fading smile. I could feel the waves of embarrassment coming from Dad, and it made me blush. The birthmark on my face seems flushed, livid. I shrank into myself. You can see that too: I'm sort of pulled inwards, arms pressed against chest, neck retracted, torso stiff. The arm never reached the shoulder. That's the story of me and my dad, in a nutshell. The arm never made it.

Not that he was a bad man, Joe, not at all. I can see that, especially now that he's dead. I always liked him, I would say. But his shyness was a kind of disease, virtually a mental illness. He loathed and detested being touched, by me or my mother, or anyone else, not, I think, because he was a cold man, but because he just found it all too embarrassing. Someone somewhere had taught him that touching was like being a poof or something. Probably Gramps, old Mickey Blue. There he is, three photographs away to the left, standing in front of his shovel, face as hard as malachite, unsmiling black and white. They thought about things in a different way then. They thought love was about doing what you were told.

Who's that?

Veronica was pointing at somewhere in the

55

north-east quadrant, towards the border. I struggled to make out which of the overlapping pictures she was indicating.

The one with me dressed in a tutu?

Is that really you?

Lovely, aren't I?

Were you going to a fancy-dress party?

No. It was a job interview.

Why would you go to a job interview in a tutu?

Veronica's a bit slow on jokes sometimes. I expect I'll get used to it.

No. It was a fancy-dress party.

Oh. Anyway, that's not the one I meant. Next to that.

That . . . oh, that's . . .

Then, for a split second, I found myself struggling to remember his name. Slightly bucktoothed, sandy hair, very tall, a northerner by birth, Newcastle. We were total best friends for about three years. Did everything together. Then it came to me.

That's Martin Buckle.

I haven't met him, have I?

No. We don't see each other any more.

How come?

I don't know. We just drifted apart.

It's all drift. History, friendships, being around generally. You only stop drifting when you make it to Vronky's table. But by then you're collapsing. Correction. Collapsed.

Vronky pointed to another photo at random.

What about these?

On the left, another Martin, Martin Keeble. That's his girlfriend, Sally. And I'm standing next to . . . wait a minute . . . something . . . Niven something. Something like queer . . . Niven, Niven Bender. We were all at university together. Good people. Lovely people.

Still see them?

I shook my head. Martin died, in a jet ski accident, but years after we had stopped seeing each other anyway. He'd broken up from Sally by then. Who knows where she was. Niven Bender was working somewhere in Wales. He sent me a Christmas card last year.

I began to scan the board for more old friends. Terry and Cal, moved to America. Andrew Barraclough, stopped talking to him after he lost too much to me in a game of poker. Even though I tried to give the money back. Kathy Shout, one of my best woman friends. Got married to a bloke who couldn't stand me, a feeling that was mutual. So that was the end of me and Kath. Paul Baker, with that great mane of yellow hair and the pigeon chest. Moved to Scotland with the company. He phones sometimes. Three kids now.

I looked and looked. Dozens, scores, of faces stare back at me, faces with whom I have laughed, and shared secrets, and drunk, and played stupid games, and, in my way, loved. Gone, most of them. Married with mortgages in Weston-super-Mare. Working for software companies abroad. Can't talk or won't talk. Fallen out or fallen away. Good

57

friends I haven't seen for years, not only through geography but through natural erosion.

Friends have different ways of sliding away from you. Sometimes it's quite dramatic. For instance, among the photos I can spot one drug addict, one certifiable drunk, two clinical depressives, one borderline schizophrenic who's doing six months in the Scrubs for ABH. Of the friends that remain, there are people I went to school with, people I went to college with, people I met at work, friends I nicked off other friends. Most of them, it occurs to me in a flash, maybe a good half, I . . . don't . . . I don't . . .

It's not that I don't *like* them, it's just that they're there simply because they've always been there. Like I say, life's a matter of habit. They're your accumulated history. One way or another they hold you up, they remind you who you are, insist on who it is you remain. That can be irritating too. Old friends can be like deadwood, like one of those petrified forests. You have to fight your way through, not in order to get anywhere, just to stay in the present, just to not get dragged back into the past.

Veronica was staring at another corner of the board now, a good chunk of the south-eastern quadrant. This was a distinct area . . . the same faces again and again and again. Me, Colin, Nodge and Tony. At the Munich Oktoberfest, Tony pissing down the windscreen of a camper van with the windscreen wipers going. Ibiza in

'93, '94? All on E, it was mad. Me, Tony and Nodge punting footballs at Colin just off Scrubs Lane. The four of us falling together into a perfect blue pool, can't remember where that was, was it the first 14 August?

Scanning the board and pecking at my memory, I thought to myself, we really are the last four. Everyone else had retreated into some micro-world, somewhere where mates are excluded or don't count for much. These other mates, I see them by themselves one night for dinner or a drink, or I go out with them and their girlfriend or wife, or go and see them and their kids, or take in a movie with them. But me, Nodge, Tony and Colin, we still all go out together, hunt totty, drink together, do mate stuff, take the piss out of each other, out of women, out of everything.

It's great. Or it's been great. I suppose, what with Veronica, they think it's all over. But it doesn't have to be. You don't just drop your mates, even if you are going to get married. And I'm not going to. Veronica's got to understand that. That's more a girl thing, I've always thought, a female treachery, the tendency to over-invest in a relationship to the exclusion of all else. God, I hate that word. *Relationship*. Makes me think of a boat full of relatives. Anyway, that's maybe why Nodge, Tony and Col don't like Vronky. The feared over-investment. At least I don't think they like her. Because when we all went out together for the first time – only a few weeks ago – the atmosphere was something like it must feel in Vronky's chopping room. Freezing. No movement, no give. We gave it up after ninety minutes and went home half an hour before the pub closed.

As if she was reading my mind – how does she *do* that? – Veronica said, without turning her head, *I suppose they're your best mates.*

Who? I said, although I know exactly who she meant.

She pointed to a photograph of the four of us, *circa* 1984. Tony had gone Goth, with purple hair, torn tights under his trousers, high patent-leather Doc Martens boots, and I'd had a go too, although I was dyed blond, short-haired, with pinstriped jeans. I looked at Nodge: his face very different, unpadded by fat, his head unafflicted by baldness, a different person seemed to be exposed, a person I'd almost entirely forgotten. There was a sensitivity in his face then, even an elegance, instead of that impenetrable soft, sunken wall. I had never thought of Nodge as good-looking, or happy. And he was wearing bright colours – a canary-yellow T-shirt, a pair of green trousers. It's been so long since I've seen Nodge wearing anything except grey, brown or black, I've forgotten he was once quite romantic in his dress sense. Only Colin looked much the same – badly dressed, acne-scarred, apology in his face even then, damage there even then. The cheapest, the worst clothes. This makes a pang of sorrow shoot inside me. Poor Col. Of all of them, I've known him by far the longest. Since I

60

was just a little kid and we played table football together. *I loved him then,* I said to myself, then felt embarrassed by the thought.

Colin, Tony and Nodge.

I suppose they are.

How many friends have you got in all?

I gave a blink. Tough question. I stared at the board and it stared back at me. Scores of the faces were of friends, or of people who were *once* friends. Ay, there's the fucking rub.

I have no idea. I know I have quite a few. More than the average thirty-year-old, I should imagine. The average would be . . . what? Ten really good ones. Ten more peripherals. A score or so right at the outside edge, virtual acquaintances. A few left over from school, a few more from college, a few picked up at work, perhaps an ex in there somewhere. One or two borrowed or stolen from other friends. An ex-flatmate or two. Not as many mates as I used to have, that's for sure.

And why did I get this feeling they were about to take a further tumble? Because they always do when you get married. Another bunch of old pals down history's perpetually flushing bog.

I continued, hardly knew how to stop.

I'm not sure what a friend is. Is it just someone you like? Can it be someone you haven't seen for ten years and have no intention of seeing again? Do friends expire? What's the difference between a friend and an acquaintance? It's very hard to say.

Well, why don't you try?

What does it matter?

61

Because we have to do a list of invites for the wedding.

Ah fucking ha.

Like I told you, I've booked the hall now, but as it turns out they can only physically seat sixty people. It's not very many, not once you've included family on both sides.

Her tone had changed suddenly, utterly. From being relaxed, dreamy, Veronica was being brisk and efficient. It's funny, since we decided we were getting married, briskness and efficiency have surfaced much more decisively in her personality. I know that she *is* brisk and efficient. She's very successful in her chosen field – one of the youngest pathologists at her level in the country. It's just I thought it was something she dipped in and out of through necessity, in order to bring home the bacon. A necessary affection. Now suddenly I had this feeling I was being dealt with, like a situation. I was a circumstance that she had to be on top of, so to speak.

Still, getting married is a stressful business. If we're going to be together for life, there has to be give and take, I suppose. That's what everyone says, isn't it?

So what you trying to say?

You're going to have to make up your mind who your real friends are. Because there's only going to be room for about twenty of them at the wedding, if they all bring a guest. Most of them – the ones that aren't total losers — are going to have girlfriends or boyfriends by now, after all.

Is that a crack at Tony, Nodge and Colin?

It's a joke, Frankie. Like you wearing a tutu. By the way, do you have any girlfriends?

Of course I do.

Have you slept with any of them?

Oh my God.

No.

Veronica gave a deep, resonant sigh. Then she turned away from the board and towards me and said, *You know when you proposed to me at Angel Eyes?*

Of course.

Angel Eyes is a restaurant in Islington, very romantic. Very sophisticated. Very fucking expensive.

Do you remember I said that the most important thing in a relationship is honesty?

I couldn't remember anything of the sort. I nodded vigorously.

Well, those aren't just words. They're not just noises you make. They mean something. Do you understand? I want you to start telling me the truth.

She turned back to the photo board.

And by the way, I know your nickname.

What nickname?

Jonathan — Nodge — told me that you were called Frank the Fib. He seemed to think it was very funny.

Fat fuck Judas pompous little scumbag tosser.

Oh, no one ever calls me that any more. That's just

a stupid name I had at school. It was just a joke. I'm as honest as most people.

That's what worries me. So who do you want to invite?'

She shook her head, for no apparent reason. Her red hair moved not at all, so short, so severely gelled. It turned out that it was dyed. The roots pushing through. It's all illusions nowadays, isn't it? Estate agency, self, appearance, relationships, friendship. No, not friendship. I couldn't let myself believe that.

I felt breathless at the barrage she'd just unleashed. I excused myself and went to the loo, just to recover. Where did *that* come from? Jesus. And yet a part of me saw that she was right, or wanted to believe that she was right. It would be so good to have a life with a solid set of rules. I've always wanted to follow the rules – that's half the reason I lie, so that it can appear to others that I am following them. *Really* doing it is just too difficult. And it would be so good to be able to commit yourself to a set of private principles. But it's just not realistic. Everyone lies about ten times a day. You might as well try and abolish gravity. A wedding certificate isn't going to do away with it.

When I returned from the loo, I saw that Veronica was sitting at the David Wainwright Rajasthani table – practically everyone in the street has one – and was fumbling with a small plastic box. When I drew up close, I saw that what was in the box was a selection of drawing pins with different-coloured plastic heads.

I've had an idea, she said.

I've had one too, I said, and I drew both my hands around her chest to bring the palms in contact with what I could find of her breasts. There's something about Vronky that drives me crazy. I can't keep my hands off her. It's the poshness, I think. Those rounded little vowels. They just make me *sweat*.

She pushed my hands firmly away, then shot me a look. I think I'm going to get to know that look. Like briskness and efficiency, I had previously thought it was something she just used in her job. But now I see that it's kind of a look that says *you think this is a game, but it isn't a game. This is life. This is what women know and you have still to learn.* It's a complicated look. Not so bad as it sounds, but bad enough. I decided to shake myself up a little. Stretch my neck, widen the eyes. Give the appearance of paying attention.

So who do you want to invite to the wedding?

I haven't really thought about it.

Veronica's face darkened slightly again. Wrong answer. You always have to ask yourself these two questions when bowled a googly. Shall I give the truth? Or shall I give the right answer? There's quite a big difference.

Frankie, we have exactly two months and three days left. I've organized the church. I've organized the hall. I've arranged to have the invitations printed. I've sorted out the wedding list. And what have you done?

65

I was about to answer when I realized that, as a question, it was rhetorical. It was not an invitation for me to catalogue the tasks germane to the wedding that I had performed, of which, in fact, there have been several. It was a request for me to appear contrite.

Right answer/Truth.

You see. Look. I hate this, Frankie. I hate hearing myself nag you. You know it's not me. It's just – I don't know. We've got to start doing things together.

Veronica was softening in the face of my contrition, to show that I was not simply a difficult colleague at the office, but her man, her lover. Her betrothed. She leaned closer to me. It was pleasant. I felt soothed. I looked up towards her face, and she smiled. I noticed she had developed a white spot, quite large, just at the join between her bottom lip and her top, on the right-hand side. This made me pull back slightly when she moved forward to kiss me. I'm fastidious about that sort of thing. But she didn't seem to notice. Just a brush, lips against the cheeks. Already we were doing tongues less than we used to. It's one of those transitional phases everyone talks about, part of the pre-marriage phase. I've managed to isolate five of these staging posts so far. Pre-proposal. Proposal/Pre-marriage. Marriage. Kids. Death. I escaped contact with the spot, anyway.

I'm sorry, Frankie. I didn't mean to snap at you. It's just that – it's a month to get the invitations ordered and printed, another week to send them out.

That only leaves – what, five weeks. No, four. People need to know well in advance. And we're already late – or later than most, anyway.

I'm sorry. We ought to be getting on with it I suppose. I could have done more. What's this idea you've had, anyway?

I indicated casually towards the pile of coloured pins on the table.

Veronica studied the array of photographs. She stuck her tongue out slightly, which I always feel makes her look like a retard. The slightly mismatched eyes, one discernibly larger than the other, searched out images, processed them.

It might be silly. Or it might be fun. But I thought we could spend some time deciding who we're going to invite.

Deciding who *we're* going to invite. But they're my friends, mine, mine. Or does authority have to be yielded up to the collective? Is that part of being married? Is it part of being pre-married, like not using tongues any more?

Veronica looked quite agitated and excited. She jigged around in front of the board, shaking the box of pins.

Listen, it'll be a laugh. We'll start by colour-coding them.

What?

Colour-coding them. We'll give each kind of friend a coloured pin.

I assumed she was joking, but decided to play along.

How many varieties of friend are there then? I said disdainfully.

Veronica seemed to be unconscious of the irony.

Oh, loads. For a start there are friends you don't like. I've got plenty of those. Then there are friends you do like, but never bother to see. Then there are the ones you really like a lot, but can't stand their partners. There are those you just have out of habit and can't shake off. Then there's the ones you're friends with not because you like them, but because they're very good-looking or popular and it's kind of cool to be their friend. Trophy friends. Most of the time they're what I call VCSPs, although you can be a trophy friend without being a VCSP. It's just that the two tend to go together.

What does VCSP stand for?

Very Charming Selfish People. I've got two of them, and a third borderline. They hold you on a string. Then when they feel you're getting far enough out for the string to break, they pour the charm on, draw you back in again. Make you feel like you're the only person in the world. For about ten minutes. Then when that's done, they let go again, because other people's strings need drawing in. They go for quantity rather than quality. They need the fix, the drama. They need to . . . beguile people so that they can feel real. Know anyone like that?

Not really, I lied, thinking of Tony.

Then there are sports friends. There are friends of convenience – they're usually work friends. There are pity friends who you stay with because you feel sorry for them. There are acquaintances who are on probation as friends. There are –

Enough. Have you got any idea how ugly – how **clinical** *– this sounds?*

Don't be silly. It's just making lists. Boys like that, don't they?

Now that she mentioned it, it did sound rather appealing. Parcelling it all up, nice and neat.

Friends come in loads of different varieties. And that's just the start. If we're going to decide which ones to invite to the wedding, we have to take in other factors. How offended are they going to be if they aren't invited? Did they invite you to their wedding? Are they going to kick up – just being practical – with a decent wedding gift? Are they going to get horribly drunk and embarrass everyone? Do they like me? Do I like them?

Now I was really getting rankled.

Frankly, Veronica, it doesn't matter whether you like them or not. They're not your friends.

Maybe. But it's our wedding. It's my day, so the books say. I've got a right to a say.

There are different kinds of pause, with different lengths, different weights, different textures. The pause that followed this last sentence was complex. It had weight, a lot of weight, it felt like it was pressing down on the room. And it went on for a long time. And it was charged with all kinds of hostility and anger and perplexity. It had a sound too. For a long time I couldn't work out what it was, then I recognized it. It was the sound of

69

trenches being prepared and dug. It was the silent scrape of shovels. Trench preparation is characteristic of struggle that typifies the early stages of any long-term relationship. I know, because I've started lots of long-term relationships. I've just never finished them, that's all. All those lines being drawn that, once completed and established, will be nearly impossible to redraw. And those lines represent power.

After the silence had continued eating away like acid at our skin for about four minutes, I decided to throw in the towel, but – and this is important – *without grace*, in order to try and communicate that the fortification she was establishing was only a temporary one which could be subject to reconstruction. It needed to be made clear that no principle had been comprehensively conceded.

OK. Have your own way. Let's parcel them out and pack them up.

I took the box of pins from Veronica, removed a purple-headed pin and stabbed my old friend Ron Pearce – living on the Purley Way, lost his gonads about 1993 in a mind-meld with a woman who had all the personality of a polystyrene cup – through the heart. He was standing in front of a road sign somewhere in Germany, *circa* 1989, grinning and pointing to a village sign which read *Minge*. It was a good holiday. Ron caught scabies from a barmaid. I wiggled the pin in his chest, as if he were a voodoo doll.

70

Expired. Ron Pearce is history. He's a husk, a busted flush, a nowhere man.

Veronica nodded sagely.

So, purple pins are for the undead.

Let's say so.

Who else is a zombie?

Violently, I shook the box and exposed a handful of purple pins. I picked them out gingerly and held them in my palm. Ralphie Waterman got it in the head, fell at the battle of the Fulham Five-a-side, when he got the hump and head-butted me. That was the last time we ever spoke. Mad Ian Sprightly and his girlfriend, Susan, got one each, both in the guts. We were close until I tried to climb into bed with Susan after one line of chop too many. I was lucky to escape with my head.

John Sadler I tried to stab in the eye but got him through the nose instead. I don't know why we stopped seeing each other, but we did; last sighting, 1991 in the Bush Ranger. It was cordial, worn out. More pins and more pins. Katie Calhoun, who I loved and who fucked me up, broke my heart. Take that. No, take two. Philippa Fat Arse Booth, who got the hump when I made a pass at her, although she'd spent the previous three years flirting with me. Take *that*. Right in the ear.

More and more and more. At the end of it there were about twenty visible purple heads protruding from the board. I seemed to have broken out in a sweat.

71

I turned to Veronica and I said, *You know what? This is fun.*

Told you so, she said diffidently. Then she threw me a smile, showing all those tiny teeth, twice as many as a normal person, I'm sure, like Chiclets in pink Plasticine. The top layer had lipstick on them that matched her chilli-pepper hair.

It's like a kind of . . . I don't know. Cleansing. Like scraping off barnacles or something. The, the weight of those people. It's gone. More. I want more. Make me lighter. Make me like air.

Well, the rest probably aren't going to be so much fun. The gradations are finer. It's less purgative.

Look, I've got some green ones. What shall we do with green ones?

Let's do . . . good friends you don't like.

My brow furrowed. It really does, my brow. It's not just an expression indicating puzzlement. Great valleys and troughs appear on my forehead. Despite being a liar, I can be an open book.

Isn't that a contradiction in terms?

Not in the least. Some of my friends are completely hateful. They serve other purposes than being liked. Perhaps they get me into a social circle I want to be part of. Perhaps they just have good dress sense, and they're beautiful, and I want to be seen walking down the street with them.

I don't know that I've got anyone like that.

I stopped and thought. Then rammed the point through the left temple of Vinnie Moran, who I take with me to Rangers games sometimes. He's handsome, fashionable, supercool. He's also a violent, cruel bully. For many years I've convinced myself that he's a rucker, a lad, a good laugh. But he's actually just a prick.

There were only a few more green pins – one for someone I saw from Farley, Ratchett & Gwynne because he puts a lot of business my way, and one for a woman who spends most of our evenings together telling me what a sexist and potential rapist I am. To my surprise, I found my eye drifting back to the quadrant containing the images of Colin, Tony and Nodge, and at one point I had a green pin travelling in that direction. I thought to myself, *Do it now. Finish them off. Kill them all*, but instead I diverted it to the bloke from the office.

We did a few more – friends who had partners from hell, friends who were cheap, friends who would be an embarrassment on the day. We'd pinioned all my ex-girlfriends to the wall with yellow-headed barbs; I let Veronica do that. She seemed to get a kick out of it. But by now I was getting bored, and anyway Veronica had to leave to go to her reiki class. For someone trained as a scientist, she has a remarkable array of irrational beliefs. I have since learned that her concern for the feng shui of Dirty Bob's flat in Shepherd's Bush was far from artificial. The flat she did buy in the end – not from F, G & R – I tried to talk her out of, but she was determined that the vibrations were good.

I stared at the last colour in the box, a powder blue.

How about making that for the untouchables? said Veronica. *You know, the blue chip chums, the friends who are beyond criticism, who you would trust with your life, who would stand by you and so on and so forth.*

I nodded, and immediately sorted out three pins. As a kind of apology for the thought I had had a moment previously, I awarded one to Tony, one to Nodge, one to Colin. Veronica made an annoying little choking noise in the back of her throat.

Something funny?

No.

I thought you believed in being honest.

I do. It's not funny. It's just a bit sad.

What do you mean by that?

I was trying very hard not to bridle, but I felt particles of bile burning the back of my throat. Veronica softened palpably and put her hand on my arm.

I'm sorry. I don't mean anything by it.

Now you're being dishonest.

Another pause, this one in which things were fermenting, being considered, in which words were being carefully shaped. Then Veronica said, *All I'm saying is that from what I could tell when we met, things seemed a little bit tense between you.*

That's because you were there.

I know. But that wasn't all of it. I didn't think there was any . . . love between you.

This raised my anger another notch.

Oh, don't be such a . . . a girl.

74

No need to be embarrassed of the word.

I'm not, actually. Love. Love. Love. Fa de la. Love.
I love my friends. Tony, Colin, Nodge.

Are you sure?

I'm a lot more sure that I love them than . . .

I caught myself, too late.

Than you are that you love me.

I wasn't going to say that.

Veronica was biting her lip now. I'd genuinely
hurt her. I felt a surge of regret and shame. But at
the same time, I thought, *perhaps it's true.* Veronica
turned to me. She threw what was left of the box
at the photo board. Tiny barbs spread themselves
randomly over the floorboards.

*Listen, let me tell you something. Because I'm good
at this sort of thing. You don't like Tony and he doesn't
like you. I can't imagine why you're friends at all. You
feel sorry for Colin and he resents you for it. The only
one who's a real friend is Nodge, I think. He cares
about you. I don't know why him in particular. It's
true, though. But you've let him down somehow.*

My eyes were watering with indignation and
fury.

*And you know all this from an hour and a half in
the pub?*

Veronica shrugged.

Yes.

Now I was seething.

*That is so totally off whack. Nodge has never shown
me any affection in his life, actually, not that that
means anything. I don't think he'd show emotion if he*

75

saw his mum set on fire by fundamentalist anti-knitting guerrillas. *It's not because he's taciturn. He doesn't have any emotions. He's a bloody great solid lump of rock. That's why he's so reliable. No passion. And I've never let him down, to my knowledge. Colin's my oldest friend and we both love each other. Yes, I feel sorry for him sometimes. But that's different from pity. And Tony's a great bloke, a total diamond. He's a laugh. He's up for anything. He's got such* **enthusiasm**.

Veronica said, *Enthusiasm is just some people's way of panicking.*

For some reason this sent me right over the edge.

What the fuck do you know? How the fuck dare you? You've only met them once! Just because they didn't like you, you're giving me all this . . . chat. Well, they're my mates. And I'll tell you something else. Tony's going to be my best man, so stick that in your trocar and inject it, you fucking graverobber.

Veronica looked at me steadily, then said, quite coolly, *Darling. Our first argument.*

Then she picked up her coat and headed for the door. But she turned before reaching it.

It's not me they don't like. They're just scared of me. It's you, Frankie. It's you they don't like. All except Nodge. And if you make Tony your best man, you'll be acting like a fool. And you're not a fool. You're just a liar. You lie too much. And what start off as habits end up becoming what you are.

I ignored this, because to deny it would be to confirm it.

The thing is, Vronky, friends are important. Friends are the most . . .

I was about to say, *the most important thing in life*, but even as the thought flickered another, censoring, overlaid it. I paused momentarily, then said lamely, *I'm just saying, friends are important.*

I knew again that I was guilty of possessing an opinion that I should no longer possess, not if I was getting married. The thought should have been amended by now. But it wasn't. Veronica spoke again, more quietly.

That's not what you were going to say.

I exhaled theatrically.

No. That's not what I was going to say.

You were going to say that friends are the most important thing in life.

I suppose so. I'm not sure. I suppose so. I don't know that I believe it though.

Why would you say it if you didn't believe it?

A good question. But isn't it what everyone does? You don't have to *believe* what you *say*. How are you meant to know what you *believe?* Sometimes – most of the time – you just have to guess. You have to say *something*, after all.

I don't know. Sometimes you just pick up opinions. Like fluff on your jacket.

Uh-huh.

And you don't always know where you picked up the fluff. But there it is, all the same.

Right there on your jacket, said Veronica sarcastically.

77

Yeah.

Veronica shifted on the floor. She was half twisted towards the door, half still in the room. She was smiling a bit now, as if this was a piece of unimportant gossip, idle wordplay. But I knew that the conversation had entered deeper waters. She wanted to know about my priorities. It wasn't unfair.

So do you believe it?

And I said, flatly, flatly enough to close the conversation, *I don't know. I just don't know.*

Then she closed the door quietly and went to her reiki class. I knew she would not return that night. I went and picked out the rest of the blue pins and stuck two or three more in each of the photographs of Nodge, Tony and Colin.

Untouchable. Untouchable. Untouchable.

She didn't understand. Friends *were* important. *The most important thing in the world, Frankie.*

I then thought suddenly that it wasn't me speaking those words in my head. Then I had the strangest feeling of standing back from myself and listening, of straining to hear that other voice. It was a woman's, familiar. It came from a long time ago, from a place that moved, and vibrated, and smelt powerfully of cigarette smoke and liniment and inexpensive, pungent perfume.

So it was that I had, suddenly, vividly, this memory. Sometimes I find myself wondering if we really do possess memories. They seem more to me like drunken, out-of-focus visitors who arrive, then disappear again, sometimes without trace, sometimes returning. This memory, at this moment, in this house by the multicoloured pinboard, arrived, through a door I never imagined was there, all wavy lines and strange, unfamiliar colours.

This was like a little film, this memory, not all cut up and fractured, as so many of them are. A film flickering in and out of focus, but clear enough.

It was a film of me sitting next to my mother, Florence – Flossie Blue – on a bus going somewhere, I don't know where. I don't know how old I was. Nine perhaps – somewhere on the cusp of childhood, where innocence was beginning to decay and recede. I registered a vague sense that the constant intrigue and fascination I found then in the world was tarnishing. Boredom was establishing itself like a strange virus, a sense that just being here, just being in the now, was no longer enough. I was beginning to itch for something, something I could not name. Still can't.

I am reading over my mother's shoulder – a magazine, *Homes and Gardens* or *Woman's Realm* or *People's Friend*, or perhaps *Reader's Digest*, because my parents subscribed without fail. *The Most Fascinating Character I Ever Met. Humour in Uniform.* I am bored, and have brought no comic of my own, and am tired of looking out of the window at the flat featureless estates of west London. I stare over my mother's shoulder and read the headline, over a line drawing, a kind of collage, that suggests a combination of laughing children, cosy hearths, eager husbands sitting down to enjoy freshly cooked food, knitting, dancing. The headline reads 'What is the Most Important Thing in Life?' in some big, bold, confident typeface, set above a white-out-of-black bullet, in copperplate at an angle, like a signature: *The Editor Writes.*

And I, bored, turn to my mother and ask the question, the very question that appears in the magazine headline, because there's nothing else to do. I don't expect her to say anything, because she never does. Too busy, always too busy. I expect her to bat away the question with a *dontbesilly* or *nevermind* or *notnow*. Instead there was just silence.

Mum, what's the answer?

I stab my finger at the headline.

She stares at me, surprised through her overlarge spectacles. Her eyes seem suddenly less milky than usual, less absent. To my surprise, she considers the question seriously. She shifts in her seat, she furrows the already deep lines on her brow, touches her lips with a finger leathered at the tip from hard, relentless work as a seamstress.

Some emotion passes across her face, an emotion I do not recognize, and that I find oddly disturbing. The mood that surrounds us, a tiny invisible bubble, switches from soft indifference to something earnest and charged.

Ah. The. Most. Important. Thing. Now that's not

*easy, is it, Francis? I shall have to think about that
one for a bit.*

She seems puzzled, lost.

Well, I suppose. I suppose it's –

The bus conductor sounds the bell, turns the
wheel of his ticket dispenser with a flourish. The
bus begins to slow, and as it does, increases in
vibration so that it feels like a great, tired cement
mixer. A newspaper, left on an empty seat, moves
in response, slides to the floor, separating its pages
and joining the mush of cigarettes, old tickets, used
paper hankies.

My mother's face suddenly composes itself, as
if a series of pins had connected with a series of
aligned holes, so that now the system could be at
equilibrium, run smoothly once more. This state
of equilibrium is confirmed by a series of vacant
nods, bobbing one after the other.

It's your friends, isn't it?

She says this with a newly discovered certainty,
as if she has just found a lost gold ring down the
sofa. *There* it is.

*Friends. They're the most important thing in your
life, Frankie. If you've got good friends, you've got a
solid base, you see. Friends help see you through.*

She says this firmly, with absolute conviction
and a kind of ferocity I don't think I had ever seen
in her before. And I look at her, right into those
watery pale eyes, thinking, but not saying, hoping
she can't hear my thoughts like mothers sometimes
can, *But, Mum. You don't have any friends.*

81

And this was true. A child, a full-time job, a husband who was shy to the point of blind terror. There was no time, and if there was time, then Dad – Dad wouldn't actually have objected, but it was out of the question. He blushed when the neighbours said hello, blushed when the postman delivered a parcel. The strength in his face, strength that had seen him work delivering coal around the streets of west London for twenty years, was reduced to a series of apologetic lines and stutters.

No friends. My father, although a well-liked man, gentle enough and well mannered, had no place in his life for them, and he didn't seem to mind. Happy in his rare moments of leisure reading the *Sunday Mirror* and the *News of the World*, listening to his Bush transistor radio, eating noiselessly the plain food Flossie cooked for him. No need for friends. Flossie was different, but she went along. Women did go along in those days, at least in the Goldhawk Road.

The nine-year-old me looks at my mother, sees that she is no longer aware of me, is staring out of the window. The bubble turns blue, ochre, grey. I was never a particularly sensitive child, yet I can quite clearly see her pain, so suddenly surfaced, like an aura or shadow around her head. I see with a shock that feels like a slap with an open hand that she is lonely – dreadfully and utterly lonely. And then and there I decide, and recite an incantation.

*I will **never** be lonely, I will be liked. **Never** be lonely, I will be liked. **Never** be lonely, I will be liked.*

With each private sounding of the word *never* I bite the back of my hand, so hard it leaves toothmarks. This thought is formed in my head like a heavy monument that starts to sink into soft ground the moment it is raised, sink from view, sink far underground. But in my memory, suddenly, I can see it, the largeness and realness of it, the determination that underpins and stabilizes it. *I will never be lonely, I will be . . .*

The bus slows further, then stops. The rainbow collapses, surface appearances are re-established, leathery, unbreachable.

Ah, here we are then. Our stop.

The mood switches back, the bubble changes colour, is forgotten to conscious mind. Forgotten until now, here, twenty years later, in a house empty apart from me, staring at my board, my board of paper friends, stuck through with dozens of small, sharp, multicoloured rapiers.

CHAPTER 4

HER HOT BUTTONS
AND HOW TO PRESS THEM

Nodge has started again. He speaks between puffs of cigarette. Nodge, despite all his ordinary Joe trappings, smokes like a Hollywood movie star. He does it with real style, holds it just so, inhales long, a deep, slightly bent wrist. A kind of Zen connection between him and it. It's a talent that very few people have got. Cigarettes and the way he smokes them are his only flourish.

Ghosht Taba. Velvety spheres of finely minced young lamb flavoured with cardamom in a yoghurt gravy cooked on a slow fire. The crowning glory of the Wazwan legendary ceremonial feast of thirty-six courses. What a huge, great, enormous . . .

A waiter glides up to the table, detached, superior. He is not Indian, rather Mediterranean.

Anything to drink, gentlemen?

Yes, says Nodge. *Could I have marbled wheaten cordial topped with a creamy nimbus cloud of white foam as beloved of the German emperors.*

84

The waiter looks blank.

He means a lager, I say, smiling apologetically.

And I'll kick off with a Margarita, says Tony.

I never thought I'd see the day when a curry house would do Margaritas. The waiter looks delighted. I'm not surprised at six pounds a pop.

We order the food. Tony has the Ghosht Taba, me and Nodge go for the Pacific Shrimp Tandoori with Escarole Salad, me because I like leaf and shrimps, Nodge because he's trying to lose weight as always. Although it isn't on the menu, Colin asks for a Chicken Madras, because that's what he always has when he goes to an Indian restaurant and he hates change. Colin just wants things to stay the same. The waiter, in a way that suggests he is being extremely tolerant and understanding of someone who is probably mentally disadvantaged, agrees to have it cooked specially for him.

We settle. The tension between Nodge and DT has faded now, back into the realm of latency, to be stored with a whole database of other complaints and resentments, carefully filed away over the years, waiting for reactivation by present circumstance. One day, the whole thing's going to blow. It's unstable.

Colin and Nodge are still mourning the inadequacies of the Rs, while DT bangs on to me about the opening of his new shop, his third now. I listen politely, but I'm still rehearsing the beginning of speeches in my head.

– *I've got some great news.*

85

– I've got some terrible news.

– I've got some news which may come as something of a shock.

Tony senses my lack of interest – one of the many things that really winds him up – and turns away to pitch in his final point of view about the performance of the current manager. QPR are perhaps the last subject that truly binds us together – or at least that we are prepared to discuss. No, not quite the last subject. Although I don't know whether our references to sex count as discussions. They can be, I suppose. For instance, now Tony is starting one of his pesting stories. He always says that he can pest a woman into bed, and he can. I've co-pested with him sometimes.

His voice is getting louder as he reaches the end of the story.

*So we're just heading up the stairs to the bedroom, so it's locked and loaded, right? I'm there. Four stairs to go, I'm counting them. One, two, three. I'm already going for my fucking zip. She's mad for it. Then she stops, and I think, what the fuck is this? And she turns round right there on the stairs. I'm **totally** binnered, right? Don't know what's going on. All I want to do is get my shreddies off. Do the business. And so she turns round, and stops. And I'm thinking, like, what the **fuck** is this? Then she looks me right in the eyes – right smack in the fucking eyes – and says – get this – she says, 'What's my name?'*

86

Colin and Nodge start to crack up. Tony's face is showing red through the tan, his teeth exposed, white.

What's my fucking name? she says. Nightmare. And I'm thinking, I have got to get this one right. This has gone too far. My kecks are almost off. And I can't get it. I just can't recall it. And you know. These things matter to a doris.

I let his voice drift in and out of focus, barely aware now of the gusts of laughter coming from all three of them. The beer is really working now. Then I become vaguely aware of the laughter dying away. There's one of those small uncomfortable gaps you get when a story has finished. Tony, always the most uncomfortable with silence, has picked up a copy of *Loaded* from Colin's windcheater and started flicking through it, stopping at the pages where there are exposed breasts.

I speak, just to fill the silence.

How's your mum, Colin?

Colin's mum has been ill for about thirty-five years. It's always polite to ask, though probably a more to the point question would be, is she dead yet?

Colin screws up his face.

Actually, she's really not well at all. I mean, really not well, this time. The hospital sent us this report. I've been very worried. I just wish that –

Tony, who hasn't been listening, suddenly lets out a bellow and begins to wave the copy of *Loaded* in the air.

This is great. 'Her Hot Buttons and How to Press Them'. This I have to read.

He gives a little giggle, a small effervescence at the back of his throat. Colin looks crushed, even slightly irritated, but doesn't say anything. Tony's looking at me when he talks. I don't give any kind of encouraging smile, because it's obvious to me that Colin is genuinely upset and wants to finish what he was saying. But Tony is an unstoppable force. Anyway, the atmosphere that would allow a discussion about anything other than surface stuff has been blown. Tony's on a roll.

Tony loves talking about sex as much as Colin likes talking about football. He pretends to be a misogynist. He pretends everything. I'm beginning to think that we all do, so much that we don't notice any more. That's a strange thought. You're pretending, and you don't know you're pretending. But why would you bother?

Anyway, Tony and sex. We go along with it. You have to talk about something. Once it was all spontaneous, full on, a giggle, like magic, the jokes, the one-liners, the just being together. An improvisation, like some record on Blue Note. Now we just go along with it.

Colin and Nodge let their conversation fade out. Nodge is peering over Tony's shoulder at a photograph of a close-up of a face of a women whose expression is clearly meant to mimic orgasm. Mouth open, eyes closed, neck stretched.

Our food arrives, occupying a small space in the

centre of outsize white china plates. it is not the usual orange and brown mess, but looks elegant and quite edible. Nothing's the same any more, not even curry. We pick up our cutlery and begin to eat, leaving a gap for what we know is sure to come. Colin begins to speak, quietly.

This really tastes of –

Tony looks up from the magazine and interrupts Colin without a qualm. Addressing us generally, he says, *What's the most times you've ever made a woman come?*

He leans back and waits for the reaction, grinning. Off to my right, I think I see Colin blush slightly and look down at his drink. Colin always drinks the same thing – Holsten Pils. I gave him a blind tasting once against Kronenbourg, Fosters and Staropramen. He couldn't tell the difference. It's not a matter of taste really. As I say, Colin just likes things to stay the same.

Nodge coughs and doesn't laugh. He considers the question disrespectful, not to himself but to women. Nodge pretends to be a feminist, like Tony pretends to be a misogynist. They're both just striking poses as far as I'm concerned. At least Colin's an honest loser and authentic Sad Bloke.

Nodge must be the only taxi driver in London who reads the *New Statesman*. Many a punter has been bewildered in the rear of his cab to hear him holding forth about the evils of sexism, racism and Third World debt.

Now his cigarette seems to drop several degrees

89

– beautifully, it must be said – as his mouth puckers.

Is this a competition?

He takes his cigarette from his mouth and stubs it out. He grinds it, like the ashtray was Kevin Gallen's head.

He starts to eat his shrimps. It's about time, since by now he's already consumed half of Colin's Madras, a good mouthful of Tony's Ghosht Taba, three trendy poppadoms and a whole portion of rice which was meant to be shared between us. I start to hum a football song, half under my breath.

Who ate all the pies? Who ate all the pies? You fat bastard, you fat bastard, you ate all the pies.

Tony shrugs at Nodge's question, those big shoulders of his tugging at the seams of his four-button linen-mix midnight-blue bespoke suit.

Tony's face takes on an expression of unconvincing innocence. One thing Tony's face could never do convincingly is look innocent. Even at rest, his face suggests a leer.

No. I'm just curious.

Nodge remains looking suspicious. Suspicion comes as naturally to his face as innuendo does to Tony's. He narrows his eyes behind his specs against the smoke still coiling from his smouldering, soggy dog-end. He's been in the sun; his neck is like a firehose poking out from that grey no-nonsense drill shirt.

Tony and Nodge don't always get along. But

although I don't much like the question, I like the way Tony throws stones into ponds. It makes him entertaining. And if Tony isn't entertaining, what's the point of him?

I'm already deciding what kind of lie I'm going to tell in response, when Colin, to my surprise, speaks in that soft, vague dither of his.

What, in, um, in one, er, session, or in one night?

Like Nodge, he has a tinge of red around the ears now, but not from the sun. Colin is embarrassed. So he has become doubly amiable, tries to affect a knowing amusement. I find it hard to believe that Colin has ever aroused anyone to climax other than, and very frequently, himself. Having looked up at Tony, he returns his stare to the bottle of Holsten Pils. This is his sixth of the night and the drink has made him momentarily bold.

The music is very loud. Not your usual duelling sitars with some bird from Delhi having a fit, but something dark and threatening; Portishead first album, I think. I call over the waiter, who nods indifferently.

Would you mind turning the music down a bit?

He shrugs. A few seconds later, the music is reduced by perhaps one tenth of a degree of a single notch. Afterwards, it will renew its inevitable upward drift as the waiters get more and more bored and anticipate a night of clubbing ahead once they've got rid of all the annoying customers.

Of course, Nodge is right. This *is* a competition.

91

Nearly everything's a competition between me, Nodge, Tony and even Colin. Colin's job is to come last, and he does it well. He's a champ at it. He always wins at that. It's one of the reasons why we keep him around.

The competitions are never acknowledged as such, though. That's one of the rules. There are lots of rules in our relationship. I still haven't been able to work them all out. Because, the rules are something else you can't acknowledge. You can't acknowledge *anything*, actually. If you've got something to say, you have to say it through the Game. Or one of the games that add up to the Game.

I'm taking liberties a bit here, thinking consecutive thoughts, talking nonsense. That's because I'm the airy-fairy one. I've got a degree and everything. So it gives me a bit of leeway to pontificate, as it were. So long as it doesn't go too far.

Tony says, *In one session.*

And I say, immediately, since I have been wondering this since Colin spoke, and also because I need some time to think, *What counts as a session?*

Tony looks bewildered. I continue. I'm fair-minded. It's important to me that when we compete – at least as nakedly as this – that the playing field is level.

And what about multiple orgasms? Do they count as just one? And if not, how many do they count as?

Tony nods his head, confirming the complexity of the problem. Nodge is still trying to look disgusted, but he makes out that he's interested in the problem *intellectually*.

A session would be from when you got an erection to when you lost it, says Tony, with a firmness of voice that his face belies. He swigs backs his Margarita and orders another one.

I shoot a glance back. It isn't satisfactory. I tap my finger on the table like an impatient teacher.

No, it doesn't **work**. *Your question was, 'What's the most times you've ever made a woman come in one session?' Perhaps I'm speaking personally, but you don't only make women come with your* **dick**. *You can make them come with your tongue, with your mouth or with your finger. Then you have to take into account accessories. Vibrators, ticklers and so forth. So whether or not you're hard isn't necessarily relevant.*

Tony looks defeated by this.

It has to be per night. Nothing else works, says Nodge, with the air of a circuit judge who is simply interested in impartiality being maintained. His face is at its best like this: droopy, serious, Eeyore with jowls. He's finished his cigarette, so he's started biting the tips of his fingers. The nails are pretty much gone, so he's down to flesh, self-cannibalization. Next cigarette is scheduled three minutes from now. The butt of the previous one still burns in the ashtray, smoke floating into my face and making my Pacific Shrimp taste like a used matchstick.

Colin nods in agreement. But then Colin has

nodded in agreement both to what I have said and to what Tony has said previously.

Something else has occurred to Tony. A neutral spirit of inquiry is still reigning, momentarily at least. Nodge is fully engaged now, despite himself. He pulls his hand across a head that is even redder than his neck, and more or less hairless apart from a kind of remnant of a tonsure at the side. There is also a sad little island just at the crown that used to be the vanguard of his hairline, now no more than a few centimetres of dark, rippling stubble. Tony speaks now, loudly.

What if it took place during the day? What if the most times you made a woman come happened, say, in the afternoon?

Without invitation, Tony raises Colin's beer glass to his mouth as he waits for Margarita No. 2 to arrive. A fleck of foam slips past his lips and on to his lapel.

Fuck my cunt!

A woman in a black two-piece suit sitting at the next table alone while her partner, presumably, goes for a waz looks across at him coldly. He smiles back, that Tony killer smile, all olive skin and pearly whites. It crushes his eyes into slits. It sends out gorgeousness and fascination and bewitchery. She is plain, way below his mark, but, flattered, she smiles back, actually blushes with pleasure. He can do it every time.

He turns away from her with an expression that suggests he has just finished a tiresomely routine

94

but necessary task and reaches for a napkin to wipe his suit clean, but it just extends the smudge across a distance three times as large. I ponder for a moment, rub the small but clearly visible birthmark that straddles my hairline, then say, *I've got it.*

Everyone looks up, as if this was important.

A session extends from the moment you take your clothes off to when you put them on again.

Colin actually puts his hand up. I think it's meant to be a joke, but the gesture looks somehow appropriate coming from Colin. Tony nods to him, as if granting him leave.

People can have sex with their clothes on.

Tony waves his hand derisorily.

Frankie's is the best definition. The best we can do, anyway. How often do you have sex with your clothes on? It happens. Certainly. But rarely. Frankie's formula is concise. We have to compromise. From when you take your clothes off to when you put them on. That's good. And multiple orgasms count as a single.

No. Not fair.

Nodge this time.

How can a multiple orgasm count as a single orgasm? It's . . . What's that word, when something's opposite to itself? Frankie, you're educated.

He says this like, *Frankie, you've got the clap.*

Help me out.

Tautological, I say, not taking offence. I'm used to it.

Tautological. I love you when you use all those syllabobbles, Francis.

Thanks.

Deadpan, derisory. Nodge carries on.

We should – nominally – count a multiple orgasm of any kind as double. I know it's not perfect, but they don't really have an exact number as such, women, do they?

Tony looks perplexed again.

Don't they?

Nodge is getting into it now. He's lit another cigarette. The waiter is clearing away the dishes and pretending not to listen.

You know, they either have one or a few at the same time. But they don't know exactly how many. Like they won't say, yeah I had eight orgasms at the same time. They'll just say, I had a multiple. You can't count them.

I'm scratching my head. Nodge sucks down half of the diet Coke he ordered after the lager, then finishes what's left of a Peshwari Naan dripping with ghee. Suddenly his tone changes to one of indifference and disdain. He turns to Tony.

It's stupid, anyway. What is it? Some kind of test of how big a man you are?

Tony shows a flash of irritation.

It's just a conversation, all right? It doesn't mean anything.

Tony turns towards me. Nodge sighs a deep sigh, but stays sitting forward on his chair.

Perhaps you're right, though, Nodge, says Tony, having clearly made a decision to repair fences.

Yeah. Perhaps you're right. You can't be exact about it. Multiples count double. Fair enough, Frankie?

It makes sense. Like, one clitoral, one vaginal.

Colin? says Tony.

Colin smiles, says nothing, going along as always.

Nodge?

Nodge takes a deep breath.

It's stupid. How do you know the women aren't lying, anyway?

Of course you can tell if they're lying, says Tony, fidgeting with the menu.

It's a more interesting selection of puds than usual, which isn't to say they aren't horrible. Dry Carrot Tart is the most attractive. Then there's Barfi, which turns out to be one of those Technicolor horrors you see in Southall market, and something called Ras Malai – sour milk and flour patties served in sweet thickened milk. Tony goes for a basic Kulfi, while Nodge orders the Ras Malai. Me and Colin pass.

How?

Because when they really come they . . . they sort of bunch up. Inside, you know. You can feel it. And they go into a flush.

*Not **always**.*

Tony sighs and rolls his eyes.

*You're just trying to sabotage the whole thing because you think it's . . . improper. As if you've got so much more that's interesting to talk about. Who **have** you had in the back of the cab this week, anyway?*

Nodge's redness seems to deepen very slightly. As I have said, he never, ever loses his temper, because that would mean losing control, but sometimes you sense a kind of volcanic rage inside him that is expressed as disdain, or a haughty distancing.

That's not it. I'm just saying you can't always tell, he says coldly.

There is a long silence. Some breach has been made in the atmosphere. It often happens like this – what starts out as an innocent joke, ends up as a battle. It's as if the basic structures of our personalities are too exposed nowadays and graze against each other all the time. We can't be bothered or we are unable to erect a buffer zone. Still, we cling together. And it's not only out of habit. I'm sure that underneath it all, we really *do* like each other. But what good is that, if it's always underneath?

If I let the silence settle the temperature will continue to drop, so I start chattering on. I like to build bridges, despite everything. So does Colin, but he doesn't have the tools. Anyway, nowadays there's plenty of opportunity. I look at them both imploringly.

Boys, boys. Can't we all be friends?

This was, I immediately see, clumsy, a mistake. Now they've deflected their anger from each other towards me.

Don't patronize me, says Nodge, lighting another cigarette.

Tony just grimaces and nods. I plough on regardless, trying to clear the choppy water.

OK. This is the way it stands, then. The question is, how many times have you made a woman come, in one session, counting a session as from the moment you take your clothes off to when you put them on again. Multiple orgasms counts as two, but you have to take your partner's word for whether she's had one or not. Same goes for singles.

*So, what the thing is is, how many times have you made a woman **say** she's come?* says Nodge, pulling so hard on the cigarette that you can see the tobacco actually regress into ash. The thought comes to me, oddly: *transformation.* Plant to fag to fire to smoke to . . . I lose my way and flick the thought away from me as if it too were a dog-end, and continue.

It's the best we can do. In the circumstances.

OK.

Tony seems satisfied now.

So who's first?

Why don't you go first? Since you're the one who brought it up in the first place, says Nodge.

Since you're clearly dying to tells us all, I say.

Yeah, says Colin.

Or, at least, I see his mouth move to make that shape. The music's too loud, Colin's too soft.

Tony pulls his lips up tight against his teeth, as if he didn't already have the answer worked out long ago. His eyeballs move up towards the ceiling a couple of degrees.

I did make a baker's dozen once. That's without multiples.

Nodge laughs out loud. Then he points out of the window, up at the sky, and says, *That's something you don't see often.*

What? says Tony.

All the way up there. A whole flock of them. And in formation too.

I'm straining to look now as well.

What? Where?

Pigs, says Nodge.

I laugh, and turn back to Tony, who is throwing his head back to displace his fringe, which is always falling in his eyes. Women find this sexy, I am told.

I say, *Thirteen singles is biologically impossible.*

Tony shrugs, like he doesn't care whether we believe him or not.

She just had a hair trigger. It's not like I'm saying I'm a –

What? Stud? A super **pants** *man. Of* **course** *not,* says Nodge.

I just had to touch her in the right place and . . . ptttft.

Ptttft?

No, not ptttft. More like . . .

Tony makes a sound like he was lifting barbells that were too heavy.

Nodge is still trying to separate himself out from the voyeurism of the conversation. He wants to be lofty, analytical.

And this took place over what period exactly?
A night. We were awake all night. I was on E.
Hold on, I say. *That doesn't count then.*
Nodge nods censoriously.
That's right.
Colin nods too, but says nothing.
It's like using steroids if you're a body-builder, I
say.

Tony pretends he's outraged. He spreads his
palms outwards. Innocence.

Yep. You got to be clean, says Nodge.
That's stupid, says Tony. *Like, if you've had a few
glasses of wine, it doesn't count either?*

This brings things to a halt momentarily.

That's a fair point, says Colin. *That would change
the number of organisms.*

This time Colin is audible and we all laugh. Once
he has worked out why, he starts laughing too.

Orgasms, I mean.

He is embarrassed. He has a T-shirt on that reads
'Silver Valley Silicon'. It's the company he works
for, in Perivale.

*Right on, Col. But look. The two things are different.
Alcohol is a negative factor. It can only decrease your
performance. E **improves** performance*, says Nodge.

He looks pleased with himself, an expression
that is always hiding near the surface of the folds
of his face.

But Tony won't give it up.

*How would you know? You've never done an
E. Besides, it was only me that was on one, not*

101

her. And it's her orgasms that would be affected.

He turns to Colin, who was the most recent person to give him any support.

Colin, you're neutral. What do you say?

Colin looks immediately uncomfortable. He hates being forced to take a position. I watch his face. It is unbalanced. One nostril is bigger than the other. The French crop shows a whorl on the right side of his crown. One lip is thick, one thin. The right eye is narrower than the left. Perhaps this is why he's always seeking to balance things up. More likely, though, he's simply weak.

I can see both sides, I suppose. But –

Look, I'll tell you what . . . I'm speaking over the top of Colin, which is something that is no longer rude since it has been established by custom. *We'll have two categories. Class-A sex, which involves the consumption of Class-A drugs. On that count, let's say Tony wins . . .*

Not, of course, that this is a competition, says Nodge, with mild, indifferent sarcasm.

Not, of course, that this is a competition, but a general inquiry into the nature of human sexuality. But what about Class-B sex? That's involving soft drugs – alcohol or puff – or nothing at all. One session. Where do you stand here, Tony?

Tony takes it in good part. No one believes the baker's-dozen story anyway. It's just a shot across the bows.

You'll have to give me some time to think then. I

102

accept the category, though. Nodge, what about you? What's your personal best Class-B sex?

Leave me out of it.

He raises his hands like he was halting traffic.

That's so typical. Nodger Cromwell, the Shepherd's Bush succubus, I say.

What's a succubus? says Colin.

He looks puzzled. Colin always looks puzzled. But at least he has the honesty not to hide his confusion. Or the honesty has him. Perhaps honesty itself is a succubus.

A succubus? It's like . . . like a vampire. Feeds off your energy. Puts nothing back, I say.

I'm trying to make it jokey now, realizing how harsh the words sound. I don't want the temperature to drop again. I want us all to get along, particularly tonight.

Tony laughs.

Bang on. Suck Yo' Bus. Good word, Frankie. Word of the week.

He finishes the last of his pudding and summons the waiter for a digestif. He chooses a twelve-year-old whisky.

Nodge isn't smiling. He hates me using *vocabulary*. He bites the tip of the smallest finger of his left hand, then says, *A succubus isn't like a vampire, actually. A succubus is a demon that preys on sleeping men. A vampire sucks blood. And a succubus is always female.*

Nodge is what is known, I think, as an autodidact. He reads books because the covers make him feel smart, even though the books are crap. He's got them all on his shelf, all the pointy heads, the great unreadables – Thomas Pynchon, James Joyce, Jeanette Winterson, Angela Carter, Salman Rushdie, Uncle Tom Cobbleigh and all. He goes to French movies that go on for ever and admires the cinematography. He even goes to modern dance, perhaps the most shit of all contemporary art forms. Closely followed by opera, of which he also professes to be fond.

As I've said, not your traditional taxi driver then. Except that he is, actually. You can take the boy out of the Bush, but you can't take the Bush out of the boy, as my dad was always fond of saying. Which is why he goes to all this effort to prove that he's not just a cabby, that he's escaped. We're all in the business of escape, one way or another.

Tony shrugs, unimpressed, not interested.

Whatever. So you're a vampire. Anyway, what about you, Colin? How many times you made a woman come in one session?

Can't remember, says Colin, a little too fast.

This is an unkind question to ask Colin, because he, at the age of thirty, has only been known to have about three or four girlfriends his whole life, and the last one was a long time ago. The thing is, he probably *can't* remember. Then he speaks again, just to get himself out of the spotlight.

Three times.

We all whistle and hoot.

*Not **bad** . . . Who with?*

Tony's left leg is bouncing up and down in its place, as if it acts as earth for his nervous energy.

Colin doesn't like this question. Partly because he's shy, but partly because he will feel he's betraying the woman he slept with. He seems to make himself smaller in his chair. It's a gesture I remember from school when a teacher picked on him. His natural instinct is privacy, but he knows he has to give something out. His lifelong losing struggle to make himself interesting, to make himself accepted, demands it. He doesn't have Nodge's confidence to hold himself within.

Tricia.

Tony's foot-tapping rate increases.

You're shitting me.

Tricia was Colin's girlfriend, season of 1988–9, I think it was. Worked in a library. Small, mousy. Her nickname was Trish the Fish. Pale, emaciated, bloodless. Colin grins now and fidgets with the salt cellar. He inverts it, makes a little white pile on the bare table.

Yeah, Trish. She was mad. Full on.

Tony turns his head away, because he's started to laugh. I'm trying desperately not to join in.

Three times. Pretty good.

I slap Colin on the back with a sudden rush of genuine affection. I *like* Colin. I like him for his vulnerability. It's a little pathetic perhaps. But it's easier to love than the armour that Tony and Nodge always are so intent on maintaining. If they feel some kind of weakness is being exposed, they

105

get cold or aggressive, whereas Colin just looks kind of sad. Sadness is more genuine, isn't it?

OK. I've worked it out now.

Tony turns back, face composed, desperate to get on before he starts giggling again.

Geraldine Pascoe, 1991. Panter Pascoe as she was known. I was completely clean, she had half a bottle of Piat D'or inside her. Class-B drug. It was between the hours of eleven-fifteen at night and approximately three in the morning. Straight sex, no oral, no accessories. One multiple, counted for these purposes as two. Final count. Seven. No, no hold on. Eight. Eight orgasms. Six of those in the first two hours. Those were all singles. The multiple came last of all. After a little nap. Timed at approximately 2.55 a.m. Woke up half the block of flats. She was a screamer. Big-time. She could have been a professional.

A professional what?

Nodge is seeking out political impropriety. Like, *Are you saying she was a whore because she expressed her sexuality?*

A professional screamer. They have them. Like, in horror movies, says Tony.

Colin brightens up. Colin is a movie buff, especially horror. Latterly, Wes Craven, Dario Argenti and John Carpenter. But his all-time favourite films are 1) *Invasion of the Body Snatchers* (Walter Wanger, 1955), 2) *Dead of Night* (various directors, 1945), 3) *The Exorcist* (William Friedkin, 1973).

You get to know each other pretty well after

106

fifteen years. I know Nodge's top ten – no probably twenty – favourite records, though not in order. I know Tony's five favourite sex symbols (Bardot, Monroe, Madonna, Herzigova, Ulrika). I know Colin's ten favourite comedies, three favourite sci-fis and five favourite westerns. They know all my favourite cartoons (*Duckman, Dr Katz, Rocko's Modern Life*). I love cartoons much more than real life.

That's right, says Colin. *It's like, they have this really good actress but they can't scream properly. It's an art. So they dub on the screams afterwards. They bring in a professional screamer. Like some models do only hands? Some actresses just do screams.*

It's true. That singer, what was her name? She screamed for movies.

Which one?

Nodge is the pop buff, or used to be until he started on Radio 3 (*not* Classic FM, he'll insist on telling you that). Still has a whole room of his house devoted to the stuff.

Can't remember. She sort of wore pigtails and sang like she was being hammered like billy-o up the jacks.

Nodge flicks through the microchip in between his ears that constitutes his pop music knowledge. He has the answer in seconds.

Lene Lovich. Had one hit with 'Lucky Number'. 197–8? 1979? An early Stiff recording.

He's right. Colin speaking. *She was mental.*

Tony looks unimpressed. He turns towards me and he winks.

So, Frankie. Do you have something you would like to share with us?

Tony is getting bored again. He's checking his watch and not bothering to hide it. My heart leaps into my throat. Does he know something about me and Veronica? No. He can't possibly.

I nibble at my After Eight. It's not an After Eight, of course, but some kind of top-of-the-range version. An Elizabeth Shaw Mint Crisp, I would hazard. No. Bendicks.

Would you like one of these? They're quite nice.

Tony is not put off.

No thanks. How many, Francis? And none of your Frank the Fib bollocks.

That's what they call me. Frankie Blue, Frank the Fib. I'm not ashamed of it. A fib is not the same as a lie, after all.

Tony focuses and gives one of his winning smiles. Tony can charm men too. You're always faintly flattered – in secret, of course – that you qualify for time with him, since he seems to be so much in demand. At the same time you're irritated that he always seems to be on the way somewhere else. His mobile, an Ericsson GH688, has rung at least four times since we've been sitting here. He's always being *sought*.

I finish off the chocolate and swallow.

Nodge didn't say. I don't see why I should.

Having suddenly worked out the answer, I've decided I don't want to play any more.

Come on, man. Don't be a Suck Yo' Bus.

108

I yawn, showing boredom and reluctance. When I speak, it is flatly, to show that I'm not trying to boast.

In one session, I once made a woman come ten times. Five multiples, no singles.

This is actually the truth. As all good liars know, you only lie when absolutely necessary.

Tony laughs artificially loud. Colin follows his laugh with an echo.

Thank you and good night. Frank the fucking Fib sterrrrrikes again, Nodge says, still looking moony but refusing to be locked out of the conversation.

Look! The pigs. The pigs are back, say Tony, looking pointedly out of the window.

I give a little shrug.

This is what she told me. Why should she lie?

It's not **her** *commitment to verisimilitude we're doubting, Frankie,* says Nodge. *And how's* **them** *for syllabobbles?*

I'm tired of the whole thing now. My mind's going back to Veronica. I know I've been putting it off. I feel a rush of determination to unload the fact right away. But before that, I think to myself, *I win . . .*

Except since I like to think of myself as grown up, I immediately bury it. Then I remember not to lie to myself, and disinter it, and double it. *I win, I win.*

It is at this moment that the killer question comes, the reason I didn't want to play any more. And worst of all, it comes from Nodge.

109

Who was the lucky girl then?

No irony now. He's being friendly again. He doesn't want to play out the China Syndrome any more than I do.

Yet I almost – *almost* – snap back the truth. If I wasn't such an old hand at dodging – because the truth can be very seductive – I might have told him. If I was Nodge and he was me, the truth would have been there like a greyhound out of a trap, because, as I say, Nodge thinks of himself as the truth teller, however much it hurts anyone. He thinks it's cowardice to duck it. Me, I think it's just common sense. It's doing the decent thing, particularly in this instance.

So it is that I say – holding back an impulse to let my eyes flick to one side when I say it, a beginner's mistake when lying – *No one* **you** *know. Some girl I met on holiday once. She was American. Perfect teeth.*

I feel sure that these details make the story more believable. See Index, Frank the Fib's Unwritten Guide for Liars, under *Details, Use of in Creating Believable Falsehoods.*

She was **definitely** *lying then. American girls read books like* How to Make Your Man Explode in Bed. *Answer: fake it all. It comes naturally to Americans,* says Tony airily, fidgeting with his mobile, then gesturing for the bill.

Which holiday was that then? says Nodge innocently.

I think he genuinely *is* being innocent, not trying

110

to catch me out. Deep in his heart, Nodge trusts me. Funnily enough, I think he's right to. None the less . . .

Did we ever meet her? says Nodge.

Now doubts are setting in. Maybe he isn't being innocent after all. You have to watch your back at all times. Little daggers everywhere.

Then I think to myself, *Don't push me.*

Don't push me, otherwise it might just slip out that the woman I've given more orgasms than any of you have managed is Ruth. You heard right. Your *ex*. Your true love star, the solid point in a shifting universe. Reliable Ruth. Reliable is right. Five times: bang didda bang didda bang bang bang. So put *that* in your Craven A and smoke it.

Nodge opens his mouth to speak again. I'm ready to strike back, on the point of cracking in the face of the truth's dirty little seductions. Then, just in the nick of time, the waiter arrives with the bill.

Tony picks it up. Immediately I know what is coming. Colin shrinks a little bit, Nodge stiffens. I put Veronica to the back of my mind for just a few more moments. Any excuse.

A hundred between the four of us. Twenty-five each. No. I had a bit more. I'll leave the tip. I'll leave thirty. OK?

And he flings down three ten-pound notes, then picks up his mobile and starts to make a call.

Me and Nodge shoot glances across the table. I pick up the bill. Including his cocktails and his choice of the most expensive dish on the menu and a dessert, Tony has consumed approximately forty pounds' worth. Colin, who's almost broke, has only had a bottle of beer and a chicken curry – a tenner in all. Me and Nodge have both, it's true, spent about twenty-five each. Colin fidgets uncomfortably, but reaches for his wallet. I know that he won't say anything for fear of appearing mean.

I need a waz.

Nodge heads off to the Men's. Tony is talking loudly on the phone now. The waiter comes over to pick up the money. They're beginning to close the restaurant down. Still talking, Tony gets up to go. I give a big but inaudible sigh. *Same old same old.* Tony takes advantage. Colin keeps his head down. Nodge goes to the toilet. I try and protect Colin. I wish just for once . . .

Still. Custom needs to be respected. I gesture over to Tony, who is heading for the door.

Tony, it's not quite kosher.

I think he hears me but pretends not to. He carries on talking. I look round at Colin. His head is down. The waiter has come back again.

Could you give us a minute?

Restaurant is closing now, sir.

I catch Tony's eye at last and begin gesturing. He looks irritated.

What?

It's not on, Tony. The bill. Colin only had . . .

Tony raises his eyes to the heavens, as if having to deal with something irredeemably trivial. He reaches into his wallet, takes out a five-pound note and flings it on to the table as if nothing could matter less. Now he's cast himself as the good guy, me as petty and Colin as pathetic. And he's still short of what he should be paying. He starts back on the phone again. Nodge has returned from the toilet. He has clocked Tony throwing down the five. He looks at me.

Ah. Leave it, Frankie. We'll split the difference.

I nod. Nodge is, when all's said and done, pretty fair-minded.

Colin goes to put in his twenty-five, and I take fifteen of it and put it back in his hand.

It's too much, Col.

Look, I don't mind splitting. Honestly.

But I know that he does. His mother takes a lot of looking after, his wage is worse than Nodge's, and the long and short of it is he hasn't got a pot to piss in. Nodge throws in thirty-five, the same as me. Colin pockets the fifteen pounds reluctantly, but I know he's grateful. Still, I'm not sure whether at this moment I'm angrier with him or Tony. There's a part of me that's sick of protecting Colin. This has been going on for twenty years, for God's sake.

Look at this!

Nodge is grinning and holding a note in his hand, a twenty-pounder.

What?

Just found this stuck to my shoe on a bit of bubblegum.

Why does that never happen to me? Because I'm

not the luckiest cunt in the world, like some people I could name.

We leave the restaurant, Tony still barking into his phone, Nodge carefully scraping bits of bubblegum off the twenty-pound note. I feel the moment of truth rushing towards me like the push of air that precedes a tube train. The situation is now ludicrous. I have to say what I need to say, and we're all about to set off in separate directions. This is typical of me. By avoiding making a decision, I've backed myself in a corner. Tony finally clicks his phone closed. We're all waiting outside, preparing farewells. Then I hear myself say it, hear it slipping out unexpectedly, like Cowper's fluid out of a cock.

I'm getting married.

Everybody laughs, except me, and even I join in after a while, just because the laughter is so infectious. And I think, out of the blue, *I love my friends*.

Love them. At least I think I do. I know that you're meant to, but it's hard to be absolutely sure. Love for friends is a bit like love for your mum and dad. You hypothesize that it's there, but you don't know for sure until one of them croaks or something. Love for friends and parents is conspicuous only with their absence, whereas with women, if it's right, you can feel it, positively feel it, a little *tang*, a little *bing*, in the centre of your chest. For the first couple of weeks anyway.

So love for your friends is largely a matter of

114

faith. And I have it, I have that faith. Tony, Nodge, Colin, my oldest, dearest friends. I love them. I would like them as well, I would, only things keep getting in the way. What gets in the way mostly is the past. Yet while it's the problem, it's also what keeps us together. I've long since stopped asking whether we *like* one another. We're just . . . friends. We're furniture in each other's front rooms, too heavy to move. Friendship just . . . sets, like some weird historical superglue. They got the job. They exist as part of my history, and you need your history, don't you? Otherwise, what are you? Who are you?

No, I say, still laughing, although letting it die a little now. *I really am. I really am getting married.*

Quite suddenly, the laughter stops, as if a plug has been pulled. Then there is only the sound of a night bus thundering past, and the thin thud of distant reggae.

In September.

Colin is the first to stop playing statues. He moves awkwardly over from where he's standing by the kerb, bends over and gives me a slightly embarrassed hug. I don't know what to do with my arms. Colin and I rarely touch.

Frankie, that's brilliant. Congratulations.

He seems genuinely pleased. Tony and Nodge, on the other hand, haven't moved an inch. Then Nodge, very deliberately, takes his cigarette packet out of his pocket, removes one filter tip with an elegance that is even more precise, even more considered, than usual.

Great. That's great, he says, in a tone that aspires to be something from neutral to approving, but sounds about as cheery as a pile-up on the M25.

Tony says, *You're joking, right?*

I shake my head. A couple walks slowly past us, so the silence descends again until they've gone. Then Tony, having decided at last that I really am serious, says, *Bit sudden, isn't it?*

I suppose so.

How long's it been?

Since what?

Since you met . . . what's-her-face.

About six months.

Nodge lights the cigarette. Smoke cloaks his eyes.

What was her name again? Something Bush, says Tony.

Veronica. Veronica Tree.

Well, says Tony. *Well done.*

I can feel the atmosphere straining to breaking point. Colin is still grinning, but you can see he's having trouble holding on to the sentiment under the weight of the growing atmosphere. I'm beginning to feel just a little bit upset.

What's the matter? I thought you would be pleased for me.

Tony, I can see, is making a real effort to bottle his feelings. He struggles for neutral words.

*We are pleased, Frankie. It's cool. It's just that . . .
just that . . .*

Nodge is looking grim.

*It's just that you haven't even **introduced** us.
Apart from that time in the pub.*

He says this bitterly, and I suppose I can understand why. He thinks I'm ashamed of them for
some reason. Which is nonsense, which is rubbish,
which is crap.

Which is true.

The silence is building up again around us.
There's no script any more. Some great rift has
opened up. When someone speaks again, finally,
it is Colin, in a voice edged with a kind of panic.

*What about 14 August? There'll still be a 14 August,
won't there?*

Tony and Colin look at me. I know that this is
a test I have to pass.

That's sacrosanct. That stays, I say.

And I mean it.

CHAPTER 5

RELIABLE RUTH ON A
BINNER SESH

The strange thing is, I didn't much fancy Ruth. I didn't even *like* her much. But the moment happened and I took advantage of it. I didn't think of consequences. But they always occur sooner or later, don't they?

It was one night back in . . . 1990, I think it was. I had met Ruth many times by then – she had been Nodge's umfriend for about six months (as in, 'This is my, um, *friend*.'). Nodge felt it incorrect to use the word *girl*friend, although Ruth called all her women friends girlfriends and that seemed to be OK, and also those girlfriends could call *their* partners *boy*friends and that was OK, and also she could call a man a *prick*, but you couldn't call a bird or even a bloke a *cunt*, in fact you couldn't even call a bird a *bird*, not to their face anyway, although they could call you a *hunk* and say you had a nice *bum*, but you couldn't say *they* had a nice *arse* and . . .

But don't start me.

They seemed happy. However, I couldn't quite put my finger on it, but I didn't feel they were right for each other. They were too much of a mirror image in a way – their virtues cancelled each other out, but their flaws refracted, doubled and redoubled endlessly.

Nodge, though, was smitten. Of course, that word has to be used in the context of Nodge. That is to say, he admitted her existence to the rest of us, introduced us, spoke reasonably admiringly of her in her absence. All these modes of behaviour were departures for Nodge, who both subsequently and previously kept his personal, most particularly his sexual, life absolutely to himself. Although she never moved in, they went on holiday together once, which is often the preamble to cohabitation in my experience – or at least one of the fences you have to clear on the way to shacked-up so-called bliss.

Nodge met Ruth while he was doing the Knowledge, poodling around London on a moped with an *A–Z* lashed to the handlebars. Ruth was the only female driver trainee there. Like Nodge, she was a misfit among the crumbling fascists, tattooed Bromley boys and Jewish melancholics who made up the rest of the ranks. It drew them together. Romance blossomed as they tested each other on road layouts and traffic flows over mugs of Nescaff at Ruth's Camberwell bedsit.

Ruth was a good few years older than Nodge, and something of a type, brackish tidal wash of the 1970s. Like Nodge, she was a puritan, with an inclination towards censoriousness and fits of sudden moral outrage. Nodge was still soft-shelled at the time, only partially developed, and Ruth provided a kind of sand to his cement. Finding a kindred spirit reinforced his sense of rectitude. They became a kind of two-strong police force, always ready with a caution for inappropriate use of language or unacceptability of attitude. Tony used to drive them both into fits of apoplexy, quite deliberately. This was inexcusable, but it was also extremely funny at times.

Looks-wise, she wasn't the jackpot, and she didn't help herself any by what was in those days a fairly widespread determination not to kowtow to some Barbie-girl ideal of beauty. This was just before Madonna had got her kit off and changed everything. To be sexual in Ruth's book was still the same as being a bim.

Ruth was average height with cut-short but unstyled black hair, a few proto crow's-feet developing around the edges of the eyes, and rather stubby legs. Her greatest USP was a remarkable pair of large, fully cantilevered baps, which she habitually kept hidden under loose black sweaters or untucked white shirts. I cannot deny that I coveted these secret globes, particularly since at the time I was going through one of those inexplicably parched periods with women which get worse the longer they go on, since your confidence begins to stutter and women detect it like anthrax fifty feet off. But I never dreamt that I would get a crack at them, and I flattered myself that I would Do the Right Thing even if I *did* get a crack.

The overestimation of my moral fibre is one of my most regular failings.

I was firmly of the opinion that Ruth disliked me at least as much as she disliked Tony, which, I should say, was a good deal. Certainly I was careful not to wind her up too much – as usual, I was trying to fit in. But to a mind that valued commitment, a *point of view*, above all else, I think she found that kind of fence-sitting even more contemptible than Tony's irrepressible – but, I thought then, ironical – jokes at the expense of anyone gay, or female, or northern, or basically not from Shepherd's Bush and exactly the same as Tony. I was wishy-washy, and that was a cardinal sin in her book. The worst thing about her was that she made *me* feel like it was too – like not knowing what you thought was a crime. And I hardly ever know what it is I think. I just make it up. Doesn't everyone?

Also, if I'm honest, I was jealous. Nodge and I, before Ruth came along, were going through one of those times when we were almost in love ourselves – in a matey, football-kicking, beer-swilling fashion. We were best mates in a way I never then thought I could be with Tony or Colin – the one of them too inflated, the other too shrunken. But Nodge and I fitted together somehow. We always had, ever since schooldays. We went clubbing together, puked in each other's toilets, nattered on the phone for hours like a couple of girls.

When Ruth came along, all that changed. It was Ruth this, Ruth that, Ruth the other. When I rang him up to come out for a drink, he would just bring Ruth along as if she was invited. When they went to a party together, they would just take *one* bottle of wine instead of *two*. That's always fucked me right off. In an argument, they would always side with each other, whatever the rights or wrongs of the case. Also, where Nodge had always rung *me*, now I always had to ring *him*. It sounds trivial, but it isn't. It's about power. It's about how much someone is needed. And I was definitely feeling unneeded at that time.

They weren't that physically amorous. I don't think I ever saw Nodge kiss her or give her a cuddle. But they were in that passionate state where they thought each other was special. And no one's special, really. Everyone's more or less the same. People who don't realize that are annoying.

So when I rang Nodge one day to hear Ruth telling me that he'd gone off to visit some sick aunt in Runcorn, I found it hard to hide my disappointment that it was her answering the phone. For a start, I thought it meant they must now be in that netherland before you start living together – it starts with a toothbrush in the bathroom and a few pairs of knickers in the drawer and ends up with a mortgage, a pot of Sudocrem and the soft crash of hopes – but also, I desperately wanted a beer. I

122

was getting stir crazy a lot then, cabin fever, and needed to go out so badly it hurt.

Instead of making an excuse to get off the line as quickly as possible, I sort of hung on. Even talking to Ruth on the phone was better than nothing when I was in one of those moods. Ruth, to my surprise, seemed equally ready to talk. It was cobblers – about Nodge, QPR (Ruth, to her credit, was a supporter), what soaps had been on the telly. But it was better than staring out of the window hoping for the phone to ring.

Then, out of the blue, Ruth said, *You don't like me much, do you, Frankie?*

That was typical of Ruth, at least I thought so at the time – tactlessness masquerading as frankness. I mean, what if I didn't? Talking about it wasn't going to help anything.

That's correct, Ruth. That's because most of the people I know are unanimous in agreeing that you're a fucking horrendous pain in the rocks, is what I should have said, but my natural inclination towards wriggling came to the fore. *That's not true. Yeah, you annoy me sometimes, and I annoy you sometimes. But it's never boring.*

A total lie. It's always boring. I continued.

We can both be a pain. But I think you're great. Really, I do.

Yeah, I think you're great too.

This was weird. I assumed she, unlike me, was telling the truth. I wrestled with myself for about half a second whether I should make my

123

excuses and hang up, and then Ruth said, *I'm sorry Nodge's not here, but I'm not doing anything tonight. Perhaps we could have a drink together.*

Sure. Why not? I heard myself saying.

Why not indeed? It was innocent enough. You and your best mate's girlfriend going out for a drink. I didn't have a binner sesh in mind, or anything like that. Just a few quiet glasses of wine, some inconsequential chitchat.

That illusion lasted about as long as it took for Ruth to walk through the door of the Anglesea Arms – in those days untarted up and full of old miserable blokes smoking roll-ups – one hour later. She wasn't exactly glammed up, but she was for the first time ever wearing a tight sweater that advertised her remarkable breasts to their full advantage. It was the only time I had ever witnessed them unstrung, and it was a glorious and moving spectacle. I fought to remain aloof. But my body is hopeless at hiding itself. This meant we had an argument right away.

What are you staring at my tits for?

I'm not.

Yes, you are. You're staring at them right now.

*Am I? Well, they **are** a bit in-your-face tonight.*

I've got a right to dress how I want without every wanker in the pub ogling me.

I'm not every wanker in the pub. I'm just this wanker. And anyway, we know each other.

That just makes it worse.

124

. . . and so on. And this was before she'd even sat down.

But it was different from the arguments we had when Nodge was there. It was more like a row between me and him – spirited, but with the underlying confidence of affection that meant we could yank each other's chain without undue offence being caused. Ruth seemed quite cheerful about it, and immediately offered to buy me a drink, which I accepted. She came back with a pint of bitter and a gin and tonic. The gin and tonic was for me.

We kept on arguing, but it wasn't a matter of hostility, simply a mode we were used to and therefore comfortable with. As I say, I didn't have any particularly strong opinions about anything, but to keep things lively I simply contradicted every point of view she tried to trumpet. For once, this did not reduce her to a state of moral froth, but to a kind of knowing laughter. We drank, then drank more. Soon enough I was well and truly binnered. The drink made her breasts appear to expand and grow in proximity, and I felt myself desiring them recklessly. The desire made me like Ruth, but also dredged up little pipkins of guilt about Nodge. Still, I told myself, it was all fluff. Nothing was going to happen. Lots of blokes had fantasies about their mates' girlfriends.

We talked about Tony. Although I knew they didn't see eye to eye, I was surprised at the weight of Ruth's invective against him.

*That guy hates women, hates blacks, hates gays. He just **hates**.*

You're wrong. It's all a wind-up. It's striking on attitude to get a response.

*You strike an attitude long enough, it becomes **you**. Things start out as a joke and end up as the thing you are. I know he **thinks** he's doing it as a joke. I know you do too. But it isn't. It isn't a joke.*

I defended Tony, but I wondered if what Ruth said was true. I thought of the way he used up women like so much Andrex off the roll, and laughed at them behind their backs. I thought of the way he called black people *niggas*, but pretended it was just because he was so *unprejudiced* he could say what he wanted without any liberal guilt shit.

It was all just a crack, wasn't it? Just a piss-take?

Yeah. Then the final bell rang and Ruth sank the last of her pint. She looked me right in the face and said she was too pissed to drive home and could she come up to my place and wake up a bit with a cup of coffee.

Even then, I found myself unable to believe that this was anything other than a genuine request for relief from intoxication, so when she threw herself against me on the stairwell on the way up to the flats and began kissing me, I was amazed. After struggling with myself for a tenth of a second or so, I kissed her right back. She started breathing like she'd just finished up the

126

London Marathon, a sign I took to mean she was excited. I felt a marquee-sized construction appear in my trousers.

We burst through the door into my flat and continued the kissing there. She smelt of untipped cigarettes and the last quarter-pint in the bottom of a glass of Directors Bitter, but underneath there was something feral and wild.

At one point, Ruth pulled herself away and said sternly, *This is wrong, Frankie. This is terrible.*

But I knew that this was only so that she could register having said something of the sort when she remembered it tomorrow. My moral sense, always ghostly, was entirely submerged by a wave of hormones and penile blood, and I started grappling to get her sweater over her head to view the famous orbs. When this was achieved, a few seconds later, all thought of Nodge finally disappeared and I fell on Ruth with a gasp. It was a wonder I didn't just trampoline off again, but Ruth clutched me to her and made noises like she was happily dying. I took this, not unreasonably, as a come-on and continued the incursions.

It was amazing. It was just incredible. She came at least five times, each time lasting an age, and I know it was for real, because when she did, she flushed from head to toe, an amazing pink glaze appearing on her skin, only to recede minutes later, then reappear again after the next session. I think it was the best sex I'd ever had, or ever will have. It was the spicing of betrayal that made it so special.

But after we'd finished and she was lying next to me, trying to justify herself by telling me how her and Nodge's sex life was crap, how he said he loved her but didn't fancy her, I realized that I still didn't like her. Also the full force of my remorse hit me, now that it was in no position to stop me getting my way. My stomach turned over, rotated by the arrival of guilt and self-disgust.

When I woke up in the morning I was relieved to find that there was just a dent in the pillow where Ruth had been. I shook myself awake, lit a cigarette and phoned Nodge's flat. It was Nodge who picked up, sounding chirpy and well refreshed. It was obvious that he was oblivious of the latter part of the evening, but I didn't know how much he *did* know. Had Ruth told him that we had gone out for a drink together, but omitted the sex? I could hardly not mention the evening at all – but if I did and Ruth *hadn't* I would be equally screwed.

Frankie, how are you? What you been up to?

Just the question I didn't want. I desperately searched around for a way to get off the phone.

Yeah, Nodge . . . I'm . . . hold on, there's someone at the door. I'll be right back.

I held my hand over the receiver desperately hoping for inspiration, but I was fucked. I needed to speak to Ruth, to get my story straight. I waited for a few seconds, then put the receiver to my ear again. I'd made up my mind. No way out.

Nodge, I've got something I've got to tell you.

What's that then, Frankie?

Ruth's voice was at the other end.

Ruth! Thank Christ. Is he still there?

I dropped my voice, hoping it wouldn't project out past the receiver.

He's just gone to the toilet. Short time no see. How are you?

Loudly.

I feel fucking terrible. I feel guilty as hell. Listen to me. For God's sake don't tell him. We didn't go out last night. You stayed in and watched TV.

Yeah.

Loudly again.

It was good fun last night. It was so rammed, though, I could hardly move, she said.

Message clear. She'd told him about the drink, but not the fuck.

*Ruth, don't **ever** tell Nodge about this. It would destroy our friendship. And we must never do it again.*

Yes, well, I might have to disagree with you there, I'm afraid. On the first point at least. Not the second or the third. I definitely agree with the third.

What!

I'll think about it, what you said, though. Maybe I'll tell. Maybe I won't. Oh, here's Nodge. Mind how you go, Mr the Fib.

And with that she passed the phone to Nodge. Nodge expressed mild surprise at me and Ruth going out for a beer, but on the whole seemed pretty pleased about it. It was obviously beyond his imagination what a shit I can be, which isn't surprising, since it's frequently beyond mine.

I never saw Ruth again. I panicked about what she said about telling Nodge, but she obviously never did. No words were ever exchanged. Two weeks later, she left Nodge for a city trader and obsessive body-builder, a man with no brains whatsoever, or convictions, but buckets of cash, buns of steel and several acres of abs and pecs. It was very depressing for Nodge, who took it hard. It wasn't as if it was simply his faith in Ruth that had gone, but all the things she represented – equal opportunities, positive discrimination, women's rights, handouts for toerags, all that stuff.

After that he was kind of less militant about things in general, drifting into a more general leftish indifference. Somehow, irrationally, I have always dated the Blairite Labour Party from this moment of change in Nodge. After that I never really believed him when he vented his spleen about the Tories, or American cultural imperialism, or the threat to hedgehogs from arterial roads. After that, I thought he was just going through the motions. It comes to us all, sooner or later, I suppose. What else is there to go through?

CHAPTER 6

COLIN'S HANDCUFFS

I am ringing on Colin's doorbell. In the walkway where I am standing it is cold, although it is a warm enough day, somewhere around fifteen or twenty degrees. Something in the open corridors generates wind, which drops the temperature. The wind brings tidings, dismal trailers from the rest of the White City Estate: the smell of chips and junk-fed babies, small cascades of ripped and discarded lottery tickets, rattling beer cans sucked dry by collapsing scumbags. The light is fading; I feel nervous for my safety, as I always do coming here. Fifty feet below me, I can see three or four kids moving down the street in the direction of my Beemer. They reach it. One of them spits on the bonnet. Apart from that, they don't damage it. It's under a streetlight, next to a well-advertised security camera.

I ring the bell again and peer through the letter-box. Of course, it's blocked off. I can see nothing but a metal grid. But I feel sure that the bell isn't working, because through the barred window to the right of the door I can see some kind

131

of shadow moving. So there's definitely someone in. Anyway, Colin never lets you down. His social schedule is not what you would call hectic.

I hold the laptop computer that I have brought round for Colin to fix tight in my arms, nervous that some white Reeboked, stone-washed, malnourished welfare burden is going to rush past and grab it. It's top of the range, cost me 5,000, built-in modem, CD, and it's a very sick puppy indeed.

I lost my temper with it when it betrayed me. My body, machinery, Nodge, everything and everyone is always betraying me. After a long and frustrating day, it deleted a file I'd spent the last six hours writing. It was the computer, not me. It was just fucking malicious, spiteful. So I threw it – one eye still on the cost of the thing – at a big soft settee. It missed the settee and hit the wall. Since then, half the keyboard strokes display the wrong letter and I can't retrieve any of my documents. I've brought it for Colin to fix. Colin's a bit of a genius at computers. He has had computer companies all over the country trying to get him to work for them, to design software. But Colin has to stay at home and look after his mum. He does just enough work to pay all her hospital bills, which are immense, since she is a hypochondriac of titanic proportions, as well as being nearly crippled by arthritis, back pain, lumbago and chronic depression.

I bang on the door with my fist – the knocker has fallen off. Immediately, a shout from about twenty yards within the flat.

132

All right. Hold your . . . wotsits.

Colin's mum, the White City dragon lady. She takes ages to reach the door, shuffling and mumbling and sniffling. I think I can smell her through the letter-box. In my mind I see her, always in a dressing gown, always with downcast eyes. A lizard's skin.

Who is it?

It's me, Mrs Burden. Frankie Blue.

Frankie who?

Frankie Blue. Francis. Colin's friend.

Frankie who?

Olive Burden. Sixty-five years old and well on the way to merciful senility. Prior to being senile, she had been depressed, and prior to that, she had simply been stupid. I had never liked her, even as a child. Even then, when she wasn't so weak, she *performed* weakness to forge tiny handcuffs for Colin. These were carefully enlarged over the years to accommodate his adult wrists.

Now she was truly weak, Colin was so enfeebled by her dependency on him that there was no escape, not until she died. Colin's two brothers had both emigrated to get away from her, and he was alone now. They could have moved out of the flat, but Olive wouldn't. She was a wicked, stubborn old woman, with a hatred of life as deeply ingrained as the coal dust on my dad's thumbs. Now that she was more or less insane, the hatred had become more palpable, less socially neutered.

I bend my legs and shout through the letter-box again.

It's me, Francis Blue. I've come to see Colin.

Colin who?

I sigh and turn back to look over the parapet. The Beemer remains untouched. I hear a shuffle behind the door, then Colin's voice, gentle, beseeching, apologetic.

Mum, it's Frankie. Frankie's here. He's broken his computer and he wants me to fix it.

You and your pewters. It's all double Dutch. I can't make head nor tail.

Colin's voice rises a decibel or two.

Sorry, Frankie. I'll be right there. She's a bit confused at the moment. I need to find the mortise key to let you in.

No worries.

I stand back and gather my Crombie around me. The wind keeps on picking up, so that it fills my ears. It sounds like a plane descending in the middle distance. After a minute or two, there is the sound of a key in the lock and the door opens. Colin gives a defeated, what-can-you-do grin. His cheap gold earring glints in the dim hall light. His eyes are the colour of sludge. His faint acne scars seem to stand up in relief, as if prompted by the chilly temperature. The flat is always cold, though it's not as if they can't afford to heat it.

Colin's wearing a QPR shirt with an egg stain down the front, a pair of faded black canvas jeans and a pair of fake Air Jordans. I hear Olive grunting resentfully in the next room and I suddenly think of asking him jovially if he's ever heard of euthanasia,

134

then think better of it. Colin's sensitive on the subject of Olive. I suppose he's bound to be, she being his mother, but I would have thought by now he would have let himself hate her a little . . . tiny bit. But then that would mean opening a crack in the door; the door behind which stands that neon sign perpetually flashing: Guess What, Loser? You Wasted Your Life.

The flat has the exact same smell I remember from childhood, the straight-out-of-the-cellophane meat pie smell, then something milky, then, underneath, embrocation, floral air freshener, cigarette butt.

Through a doorway, I see old Olive Burden sitting in a big faded wing chair, shifting slowly from side to side. There is an ad for Bodyform Sanitary Towels on the television which she is watching raptly. Colin is regarding her with fondness.

Dear old Mum. She's had it tough. Haven't you, Mum? Eh? Do you want a cup of tea?

This last remark is shouted at Olive, but she doesn't respond. I'm staring idly around the corridor. Up above eye level, I notice an old photograph that's probably been there years but for some reason I've never noticed before. It's of Colin, about four or five years old, in what looks like a brand-new school uniform. He is staring at the camera, smiling broadly. He looks happy, unafraid, an ordinary kid. It is before his acne, before his father became a drunk, before his mother went crazy. His skin is glowingly, heartbreakingly, pink, fresh and pure. His eyes are not sludge-coloured, but quite a vivid blue.

The present, reduced, Colin turns to me and beckons me towards his room, and I follow him, not breathing through my nose because of the smell. Something aches slightly at the walls of my chest.

The room is about 12 x 12. The ceilings are low; there is a single bed against one wall and, above the bed, a collage of QPR posters stuck edge to edge with Sellotape, so that no portion of wall underneath is visible. On the opposite wall is a small window overlooking the neighbouring block of flats, and next to that window, a computer table with a screen and keyboard on top. Scattered all around here are floppy disks, computer manuals, old screwdrivers, CD-Roms and a forest of wires and leads. There is a wardrobe, a chest of drawers and a few shelves with no books but dozens of videotapes. I read the titles scrawled on some of the spines: *The Evil Dead, The Howling, Dr Phibes Rises Again, Halloween, QPR Season 1997–8.* All horror movies then. I wonder if any of them conceal porn but decide probably not. Colin would simply download it from the Internet, store it on his hardware, to use with his software, when his software was hard. Or something like that.

On the floor, comics – *Viz, Loaded* – a few graphic novels, *The Sandman* and *Batman: The Dark Avenger,* and a heap of computer manuals. No fiction.

The two other walls are bare apart from a giant photograph of Claudia Schiffer and an unframed film poster advertising *Invasion of the Body Snatchers*, with one drawing pin in each corner. What is obvious suddenly occurs to me with a strange freshness: I am in a child's bedroom.

Colin is sitting down at his computer terminal now, and the light from the screen illuminates his face. I can see already that he is lost in the screen, that some part of him has dissolved into that network of electrical impulses and silicon chips that constitutes the virtual world. He has not offered me a drink or a chair.

Check this out! says Colin.

He punches at the buttons on his keyboard with an accusing single finger, until the screen suddenly fills with a full colour photograph of a well-known film star being fellated by what appears to be a twelve-year-old girl.

Colin giggles, and jigs about in his office chair, rotating it twenty-five degrees one way, then fifty degrees the other, then back again. He is in his element here, among his darker impulses and domestic electricity. His blink rate is up, his leg twitches like Tony's does when he's down the pub, or about to close in on a new woman.

That's pretty wild, I say, feeling a bit sick. I'm not sure the girl is even twelve. But I don't say anything else. I don't judge my friends, like Nodge does.

That's nothing. You've got to see the 'Horse, Donkey and Other Equestrian' page. I think it's http backslash www stop pony and cart stop com.

That would be nice. But I've got to get back to the

office quite quickly. I wonder if you could just have
a quick look at my portable. It seems pretty fucked. I
threw it at the wall.

Colin looks momentarily depressed, even a little
shocked.

You threw it at the wall?

Yeah. It destroyed a file. For no reason whatsoever.
So I threw it at the wall.

He tuts, with genuine disapproval. I know he
thinks that this is both childish – since computers
can only do what they are told to do – and immoral.
He is far more shocked by the idea of me doing
damage to this laptop than the idea of some poor
woman being reamed by a Shetland pony, or a kid
sucking a movie star's todger. He swings round on
his chair to directly face me. His eyes, however, do
not meet mine, but settle right away on the laptop.

The r7685x. With or without modem?

With.

33.6?

Yeah.

What's the CD speed?

Does it really matter, Col? The point is, it's not very
well and I need it fixed. Do you think you can do
anything?

Nice machine.

He fondles the casing as if he were a mother
holding a child. He switches it on, punts at a few
buttons, then says immediately, *It's got a virus in it.*

What?

A virus. You've heard of them, I'm sure. People

design them to mess up other people's computer soft-ware. Bad people.

He giggles. It really is a giggle, not a laugh; small, a fast repeater, goes on much too long, no real humour in it.

Of course I've heard of them. Farley, Ratchett & Gwynne are plagued by the things. It seems estate agents are among hackers' favourite targets.

Colin gives another little snigger.

Have you downloaded anything recently? he asks.

Sure. I download stuff all the time. From the company computer, from the Net, from e-mail.

Have you got anti-virus software?

No.

You need some. I'll design some for you. And I **think** *I can retrieve what you've lost. Although I can't be sure. As for the keyboard giving you the wrong letters . . .* He punched at the keyboard. The 'a' produced a number 8, the 'b' an asterisk. *That looks like hardware damage to me.*

That's bad, is it?

Yes. But it's not necessarily fatal.

And with that, he switches off the laptop and summarily rips the back off and begins poking around with a tiny screwdriver. I watch amazed as his hand darts from tiny circuit to tiny cir-cuit, at bewildering speed. He talks to me while he works.

Have you any ideas about what we're going to do for 14 August yet?

Not really.

139

For some reason, the whole idea of 14 August fills me with apprehension and gloom. Colin seems to relish the prospect. He always does.

What about this? We'll start off by getting binnered. Then down to Thorpe Park and have a go on all the rides. Then go-karting in the afternoon.

We did that two years ago.

Oh.

His attention is on the guts of the computer again. I'm finding the silence a bit uncomfortable. I think back to the disaster with Vronky at the pub, heretofore the one and only meeting between my marital future and my social past.

What did you think of Veronica then?

This is quite badly damaged, you know. What did you do to it?

I was aiming it at the settee, I mean sofa. I missed.

I pick a greeny out of my nose and flick it. It seems OK in this environment, even appropriate.

Veronica. What you reckon?

Oh. She was nice.

Just nice?

Umhmmm. She was great. Amazing legs. I think you're going to have to leave this with me.

Veronica is clearly a subject Colin is uncomfortable with. But for some reason I have trouble dropping the topic.

Do you know, she said something very funny. Well, it made me laugh.

It's going to be touch and go. The hard drive is quite severely compromised.

She said she didn't think we really liked each other. Me, you, Nodge and Tony. Stupid, isn't it?

Colin looks up suddenly from the computer, his face an unreadable mask.

That's a strange thing to say.

Yeah. Stupid, isn't it?

A very strange thing to say.

There is a short pause, before Colin turns back to the computer. I can't work out what he is thinking, but whatever it is, he's forgotten it again now.

I don't know if I'm going to be able to rescue this.

But I need it. There's all kinds of stuff in there.

Didn't you back up?

Of course I didn't back up. It's nearly brand new, top of the range. Why should it go wrong?

What sort of stuff?

All kinds. Very, very important. Vital.

Colin whistles like a greedy plumber.

I don't know, Frankie. It's pretty badly hurt. Could take me a couple of days. What about golf?

Hmmh?

On 14 August. We could all go and have a game of golf. Maybe over at Perivale. Then take it from there.

Great. Whatever. I'll check with Nodge and Tony. Can you fix it?

Colin looks up at me as if I'm simple-minded and says, *Of course I can fix it. It's just a matter of time. I've got to take Mum to the hospital tomorrow, and she's got physiotherapy after that, then an appointment at the Mental Health Unit –*

He stops, looks thoroughly confused for a moment.

141

The nine-year-old whose room he inhabits suddenly appears in that prematurely worn face. He looks at me, almost uniquely, right in the eyes.

She's very ill, you know, Frankie.

I can't help myself. I glance at my watch. I've got an appointment in Hammersmith in fifteen minutes. Just about enough time, if I motor it.

Sure. I know. She's been ill a long time.

No, but, Frankie. She really is ill now. They've found something on the X-ray. I don't know if . . .

I look vaguely in Colin's direction, pat him on the back, glancing again at my watch as I do so.

Colin, she's going to be fine. She's as tough as old boots is Olive. More's the pity, eh? Just kidding, just kidding. I'm really sorry, old fruit. I've got to hurry off. I've got a flat to show. If I can just do another 200K's worth of business, I'm up for a big bonus this month. Listen, we'll have a drink, eh? I'm going to owe you a big one if you get that stuff back for me. Can I just leave it with you then? Maybe pick it up Friday afternoon?

Colin pauses for a moment, as if he wants badly to say something else. But then he slowly and deliberately nods.

Friday, yeah.

Excellent. You're a pal, a mucker. I'll give you a bell, all right?

Yeah. Give me a bell.

He says this lifelessly, almost under his breath. I start to charge towards the door; to my left, I see Olive Burden in exactly the same position as when I came in.

I yell, at the top of my lungs, *Bye, Mrs Burden.* Then, under my breath, *Die soon!*

I see her move very slightly. Her mouth works, then works harder. Then she says, *Colin who?*

And I laugh, and I'm out of the door, out of the smell and the constriction, and I look over the balcony. The Beemer seems OK. Colin who? Colin who? Poor old loony that she is.

When I get down to the car, I see that both the registration plates have been pulled off and one of the lights has been kicked out. I get in to start the car. The battery's dead. I go to the bonnet and lift it. The battery's gone. I kick the wall and swear pointlessly at the BBC building, just visible in the distance.

With my mobile, I call the AA and sit back to wait. I consider going up to Colin's flat, but decide that I can't afford to leave the car. I know it could be hours. I crank the seat back and let the recline go obtuse. The voice in my ear that followed me out of the flat repeats, *Colin who?*

I look up at the block of flats and imagine I can see him for a moment, but it's just a shadow, or more probably a dosser. It occurs to me how sorry I feel for him, and simultaneously how angry. *Loser* . . . I wonder if it was always like that. I don't think so. I *know* it wasn't. Once upon a time, Colin was truly my best friend. Once upon a time, I realize with a strange shock, I loved him more than anyone else in the world.

CHAPTER 7

A CHILD'S THEORY
OF GAMES

Colin was not my first friend, but he was my first Best Friend. I don't have to think twice to remember. His mother was a housewife, his father – who knew? Who cared? You don't talk about those things when you're nine years old, which is when we became mates. You don't talk about what you're going to do with your life, or how much you've failed to do with your life, or who is sleeping with who, or how much you've been hurt, or how the telly isn't as good as it used to be. You don't talk about your disappointments, or whether or not you're happy, or how much money you're making, or how paralytic you got last night.

You just played games. Honest games, that had names and rules and horizons and borders. You knew where you were with that sort of game. You won, you lost, sometimes you drew. They were exciting, fun. Innocent, I suppose. Not like the games you learned to play when you were older, the invisible ones, where you only learned that you had lost – when you only learned that a game was being played – when it was too late. The games that hurt.

Not fair, not fair.

When I say that Colin and I were friends, I mean the word in a different sense from the way I use it today. We were together, we were – not one person exactly, more like two sides of the same person. I don't know if we loved each other. It went beyond that. It was like – this sounds silly, I know, but it's true – it was like I imagined marriage would be when I was older. I thought that being married would be like being with Colin. When I was big and had a wife, she and I would play games together, laugh when we saw each other by accident in the street, chatter nineteen to the dozen about nothing in particular, go on adventures. We would make each other feel complete without losing any part of ourselves in the process.

I knew, incidentally, that I would get married, because it had been predicted by the numbers on a bus ticket. It was a game we played – as I say, life was full of games then, declared and identified as such. You would check the numbers on the bus ticket, of which there were five. The first two indicated how long you would live (73), the next one how many wives you would have (4) and the last how many children (2). Some people did it all the time, changing their prediction with each ticket. Me, I did it just the once – otherwise it

145

just seemed pointless. It would have been cheating. Rules are meant to be kept.

To this day there is still a part of me that believes I will live until seventy-three and have two children. As for the four wives – I don't know. To be honest, I'm losing faith. By the age of thirty I should have been on my second by now. Why have I waited so long even for the first? I don't know.

Maybe I've been waiting for Colin all these years. Some version of what we had. Veronica is the abandonment of that hope, perhaps. That's good. It means I must be growing up.

I used to – I still do – take my games seriously. Colin and I understood that if you didn't take them seriously, there was no point. But it was a very exact kind of seriousness – earnest without being vexed, light without being flippant.

We each had our own areas of expertise, games in which we expected to triumph. For me, it was ping-pong. There was an ordinary kitchen table in my dad's garage where we set up with a net, and we would go into that garage and play – I'm not kidding – for *hours*.

I had a square bat, green flat rubber, pimples facing inward. Inherited from my dad, quite a fine player in his day. It was a Slazenger Victor Barna. Colin played with a classic round bat, no foam under the rubber, pimples out. Very solid, very reliable, good to block the ball, good for defence and for deadening your opponent's spin. But the Barna – it was, it was more than just a bat. It could send that Halex Threestar ball every which way – the backdrop loop serve, the drop, the high-spun lob, the topspin backhand. It was a wand, it was a mace.

I played that ball like one day I would play at life – in deadly earnest, aggressive, a little unpredictable, not always thinking out every move, but by force of will always one step ahead. Watching that little pale globe leaving the surface of the bat, steady as if you had sent it straight, then hit the table and *spin*, forty-five degrees, fifty degrees, sixty degrees. If Colin got to it, sometimes it would just fly off his bat like a comet. On the balls of my feet like a boxer, knees slightly bent, moving from the waist. Deadly.

Colin, on the other hand, his game was table football. *Not* Subbuteo – neither of us ever got the hang of that for some reason. This was based on tiddlywinks, with the base of each player a flat disc the size of a new tenpenny piece. You flicked the counter from one end of the pitch to the other. Colin, he was precise, organized. He never went for the fancy shot, always played percentages. Slow and steady wins the race. He was the tortoise, I was the hare.

I remember his baby face, pre-acne, creased up in concentration, ready to flick, never more than two or three inches, whereas I'd always go for bust, the big one to the other end of the pitch. Bad strategy. Always my problem. Seven or eight times out of ten, he'd take me, not spectacularly, by the odd goal or two. It was enough. Colin never wanted life to be spectacular, even then.

Baby-face Colin. I wish I'd kissed him, before it was too late, before we were both self-conscious, grown. In my memory, I hold him in my arms and crush his bony, delicate body to mine. Colin, with his furrowing brow, the steady flick, flick, flick. We would stand and watch sycamore helicopters fall from the trees, capture them, and try and make them land on a spot on the ground. We would share Blackjacks and Fruit Salads, we would spill white Sherbet Dabs on our shorts.

There were other games in which we were more evenly matched. Luck games like Monopoly, Ludo, Sorry!, Snakes and Ladders. Although somehow I seemed luckier than Colin. Luck, I have always believed, is a quality you have, like blue eyes or grace. Nodge, for instance, has always been luckier than me. It drives me crazy.

Skill games, draughts and chess, and Chinese chequers. Paper games – battleships, hangman, noughts and crosses. There were quizzes, from books, or on the Magic Robot, which magneti-cally swung to the correct answer. There was Spy Ring, Totopoly, Escalado, Cluedo, Formula One, Campaign, Risk, Go, Escape from Colditz, The Battle of Little Big Horn. If it was sunny, there were penknife games, when we threw a small, unfolded blade into the grass in my back garden. You tried to stretch to it with your foot. There was football of course. Catch with a tennis ball – two misses and you were down on your knees.

There were toys – the Man from U.N.C.L.E. Starsky and Hutch. I had the Gold Attacking Martian Robot whose chest opened and a gun fired, whereas Colin had the Dino Robot, whose metallic head opened to reveal a dinosaur inside. I had a plastic Starship Enterpise Play Station, Colin had Steve Austen the Six Million Dollar Man and Oscar Goldman, his boss. I had Chewbacca, Major Matt Mason, Evel Kneival, Action Man, Dobie, Kojak, Huggy Bear. He had a model Ford Torino, Captain Scarlett and the Mysterons, the Bond car, Planet of the Apes action figures. Between us, we had them all. And we would lend them to each other, even our very favourites, without question or hesitation. We knew they would be safe in each other's hands.

Every day was another contest, especially in those long summer holidays, when we lived in each other's houses – or, in Colin's case, his flat – slept over, exchanged secret codes, swapped comics.

We went on adventures too. Perhaps to the paddling pool at Kensington Memorial Park, cobalt in the August sun. Colin and I splashing each other, bombing, having underwater races, playing 'It' around the pool perimeter as barking mothers commanded their children. Ours let us go alone. It was thought of as safe then. His body coffee ice cream, while mine turned a baffling pink. Shouts of laughter. Absolute presence in the day, in the hour, in the second. Such luxury then, with no past, and only the slightest trace of future in our minds.

Once we even went on holiday together. Colin came with me and my family to Cornwall, me vomiting in the Austin Allegro on the way down, while Colin stood slightly apart, indifferent, reading *Silver Surfer* in the dull light. He didn't try to comfort me; children don't assume those responsibilities, they aren't expected. You knew your limits, exactly. I didn't mind.

What did we do on that endless white beach, the dunes scattered with sharp, tall grass, the English green seaweedy sea? What did we talk about? I can't imagine. It wasn't necessary to talk then. That's how close it was. Now, when I go out with a friend, even my best, my closest, my least vengeful friend, and we sit in a pub, or walk in the park, words need to be spoken, like talismans warding off silence. Ten, fifteen seconds and it starts to be uncomfortable. Someone has to fill up the space, or . . .

Or what? Intimacy, that's what. That's not allowed any more, now you're grown up. But for Colin and me, silence was our currency, all the different kinds of it. Excited silence, anticipatory silence, glum silence, angry silence, concentrated silence. We saw then what we have now lost – that the words didn't matter, that words were screens behind which to hide. We had our silences. We lived in them like the fish we saw darting in the grey pools at the edges of the beach

150

as we searched for red crabs and starfish and jellyfish.

I remember the beaches being empty then, and just the two of us walking towards the low, flat horizon, the sea sucking at the sand, bubbles pulling through the holes that the hermit crabs left. Distended shadows of seagulls showing against yellow cliffs. Greenstones, granite, black slate, molluscs on black rocks like remnants of foam. The sheer brute randomness of the rocks, as if they had been dropped in one piece from a great height and had then shattered. The suck and wash of the sea. Changing weather, beating wind. Adults looming in the distance, another strange species like the weird anemones in pools.

There were chaps inside our legs from all the walking, nylon swimming trunks caked in mud. Colin and me, the beach, silence, clarity, singing air. We were absent, out of our selves, in that child's way, and this enabled the connection between us to stay charged.

It was . . . holy, I think. I know that's how Colin saw it – saw it in an almost literal way. I can be sure. Because he put it on paper. He *painted* it.

Colin was not a particularly talented child. His parents, Olive – sane then – and William, Billy B. as he was universally known, were assiduous in making sure that he completed homework, and the small projects he returned to the class once or twice a week were always well presented and on time. Unless it was mathematics, for which he

151

had an undoubted gift, the content was usually mediocre. Colin was one of nature's C-students who nevertheless managed to achieve consistent Bs through effort and application rather than flair. But the writing his work was presented in was almost pathologically neat. If everyone finds their own way of tidying up the world, it seems to me now that Colin then attempted to beat down all the uncertainty and shapelessness that make up a child's life through the shape and precision of his writing. It won plaudits from the teachers. It was truly miraculous, and in a school where merit in handwriting was considered – for some reason – to be a primary qualification for survival in the adult world, it became Colin's chief source of status in a place where he otherwise found only indifference.

This much-admired graphic precision, however, was a hindrance in other fields. When sitting exams, Colin never finished in the allotted time so concerned was he that each letter should be correctly formed on the yellowing woodpulp we used as paper. Also, the concentration necessary seemed to involve the protrusion of his tongue, making him look simple-minded – which, in a certain way, I can see now, he was. This led to constant ribbing by other pupils.

In those days, of course, I did not join in.

Colin and I were not competitive at school in the way we were at games – as I say, it was as if the playing out of that instinct on boards, fields and ping-pong tables bled the relationship of its

152

conflict. This was just as well, because I was a kind of mirror of Colin in that I was a natural A student who was too lazy to make the grades, and was happy to drift along with the same Bs that Colin had worked so industriously and single-mindedly to achieve. My mind always raced ahead of his, like the hare's mind it was, while he cautiously, step by step, moved premise by stumbling premise through to a rigidly adopted conclusion. But our – artificial as it turned out – equivalence on the field of study helped to maintain the idea that he and I were essentially equal for a long time.

The number of areas in the school timetable where we actually *were* equal was limited. I was better at sport, English, geography, history – you name it. Facts, interpretations, remembering – it was like breathing to me, while Colin struggled and wrestled with his own limitations. I always made the first eleven at football, while Colin, with his small, weedy frame, his slight, persistent asthma, always got picked last, and walked shamefaced towards a complaining or indifferent team.

My success at football helped to override the natural shame I felt at the birthmark on my face. I would often make a wish that that birthmark, raspberry-coloured, the shape of Australia and protruding half an inch beyond by hairline on to my forehead, would disappear, perhaps after pulling a chicken wishbone, or once every year with a silent prayer after blowing out the candles on my birthday cake. But only scoring goals at football seemed to work. The more goals I scored, the more applause I received, the more it seemed to pale and fade when I looked at it in the mirror. Once, when I scored a hat trick, I thought it had gone altogether. But it always returned. It was one of the things that linked me with Colin, because it announced my difference, my seemingly inescapable role as misfit.

Only in art classes did Colin and I have anything like the same natural ability – which, in fact, was a kind of lack of natural ability. We were both hopeless in our very particular ways. I was slapdash, all over the place, impatient. There was a flair of some kind there – so the teachers informed me – but to corral it into the shape of a meaningful painting or portrait involved, for me, an impossible amount of patience. I couldn't sit still that long, my hare's mind running ahead to the next moment ahead of this one. Each attempt I made to represent something of real life on the paper, although energetic, and sometimes imaginative and colourful, was technically hopeless.

As was often the case, Colin's problem was the converse of mine. His pictures and paintings were painstaking and meticulous, and he was extraordinarily good at copying material that appeared in two dimensions – a photograph from a newspaper perhaps, or flowers on a calendar. But when he was asked to think in an extra dimension – copying something from real life, for instance, or using his imagination to paint thematically – he would fall

154

apart. His pencil or brush seemed to freeze on the page; the mental equipment simply wasn't there. Perhaps nowadays it would be recognized as a mild form of autism, that extreme literal-mindedness he possessed, that exactitude, that simplicity. Yet it was that I loved in him – a kind of absence, an insufficient ability to dissemble or disguise himself.

Anyway, I remember on one occasion that the art teacher, Willy Knocker – a ludicrous character with a name to match who actually wore a beret when he painted, smoked in defiance of the rules in class and affected a bohemianism that in Shepherd's Bush was thought of as somewhat pathetic even by his audience of ten-year-old boys – asked the pupils to paint a picture on the theme of love.

At the announcement of the theme, Colin looked frozen, the posture he always adopted when confused. I, in the meantime, had already begun to attack the paper with a series of reds and purples, and even scarlets, since there was an edge of sexuality appearing in my idea of love by then. The mess I put on the paper suggested hearts, roses, the lips of a kiss – a child's cliché of the idea of love.

Today I would probably draw handcuffs.

We had two hours to work on this painting. I would occasionally look across to Colin to see how he was getting on – in a different kind of class, I would have tried to help with a proffered fact, or a sneaked calculation to make his marks look better. But in art I was helpless.

To my surprise, Colin had lost his frozen look and was working on the large stretch of sugar paper. His face was abnormally close to the paper, his tongue protruding as if he was doing his best handwriting. There was a slight flush to his face. When I caught his eye once, to give him the reassuring wink I would offer when I felt he was in trouble, he avoided it and bent back to the painting without acknowledgement. I shrugged and went on with my mess.

I ran out of patience after the first hour. Standing back from the painting, I could see that what I had done was a disaster – lacking in method, thoughtfulness, any kind of discernible technique. It looked as if a tin of plum tomatoes had been spilled into a dish of custard. Giving up the struggle, bored, I scanned the room for distraction.

Many of the other children had finished and were whispering, giggling, forging paper pellets and dipping them in paint to use as missiles. But Colin, four desks away, I noticed was still bent tightly over his palette, his sparrow's chest tracing the slant of the surface. His face was crumpled into a wad of concentration. Crooked teeth, crooked hair, the quiff standing up outlandishly from his crown, untamable. The muscles in his tongue had described a point at the end of it rather than a soft contour, always a sign that he was working to his absolute limit. I wanted to walk over and see what he was doing, but Knocker's avowed bohemianism stopped at any relaxing of discipline. Each pupil was to wait in silence at his desk until the lesson was finished.

Eventually, the bell for the end of the period rang. Knocker had already collected my painting with a grimace and was completing each of the other rows of ten desks. I left my seat, but instead of heading for the door went to where Colin sat, even now with head bent, brush working the paper with that doleful determination of his. He seemed to sense my approach and looked up towards me. At that moment, to my amazement, he sort of . . . reared up. A kind of panic appeared, registering all over his body as a slight tremor. As I progressed towards him, he started looking about wildly. I had seen him do this before, when cornered by some of the rough kids, but had never seen anything like it addressed to me. A look of puzzlement rippled across my face. Then Willy Knocker spoke from behind me.

Blue, the lesson's finished. Get out.

But, sir, I –

Shut up. Get out. Do it now.

I saw a shadow of relief pass over Colin's face. The expression in his eyes changed to a kind of welcome. He gestured at the playground as I retreated towards the door and mouthed as he pointed, *See you there.*

Knocker now stood over Colin's desk. The

harshness in his voice, adopted to clear the classroom, continued to rattle in the air.

*Come on Burden. Christ, that's what you are, isn't
it? A burden, a weight on everyone's shoulders.*

Then something odd happened. Knocker, who
had clearly been in a rush, hovered momentarily
over Colin's picture, then paused altogether. The
classroom was practically empty now, but I hung
back, waiting for Colin. Knocker picked up the
sheet of paper and held it at an angle to catch
the light. He gave a quick, not unkind smile,
then glanced at me by the door, then back at
Colin, whose nervousness had increased at the
unwelcome attention. When Knocker spoke, it
was more softly, and without the brisk dismissal
that had characterized his voice a few moments
previously.

Yes. That's good, Colin. A very good effort.

Sir.

I could see then, bewilderingly, that it was not
only Colin but Knocker too who was embarrassed.
It was the way he gathered up the painting a little
too quickly, the way that instead of putting it on
top of the pile, he slid it into the middle and began
to hurry away to his desk with a too sudden shift
back to his previous tone.

Well, then. What are you waiting for? A big kiss?

Sir. No, sir.

Disappear then.

Colin was always tongue-tied with the teachers.
He sauntered towards the door, where he now saw

158

me standing, a shadow of blush still on his cheeks. His hands were daubed with paint and he reached out, as a joke, towards my hair. I laughed and dodged, flicking some of the paint from my own hands on to the front of his clean white nylon shirt. It showed like a spray of red over his heart. We began to run down the corridor, him chasing me brandishing his hands. A teacher saw us and called a halt, and we fell into step. By now we were both breathless. We stopped at a drinking fountain and Colin bent to suck the thin jet of water.

What d'you do a picture of?

He raised his head, but didn't look at me.

Dunno. Nothing. It was stupid.

Mine too. Looked like I'd spewed my ring.

He laughed.

Me too.

And he caught me by the hair and rubbed, imprinting blue paint on the front hemisphere of my rough-cut fringe, staining my birthmark.

The normal rituals of playtime were gone through – running, water bombs, 'It', football with a crushed-up newspaper – and by the time the bell rang, I had almost forgotten the oddness of the scene with Colin and Willy Knocker.

Colin and I separated for the second half of that afternoon. The streaming system, defined by the size of the intake rather than rules of meritocracy, meant that we split up for many of our lessons. So it was that I walked along past the art studio on the way to – whatever it was.

159

I looked in and noticed that the room was empty. On Knocker's desk, the pile of paintings he had just collected. The scene of the two of them came back to me, intrigued me. I opened the door and went in. The air smelled of oil, chocolate, radiators.

When I reached the pile of paintings on the desk, I remember that I suddenly felt absurdly furtive, as if watching something secret and grown up and forbidden through a hole in a wall. I began to sort the sheets, looking for Colin's effort. The other paintings, it was a relief to see, were quite as bad as mine had been. Whatever the word love suggested to a ten-year-old mind, it was clearly pink and amorphous and involved cartoon hearts and badly drawn stick-figure mothers.

I knew which was Colin's painting before I read the inevitably perfect inscription of his name at the bottom. Even though upside down, I recognized the place he had depicted. He had made it out of powerful, bright colours – stark yellows, a blue sky the colour of the last stage of a Zoom ice lolly, pillar-box reds.

It was a bad painting, I suppose, as bad as the rest of them there. But it had a certain quality, and perhaps this was the quality that made Knocker pause and think about it. I couldn't see it at first – my child's mind was puzzled at the attention it had merited, and the palpable embarrassment of its author when I had approached it.

The scene showed an island, an area of yellow land enclosed by water. There were green hills in the background, gulls, a beach, all the normal images that would crowd a child's mind when thinking of the seaside. A cartoon sun shone from the sky, too round, too yellow. It was entirely unremarkable.

What was strange, however, were the two figures portrayed running on the white beach. It was strange at first because they were so obviously alone on this island and simultaneously dwarfed by it. Most of the other paintings represented people large, in the foreground, dominating the scene. This was just a wide, empty beach with two figures on it. All Colin's time must have been spent working on these tiny pale figures, overwhelmed by the colours that pressed down and around them.

The contorted angles of their limbs suggested that Colin's intention was that they were running. Two of the sticks that held out from the approximate bodies joined together; the figures were holding hands. Discernible fingers twined round each other. One had blond hair, the other brown. There were what were intended to be rivulets of water spreading down their lobster-coloured legs.

Staring at the picture, I began to understand what had made Knocker pause. Despite the spills of paint and the botched perspective, the flatness (Colin, as I say, saw everything in two dimensions), there was some odd radiance about the picture. It was something to do with the figures, not the background. Although badly drawn, there was something mysterious about them. A pale halo surrounded them in a slightly more dilute whiteness than the rest of the beach, as if they were enclosed in their own private air. Their faces were indistinct, but their expressions were meant to indicate joy, and somehow this was miraculously communicated in a few crude lines. One of the faces, the brown-haired boy's, was blurred, indistinct. The other – the blond's – was, in contrast, drawn with bold exact lines, delineating eyes, mouth, nose etc.

I knew at once that it was meant to be me – although it looked nothing at all like me, Colin hadn't the skill – and yet I didn't understand why I was clear and Colin was blurred. Only years later did it occur to me that Colin could not see himself and used me as a kind of mirror, or sounding board. A lifeline, even, to the outside world.

I stared. It was hard to explain; the thing was junk, but there was emotion in it, as if emotion had been layered on to the page directly. And the emotion was the one Knocker had asked for: love. Of course, none of these things came to me in words as they do now, but in a complex of feelings and intuitions, unarticulated. I understood why Colin had been embarrassed, though. Even at ten years old, you have learned that expressions of love – for boys, at least – are ridiculous, sissy, dopey. What possessed him to paint it I couldn't imagine – it was like taking his clothes off in public.

As I stared at it, I felt my skin creep with embarrassment. I realized that Knocker couldn't have known it was meant to be us two, despite what I had thought to be his knowing glance towards me. And yet underneath the embarrassment – a taught feeling, a learned response – there remained another layer of emotion, which I could hardly face up to, that of a returning love, and of gratitude for the picture and Colin's simple passion. I forced myself to shake it off, like a dog shakes off water, leaving only my embarrassment and a kind of rage at being violated. I never said anything to Colin; when the paintings were given back the next week. I avoided his eye and was relieved when, after the lesson was over, I saw him stuff the picture into his satchel before anyone else could see it. As ever, he had got a B for his efforts.

The thing about it was – I know this is often said about childhood, and often wrongly, but in this case it seemed to be true, perhaps for the last time – our friendship was so uncomplicated, so without artifice. Or to be exact, the artifice was in the place it was meant to be, out in the open, codified, ritualized. On the games board, over the net, on the pitch. That's where the complications were located – not in the friendship. The friendship was clear blue, unsullied. Which was odd in a way, because children – like their strange and distant relatives, adults – are stuffed to the brim with passions, and longings and needs, and reckless furies. I wonder now how we confined ourselves, how we cut ourselves off from all the dross and mess; or perhaps I have simply misremembered.

Anyway. It was a golden time, a friendship without malice, or complication, or heartless calculation, a friendship as natural as breathing, an unspoken love that submerged and renewed.

It didn't last of course. I sold him out in the end. It wasn't because of the painting. It was just . . . life, with all its blind hammerings out. I broke what there was of his heart, I cracked his soft little tortoise shell with one well-aimed blow. I didn't want to, of course. It just had to be done. That's the way it is with friends. Sometimes, whatever you've been through, however deep the love, you have to cut them out, cut them off. It's all in the name of progress, of moving forward. Life's movement requires a sort of ruthlessness or you get . . . bogged down. Things change, and, as they change, things break.

CHAPTER 8

THE ART OF PRAYER

I am at Veronica's flat after finishing work on a Thursday night. It is less than two months before our wedding is due to take place, at the Church of the Holy Innocents by Ravenscourt Park, 200 yards from my house. I am waiting for her to come back from the morgue.

That's a nice phrase. That has a ring to it. 'I'm just waiting for the wife to get back from the morgue. Oh yes. She chops up the dead to earn her crust, you know. The money isn't so good, but she finds the work extremely satisfying. That's so important, don't you agree?'

What am I doing? Marrying someone I've only known for a matter of months who spends a good forty hours of each week filleting people like a fishwife goes at a mackerel. I must be insane. Like Tony has said – since my proposal – I'm only thirty, I've got a good five years left in me before I need to be *got*, before the gut begins to sag, before my stock begins to drop, before Commitment beats out Freedom once and for all.

And yet I ache for her. Sitting here, I imagine her in the car, stopped at red lights, stuck in traffic. I urge the cars in the jam out of the way, I beg the lights to change. Something in me calls out. It's fucking weird. I don't think I like it. I didn't know love felt so much like dependency, like nakedness.

Or is it love? Perhaps it's just my todger talking, sending out static, blotting out sense. It can do that. It almost exists in order to do that. How are you meant to know any of these things? What does certainty feel like?

I've been thinking and thinking, and I think this: I don't think I can go through with this marriage. I've been waiting for the right moment to tell Vronky, but it never seems to arrive. I always back off. It's not a matter of whether it's what I want to do any more. It's just all got too big to simply fold up and put back in a drawer.

Or is that a rationalization? Perhaps I don't want the right moment to arrive. Christ, I don't know. I just wish things could be settled, one way or the other. Not knowing, that's the definition of true torment. And the clock is ticking, layers of events are unfolding that make it harder and harder to back off. It's planned that way, no doubt. History has arranged it thus, in order to better fuck everyone up. One of its specialities.

The church is booked now, the hall is booked, the invites have been sent out, the car has been arranged, the honeymoon is bought and paid for.

To go back on it now would just be so . . . inconvenient.

I shuffle around the flat pointlessly, inspecting it nevertheless with a professional eye. I strongly advised Vronky not to buy it. It's in a nasty part of North Kensington, a single bedroom in a converted house. No one has yet seen who lives downstairs. But there are endless comings and goings, steel doors and the constant faint complaint of some tetchy mutt with a close but impure relationship to a pit bull. It all suggests to me one thing: a crack house. But Veronica thinks it's wonderfully gritty.

She bought it because of its *feel*, because it seemed welcoming and friendly. I said to her, it's a flat, bricks and mortar, you're buying an asset, not Paddington fucking Bear. But she kept going on about its vibrations.

What a paradox people are. This I know from selling houses. On one shelf of Vronky's flat I can see this huge, intimidating volume, *Gray's Anatomy*. Pure science. Right next to it, *Astrology, Destiny and the Future of Mankind*. Pure shite. How can someone so smart be so dumb?

It's a question I often ask of myself also.

Anyway, she had her friend in who's a feng shui master and this friend told her it was perfect. So that was that.

Now I wander around, waiting for Vronky to get home, wondering if she might have been right, but doubting it. Idly, I study the other books on IKEA shelves which I have helped to construct. There are books on Sufism, Buddhism, Zen, Vedantism, Hinduism, Jainism – you name it, she's started it. There's *Bridget Jones's Diary*, *Emotional Intelligence*, *Men are from Mars, Women are from Venus*. There's Austen, Brontë, Eliot, Woolf (Virginia) and Wolf (Naomi). Toni Morrison, *Jazz*. An unread copy of Marina Warner's *The Beast and the Blonde*. It's your basic New Age Lite-cum-middlebrow thirty-something female canon. It'll do. It gets me far enough away from Shepherd's Bush, so to speak.

The flat, then. Sure, it's got nice big windows, bare floorboards, a decent-sized kitchen, high ceilings, original fireplace. All the bits and bobs that get the girls wet. But there's stuff that worries me. First, the estate agents she got it through – Bartlett and Bugle. I know, without a shadow of a doubt, that B&B are the dodgiest, shadiest, most reprehensible estate agents in west London – and I say that with a degree of admiration. They deal with freeholders who make Dirty Bob look like the Pope. B&B – or Bumfuckem and Billit, as we in the trade call them – knock themselves out half a percentage point cheaper than everyone else in the neighbourhood. Of course, just by sheer luck, they must shift a few decent properties, and maybe this is one of them. But I don't like the look of the two big thirsty trees in the street out front, combined with a brand-new paint and plaster job inside. Just right for hiding any inconvenient cracks.

Also, I've never heard of the freeholder, despite

having sold property around here for around ten years now, and the extreme low level of the service charges over the past five years suggests something isn't right. Everything points to a nasty surprise waiting in the wings, or in the roof space, or under the floor. Still, I suppose I admire her for doing what she wanted to do, buying the flat she wanted to buy. She's very independent and I respect that. Up to a point.

I sigh and look at my watch. She's late. I can't say I'm exactly looking forward to the evening anyway. I've resolved – since I've decided to ask Tony to be my best man – to make Veronica and Tony like each other, or at the very least tolerate each other. When they met that time in the pub, Tony spent the first half hour trying to charm her. Meticulously, she refused to respond, and after that he went into a sulk and they barely spoke. Tonight I'm going to try and mend a few fences.

Unfortunately things have started going wrong already. We planned a quiet drink, the three of us, down the Anglesea. I was going to ask Tony there, oil us all with a few bevvies, and then do the best-man thing. Then Vronky said that she'd suddenly found out that someone called Christopher Crowley, who the same friend who does the feng shui believes is a spiritual genius, was putting in an appearance at Kensington Town Hall on the same night, that is to say tonight. It was only for an hour, so could she go to it and meet us afterwards? Fine, except that when I spoke to

169

Tony, he decided he wanted to go too. I thought he was joking at first, but he insisted. Now we're meeting at the Churchill Arms, all going to see this guru, then going down the Anglesea afterwards. I tried to talk him out of it, but he wouldn't let go. Veronica, innocent fool, was delighted, and started to say how that perhaps she'd got Tony wrong after all. If she only knew Diamond Tony's other nickname: the Wazir of Wind-up.

I hear Veronica's key in the door. It swings open and she hurries in. She looks smart, well groomed, as if she's spent the day quietly behind the screens at a bank. The red hair has nothing out of place. Her face is in a grimace, the small teeth just showing. She barely looks at me. Despite myself, I glance at her hands to see if there's any blood on them.

Hi, babes, she says, all of a dither. *What time is it?*

I darken my voice a shade.

Nice to see you too. Babes.

She checks herself, stops in her tracks, then moves towards me with an apologetic expression creasing her face. She kisses me full on the lips, holds me for a second, kisses me again and shoots me a big sparkly smile. Then she continues on her interrupted route towards the bathroom.

Sorry, Frankie. It's been a bad day. I'm sure you don't want to hear about it. What with your weak stomach. Anyway I know I'm late. Can you check that clock?

I peer through to the kitchen, where the only clock in the house is located. Veronica by now has her coat off, has slipped her shoes off and is at the bathroom door.

It's just gone seven.

Right. I've got about fifteen minutes. Is Tony still coming?

I think so. We're meeting him at the Churchill first.

Strange choking sounds begin emitting from the plumbing system. Veronica is talking to me behind the door now.

Isn't that sweet? And I thought he . . . Christ, what's this?

What?

The water's gone . . . yellow. No, **brown**. *It's filthy.*

Let it run for a while.

More strange, apocalyptic sounds from the plumbing system. After a minute or two, I hear the toilet flush. I study the ceiling, noting small hairline cracks that work their way out from beneath the cornices.

How's the water?

Better. I'm going to have a quick bath. It smells a bit of old eggs though. Listen, can you pass me my book. It's just in my bag there. Red cover. The Art of Prayer.

Got it.

Stick it round the door, will you?

I push the book round the door and sit down

171

at the kitchen table to wait. There's a small colour pamphlet that shows a kind of sun, or centre of emanating energy, on the cover. Written underneath, it says, 'Christopher Crowley of the World Spiritual University: Power of Symbol, Call of Myth'.

Inside, there is a small photograph of Crowley. He is white, handsome and tanned and wearing a well-cut grey suit. He has a Californian smile, although I understand from Veronica that he's originally from somewhere in the Midlands.

I pick at snippets from the rest of the leaflet. Somewhere on the back shelf of my conscious mind, I hear the water draining away from the bath. I carry on reading. The World Spiritual University, it turns out, is holding a number of seminars that month.

– *Thinking Positively. Releasing the power of the positive mind. Methods and techniques for PMA (positive mental attitude). How to disarm others' negativity. How to harness the phenomenal power of thought.*

– *The Art of Relationships. The four essential relationships. How to avoid being blamed and blaming. Ten principles of successful, harmonious and loving relationships.*

– *Inner Values for Leading, Learning and Living. You are never more powerful than when you are being yourself. Shedding light on the inner recesses of yourself. How one leads not from the back, or the front, but from within.*

172

– *Building Self-esteem. The secret of sustained success. How to discover your hidden, spiritual self. There will be exercises to help develop self-acceptance.*

– *Managing Your Self. You cannot manage external forces of change. What you can manage is your ability to respond to change. This is your response ability, and every response is your choice.*

I yawn and put down the pamphlet. It all seems reasonable enough. I wonder why it makes me so irritated. I think because it threatens my basic world-view, philosophy and religion, which is No one Knows Anything. Maybe I'm wrong. Who knows? If no one knows anything, that must include me. Which means that one possibility is that everybody knows a lot.

I check the clock again, walk to the door and yell.

Seven-fifteen. It's time we made a move.

Immediately, as if she has been standing, coiled, behind the door, Veronica emerges. She is pink and smells of sandalwood, or at least what I imagine sandalwood would smell like if I had ever smelt any. The squashy nose is slightly wrinkly now as well from being in the hot bath. Her legs are about three-quarters exposed by an elasticated microskirt. On top, a white blouse of some kind of see through material. Her hair, gelled, has had the brightest part of the red toned down. She looks very sexy, the lazy eyelids somehow heavier than ever after the bath. She's terrific in bed actually, a real romper; probably something to do with

173

compensation for spending all day with death. She gives me a brief smile. Her eyes indicate that her mind is elsewhere, running through a private check-list. Mobile phone in bag? Got purse? Tampax – she's due. A couple of johnnies, just in case. Keys. In her hand she's still holding *The Art of Prayer*. For some reason this irritates me far more than anything in the pamphlet I've been reading. She moves towards the door. The way she moves is slightly stiff, as if she has to work out which limb to put where before she places it like Bambi while he's being tutored by Thumper. It's not graceful, but it's affecting, slightly gawky.

OK. Let's get off then.

She pulls on a red knee-length wool coat, slightly flared from the hips, and opens the door. She sticks the book in the pocket, and I follow her out of the door.

As we walk down the stairs, I say, *Planning on a bit of a pray, then?*

I say this unnecessarily nastily. I can hear the edge of complaint. For some reason I can't stop myself. Veronica simply ignores me.

We get into the Beemer, the smell of soft leather mixing with the hypothesized sandalwood. She takes off her coat and throws it on the back seat. The book catches my eye again. It's still irritating me. I feel myself gravitating towards a fight. She takes out a small packet of sugar-free chewing gum.

Aren't you going to say grace before you eat that?

174

This time, she turns on me, teeth exposed.

What's the problem, Frankie? Am I doing you some kind of harm by carrying a book about with me? Does it offend your commitment to pig ignorance?

I start the engine. Although I don't want this, this is also what I want.

Not at all. I'm a big fan of intelligent books. As you know.

Emphasis on intelligent.

Oh, And is this one not intelligent enough for your fiancée to be reading? Is it an embarrassment to you?

I pull out into the street and towards Ladbroke Grove. An Escort, shaped like something that's been trodden on, tries to push in front of me from a side turning, but I won't let him go. The driver winds down his window and shouts something at me. I give him the finger and press doggedly on to the junction, braking aggressively. I myself have no idea why I'm making such a fuss about the subject. Something pulls me forward, though, further into the argument.

No. But I do think that prayer is an exercise in wishful thinking by people who are more hopeful than analytical.

So you're saying I'm thick?

I'm not saying that you're –

Of course I'm thick. That's why I'm a highly trained scientific technician and you're an estate agent.

Long, long pause. We make our way up the Grove towards the junction with Holland Park Avenue. I'm still trying to work out what's eating me, when Veronica says, quietly and without aggression, *Do you ever pray?*

Pray? I say, as if I have no idea what she's talking about.

You know. Get down on your knees. Humble yourself. Ask for help.

I don't need any help. I can look after myself.

I am surprised at the force and anger with which I say this. Veronica shows a slight recoil in the seat. I shift about, fidget with the radio dial. We're turning into Notting Hill Gate. Time to make amends.

I'm sorry, Veronica. I'm a bit on edge at the moment. I'm within a whisker of getting my bonus for the month and we need it to help pay for the wedding. It costs a fortune, doesn't it? And all for what? We haven't stopped bitching at each other since we decided to do it. Come to that, I haven't stopped bitching at everyone else. It's the stress, I suppose.

Veronica doesn't say anything. I hear myself babbling on.

It's just the pressure of the thing though, isn't it? Couples who are going to get married go through this. It's inevitable. Part of the process, I think. You have to learn to live through, through . . . vicissitude. And it makes sure that you mean it. I mean, if you don't change your mind after all this aggravation, you must mean it, mustn't you?

Still Veronica is silent. This time, I can't think of anything else to burble, so I shut up. After a few

176

seconds she speaks again, in exactly the same tone, gentle, not aggressive.

So. Do you?

What? Mean it?

Do you ever pray?

Why do you keep going on about it?

It's only the second time I've asked.

Of course I don't pray. Who's there to pray to? Father Christmas? Twinkle, the little star?

*When's the last time you **did** pray?*

Jesus, can't we talk about something else?

I shout this, quite loudly. Veronica recoils once more. I feel more furious than ever, a tight, hot ball in the centre of my stomach. Then, to my amazement, I feel a single tear on my cheek, and the anger begins to dissolve and transmute into something else, something much softer and sadder. When I speak again, we have reached the Churchill. I reverse the Beemer into a tiny space, first time. Neither of us moves to leave the car. My voice has gone small.

I haven't prayed for a while. Probably once in the last ten years.

Did it work?

No.

What did you pray for?

And almost before she finishes the question, I hear myself say, cold and dry, *I prayed for my dad to die.*

Veronica doesn't react. Her hands are tight-clasped together. I want this to stop. Through the

177

window of the Churchill, I can see Tony moving towards an empty table. I want to go and join him, talk about the football. Have a beer, speak rudely of women behind their back. I don't want this . . . mind-fuck. But somehow I can't move.

Then I feel a shrinkage within me, a shrivelling, as the memory slides upwards into my conscious mind. Dad on a pink-framed hospital bed, his face all yellow and tight, his mouth open, terrible sounds coming out. I feel the words being sucked out of me like they were being pulled by vacuum out of a tiny broken window on a plane in the stratosphere.

He had lung cancer. All that coal dust, I suppose. He never smoked. It hurt. It hurt him. I didn't like to watch it.

For no reason, I reach over and switch the radio on and off with my index finger. The engine is switched off so it doesn't operate anyway. Then I say, in what sounds to me like a very matter-of-fact voice, as if I was making arrangements for dropping off the laundry, *So I went to a church and got on my knees and prayed for my father to die. I composed a long prayer to God. All the reasons he needed to let my dad off the hook. What a good dad he'd been to me, how hard he tried. Although he couldn't touch me. Too shy. How I would believe in him if he would just let dad slip away. How he could take something from me in exchange. An arm, maybe. 'Cause it was hurting Dad.*

Veronica nodded. I was unaware of her now. I

heard that my voice had splintered, become faint. The sulphur lights outside turned everything yellow. Her voice drifted over the space between us.

You were close to your father, weren't you?

I nodded.

I suppose so.

I wish I'd known him.

Me too.

I watched traffic lights change from green to amber to red. My voice, when it came again, didn't sound matter-of-fact any more.

All this stuff you do without choosing it.

He was my best friend, you know.

I sound as if I have only just discovered this thought. Then I realize, I have. I have only just, this moment, discovered it. Now I do, at last, look at Veronica.

The thing is, I never knew it. Neither of us knew it, not until he died. You don't, do you? You don't talk about things like that to your dad. At least, I don't. Didn't.

Veronica goes to get out of the car, to gently end the moment, seeing that it is hurting me, but now I am gripping her arm tightly with my hand. She has shifted a secret wedge from inside me, uncorked some fat genie.

*No. **Listen.** I stayed in that church an hour. I was on my knees all that time. I'd never been in that church before. As a matter of fact, it's the one we're getting married in. At Ravenscourt Park. There were little red prayer mats, but I never knelt on one. I wanted God*

179

to know I was serious. That I wasn't taking any little comforts. When I came out, my knees were raw. Big splinter in one of them.

The thing is, I thought it was going to work, which was strange, since up to that moment I was not a believer, not into that kind of thing. I thought it was all crap. But I prayed so much. So much. Then I came out, I came out and looked back at the church and thought, there's thousands of these fucking things, millions of them. They wouldn't have built them all for nothing, would they? Well, would they? All those clever men.

I shake my head, once, mystified still. I can't meet Veronica's eye. I can't stop talking.

*The thing is, my dad was a good man. Worked all his life, never had a bad word for anyone. A deserving case, if ever there was one. And I'd put in the work. And I didn't ask for anything **unreasonable**, like asking for him to recover, because that would have been pushing it. I just wanted him to go easily, quickly. So. My knees were bleeding, I swear. I had a headache from so much praying. When I went back to the hospital, I thought he would have slipped quietly away. I was sure of it, for some stupid reason.*

I stopped speaking. I felt I was choking. Suddenly I didn't want to continue.

Veronica spoke so gently, with such an aching sympathy. But all she said was, *Frankie.*

I felt my cheeks soaked now. I had to keep talking. I had no choice, now. *Frankie,* she said.

I went back to the hospital, and I was walking down

the corridor, and I was maybe a hundred yards away from my dad's room. And I heard this screaming. And it was the worst screaming I'd ever heard in my life. Like a . . . banshee or something. Everyone in the corridor was glancing around in the direction of the room. And as I got closer, I knew that it was my dad. Then I realized, he was screaming my name. Like this . . . My voice went very, very quiet. *Francis. Francis.*

A woman parking warden went by, peered momentarily in the car. She smiled, and I smiled back. Then I said, *He never called me Frankie. Don't know why. That's beside the point, I suppose.*

I can see Tony smoking a cigarette by the window of the pub. He is talking to a girl, touching her on the shoulder. I turn back to Veronica.

He was saying something else too, though it was a while before I could hear what it was. Then I heard. It was, 'Stop this! Stop this! Stop this!' As if he was **outraged**. *As if no one had the* **right**. *He was a very proud man, was Joseph. His name was Joseph. Joe Blue. And do you know what I did then? Can you imagine what I did?*

Veronica was taut in her seat. She shook her head.

I walked away. I turned and walked away. Right there, half-way down the corridor to his room. Voice in my ears. And there was no one else to see him, no one other than my mum. He never had any friends apart from me. But I couldn't stand it, see. He took a whole week to die. But I couldn't . . . I

181

just couldn't . . . My voice had fallen to a whisper, but now it strengthened with anger. *I never went to see him again. Because he wasn't my dad any more. He was just pain. And I hate pain. Pain and age and loneliness. All that **fucking** stuff. All that . . . **not-fair shit**.*

I sat back in the seat, shocked with myself. Veronica reached over and brushed the back of my hand with her finger. It felt good, it felt sweet. I had never told anyone that story before. Not Nodge, not Colin, not Tony, not Martin Buckle or Niven Bender. So why did I tell Veronica? And why did I tell her now?

Because she's a dissector of people, that's why. Because she knows how to get *inside*. With her tiny, soft little knives.

Suddenly there's a loud rap at the window that makes us both jump.

CHAPTER 9

THE VIOLENT NEMESIS
OF CHRISTOPHER CROWLEY

*W*oo hoo! It's Tony. It's clear he's already been drinking quite heavily. I can smell it on him. He's swaying slightly. From the sniffing, snuffling and nose-wiping he's doing, I would guess he's been doing a line or three of how's-your-father.

Immediately I re-present myself. It occurs to me that this is something I always do before I meet my friends. I arrange to become cocky, tough, knowing, wry, all with a shrug of the muscles of my face.

Diamond Tony!

Frank the Fucking F, the F, Ffff . . . oh, sorry, Frankie. Frank the fucking incredibly honest person. The doris doesn't know your nickname, does she? No offence, Vronky. Come on then. Come and have a beer. We've got fifteen minutes before Mahatma Gandhi reveals the secret of the ages. I've got them in to celebrate. An end to all the doubts. Two pints and large Baileys for you, doll. Stop being all smoochy woochy fucking poochy. I hate marrieds. Whoops. You're not yet, are you? Married.

He flashes one of his very best charming smiles, half little boy, half satyr, full power, right at Veronica. I can see her pause, then pause some more, then give in and begin to laugh. Tony ceremoniously opens the door, and puts out his arm for Veronica to hold on to. Out of his unbuttoned shirt falls the gold horns and the hand, which Tony is never without. Veronica takes his open palm – big, soft, tufts of black hair on the back – and Tony begins a stumble towards the door of the pub.

I gather myself, muster my emotions, slide them into some cold box at the back of my head. By the time I'm out of the car, I'm pulled together, in control. I wipe my salty wet face with the sleeve of my jacket, three or four times until it's dry, then walk into the Churchill Arms. Tony is already sitting down at a corner table with Veronica. As I walk in the door, he beckons and waves, gives a loud call so that half the pub turns round to look.

Frankie!

I walk over and sit down, and take a long draught at the beer Tony has ready for me. He's wearing a beautiful chocolate-brown cotton drill suit, which is improbably, but definitely, complemented by some kind of Versace blue shirt. His shoes are square-toed Gucci loafers. He's talking nineteen to the dozen, coke-powered, to Veronica about his job.

*Hairdressing is more than just cutting hair. It's a total **experience**. Do you know what I mean? Yeah? Maybe that sounds pretentious. I don't **know**. But when people come into the shop, they want to enter a whole* *different . . . world. And that's what I give them. A bit of glamour, a bit of chat, a new look. I had Ewan McGregor in last week, monster bloke, we're mates really more than anything. He said to me, he said to me, I don't come here for the cut. It's the total vibe, the total **thing**. That's what I'm good at. Something else. Alex – Alexander McQueen – was in yesterday to have it **all** off. You know him? The designer? Yeah? He's a lovely bloke, no side, not a whisper of it. Anyway, **he** said much the same thing. He feels . . . **easy** there. So he says. Easy, that was the word he used. When we were talking. So anyway. It's **both**, isn't it? It's a down-to-earth thing, and it's kind of glamorous at the same time. You've got lovely hair, Veronica. Who does it for you? It suits you. Perhaps a little more off at the nape. Turn round, will you, for a moment.*

Veronica turns round and Tony puts his hand on her neck, raising the hair, half-stroking it, tracing the line of the cut with his finger. Veronica gives a slight shiver.

No disrespect to whoever did it, but it's a big ragged. I'd take it up a bit shorter, tighter, I think. Come and see me. No charge for you, beautiful.

It's going well. Veronica seems much more relaxed than last time. Her body language is softer, her eyelids have drifted down further. I'm pleased. I feel a sudden surge of confidence and in a gap in the conversation, I lean forward and say, *Tony, there's something important I want to ask you.*

Tony takes a sip out of his glass, then puts it back on the table. He begins to finger the gold horns around his neck. He's looking at me, but he's looking past me at the same time. Tony's attention is always switching between spotlight and floodlight. He's always half checking that someone more important isn't in the room.

Veronica and me were wondering. Well. It would mean a lot to us –

Suddenly Tony's glance is right past me and on to the far corner of the room.

Richard! Hey!

He glances back at me. It's clear he's only been half taking in what I've been saying.

Sorry, Frank. I mean, Frankie. It's Richard Bloke. You know, from the Big Green Tree Tomatoes. Great guy. I'll be right back. Give me a moment.

And with that he's up on his feet and embracing a tall, wasted, slightly embarrassed-looking man standing by the bar who I vaguely recognize as the lead singer of a minor indie pop band.

Veronica and I sit in silence for a moment.

I say, *This always happens. You can't walk down the street, go to the pub, go for a shit with Tony without him bumping into someone. The most you can ever hope to spend with him is about ten minutes.*

Sure. He's afraid.

I bridle slightly. I've already forgotten her kindness in the car.

*I don't see why you always have to see something in everything. He's just popular. People **like** him.*

He doesn't.

What?

186

Like him.

This is great. I'm marrying Dr Katz.

One of my favourite cartoons. He's a psychiatrist. Veronica, disappointingly, doesn't seem to get the reference. Just then Tony swings back over, pointing at his watch.

Richard's got a gig. He's got to hurry off.

I glance over to the thin man's table. The other man he's with has just bought him a fresh pint. Richard Bloke settles down and seems in no hurry to drink it. Tony gestures at his watch.

I suppose we had better be getting over there.

We all get up. Tony looks slightly taken aback, slightly disoriented, but he quickly gathers himself again. As we head towards the door, he says to Veronica, *So who is this geezer?*

Veronica says, *Christopher Crowley. I don't know that much about him. He's written a few books about myths and symbols. Honoria – my best friend – thinks he's great. I'm not making any promises. I'm just interested in keeping an open mind.*

Tony's checking his Psion Personal Organizer while Veronica's talking. Then he says, *Yeah.*

And when she wanders out of earshot, a few seconds later, he grins and whispers to me, *I'm looking forward to this. Christopher Crystalwaver the Californian Cunt.*

This confirms my initial suspicion that Tony is perhaps not yet ready for the Higher Path.

We arrive at the Town Hall. The lecture is in a small anteroom next to the Parking Control offices.

It is purpose-built, red-brick. Not very spiritual. Tony goes off to the toilet for a few minutes, more likely than not to top up on nosebag. He's already moderate to severely pissed.

Inside, the room is full of maybe seventy grey chairs, and there is a podium at the front. There is a small back projection of wisping white smoke and the low drone of some ambient music. The hall is maybe half full. There is nothing to distinguish this audience from any other in particular. Perhaps slightly more women, and the women younger than the men, who all appeared to be beyond forty.

Tony, who has returned from the toilet sniffing like a famished anteater, and myself are definitely the youngest men there, but there are perhaps half a dozen younger women. A single poster on the wall announces *Christopher Crowley: Power of Symbol, Call of Myth*. Underneath, there are some biographical details. Apparently Crowley had lived on the West Coast of America for the past twenty years, but had in fact grown up in Birmingham.

Just then, a door opens at the side of the podium. A man wearing the worst suit I have ever seen in my life walks in. It's cheap fawn cotton, with wide shiny lapels that have remnants of breakfast on them.

The killer detail is the fact that the trousers have not one set of belt loops, but *two*, arranged in parallel. Through each set, a wide, obviously cheap brown belt. The man's shoes are grey, the colour and shape of mullet.

Is that him?

A rattle of parched applause breaks out around the hall.

The man in the bad suit taps a microphone and begins to speak softly, with a gentle, slightly effeminate voice. He introduces himself as John Jeremy Vaughan of the World Spiritual University. He thanks the audience for being so patient, makes an acknowledgement to the Leisure Services Committee of the council, rubs his lapels with the back of his hand, dirtying them still further. Then, cursorily, he gestures towards the side entrance and says portentously, into the malfunctioning, feeding-back microphone, *Please put your hands together to welcome, all the way from Orange County, California – Christopher Crowley.*

Through the door a tall, clean-shaven man with blond hair appears. As in his photograph, he is astonishingly good-looking, like something out of a Gap ad, young and lithe, although he is clearly in his forties. His clothes are all immaculately pressed. His jeans, disturbingly, have a crease down the front. A smile which is easy, constant, unforced. The only note of affectation is that he wears no shoes or socks beneath the jeans. His shirt is a surfer short-sleeve, and he is deeply tanned.

When he speaks, I can hear that the traces of his Brummie accent are still identifiable, but submerged under a generic mid-American burr. His voice is resonant enough to carry without the microphone, so he switches it off. *Thank you, John Jeremy. Welcome to Kensington Town Hall, and thank you for taking the trouble to attend. I hope I'll make it worth the visit. At only five bucks a ticket, I should say I've got a fair chance.*

There is laughter. Crowley makes a large gesture with his hand towards the crowd.

I'm going to talk today about myths and symbols and how they shape our reality. But first, please bear with me. I want to do a little experiment and you're going to be my guinea pigs.

He gives a big, wide, game-show-host smile.

Does anyone have a five-pound note?

A good number of hands go up from the audience, including Veronica's. I feel for my own wallet and discover a fiver poking up from the worn pockets. I raise my hand too. Tony puts his hand up and, *sotto voce*, says to me, *I like magic shows.*

His voice is slightly slurred but audible. By now, there are about thirty hands up and, smiling all the time, Crowley passes about the audience, taking five-pound notes from outstretched hands, placing them in a little metal container about the size of a small waste-paper basket. When he comes to take our five-pound notes, he leans close to me. He smells of ocean. It is strangely pleasant.

After five minutes, Crowley has gathered up a good handful, amounting to what must be close on £150. He returns to the stage and sits down, placing the metal container in front of him. Then he slowly takes out a box of matches, strikes one and throws it on top of the notes. Very quickly, they ignite. Flames and smoke billow out of the container. A few people gasp, but slowly a number of the audience began to clap, delighted by the audacity of the act.

What have you just witnessed? says Crowley, very quietly but still audibly, having not moved an inch out of his chair.

Daylight fucking robbery, says Tony, to my left, not really under his breath.

Crowley continues, now standing and addressing the audience, hands clasped in front of him. He takes a jug of water and pours it into the smoking bowl.

*What you have just witnessed is the destruction of a **symbol**. And the emotion that you felt subsequently – whether laughter or anger – is the power that that symbol holds over us.*

*Everything – and I mean everything – is a symbol. Everything is a network of meanings that we ourselves create, then impart value upon. The meanings in fact **are** the values.*

I feel Tony shifting on his chair next to me, clearly irritated. I can hear him muttering threateningly, *What sort of magic trick is that?*

Money, to Tony, is sacred. Which, I suppose, is the point that Crowley is trying to make.

Crowley continues. I kind of like the flourish he has just executed, but at the same time he has a smugness that is irritating. Also, I don't buy the John Denver, Rocky Mountain High, molasses and corn dogs intonation of his voice especially when there's a good 20 per cent of Jasper Carrott mixed in.

What is money? It is a piece of paper, an agreed codification of value. It is congealed energy. It is the most sacred emblem that our society possesses. But it has no meaning except that which we bestow upon it. Nothing is anything except that which we say it is. The world simply is. But we embroider it, pump it full of colour, tear it apart and put it together again.

Crowley continues in this vein for fifteen minutes or so. To be quite honest, it is very interesting, despite the annoying crease in his jeans. What he seems to be trying to say is that we know fuck nothing, so we make stuff up to put into the empty space. The stuff we make up doesn't make very much sense, but *for that very reason* we believe in it with a passion. Because if we *acknowledge* that it doesn't make sense, we risk going nuts. Or something like that.

I am becoming quite absorbed in the whole thing, and am only vaguely aware of Tony breathing heavily in the chair next to me. The next thing I know, Crowley turns to the audience, as if finishing his speech, and says. *Any questions so far?*

Out of the corner of my eye, I see Tony's hand shoot up. He is rigid in his chair. Crowley clocks him, gives an easy smile.

Yes. Over there. In the smart suit.

Tony flexes a bit, pulls up his collar.

Can you give us my five pounds back?

Veronica glances across sharply at Tony, then at me. I lean over and whisper in her ear.

Don't worry. Tony always likes to make a theatrical gesture.

Veronica doesn't look convinced. Nor should she be. All the rows in front are craning their necks to see who has spoken. Tony clearly doesn't care. I know him in this mood. The shit is going to hit the fan. Or possibly the other way round. He is standing up now, staring at the ashes of the banknotes on the stage.

I'm sorry?

I said I want my money back.

Very calm and controlled. Polite. Crowley beams Tony a smile that radiates inner peace and serenity. He gives a faint, fatal shake of the head. I want to shout out to him, *no, no. Give him his money back.* But I know it won't do any good.

I'm sorry if I've upset you, Mr . . . Mr . . .

Diamonte. Anthony Diamonte.

Tony gives an almighty sniff in a final, unsuccessful attempt to clear his running nose. He is coked up to, and beyond, his eyeballs.

Mr Diamonte. I am sorry if I have angered you, or disappointed you. I had no wish to do so. Everybody's angry. There's a lot in this world to be angry about, after all. But what is it? What is anger? Nothing more than fear, surely.

Christopher Crowley raises a tanned arm and beckons generously to Tony.

Would you like to come down from the audience? Sit with me a while. This gathering, after all, isn't only about me. Perhaps we could talk together.

He beckons again, like a customer to a waitress.

Tony pushes past Veronica and out into the aisle. He's totally lary. Immediately, the audience begins to clap. Veronica hisses and looks round desperately. Worried, I tug at Tony's jacket as he pushes past.

193

Tony. Come on. I'll give you the fiver.

*That misses the **point**, Francis. 'Scuse, Veronica. Got your tools from the chopping shop with you, by the way? I might have a client for you.*

Then he moves down the aisle towards the stage. As he reaches the podium, Crowley stands up to greet him and reaches out a hand, which Tony takes and gives a short shake. The audience applauds more loudly than ever. I can just about hear Tony speak over the sound of the swelling applause.

Are you going to give me my fiver back? Or what?

Crowley shakes his head again, sadly, smiling ruefully. Then he sits down on the floor, crosses his legs and calmly addresses the audience.

One day, after Chuang Tzu's wife had just died, a disciple came upon the old Zen master at home, singing and beating time on a pot, whereas he had expected to find Chuang Tzu dressed in the white of mourning. He demanded to know why the philosopher was behaving in so unseemly a manner. Not to shed a tear over a dead woman's body was bad enough. But to make merry and sing and shout when she lay dead, was that not blasphemy and disrespect of the dead? No, the bereaved husband said. His wife had died and he had felt the loss. Now she was dead, passing from one aspect to another, like the seasons go from summer to autumn to winter to spring. If he were to weep and cry, he would show his ignorance of those laws.

Tony looks momentarily bewildered.

What does that mean?

Crowley looks faintly pained, but compassionate.

It means whatever you want it to mean.

Tony wrinkles his brow in a crude imitation of genuine curiosity.

What do you want it to mean?

Crowley breathes out, as if struggling with the whole firmament of human ignorance and stubbornness in the face of plain truth, and then says softly, *Does anything in the end finally mean anything?*

Tony nods thoughtfully, as if he is overtaken with a sense of profundity.

Now there's a thought, says Tony. He gives a big double coke sniff and rubs a line of snot away from the bottom of his nose. *But what I'm **trying** to say, Mr Crowley, is what does it mean with respect to my five-spot?*

Crowley gives a weak smile.

It means your five-pound note has gone. It means the symbol has been stripped of its power.

Tony nods again, more vigorously now, as if at last understanding a deep philosophical paradox.

It means, leave it behind. Move beyond it. But what have you really lost? continues Crowley blithely. *You have lost a pattern of meaning. Now all you have to do is lose your attachment to it. Do you understand?*

Tony stops nodding and says evenly, *I do. Yes. Thank you.*

There is a ripple in the audience. Crowley nods, gives a big, long knowing blink.

But, Mr Crowley –

Chris.

*Chris. I want to ask you. Do **you** understand?*

I groan, knowing by now exactly what is going to happen. Tony pulls himself up to his full height. Crowley is still smiling away happily.

Do I understand what, Tony?

*Do you understand, Chris, that you are **dead**, you fucking thieving cunt?*

It is now that he grabs both of Crowley's shoulders, steadies himself on the podium, and head-butts him, bam, on the bridge of the nose. Crowley goes down like a log, claret spurting immediately. He gasps and his legs give way. Suddenly, he's shouting, but his mid-American accent has disappeared completely. Instead, thick, gasping Brummie vowels fill the hall.

Yow fooker. I'll fooking 'ave yow, mate.

With that he swings out at Tony, but misses completely. Tony gives him a kick in the ribs, then bends down towards him. I'm on my feet, running to the stage to restrain Tony. By now he's reaching down towards Crowley and grabbing his shirt. The audience is screaming and shouting.

I can hear Tony saying, *Calm down, Mystic Meg. This is just, you know. A Symbolic thingy. A pattern of whatchamacallits.*

He thumps him on the bridge of the nose, making Crowley whimper loudly.

***This** only means what you make it mean.*

Another kick. Then he pushes Crowley back down on the floor. This time he stays there. I pull Tony away. He shouts back at Crowley:

*Get over it, **maaan**.*

196

The room is in total chaos. I look around the room for Veronica, but she's disappeared entirely. I drag Tony towards an exit, worrying that someone might have called the police. He flings his arms around me. I realize that he is very, very drunk. I strain to understand what he's saying, then, once I've succeeded, regret that I made the effort.

Frankie, you're my best mate. My mucker. Don't get married, Frankie. Stay with the boys. Have a laugh. You've got years left in you. And you're giving it all up. For a bit of regular gash.

His breath pours out into my face, beer and Hula Hoops. Even though I think he barely knows what he's saying, I feel shocked.

That's not why I'm doing it.

Why then? What other reason would you want to do it for?

Why? I'm doing it because I want to . . . I stop, stumped for a moment . . . Because I want to . . . connect. I want to stop being just myself and start being a bit of something . . . of someone . . . else.

I can hear police sirens in the distance now. I drag Tony by the collar out into the corridor and he staggers behind me, holding on to my shirt.

Tony brings his lips inwards, looks up at the blank white ceiling with wheeling eyes, then turns to me with a voice that is empty, strangely sober.

You're a pretentious twat, Frankie. And what's more, you're wrong. Let me tell you something. You're always alone. Whoever you fuck, however many times you fuck them, whoever you marry or don't marry.

You're on your own. Just you, your brain and your cock, walking around, walking around. Believing anything else is just Walt Disney, it's just Steven fucking Spielberg, it's just, you know . . . you know.

I've got Tony out in the street now and I'm trying to drag him as far away from the building as possible. His suit is covered in dust and street dirt. There is a fine film of white powder under his nose – another reason it's important he doesn't get hauled in front of the filth. Tony finally hawks up the word he's been looking for.

A . . . a myth. Like what that Brummie cunt was saying.

*That's not true, Tone. I don't believe that. I know it's not Walt Disney. But I just want to be normal. I want to fit in. I don't expect happy ever after. I just want a **change**.*

The siren turns out to be an ambulance rather than a police car. I'm still propelling Tony along the street. I don't think he's heard a word I've said. In the distance, I can see Crowley being helped out of a rear exit door. I let go of Tony and he collapses slowly to the ground. He's drunk enough for me to forgive him.

You're a vicious bastard, Tony, I find myself saying softly.

But I've known that since the beginning, and it's never made any difference to him being my mate. In fact, it was his cruelty that brought us together in the first place.

CHAPTER 10

DIAMOND TONY'S
BIG STING

If Colin was my first best friend, chrono-
logically, I suppose Tony was my second.
He supplanted and eclipsed and, in a sense,
destroyed Colin, or at least froze him, stunted him,
cut off his potential to become more than what he
was. With my help, of course.

In a sense, though, he merely completed a
process that had already started long before. For
me and Colin, things had already changed, had
begun to fade, after we both arrived at secondary
school. Many of my friends – the lesser-ranked
ones, and they all fell short of Colin – had been
cauterized, cut off. Condemned to the surly pit of
Goldhawk High, what would nowadays be called
a sink school: kids with dirty chops, vitamin
deficiencies, calloused fists who said fucking *in
front of the teachers*. Three-quarters of my friends
went there, or to one of the other holding cells
in the district – Clem Attlee Comp or, worst
of all, St Bart's, where they wore second-hand

199

clothes and the bad boys fought to the blood every day.

But Colin and I were the cream, so called. There was a remaining grammar school in the area, and both our parents put us up for it. Typically, I sailed through, while he scraped in, on final appeal. Maybe he'd have been better at one of the other places; here he was assured of being at the bottom of the pile. But his handwriting and his extraordinary ability at maths and with computers got him in at the last gasp.

The grammar had smart uniforms, peaked caps, new buildings. Colin and me were scared at first, and stuck together, tried to hold on to what we had – the little enclosed world in which nothing much mattered except each other's company, each other's approving silence.

But tides and currents were seizing us; they come at you in life, I know now, from all directions, great irresistible waves, with indifferent, cruel crests. We were now part of something much larger than ourselves, and, moreover, something with a different set of rules from those we were accustomed to living by. I knew that I had to learn, and fast. Colin, though, I felt even then, was adopting a different, fatal strategy. He began to retreat, to hide. And you can't hide. There's nowhere to go.

We were still the tortoise and the hare. Somehow the new school defined more precisely and more boldly the animals that we were, each role a defence against the new powers ranged against us.

It was a Thursday afternoon when the hairline cracks that spidered across the dam we held against the rushing world opened and let the entire structure give way. I am allowing myself to remember it now, although in the past I have always turned my mind's eye away because of the emotions it evoked in me, a kind of putting fingers in my ears and whistling.

I think I have been terrified of weak people ever since Colin.

There was – of course – a bully in the class. It wasn't what you would describe as a full-time post and it wasn't as bad as it sounded. But the bully, of course, was Tony. Not named Diamond Tony then, not even Tony: just Anthony, Anthony Diamond. (He insisted on the anglicized version of his name.) Behind his back, I heard him called Tony the Spic or Spaghetti Boy. But only ever behind his back.

Tony, in truth, had no real need to bully anyone. He just hadn't realized it yet. He was good looking, funny, clever. A tall, heavily built boy, with very short hair and those lazy eyes that moved very slowly around the room, pausing to assess. Olive skin. Big full lips. Languorous, slow and graceful. Eyes edged with frost behind their warmth. His uniform carefully customized – trousers taken in, blazer nipped and tucked, beautiful crisp linen shirts.

Quite apart from his elegance, there was something in Tony that was adult – a kind of standing back from the world, a larger gap between stimulus and response than the other children possessed. It gave him power, and, having it, he felt impelled to use it. Of course, nowadays he is more nakedly temperamental. But that has to do with all the booze down his throat and all the industrial quantities of bugle going up his nose.

He was the strongest boy in the class – not just physically, but in his ability to size up situations, to assess weaknesses, to think quickly. Even some teachers were nervous of him – he had a kind of talent for hurt, a guided-missile capability for finding out the vulnerable parts of each individual. This, of course, made him irresistible, and he soon developed a court, I suppose you might say a gang, although that suggests something more formal than it actually was.

I think I wanted – no, I am sure I wanted – to be part of that court, drawn as children are to the strong, the fearless, the ruthless. But I was identified with Colin, who by now had severe, disfiguring acne to add to the awkwardness and gentleness of his personality. And, of course, I had my own facial disfigurement, the raspberry-coloured patch, and my own mental disability, my cleverness. So I was consigned to Colin's wilderness, although not so far, not so deep, because I was known to be tougher than my acne-ridden friend, and because I was good at games and because I could punch. Nevertheless, I did not quite qualify as a real person in the eyes of Tony and his retinue.

But I was close enough to want it, and want it badly.

And then my chance came. My chance to move onward and upward and away. And I took that chance, and in the process got myself three things: a nickname, a new friend and an enduring sense of shame.

It happened after Tony destroyed a teacher. A teacher who was otherwise famous for his acuity and toughness with the kids. Laid him to waste. It was awesome, and became legendary. After it happened he became untouchable. After that you had to be with him or against him, you see. Which is why, when Colin . . .

But I will come to that. The legend goes as follows. Everyone who was there will have a different memory of it. This is mine.

The teacher – Tony's victim – was Dr Fred Koinange, a handsome, English-educated South African religious studies teacher who managed to achieve a kind of dignified disdain towards the children. He was an impressive and grave man, with an air of faint sadness, who, we had heard, had lost several members of his family in the struggle against apartheid. His younger brother, so the story went, was tortured to death by the security forces.

He was black, of course, and although this was not much of an issue among the children – who saw Authority before they saw anything else, and Koinange had Authority, inborn as well as acquired

– Koinange knew that it was a difference that could be exploited with particular ease. All differences sooner or later were – if you were slightly too tall, or slightly too clever, or slightly too poor, all these things would eventually be used against you. It was the speciality of all children to find out the Other, and Tony was master among specialists. Koinange, knowing well of his cruelty and dexterity, hit him at once and stamped hard on him from the first. What's more, as a kind of pre-emptive strike, he got personal. That was his mistake.

Tony had one Achilles' heel, his established and well-known weak point. He was Italian – both by place of birth, Calabria, and through Sicilian parents, who were respectable, but poorly educated wine merchants. I heard that when he first came to school, at the age of five, he was very dark and almost unable to speak any English at all.

Since those early days, for reasons only known to himself, he had come to hate his Italian background and was determined to establish himself as English through and through. He never spoke Italian and was claiming even then, at the age of twelve or thirteen, that he had forgotten how. Instead, he spoke a carefully enunciated, almost wilfully urban London guttural, exactly like that of any Shepherd's Bush housing trust glue snorter.

Koinange smelt out Tony's weakness from the first. He was a skilled mimic and could use this power to devastating effect, because he could summon and aim laughter like a stand-up comic.

Mockery was the weapon with which he kept his classes tame. So when Tony overstepped the mark, as he occasionally, and usually deliberately, did, Koinange managed to muster an Italian accent adequate enough to torment him.

There had at this time recently been a record in the top ten by a ridiculous pastiche-Italian called Joe Dolce, who pandered to English prejudice about that nationality. His persona was that of a rotund simpleton whose horizons were bounded by mamma, spaghetti and ice cream.

His hit song – his first and last – was called 'Shaddap You Face' and, when provoked by Tony, Koinange would saunter up to the boy's desk, thrust his face six inches away and launch into a cod version of the song to a hurdy-gurdy tune.

The last line of the chorus was the same as the title. *SHADDAP YOU FACE.*

The impersonation was poor, but it was enough; the classroom would erupt into laughter, turned like knives against Tony. The last four syllables were spat out with real menace to add to the effect. The swell of laughter neutered Tony, as Koinange knew it would. But it enraged him too. He vowed revenge. His lazy eyes became ever colder.

This eventually came one Tuesday afternoon during a double lesson. The whole episode was planned. I know as much because me and Colin heard Tony boasting before the lesson that he was going to 'get' Koinange.

I'm going to nail that stuck-up twat. Just you watch.

He won't fuck with me again in a hurry. In an hour's time he won't know what hit him.

He wasn't boasting to me – I was, with Colin, too much of the outsider, too much of the little freako. But he noticed us overhear him and gave me an icy glance that was unquestionably a warning.

The subject under discussion that day with Koinange was 'Do animals have souls?' It was a liberal kind of school, Godolphin Grammar, and the religious curriculum was very loosely adhered to. Thus religious studies became a kind of talking shop for any issues that were raised. This was the early 1980s, and green issues, including animal liberation, were topical. This class had been flagged in advance, which is why I suspect Tony had his strategy so well planned.

The class began, as was normal, with Koinange stamping his authority on the unruly class. Two girls were gossiping; Koinange's tactic was simply to stand in silence and fix his eye on offenders. Some hidden power in him did the rest, shaming whoever he turned his gaze to. Often, this was Tony, trying to maintain his status as dominant male. On this occasion, however, he was entirely quiet and sat at his desk.

The lesson began. Koinange, despite his instinct for discipline, was schooled in modern teaching methods. This meant not just preaching from a pulpit to a stunned, indifferent congregation but getting the children *involved*.

This too Tony knew, his lazy eyes still for once,

fixed on Koinange. He sat and waited while Koinange began with a reading from the Bible, then a brief extract from an Animal Liberation Front manifesto. The class obediently listened and waited for the teacher to finish. After a while he put down the books and turned to the class.

Now. How do we approach a matter like this? What kind of avenues should we explore? Anyone have any bright ideas?

Tony's hand shot up. This in itself was unusual – Tony rarely moved at anything faster than medium speed. But Koinange was not suspicious.

Tony. Va bene. Come sta?

Sir. Do you have a pet, sir?

This was the clever part – the affected innocence of it, along with the intuitive understanding that Tony had of what Koinange would do with the question. Koinange was, unlike some of the teachers, intensely private about his personal life, knowing that the slightest detail could provide ammunition for restless children. Tony knew this, and he guessed that the question would be turned around, and it was.

None of your business, Signor Diamonte. What goes on in my life is my affair. Capiche? But your idea is good. Do you believe your pets have personalities? Do you believe they have thoughts, emotions? That they can understand you, in short? Who here has a pet?

About fourteen hands in the class of thirty went up. I kept mine down; although our family kept two cats, I had learned, automatically, to keep my hands by my sides in class, as I came to understand that cleverness or eagerness to learn, especially among the already marked, the already scarred, was not to be displayed, any more than was stupidity. Both were hateful in the eyes of the great and average mass of B- and C-graders.

Although Tony's hand on this occasion went up, it was a sly half-flag, designed not to attract early attention. Koinange picked off a few of the other kids first, who told stories about their goldfish, cats, hamsters. Unusually, Colin was emboldened to speak, about the rabbit his mother had bought him for Christmas. As he spoke in a voice too low for most of the children to pick up, Tony's hand got higher, but he did not stretch or speak. The appearance he maintained was that of someone largely indifferent to whether he was picked out or not. Nevertheless, sat as he was – deliberately? – a few desks from the front, Koinange finally picked his hand out of the cluster.

Diamonte, do you have a pet?

It's a dog, sir. A Labrador. We've had him since I was a little boy.

A dog. Good. It is very common to suppose that dogs possess personalities. They seem to respond to us in a way that is almost human – to pine, to love, even to express humour. But I wonder. Is this something we project on to the animals, from our own minds? Do we humanize what are no more than . . . than . . .

Dumb brutes, sir?

Well, that is a little harsh perhaps. Your own

dog, for instance. Surely, you think of him as more than –

Oh no, sir. He's a very stupid dog. He thinks he is clever, but he is stupid. When we try to teach him tricks he gets them all wrong. And he's dirty. He piss – wees on the carpet.

Giggles broke out. Tony did not join in. Koinange held up his hand and the noise ceased.

Not much of a dog by the sound of it.

No, sir. He should be put down really. He's no good.

Tony said this with an unpleasant edge to his voice that suggested he wasn't joking. Koinange was clearly surprised – all the other children had launched into paeans of praise and affection for their chosen pets. The class remained silent. An odd atmosphere was developing – a sense that the conversation was straying to the edges of what Koinange deemed permissible. The teacher seemed slightly fazed now, unsure whether or not he was being taunted in some strange way.

Surely not. To have this pet of yours put down? Do you have no feelings for – what is – what is the dog's name?

This was the moment that Tony had been waiting for. Had in fact designed. But even at this moment, he held fire, his low and clever mind calculating as always. There was an extended pause.

I don't know, sir.

Koinange immediately became irritated, convinced now that Tony was playing a game with him, was deliberately cheeking him. Yet he wasn't clever enough to know which game it was.

Don't be silly, boy. How can you not know the name of your own dog?

I . . . I just don't want to say, sir. It's kind of . . . a secret.

Koinange, now infuriated, walked towards Tony and stood in front of his desk. He launched into his mock-Italian Joe Dolce impersonation on cue, face six inches from that of the boy.

Shaddap You Face!

Koinange began to prod him, gently at first, then more firmly with a finger.

Shaddap You Face!

The class began to laugh, then stopped dead as Tony spoke at last. The word that came out was spoken with exact neutrality, but with a deadly clarity that transmitted above Koinange's mocking song and to the corners of the class.

Nigger, sir.

Koinange looked as if he had been slapped. He stopped singing immediately and colour drained from his face. He saw the trap, all at once, how it had been planned from the first; but the knowing was no good, it was too late. The knowledge just compounded the outrage. There was a slight shake to his hands as he spoke again, with a deadly quietness. Outside, a playing-field whistle blew.

What did you say?

Tony regarded him innocently, gave a shrug, as if to say, You *pushed* me to it. You *made* me do it.

His voice, however, was laced with contempt now. He knew what he wanted from Koinange and he knew that he was going to get it. When he spoke again, the words lashed the air.

I said Nigger, sir. My dog's name is Nigger. He's a big stupid dog, a dirty, stupid black mongrel.

The moment held now; something was going to topple, and Tony knew it. The slightest push. He just gave the faintest of smiles, the most infinitesimal registering of triumph on his face. It was enough to seal that triumph absolutely.

Koinange took a step back, raised his hand and smacked Tony with his open palm across the face. The boy fell back on to the floor; even now he did not lose his composure entirely, although his eyes began to smart with tears. It was a very hard slap, almost a punch.

But, sir, you asked me what my dog's –

Koinange struck again, this time with the back of his palm, hard. A gold ring on his finger cut Tony's lip. The impression of welts was established immediately. Twice more; this time a thin line of blood emerged from his nose. Then Koinange seized him by the shoulders and began to shake him, wordlessly. Tony, although crying now, was also smiling, an empty, violent smile. He knew he had won. This fact began to settle on Koinange too. Gradually he relaxed his grip and took a step back, standing stock still before the stunned class. Then he simply turned on his heel and went out of the room, leaving the door open.

Tony did not make a move to adjust his disordered clothing, his bleeding nose, the rising marks on his cheek. He sat himself upright, shook himself down. The impression he gave was one of consummate self-control and returned arrogance. Mayhem broke out in the class. Suddenly, through the open door, as if planned, another teacher appeared.

What's going on here? What the hell's all this noise? Where's Dr Koinange?

The teacher then spotted Tony, still collapsed on the floor.

Jesus Christ, boy. What happened to you?

Tony's demeanour suddenly changed again. The composure of a few seconds ago gave way to carefully orchestrated tears. He transformed himself into someone truly pathetic and forlorn. His face was very clearly marked by physical blows, an instant dismissal offence for any teacher.

Sir. Mr Koinange, he . . . I . . . oh, sir . . .

Tony affected to be unable to speak any more. At random, the teacher turned to me, sitting as I was at the front of the class. Or I presume it was at random. I think in those days I had a reputation for honesty, for being above the fray. It was one of my qualifications for being a freak and a misfit. Clever and honest, I was, whether I liked it or not, In With The Enemy, and this was one of the causes of my exclusion.

You, Blue. What happened here?

I saw at that moment how many truths there were to each situation, and how the truths you

212

chose had to do with where your loyalties lay, to whom your sentiments were attracted. Although I had a sense some wrong had been done to Koinange, that he had been tripped up, Koinange was a teacher, Tony a pupil; the way forward, for me, suddenly clarified, was not in doubt. I saw the way to escape my status as outsider and took it.

Mr Koinange punched him, sir.

What Koinange did was less punch than slap, but only slightly, so it was merely the tiniest fib. But it felt wonderful to speak the words, to deliver skewed judgement. Suddenly the classroom broke out into an excited, shocked babble.

He did, sir –

Because he –

Asked the dog's –

It was only –

Tony didn't want to –

The teacher held up his hand and shouted for the class to be silent. He turned to me again.

He hit Diamonte? That's ridiculous. What for? Blue?

He just told him the name of his dog, sir.

The teacher, bewildered, stopped for a moment. The class went silent. Then, tenderly, he knelt down by Tony, who had made himself seem much smaller than he actually was and had continued crying pitiably.

You'd better come with me, Diamonte. You too, Blue, since you seem to know what happened. I think we should go to the headmaster's office right now.

He took one last look around the room.

Burden, you too.

Like me, Colin was thought of as a plain dealer. He walked across to join us like a terrified rabbit, sensing already perhaps that he was going to have to make some kind of terrible choice. As we walked down the corridor together, Tony watched me out of the corner of his eye.

The interrogation by the head was simple and short. It turned out that Koinange had already been to see him, briefly, and had done his best to put a decent gloss on events. But one sight of Tony destroyed any sympathy that the head might have had for the hapless teacher. The sight was shocking. His face was cut and bruised, and stained with filthy tears. He had been careful not to wipe away any of the blood.

I knew I had helped to put Koinange into deep trouble. I said nothing about how Tony had planned the whole thing from beginning to end. Above all, I didn't rat – it was one of the rules I was beginning to learn, the rules of the new games that didn't have names.

The headmaster, an avowed liberal who believed in informal, child-centred teaching, had issued strict instructions against any form of physical punishment of the pupils, a fact that was well known at all levels of the school. Tony had certainly known it well. The head was clearly particularly humiliated that the blow had been struck by a black teacher since he actually operated a strict quota system for ethnic minorities that had come in for a lot of flak from more traditional teachers at the school. Koinange had been a personal appointment, hard fought for, since his actual qualifications had fallen short of what was normally necessary for a teacher at Godolphin's. I could see that he was furious with Koinange, that he thought he had been betrayed. Towards the end of the interview he turned to me.

Blue, Mr Koinange has admitted striking Tony Diamonte. But he says the whole thing was deliberately planned to provoke him. Do you know anything of this?

I felt Tony's powerful presence by my side. I searched my conscience. So far, everything I had said had been the truth, albeit an edited version of it. My mother and father had always told me to tell the truth. Mr Koinange himself told me that to lie would be punished by God. And right there and then, I made up my mind what to do.

Absolutely not, sir. It wasn't like that at all. Mr Koinange just attacked him. Diamonte was only telling the truth, after all.

The particular cleverness of Tony's scam being that his parents really *did* have a dog called Nigger, Sicilians not being much noted for their enlightened attitudes towards race.

The head exhaled. He believed me. It was at that moment I understood the enormous power of the lie. The beauty of it.

Then the head turned his face to the terrified Colin, fixed him with a penetrating eye.

Burden, what do you know about this? Was it planned?

Colin gulped and glanced around him, as if looking for a door.

Tell me the truth, Burden. Did Diamonte plan this in advance?

Colin writhed and shook slightly, pulled his lips together, then said, *Dunno, sir.*

Both Tony and the head glanced at him furiously. Inside my mind, I begged him to stand up for Tony, to do what he needed to do. Instead he just looked shifty, suspicious. He was undermining the whole scam.

What do you mean you don't know? Either something was planned or it wasn't. Either you knew something about it or you didn't. **Did** *you know something about it?*

Sir, I s'pose so.

What? What did you know?

Long pause.

Dunno.

It was as close as Colin could come to lying. Not enough. The head let out a sigh of frustration, then waved his hand in dismissal. We were let out of the room together. Tony ignored Colin, but looked slyly at me and spoke to me, I think, for the first time since we had been at school.

Blue, I always thought Mummy told you not to tell lies.

It wasn't a lie, I muttered, still flush with the moment, the power of it.

*You **knew** what was going on. Don't bullshit me*, said Tony.

It wasn't a lie, I repeated, more clearly. *It was a fib.*

Tony turned his head upwards and laughed to the ceiling, a big round juicy laugh that made a teacher twenty yards in front turn and shhhh him. He quietened down.

A fib. Not a lie, a fib. That's good, Blue. Francis the Fib. Frank the fucking Fib.

He smiled at me, one of his dazzling smiles, accepting me, approving of me, *noticing* me. Embarrassed, shocked by his swearing – it was still taboo in our house – but delighted, I smiled back. And then he ran off and was gone, chanting, *Frank the **Fib**, Frank the **Fib***.

And so I had a name. A big improvement on Scarface or Freako. And with it, you might say, I acquired an identity, a persona. Persona was a word I learned when I was at university.

I also learned there, of course, that the word *persona* – person – means, is identical to, the Latin word for *mask*. Which makes perfect sense to me. What I didn't understand, and still don't, is once it's there, why can't you ever get it off again? It gets so . . . stuck.

When I made a secret wish after snagging the long part of the chicken wishbone that Sunday lunch time, for the first time that I could ever

217

remember I didn't wish for my birthmark to disappear. I wished instead for Tony to become my friend. I wished that I would no longer be the outsider. And to my amazement and barely hidden joy, my wish began to come true. Tony, the kingpin, the keeper of the court, began speaking to me.

The fact that I hadn't ratted – had positively stood up for him – meant something in the schoolboy code, that first unwritten game in which I was actually aware of participating. He grinned at me the next day when we came into class, gave a friendly nod. Up until that moment, he had completely ignored me. I didn't like him much, was scared of him even, but I was flattered. For the first time, I felt I could be a *someone*. That I might escape the invisibility that the combination of difference and shyness and cleverness had imposed on both Colin and me.

Nothing happened for a while after that. Colin and I continued the same as ever – walking home together, kicking a tennis ball down the street, stopping at each other's houses before going home.

More often than ever now, Colin came to my house rather than me going to his. Something, I knew, had happened to his father. This was not something Colin had told me but that I had overheard from my parents one night, sitting on the stairs before bed. My mother went to bingo with Colin's mother once a month – that practically constituted her entire social life – and we were in fact distantly related, Olive Burden being my mum's uncle's younger half-sister. That made her a semi-great-aunt to me, I think, and Colin some sort of weird, disconnected cousin. Also Colin's father had worked on the coal round with my father years ago. For some time now he had been at a saucepan factory in Acton, but then he had been sacked for being drunk while on shift.

I knew that Colin's father drank. Sometimes he loomed over me at Colin's house, and I could smell it on his breath – brandy, usually. Since losing his job, the smell had got worse. Often when I went round, he would rant and scream in a way I could never imagine my father doing. I was shy because my father had taught me to be shy, because he himself was that way. Colin was shy because his father, I realized years later, badgered him, bullied him, belittled him, struck him and his mother with his fists, stripped him of confidence and sentiment and hope. Sometimes there were strange bruises on his arms and body when he dressed for PE. He never said anything about them; if pushed, he would say that he took a fall playing football.

The bruises became worse, more frequent, after Colin's dad lost his job. Still Colin said nothing. But when I suggested going back to his house he would always make excuses. Then he would come back to our house and stay for as long as he could. Eventually it got to a point when my mother actually had to ask him to go home, when tea was being served. He always apologized and went off right away. I would watch him disappearing into the distance, hanging back, as if elastic was mooring him to our street, to me and my house. In a way it was; sooner or later it had to snap.

At school, my life was changing. I had filled out physically and discovered skills at football and cricket that made me more and more in demand. Colin remained the last to be picked for any team. Tony had kept up his interest in me since the day with Koinange, offering daily hi's and howaryas? He had also shown a worrying iciness towards Colin, more disturbing than his previous indifference.

But his interest in me made a positive difference to my life. Other boys there, boys who had previously had nothing to do with me, began to acknowledge my existence. Even then he was a trophy friend. If a prank was to be played on a teacher, I would be enlisted along with the rest of Tony's crew. If a new joke was making the rounds – something cruel about Ethiopians or the disabled, who were universally categorized as *spackers* – Tony would include me in the circle where the joke was told, would invite my laughter, which I learned to supply whether the joke was funny or not. It was just one more kind of fib, after all.

All this had a real effect on me: I began to get bigger inside, less frightened of the outside world. Something in my walk changed, something in the way I held my head. Colin, conversely, seemed to shrink as I grew. Sometimes, I would be heading off with Tony's gang and I would see him lurking around the corner of a corridor. I knew he was waiting for me to separate myself, so that we could go and talk, and play together. But lately, when I saw him, he had begun to irritate me. It wasn't that he was clingy, but it was increasingly clear that he was weak, which was almost the same thing.

Meanwhile, Colin's father began to get a reputation around the school. His drunkenness had become public. Not only was he involved in fights at the local pub, but he had been seen sitting on park benches near the school clutching cans of beer and cider, unshaven and bedraggled. Colin never said a word about it, but kids would whisper sometimes when he was in the room and throw glances at him.

Tony and I were by now if not exactly mates, then approaching something of equivalent status. We had formed a partnership at football, him at the centre, me on the left wing, finding his height with long, looping, well-timed balls. Crossing the ball was a special skill of mine; I would send it on to Tony's waiting head with devastating precision. It delighted him – sometimes on the pitch, after nodding in another goal, he would hug me in full view of the other kids. On a few occasions, we hung outside the school gates together, smoking cigarettes that he supplied, while Colin walked home alone. I didn't have much to say for myself, but this hardly seemed to matter. Acceptance is a strange thing, it seems to arrive unasked for, and the moment you make an effort it eludes you.

At first this was maybe once a fortnight, but I found myself making excuses to Colin more and more. Tony was cruel, but he was funny, and he had power, and he had friends. He defined the group, and if you weren't in with the group at school then you were no one. And I had discovered that I didn't want to be no one any more. I wanted to be liked. I wanted to matter.

I didn't realize then that there was a price to pay. I found out during one free period, just before the summer term broke up. I was thirteen years old and coming out of my shell, while Colin retreated into his. I felt nevertheless sure that somehow Colin and I would always remain friends – I always believe I will always remain friends with those I love, until the world proves differently, as it does again and again.

It had started even before I walked in the room. There was a gathering of boys together in the corner, just to the left of the chalkboard. Laughter gathered in the air; not the innocent kind that followed a well-delivered punchline or a fresh anecdote. It was laughter that cut, the laughter of attack.

There were about fifteen boys in the room. Nodge was there, standing slightly apart from the others. Like me, he was part of Tony's group – albeit a separate part, so we barely knew each other. I knew, though, that he was one of the few boys Tony really respected, because even then he was so stubborn, so immovable.

Then I saw Colin behind the gathering. He looked hunted, pale as bread. His body was drawn into itself, compacted, and his head slightly further down than it always was. He didn't notice me enter. It was cold, early in the morning before the heating system had fully warmed the air in the draughty corridors and classrooms. You could see your breath.

Then I saw Tony in front of the smaller mob of five or six boys who surrounded Colin. Tony was slouched, hunched, walking with a wobble. I thought at first he must have been ill, then at once I realized he was acting a role. There was drool at the side of his mouth. He fell over and the laughter increased once more, while Colin seemed to retreat still further.

Tony got up again. Now I could hear him speak, in a mock-slur, as he once more swayed and faked an off-balance stagger.

Gshh shoo fuckin bsstrd, gis a drink. Come on na, just a little one for yer auld mate Billy. Whatchoo looking at, ye BASTARD? Ah, now, ye me best pal.

It wasn't a funny or a good impersonation, but it was raising laughter none the less. He put his arm around Colin, who now looked as if he was going to be physically sick. I knew at once what Tony was doing. Unlike Colin, who had taken after his English mother, Billy Burden had a strong Glaswegian accent, which Tony was imitating, badly.

Ye na, ye ma son, and . . . He threw his arms around Colin and pretended to cry. *And I love ya, by* **Christ** *I do. But I just . . . I just want just the one drink and I'll buy ya some fuckin stamps for ya birthday, och the fuckin noo and hoots, you cunt, honest I will.*

The laughter swelled into an ugly balloon. Colin, I knew well, collected stamps in lovingly tended albums. All the stamps were worthless, but he liked the colours and patterns and the ordering that could be achieved, by country, by colour, by price. As with his handwriting, it was a way for him to get to grips with a world that was falling out of control.

Colin looked up. I felt a wrenching in my stomach as he caught my eye. I knew I had to do something, I even moved to do something. But I'd started to be a somebody instead of a nobody. And I didn't want to give it up. To stand between hunter and prey – it was like ratting. It was something you didn't do. I wasn't scared of being physically hurt. I was afraid of being thought of as someone like Colin.

Something changed in Colin when he saw my face, when he saw what was in it – or to be more accurate, what was absent from it. He knew at that moment I wasn't going to help him, that the last thing in his life that he trusted had failed. Then it was like watching mercury disturbed: a rippling across the face, a strange development of reflexes that tightened his mouth, forced his eyes into slits, lengthened his neck.

Ah now, Colly, Colly me little feller. I think am ganna be sick. Could ya pass me that school cap of yours? I'll get it cleaned out for ya, och I will.

Tony began to fake awful retching noises. Colin's changed face turned towards him and held the large, dark globe of his head in its gaze. I knew then that Colin was about to make a fatal mistake – fatal for a tortoise. I saw his fists bunch, saw the knuckles whiten. Then at once he struck out, catching Tony clumsily, not on the cheek but on the forehead. Tony momentarily looked stunned, then reared up. The laughter immediately seized. When Tony spoke again, it was in his normal voice, compacted, tightened, openly threatening.

*You little **mongol**. You fucking sell me out to the **head** over Koinange. Now you think you're a big man again. But you're not. You're. A. Tiny. Little. Prick. In fact, let's see it, shall we? Let's see that tiny thing that barely qualifies as a cock.*

Tony and the rest of the mob fell on Colin. I heard something that sounded like a yelp, then a scream. Still my feet were rooted to the floor. I wanted to turn and run, but I couldn't help watching. I knew they weren't hitting Colin. What they were doing was worse than that.

Colin was struggling like crazy now, but he didn't have a chance. I saw his shoes come off, then be thrown out of the open window. His socks followed. Now Colin was silent, panting, all his energies turned furiously to try and prevent what was coming next. I saw his trousers come off and his sad little underpants. They too went out of the window. Colin began to sob hysterically. I could hear Tony's voice shouting over the racket.

Crybaby! Crybaby!

Girls were giggling nervously in the corner of the room. Colin was naked now, his tragic, unformed penis a small worm under the white neon.

Crybaby! Crybaby!

It was only now that I turned and ran, as I saw the lower half of Colin's body naked on the floor. The other boys were standing back and laughing, while my friend, my best friend, lay on the floor and tried to cover his privates with his hands, shaking with anger and humiliation.

It was then I heard Nodge's voice, saw him move in between Tony and Colin.

Give it a rest, Tone. Enough's enough, eh?

Tony glared at him. But Nodge was big and solid and, as I say, totally stubborn. Tony took a step backwards. Colin wept on the floor. The scene was static. Then I turned, and I ran and ran, ran down the stairs and out into the playground. I could still hear Tony's voice in my head.

He's a fucking crybaby!

The clothes were scattered forlornly in a pile, by the line that marked the long side of a tennis court. I fetched them desperately up and turned and ran upstairs.

By the time I got back to the classroom, Colin had gone, and the boys and girls were sitting at their desks waiting for the next lesson to begin. Tony was laughing, unrepentant – there was a small red mark on his forehead where Colin had caught him. Nodge was staring out of the window, apparently disconnected from events now.

I knew where Colin was without asking. There was a boys' toilet two doors along. I made my way down the corridor holding the pathetic pile of clothes. More than once, in my rush, I dropped a shoe and had to run and retrieve it. The heating made a noise as it cranked up like breaking metal. I pushed through the door. The toilet appeared to be empty, but one of the cubicle doors was closed. The urinals began to flush automatically. Above the sound, there was a small sobbing noise. I made my way towards the locked door. When I spoke, my voice sounded tiny, ridiculous. I remember being unsure of what it was I was meant to sound like, what tone I was meant to adopt.

Colin. Colin, it's me.

The sobbing continued. There was a slight movement inside.

Colin, are you all right?

I looked under the cubicle door. I could see his ankles, bluish white. There was a small puddle of water on the floor where someone had missed the seat. A scrap of hard toilet paper.

Can you hear me? I've brought your clothes back.

I knew that it wasn't nearly enough. That there

was something craven in the very act of trying to obtain absolution through a gesture so trivial, so after-the-event. Nodge had particularly disgraced me by stepping in, when it should have been me, Colin's best friend, who stood between Tony and his prey. It was at this moment, I think, that I began to cast Nodge as a self-righteous prick. It was my only way of defending myself against my own shame.

The toilets finished flushing, leaving only the sound of our breathing, him on one side of the rusted metal door, me on the other. I could smell urine now, for the first time. I prayed no one would walk in. Still no answer from Colin.

Come on, Col. I . . . I . . .

I sought for the words that would heal the wound between us, that would put together what had been broken. Then I did not know there was an invisible world within us, in which events move on, irrespective of what we want. Connections here are made and unmade, opportunities are offered, taken or refused. Tentacles of connection reach out or are withdrawn, sometimes suddenly, sometimes gradually. Tectonic plates move, unseen, and cannot move back. So no words *could* come, not without being fake, or melodramatic, or unbearably true.

I heard Colin begin to cry again, then I turned to face inside me what I already knew. Whatever was between Colin and me, whatever love had been there, had now cracked, or transformed, diminished. It had, I suddenly knew, been coming apart for a long time, and my betrayal in the classroom was simply a symptom of this. I was craven, I knew. But at the same time, as I silently pushed Colin's trousers, pants, shoes and socks into the gap under the cubicle, there was a lightness that entered into me. I had outgrown him. He was a drag on my . . . on my career. My lifelong vocation of wanting to be liked, by people I wanted to know. It's the start of ambition. It's the end of simplicity. It's recognition of the way things are.

I knew that the door now would remain locked, and I knew that was the way I wanted it to be. Colin on the inside in that cramped, sealed-off space, me on the outside, with doors into doors into doors. I turned away and moved back to the classroom. The lesson was about to begin. The teacher pushed past me towards his desk at the front of the class. Tony winked at me and, God help me, I winked back. The teacher scanned the desks, read the roll call. The room had warmed up at last. I looked at Colin's empty desk and I felt – nothing. I felt nothing at all.

CHAPTER 11

NODGE, OR, STRICTLY SPEAKING, NOJ

I'm at the park with Nodge, or strictly speaking, Noj. It's Jon spelt backwards, of course. He's taking his sister's girls, Florence and Dilly, to the swings for a couple of hours at Ravenscourt Park. Dilly has her friend Ben with her. Nodge likes children, and anyway one of his many highly developed senses of duty is familial. We're sitting on a park bench, watching the two sisters, one four and one three, rock back and forward on a seesaw. We're not saying much, then right out of the blue Nodge says in that low, neutral, classless, slightly sinussy voice, *Why are you getting married then?*

Nodge always likes to come straight to the point. It's one of the ways he sells himself to the world – as straightforward, down to earth, no nonsense.

He is smoking a cigarette, a Craven A. That's typical of Nodge. I don't believe he likes Craven A cigarettes at all – he often chokes on their strength, and when I tried to puff it once, it rasped in my throat like I was swallowing a tiny burnt fir

230

cone. But the point is that Craven A cigarettes are honest. Tobacco rolled up into a bit of paper, for the smoking of. No knives cutting silk, no cowboys in hats on prairies. It was how Nodge saw himself precisely.

Today he's wearing black trousers, black boots, a grey sweater and a moss-coloured waterproof jacket. I don't think I have ever seen Nodge wearing a bright colour – not a single bright colour. Not since schooldays anyway. Even, at the fancy-dress party I had recently – the theme of which was, naturally enough, cartoons – he turned up, predictably, as Eeyore, entirely in well-pressed grey felt complete with a forlorn tail. (I went, originally I thought, as Cornfed the Pig from Duckman. No one recognized me. Tony was a convincing Joker from Batman, Colin equally believable as Butthead. Or was it Beavis?)

Everything today, as ever, is pressed and clean, as if it was laundered and ironed an hour earlier. His movements are precise; his cigarette smoking is elegant – one could almost say beautiful, were it not a ridiculous thing to say. His hands are delicate, with long thin fingers quite in contrast to his imploded steamed-pudding face.

I am holding a can of Lucozade. I take a swig, wipe my mouth with the back of my sleeve, leaving a small white slick about four inches long. I cough and consider whether or not I should answer, and if so, how truthfully. I wasn't sure how truthfully I was capable of answering.

231

Why? Don't you like Veronica?

Nodge sniffs and reaches for another fag. His fingers are yellow.

As a matter of fact, I do. She was all right. Head screwed on, I thought. That's not what I was asking. What I was asking was –

I wave a small cumulus of cigarette smoke away from my face.

I know what you were asking. And it's a stupid question. After all, why does anyone get married?

I'm not asking why anyone gets married. I'm asking why you're getting married.

I might as well ask why you aren't getting married.

It's not the same. Anyway, it's me who's asking the question.

I become irritated, although I'm not sure why. After you've known someone as long as I've known Nodge, no conversation takes place in a vacuum. Each phrase uttered, each sentence delivered, is part of a continuum, a larger, three dimensional pattern that occupies the present, but stretches back deep into the past and contains an array of threatening implications for the future. With Nodge, for instance, I know if I concede some principle now, it will be filed away, used against me at some unspecified, as yet unarrived moment.

Meanwhile, history – the past – has taught me that Nodge is a kind of echo chamber. He sits quite still, smoking those honest Craven As which I don't believe he likes, and either listens or asks nosy questions. But you ask him something about

232

his life, what he thinks, feels, and he'll just shrug and duck the question, then sit quite still until the weight of silence builds up so much you find yourself gabbling, telling him everything while he puffs honest smoke like Thomas the Tank Engine.

UNCLE JON!

Dilly, Nodge's niece, is running towards us, crying with the full force of her lungs. Nodge casually but precisely stubs out his cigarette and leans towards her. His face opens with a kind of tenderness. This surprises me. I didn't know Nodge had those kind of feelings. Soft ones.

What's the matter, sweetheart?

She jumps up and throws her arms around his neck, weeping bitterly. In the background, Ben is chasing another little girl who was at the playground when they arrived, someone neither of them has met before.

Uncle Jon, Ben says . . . Ben says . . . Ben says . . . She can't get the words out, she's choking so much with fury and upset. *Ben says he won't be my friend. Ben's got a new friend. They won't let me play with them.*

She begins to cry again, and Nodge gives her another hug.

Well, then, Ben's just silly. Because you're the most beautiful girl in the playground and if Ben doesn't want to play with you —

*I don't care. I don't want to play with **him**.*

Come on, darling. That isn't true.

233

It is true. It is. I'm not going to be anyone's friend ever again, not never. Not ever.

She screws her face up in a rubbery grimace. Nodge shrugs, looks at me. Ben is enjoying himself, completely ignoring – possibly enjoying – Dilly's abject tears. He's hugging the new girl; it is a deliberate attempt to taunt Dilly. She glances, then looks away.

Dilly, look. The swing is empty now. Why don't you go and play on it?

Dilly brightens up. In an instant, she's turned on her heel and is heading for the swing, face still wet, nose still stained with snot. Ben ignores her still. Meanwhile, Florence is playing with another little boy. They are laughing together and holding hands. Nodge turns to me again, raises his Gallagher unibrow and gives me a *kids, who'd have 'em* smile.

You've got it all to come, Frankie.

I don't know about that. Just because I'm getting married doesn't mean I have to start breeding.

Hmmmh.

I recognize this hmmmh. Nodge has several different and distinct hmmmhs. This particular one means that he doesn't believe what I'm saying, that I'm just pretending to stand aloof from the idea of children because it preserves my idea of myself. It's a very irritating noise.

Kids aren't for everyone.

Hmmmh. So . . . Long pause, deep honest drag on honest cigarette. *Why are you getting married then?*

234

I shift uneasily in my seat. Nodge has a way of getting you to talk in the end.

I don't know, Jon. To be honest, I haven't stopped asking myself that since I popped the question to Veronica. I just know that it feels like the right thing to do.

Silence.

More silence.

Puffety puff. I can't take the pressure of the silence any more. Nodge is used to it, sitting in a cab all day with only his own company.

Obviously, I'm not getting any younger. There's like . . . it's like there's a weight pressing down on me, a pressure. I don't know where it comes from. I'm thirty years old after all. I looked in the mirror the other day and there was fucking hair coming out of my ears. Like an old man. And everyone else seems to be doing it. Not that I'm just going along with the crowd. Veronica's terrific, she really is. I mean, I know she seems a bit off with people sometimes, but that just comes from being with dead people all day. We're easy together, it works. And I'm tired of being out there in the meat market. You get to a point when you want things to be, I don't know, settled. A line drawn somewhere.

He nods. I look around the playground. Now Dilly is playing with Ben again, and the new kid as well. Dilly actually has her arms around the new kid and is giving her a kiss. Florence is playing chase with the other kid, laughing at the top of her lungs. All around the playground, singles and pairs of parents stand silently, never acknowledging each other at all. The thought comes to me. *We close up like clams as we get old.* Distance is one of the ways we stop being children.

Then I say, *I guess I've been thinking that I've never committed myself to anything in my life and that maybe, just maybe, that's where I've been going wrong. Always hedging my bets, waiting for the better offer. It's no way to live. You have to plant your feet, make your stand. Life changes, and you have to change too. She's lovely, Veronica, she'll make a great doris. She's kind, loves me. She's intelligent and warm.*

I try to resist saying the next thing, but I can't. It's too deeply ingrained. Reflexive.

And she's a terrific shag.

You *have* to do that from time to time. Drop in a joke, something that establishes that you're blokes together, that you each possess cocks, that you're not getting too serious, not for too long. There are limits. Balloons have to be punctured beyond a certain level of inflation.

Nodge, a puritan who has, and has always had, the trick of making me feel ashamed of myself, gives a thin smile, acknowledging that the *I'm when all said and done a bloke* strategy has been, as is conventional, deployed. Then it's back to the nod, smoke, nod. He wants more. I try to just let the silence pile up, but it's too uncomfortable, too intimate.

No, I'm kidding. Anyway that's not the reason I'm marrying her. I'm . . . it's . . . because . . .

What I want to say is, why are you asking me this? Why don't you just be happy for me, and slap me on the back and wish me luck? Honesty, concern – it's overrated. It's a form of hostility.

It's an excuse for a party, isn't it?

I see, even before I deliver these words, how pitiful this is. Where do I get this stuff from? Then, out of the blue, the real answer comes to me, like a blazing sign in Piccadilly Circus. As I stare across at Nodge in his grey and brown togs, and his faint disapproval, and barely concealed judgement, I think, but don't say, *It's because of* **you**. *You and people like you. My friends, so called. I've had it with you, the lot of you. You're a game that's been played out, an emotion that's been used up, a drink that's been finished, a Craven A cigarette that should have been stubbed out years ago. You're a habit I've got to break, an existence I've got to leave behind. And Veronica, she's a ladder that was left lying out in the yard. And I'm going up. I'm going up, up and away.*

I want to be normal, and I'm getting less normal as each year passes, as dorishood, coupledom, becomes the norm. I want to be respectable. I don't want to be the misfit again. Never again.

But are they, my friends, really what I'm getting away from, and is Veronica really where I'm getting to? What are the other forces at work? There are always other forces at work. I'd ask Nodge, but Nodge finds it hard to talk. He finds it easy to

237

speak, but hard to talk. Anything that goes beyond a certain point, the shutters come down.

It wasn't always that way, I sometimes remember. I say sometimes, because there are things between us that I'd sooner forget myself. Not because they were unpleasant. That's the point. It's because they're unsettling.

For years I haven't thought about this, been determined not to think about it in fact. But getting married is a light shone into dark places. The light sometimes makes me squirm, so I endeavour to switch it off again. But sometimes it gets stuck. You click and click and it just stays on. Then Nodge speaks, looks at his watch. I pay attention, hoping that it will stop the memory-dominoes that have just started tumbling.

Decided what we're going to do on 14 August?
Colin suggested playing golf.
Not a bad idea. What do you think?
Sure. Why not?
OK then. Look, I've got to get the kids back.
Fine. Catch you later then.
Later.

The dominoes are still toppling. Walking away from the playground, I look back at Nodge, catch him in profile. He doesn't know he is being seen, and I stare at his face and wonder what it is I like about him any more. I can see at this moment there is tenderness there, but it is so . . . buried. Unexcavatable, a deep seamed mine. Perhaps I don't like him at all any more. Perhaps he scares me. But why should he scare me?

That's what the light's been showing up, that's what the dominoes are heading towards, naked and weird. It comes to me at night, when the noise of a boom box wakes me up from a passing car, or the roar of a giant motorcycle. My eyes pop open and I'm suddenly not here, still in my bedroom, but at a different time, in a different world, in my mother's house, fifteen years ago.

CHAPTER 12

MORNING GLORY

I suppose I'd only known Nodge a year or so at the time. We didn't talk much, even after what happened with Colin. He was moved to a different stream from me, Colin and Tony shortly after the debagging. But we were both good runners, and he and I at the age of fifteen paired up on the 100-metres relay team. Stocky and broad but without the overcoat of fat he carries with him now, his powerful legs gave him the perfect build for the sprint. We both ran for the school; I was often clumsy with the baton and I noticed him because, when I dropped it, he was the only one in the team who would commiserate rather than bellow at me. Like I say, he was different then. Softer. He's kind, Nodge. I often forget that, for some reason. You wouldn't guess it. He hides it, like everything else nowadays.

He was almost flamboyant then. I remember he had a big alpaca red sweater, some corn-coloured trousers and an early crude version of training shoes. There was something exotic in him that has since become concentrated all in the gestures and rituals of his cigarette smoking, leaving his remaindered self washed of tone.

His walk home would take him in the same direction as me and Colin, so we began to fall in line together, kicking cans home, smoking illicit cigarettes by this time in the greasy spoon which lay half-way between the school and our homes. Even then his smoking style was admirable. I tried to emulate him, but always looked gauche in comparison.

Nodge had a mordant sense of humour; he was dry then, although nowadays he seems to have decayed into cynical. In his quiet way, he was daring, vengeful. When a teacher bullied some innocent kid, he would put sugar in his petrol tank. He never stood back from a fight either – when someone was picked on, he would stand like a taut hippo in between victim and aggressor, daring them to strike. Nodge was always for the underdog. That was why I started out liking him, I think. And I suppose it's why he took to Colin also, although they were never that close. But he understood what it meant to be weak: the price, the shame.

Nodge, though, was tough. There was something leathery about him, something indestructible, and the indestructibility became more pronounced as he got older. Again, it seemed to become sort of debased into insensitivity later. I sometimes think some secret disappointment soured him at some time in the last decade, transforming all his virtues into their darker opposites. But I could

241

never guess what it might be. Or perhaps I never wanted to guess.

Anyway, after a few months of walking home together and running in the school team, we began to hang around in the evenings. Fifteen years old is a nether world – too old for childhood, too young for the pub. So on summer evenings, we would just go out and walk together, purposelessly, indulging sometimes in acts of petty vandalism – stealing road signs, firing air pistols at scurrying birds, always missing, deliberately.

Sometimes we would bring Colin with us. Not much would happen, but there was something about Colin – something he did on one of these evenings – that has remained with me since, still vivid. I have talked about it with Nodge and Tony since, and it has made us wonder about what lies underneath Colin's apparently bottomless mildness.

On this occasion, Nodge, Colin and me were walking home and I had the air pistol, and I drew double-quick and just let loose at a pigeon – for a laugh. I meant to miss, as usual, but I hit it on the wing. The bird made a strange gagging noise, recoiled, then began to bleed. It staggered. It was crippled. Clearly it would not fly again.

I felt vividly shocked and disgusted, horrified and helpless. The bird started to squawk now, in a cry of what sounded like pain. Nodge looked at me and I looked back.

What we going to do?

I don't know. It's . . .

We'll have to . . .

Colin very quietly looked up at us and said, *We should kill it.*

Nodge and I shook our heads, appalled.

We can call the vet.

We could put it in a splint.

Your mum'll know what to do.

But Colin hadn't moved. Then he said again, in exactly the same flat tone, *No. We should kill it.*

Then, quite calmly, he walked over to where the bird was, picked up a rock that made up part of a loose garden perimeter backing on to the pavement and with one motion smashed the rock down on the bird's head.

That's done.

The bird's body kept moving. Colin brought it down again, and again, until its head was just a red mess on the concrete. Then he looked up at mine and Nodge's frozen faces.

It's dead now.

Then he began to walk on. Me and Nodge didn't say anything, but began to follow him. And for the first time in my life, I was scared of Colin, scared of what was dark inside him.

But such drama was unusual and extraordinary. Mostly, though, we just dragged around the streets in different, harmless permutations, dreaming of when we wouldn't be there any more. Nodge would always talk about how he wanted to travel, though I suppose at that time it meant more to him than just being a taxi driver. He would go into travel agents and ask for all their free brochures and sit on park benches with me, poring over the pictures of sunlit perfection.

Look at this. Sri Lanka. The whiteness of that beach. Can you believe that sea? China – a traditional village. Probably full of tourists now. But just look at it. Isn't that something? Jamaica – 'A Jewel in the Caribbean Sea'. Mad. Easter Island. Look at those weird faces. That one looks like Colin.

And so on. He would spend hours doing this, dreaming of how he would go here and there, lie on that beach, explore that rainforest, climb that mountain, dive into those caves.

But there was one thing he kept coming back to, though I don't know why. He had a thing about Fiji. He'd seen the pictures in the brochures from the air, the iridescent, psychedelic blues and greens. He'd been to see both versions of *The Blue Lagoon*. He'd got a picture of Brooke Shields in a grass skirt up on his wall. He had every brochure on Fiji ever published.

Look at that, Frankie. It . . . it's paradise. No one about. That blue. The coral reefs. God, to scuba-dive a reef like that. There are sharks out there. Then, the people used to be head-hunters.

He knew it all. That there were 322 islands large enough for human habitation, but there were thousands more. That there were seven basic kinds of coral – his favourite was the elk-horn fire coral, with its beautiful curves and whorls, which, of course, he had only seen pictures of.

244

He knew about *kava*, the ceremonial drink, about the traditional roasting of meats in the pit, about the fire-walking, the spearing of the stingrays, the *meke* dance. Fiji was his dream, his Shangri-La, his own private Blue Lagoon.

To this day, however, he has never got further than that trip to the Oktoberfest, plus, on one occasion, a cheap weekend in Ibiza.

On these dreaming and wandering walks, Colin might be with us, and sometimes, but rarely, Tony, who seemed even then to have more of a social life than the rest of us put together. But on this occasion, this deliberately wiped-out and until now edited occasion, it was just me and Nodge.

It was a Friday evening. Mum and Dad had gone away for the weekend, leaving me with the key. As it happened, we knew of a party that night being held by a friend of Nodge's brother, Trevor, three years older. It was in the back room of a pub in one of the nastiest parts of the Bush, near Colin on the White City Estate. Nodge's brother was known as a bit of a villain. He'd been cautioned two or three times for petty theft and selling a bit of puff, and he was loud and vaguely malicious. But he told us that he could get us in, and we were ready to do anything that would take us away from the monotony of trudging the streets between Shepherd's Bush and Acton High Street, tossing pebbles at cats and glaring hopefully, pitifully, at strolling girls.

That night we began to indulge in an extended

fantasy about what might come about. The emptiness of the house, the imminence of the party. Perhaps a miracle would occur and we would lure two girls back, although if we had done I'm not sure we would have known what to do with them. We were both reluctant, resentful virgins, rammed to the extremities with unfulfilled sexual desire.

At six o'clock, Nodge arrived at my house. The Goth/New Romantic cult had begun to root itself in the inner suburbs and Nodge had had a go. It didn't seem so much against his character in those days. His hair was bleached and he wore a ripped fishnet T-shirt, cut-off jeans with high, fifteen-hole black patent-leather boots. I was resplendent with wash-out-in-one-go violet hair, a black shirt and vinyl trousers.

The party didn't get started until eight-thirty, so we had time to kill. Nodge's brother had gone into an off-licence and bought him two bottles of cheap red wine, which Nodge carried, one in each strangely delicate hand. I opened a bottle and we sat down at the white melamine kitchen table with two whisky tumblers and began to drink. We had a few records to play. The Human League, Joy Division, Fad Gadget.

My mother was a keen, though not particularly skilful, gardener. There was a twenty-foot patch of land at the back of the house which was turfed and edged with rockery plants, evergreen bushes and small hardy perennials. The flowerbeds were in bloom. Nodge stared out of the window, pulling at his drink, already growing bleary eyed with the effects. At the centre of the strip of tended land on the left-hand side of the garden was a cluster of heavenly blue flowers, in perfect bloom. Nodge's heavy lids raised slightly when he noticed them.

See those blue flowers?

He lazily raised a hand and gestured in the general direction of the garden.

What about them?

Nearly three-quarters of the bottle of wine had already gone. It was sticky, sweet, foul, but we swallowed it anyway, grimacing theatrically.

I think they're Morning Glory.

He nodded, as if doing so would add to the gravitas of the announcement. I felt I was expected to react in some way. There was a long pause before I began to formulate a sentence. Already the room was rotating slightly in front of my eyes. All I could manage was, *What?*

The record came to a halt. I moved unsteadily towards the turntable and substituted another.

They're meant to be hallucino . . . hallucinogen . . . They make you see things. Trev was telling me, the other day. Ways of getting off your face. Nutmeg, for example. If you eat a whole one, you start to trip. Banana skins. There's these mushrooms that grow on golf courses. And Morning Glory. Heavenly Blues. Something like that. They're like acid. You have to eat a lot of them though.

I coughed.

I'm not eating flowers. I'm not a fucking hippie.

Nodge waved away this objection with his thin white hand.

You don't eat the flowers. You eat the seeds.

I screwed up my face.

Trev says it's quite good. They taste fucking horrible, but you get visions of things. The world lights up. He said it was like listening to a record which only ever had dust on the needle and then suddenly the dust came off and you heard it properly. Why don't you go and have a look and see if your mum's got any?

I thought about this for a moment.

I don't want to have visions.

Of course you do. Nodge was up on his feet now, unsteadily. *Everyone wants to have visions. It'll be like . . . like being in Fiji. Everything'll be blue. Everything'll be liquid. There'll be . . . elk-horn fire coral. Come on. Where does she keep them? I bet they're in the cupboard under the stairs. That's where parents always keep their crap. You can find anything under the stairs. Drink, rat poison, glue, feather dusters, candles, trowels, entire families of Pakistanis. Anything.*

This was in the days before Nodge acquired his sensitivity towards ethnic minorities. I didn't take any notice. Nodge opened the door of the stair cupboard and began banging about inside. I could hear heavy objects falling from shelves. After a few minutes, he emerged from the darkened space, grinning from ear to ear.

Here you go. Two packets of Heavenly Blue. Jesus, that's some cupboard. I'm sure there's something fucking living in there. I was afraid for a while. It's dark, you know. Black as . . . as a . . . very black thing.

I stared dumbly at the two packets he held in his hand. Pictured on each were photos of the flowers in the garden, shown giant in the foreground against a perfect blue sky. With a single movement, he tore the tops off each of them and emptied the seeds on to a saucer on the table. They were pinhead-sized and there were about a hundred of them in all.

I'm not eating those. They've probably got fertilizer on them. I'll probably get something sprouting in my guts, if I don't die first.

Ah, fuck it. I'm game, said Nodge. Nodge was up for anything in those days.

Suddenly I felt the need to show him that I wasn't afraid. He was always the one who took the initiative, who took the big step. Like when he stopped Tony attacking Colin. I wanted to show that I had some bottle too.

What the fuck?

We said *fuck* a lot in those days. It was a way of separating ourselves from our childhood selves. It tasted good on the tongue, forbidden, adult. When my father heard me say it under my breath, when I was ten or eleven, he struck me on the face with his open hand. The only time that ever happened. I knew then I was going to say it a lot more.

I picked up half a dozen of the seeds and swallowed them at once, then shrugged.

That wasn't so bad. You can't hardly taste them.
Nodge shook his head.

You don't just swallow them. You have to chew them up. Like this.

He picked up a small handful and placed them delicately in his mouth, then began to move his jaws. Slowly, comically, his face took on a look of exaggerated revulsion.

Shit a brick, that's horrible. It tastes like earth mixed with chalk mixed with cow shit.

But he kept right on chewing, until he finally, as if in pain, swallowed. Immediately he took a swig of wine, threw back his head and began gargling. He swallowed, went white, looked right at me and said, in half-whisper, *I'm going to blow my doughnuts.*

And for a moment I thought he really was. He tensed and a slight gag reflex sounded in the back of his throat. Then he gave an almighty burp and settled back in the chair, looking self-satisfied.

Not so bad. Quite nice really. If you like the taste of foul and unspeakable things.

Seeing his expression, determined not to be out-done, I picked up a larger handful of the seeds, put them in my mouth and began to chew. Another in that endless round of competitions. The taste was truly awful and the seeds went immediately to the consistency of Cow Gum, sticking to the palate and wedging in the gaps between the teeth. I didn't want them, whether they worked or not; especially if they worked. But even then Nodge and I had developed a rivalry, which had started on the running field and, though I didn't know then, would always continue. I wasn't going to let him outdo me, or prove himself braver. So I smiled, took another handful and said. *Not bad. A bit like peanut butter with reinforced cement, peat and old chewing gum mixed in.*

Nodge, thus challenged, took another mouthful himself. We sat there, chewing at each other, each now fighting to disguise our revulsion, trying to erase the taste with baths of equally foul red wine. Amazingly, at the end of it, neither of us was sick. After five or ten minutes, the nausea began to pass.

Now we were competing to see who could drink the wine quickest. Each of us filled a glass and tried to sink it in one. The second bottle was consumed entirely in about fifteen minutes.

I was beginning to feel extremely strange. Nodge, in front of me, seemed to move about, to billow and flow, as if the water that, I had read that day in science, made up 80 per cent of him had suddenly achieved mastery over his bones and muscles. It felt unpleasant, as if I were watching everything through the thick ends of dirty water tumblers. When Nodge spoke now, it was barely more than a slur.

T'Sato. Clock.

Wha?

T'Sato. Clock. We going?

Uh.

We both tried to stand up to make our way to the party. Nodge started to fall over, giggling, and I grabbed his hand to stop him. I felt his hand round my wrist, pulling, and I yanked him upwards until

251

he was approximately vertical, then he began to fall slightly towards me. The red wine was on his breath, and tobacco that smelled sweet instead of foul. We balanced against each other, and then I noticed that the record was stuck in a groove, repeating . . .

It was at this point I always lost the ability to remember. I know people say that, I know they say they can't remember, after they've had a few drinks, and I've never really believed them. I always thought it was a joke, or just something you said to show that you had the bravery to abandon self-control utterly. But all I could ever remember is that track stuck in the groove, turning and turning, and Nodge's delicate hand in mine, and us tottering about the room, the seeds and the wine rotating my vision like a busted, boring kaleidoscope.

There is one bit I have sort of *begun* to remember, though. Since the marriage proposal, that bit has come back, although I turn my mind away from it every time it flickers up there on the blank juddering screen at the back of my head. It isn't so much a fluid memory as quick successions of still pictures, as if from a security camera. I'm not even sure it's in colour. That would make it too real, too believable.

The picture, the security camera shudder, is this. I'm on my bed in my bedroom. It's a single bed, on the far wall of the room, ten feet from a bay window. I can feel the pressure of my eyelids on my eyes, and it feels as if there is an enormous weight on top of my head. I am in pain, real intense pain that seems to stretch from the behind of my eyeballs round in a cutting curve through the entire circumference of my skull.

I feel consciousness seeping into me like a dimmer switch being gradually rotated in a darkened room. Outside, there is a hum of a motor mower, the whine of an aeroplane. It is hot. I have my shirt off, but my trousers are intact. My hair is matted with sweat.

There is a smell in my nostrils like weak, dried bleach that I do not recognize, and a pressure on my back, which is not painful but uncomfortable. There is a faint light in the room being cast through closed curtains. I can hear a ticking clock and this prompts me to very slowly risk opening my eyes a slit. Directly in front of them, there is an alarm in the shape of the Sesame Street character Big Bird. It's a joke present that my aunty, who always miscalculates my age, bought me. It says 10.05. The alarm is on the floor.

I try to stretch out and feel an obstruction. The bed seems even smaller than usual. The dimmer switch rotates another number of degrees and I try a small shake of my head, which seems to set the pain roaring again. I reach out to try and steady myself, and feel something warm and soft and slightly damp. I almost jump, believing it to be some kind of animal. But it is too still. I am bewildered, and slowly, to minimize the pain, crane my head around.

It is then that I see Nodge, eyes closed, breathing gently, in the bed with me. He is bunched up, as if a baby, but he is squat and hirsute for someone in his mid-teens. His hair is mussed, there is a shadow of soft fur on his face, stubble's mild ancestor. The expression is one of perfect innocence, even bliss. He is deep in sleep. I notice, at first, quite neutrally, that he too is topless, that the soft pressure on my back is in fact his chest, and I realize that beneath that he has one of his hands down the front of my trousers. It is gripping, quite firmly, my half-erect cock.

I do not move, trying to take in information that is simply not acceptable. I am afraid to move in case it wakes him, and in case we are forced to face this thing that I like to choose not to remember. He groans slightly and flexes. His body is all muscle at this age. I feel my own body go rigid, not in excitement, but terror. On the wall, a poster of Pete Burns from Dead Or Alive grins down at me. Mocking.

Very slowly, inch by inch, holding my breath, I begin to move towards the edge of the bed. After what seems like minutes on end, I have extended my left forearm down on to the floor. Nodge's hand feels jammed. I shift and shimmy to shake it loose, gently, in case he wakes up. I feel the nap of the carpet under my fingertips and I let it take my weight. I begin to move my centre of gravity across until half my body is flapping over the rim of the bed frame. My left leg is down now, toes touching the floor. Nodge's hand is free.

Nodge moves again, moaning slightly, and I stop moving. I feel his hand reach out for my calf. It touches and rests there. I am balanced between floor and bed, and am afraid to move in case the removal of my leg nudges him into consciousness. I wait, until my leg and arm can take the pressure no more, then something softly collapses and I fall off the bed. The Big Bird alarm clock falls over and begins to sound.

Wakey wakey! Rise and Shine!

Then it gives a little Big Bird chuckle.

I quickly roll over to smother the clock with my body. It does not stop, but it mutters under my diaphragm. I feel its vibration, the painful pressure of its yellow plastic beak. Again, I hold my breath, and crane my head to look at Nodge. I see then that his eyes have flickered open. For a terrifying moment, he catches mine, then allows them to flutter closed again. Whether he is genuinely conscious or not, I do not know.

After several more minutes, I manage to roll in a way that clicks the alarm off. Now I rise and, swiftly as I am able, I zip up my trousers and put on a shirt. I drag on my basketball boots, fumbling furiously with the laces, walking towards the door as I try to tie them. Then I'm down the stairs and out into the street and running, running, the pounding in my head exploding like so many shells on a battlefield.

I did not return to the house until that afternoon, spending the rest of the morning wandering around the streets and parks. The wine and seeds from the night before were still poisoning me; I retched in drains and litter bins, disgusted pedestrains avoiding my gaze. I must have looked a fright: catching my face in a shop window, I saw the red encrustation of the eyes, the hanging bags of a middle-aged man under my teenage eyes.

When I tentatively turned the key in the lock, scared that Nodge would still be there, the house seemed changed, charged with a different electricity. I took a deep breath and marched upstairs, preparing myself. As I hoped, all trace of Nodge had gone. There was just a dented pillow and rumpled bedclothes.

I did not see him again for a week after that. It was half-term holiday and whereas normally we would have been on the phone every day, there was only silence. Then, on the first day back at school, I was walking from my house, turned the corner in the direction of the grammar and there was Nodge across the road. We both stopped momentarily, then waved and grinned, and I crossed the road to where he was. No reference was made to what had happened that night. If anything did happen, that is. It was hard to be sure, but the circumstantial evidence was disquieting enough to my teenage mind, which reflexively, enthusiastically joined in the general schoolboy derision towards *poofs* and *queers*. Anyway. Nothing was said, not then, not ever again. It was as if it was in both our imaginations and sometimes even now I doubt that it happened.

CHAPTER 13

VRONKY'S SPECIAL DAY

W e're in my house. Veronica has been living here because she hasn't got any choice. Her new flat has the builders in. It's got rot in the roof, a supporting wall in the wrong place and seven walls in need of repointing. But the khazi still faces the back window, in top feng shui style, so that's all right. That should stop the money energy being sucked out of the house then. All the money apart from the twenty grand it's going to cost her. Us.

What made her buy that place, that disaster, against all common sense? Because Veronica is stupid. Just like I'm stupid, just like Tony, Nodge and Colin are stupid. But we have very particular zones of stupidity, very different ways of being idiotic. Our cleverness is all in different places too. That's why we can never make sense of each other.

Right at this moment I'm not sure whether it's Vronky or me who's being stupid, or if we are, or how. But we're locked into something and neither of us is intelligent enough to find a way out.

It is in the way she butters her toast that I know she's furious. There's more pressure going down on the bread than is necessary, so that you can actually hear the scrape of the stainless steel against the brittle surface of the bread. She's giving it too much attention, as if it were a complex operation. Taking the butter exactly to the edges then trimming, so that every square inch is covered.

The roses – twenty of them, red, still damp from the water in which I have kept them secretly, overnight – lie neglected on the table in front of her. She did thank me for them, but it was perfunctory, muttered through teeth that were fixed together as she spoke. A thorn on one of the stems pokes through the decorated wax paper. A card remains unread in its envelope.

I can understand why she's angry. But now I'm getting angry that *she's* angry, because it's making me feel guilty. So I put my cup down on the saucer too hard, sounding a crack. It's in order to make a point. She twists her head towards me, stretching the skin on her neck into a shifting pattern of tight, evenly spaced ripples.

What's the matter with **you**?

Her mouth is full when she says this, so a little spray of crumbs comes out from between her unpainted lips and cascades on to the table. She brushes them on to the floor, without looking to see where they go. Some disappear in between the gaps in the polished floorboards.

There's bright sunlight coming through the window. It's the perfect weather for an August day. I exhale air through my nose. It's meant to be a sigh, but it comes out as a snort.

You're the one who's got the egg on.

She untwists her neck, stares out of the window in weighted silence.

I thought we had it all straightened out, I continue. I try to keep my tone neutral.

She doesn't move. Then she turns her face away from me. Now I can hear little more than a low, even hiss of words.

You had it straightened out. You didn't exactly give me a choice.

With this, she gets up and – still not looking at me – abruptly moves to leave the room with short, fast, determined steps. She is naked, and I notice that the pinkness between her legs still seems moist, expanded from the sex. That was just thirty minutes ago. Everything seemed fine then. Days have weather, don't they? Hours have weather.

While she is gone, I sit there, knotting and unknotting the problem in my head. A fatalism then overtakes me; the problem is discarded as insoluble. I walk over to the closet and try to haul out a large white plastic cylindrical bag, only the base of which is visible under the row of my shirts that cloak it. Parting the hangers exposes the heads of a half-set of golf clubs.

Some of the club heads are caught up with the shirts.

This tangling of metal, wood and cloth underlines my sense that the day is turning against me. I pull hard at what appears to be a number-three driver. The club head will not come free. I pull again, violently, this time. There is a tearing sound. The club comes loose. Wrapped around the head of the driver, a piece of fine, powder-blue material. A scrap of my favourite shirt, a present from Veronica on Valentine's Day. Veronica, I know, is going to say that this is symbolic, this tearing of her first gift. She thinks the world talks to you through what appear to be random events. She sees meanings everywhere.

I stare at the scrap of cloth and feel some of my fury earth into the soft blue cotton. What's left decays into resignation. How could she be expected to understand, after all?

I knew it was going to be trouble when she told me which day she was born. I couldn't *believe* it. If the world really does talk to you, like Veronica says, what was it saying by arranging *that* particular collision? But then I don't believe that it does talk to you, the world. It's all just accidents, circumstance, stuff happening.

Veronica walks back into the room. She's wearing a big, pastel-pink, mumsy dressing gown. Padded, with floral designs. On her feet, there are slippers made to look like the heads of small bears. Their expressions are meant to be winsome, but they look frightened.

She still doesn't look at me. She sits down again and goes back to work on the toast. The yellow butter has dissolved now into patches of silvery oil.

When I speak again my voice is smaller than I wish it to be.

I ripped my best shirt. On my number-three golf club.

I wave the scrap of material towards her like a flag of surrender. She looks up and inspects the cloth intently, as if it bore secret messages within its weave.

Good. Her voice is frosted, unyielding. *Perhaps someone's trying to tell you something.*

I turn my face upwards, move my eyes towards the top of the lids. This immediately feels fake, a gesture I've seen on TV. I give it up and lower my head to an angle where I can see the clock. It reads 9.45. That leaves me about fifteen minutes.

I walk over to where she sits, in a slight hunch over the breakfast table. I put an arm around her shoulder and squeeze. Again, it feels wrong. She doesn't shift an inch, except to stiffen slightly. I move the arm away, let it dangle at my side hopelessly. Now she uncoils, turns to me. Her lips are pinched together before she speaks and show white where they curve towards the inside.

It's not that you even like them very much. The

261

*way you talk about them when they're not here. You
do nothing but criticize them.*

That's not true.

You said that Tony was a . . . She chews her teeth
for a second, as if balling up a word to spit. Then
she says it too fast, as if she wants to get it out of her
mouth urgently. *Cuntlastweek.* **That** *was the actual
word you used.*

Veronica hardly ever swears. She says sugar
instead of shit, fudge instead of fuck. So now I
know how angry she is. I feel faintly shocked, but
obscurely pleased. There's something sexy in it.
Seeing her stretched mouth bite off the end of the
't' with the tongue flicked hard against the teeth.

*I said that he **behaved** like a cunt. With Christopher
Crowley. With which you could hardly fail to agree.
And I said I liked him first. I said, 'Tony's a great
bloke but sometimes he can be a bit of a cunt.' It's
not the same thing as saying someone is a cunt, in
a full-time capacity, so to speak. And I didn't say
anything about Nodge or Colin.*

You did. You said that they were redundant.

I search my memory to see if this is true and
come up a blank. So I improvise.

*I said that they **felt** redundant. Sometimes, just
sometimes. It doesn't mean I don't care about them.
Anyway, I haven't said anything to you that I
wouldn't say to their faces.*

This is untrue and a slight tremor underneath the
words betrays it as such. Veronica, however, isn't
listening. When she talks, she overlaps the end of

262

my sentence. Her voice blisters, like paint under a blowlamp.

Do you know what denial is, Frankie?

Duh. Yeah. As I understand it – stop me if I get this wrong – it's what I'm in when I say something you disagree with. When I say something you do agree with, that's called facing up to things. Have I got that about right?

Veronica ignores the sarcasm. I'm not even sure that she registers it. She just carries right on.

Why are they so important to you? You see more of them than you do of me. And why do you hardly ever take me to meet them? Are you ashamed of them? Or is it me you're ashamed of?

I sit down at the table next to her. I can't say the answer, which is, paradoxically, *both*. I lean my head forward and rest it on the tips of my thumbs. The thumbs compress the flesh between them. You can sometimes tell when I've been upset because of the faint pink welt that appears in the centre of my forehead.

I'm not ashamed of anybody. They're my friends. They're my best friends. We go back years together. You just don't always like the people you – you know. Not all the time. That's normal.

I say this slightly pointedly, to try and emphasize that I don't much like Veronica at the moment, but leave it ambiguous enough to deny the intention if necessary. I knead the flesh between my thumbs. My eyes, which have been screwing closed, open. I can see through a gap between my fingers that

Veronica is pressing her thumb softly against the exposed thorn on the rose stem. A pinprick of blood appears.

I've tried to explain to you. We have a . . . what would you call it? A custom. No, it's more than a custom. It's a pact.

And none of you has ever broken it.

She says this with a slight mocking singsong, her head bobbing from side to side.

That's right. None of us has ever broken it. One year, Tony flew all the way back from France to be here. Another time, Colin had fractured an ankle and came on crutches. We arrange our holidays so it doesn't clash with it. This year is more important than ever, because . . . because . . . well, I've been trying not to tell you this, to keep it secret for Tony's sake. I pause to blink in astonishment at what I think I am about to say. *Tony has found out that he has some kind of blood disease.*

I gasp inwardly at the size and improbability of this lie. Veronica doesn't buy it even for a second and turns sharply to look at me, an expression of complete disbelief on her face.

What crap.

*It's **true**. It could be **terminal**. I mean, the tests aren't conclusive or anything. They need to be confirmed. Maybe, just maybe it will turn out OK. But what if it doesn't? How would I live with myself? And I'm amazed at your attitude. A friend of mine may be, may be **dying**, and all you think about is –*

Frankie, stop it. Just stop it.

No. I won't stop it. You're being callous and unworthy of yourself. I adopt a lofty orator's tone now, becoming more and more enfolded in the layers of the lie. *It's not so much for me. It's for him, for Tony. There'd be no competition if it was just for my sake. I'd love to spend the day with you. You would come first, make no mistake. I'd forget all this 14 August stuff. But it's very important to him, you see.*

Frankie, you're such a liar, such a liar, such a LIAR.

*I'm **not** a liar.*

That's a lie too. And if you're not a liar, why do they call you Frank the Fib?

I told you, it was a schoolboy thing. No one's called me that for years.

Well, that's what I'm going to call you from now on. Because you're the worst –

*Look. All right. **I do** lie sometimes, I admit it. But I have always – **always** – been totally honest with you.*

Really?

Really.

You absolutely swear on the grave of your father.

Absolutely.

OK.

She reaches over and picks up her handbag and starts rummaging inside. I don't like the look of this. I begin to feel nervous and rub my birthmark gently in every decreasing circles.

After a few seconds she produces something small and rectangular out of the depths of the

265

bag. I can't at first make out what it is. She waves it back and forth in front of her. Now I can see that it is a microcassette tape. For a moment, I have the mad idea that she has been bugging me.

What's that?

It's a testament. It's an X-ray. It's who you are.

Looks like a cassette that's been in the spin-drier to me.

Vronky takes out a small dictation machine and places the tape inside, then presses the start button. I hear a loud beep, then, absurdly, Tony's voice.

Hi, mate. Tony here. Long time no see. Fancy a beer? Give me a call. What about them Rangers, eh? 2–0. Look. Got to go.

BEEP.

Francis, it's mum. Can you pick me up some potatoes from the late-night supermarket. Only I've not been feeling well. Sorry to be a trouble, love. Don't forget it's your grandma's birthday next week. Call me soon. Bye.

BEEP.

Frankie, can you call me? It's Nodge.

BEEP.

Veronica has her face bunched up like a fist. I'm still confused. It's clearly a tape – an old tape, judging by the messages – from my answering machine, but I can't imagine what possible . . .

BEEP.

Giles? Hi, it's Frankie Blue. Yes. No, I'm down at Olympia now with Ms Tree. Is Rupert there? He is? OK, I'll hold.

It's my voice, leaving a message for me, on my

266

own answering machine. There is a long wait. I can hear my own voice in the background, although I still can't isolate the moment. Then my voice comes up to the forefront again.

Rupert, hi. I presume that little maisonette behind Bush Green has gone by now? Uh-huh. Uh-huh. Oh. That's a bit of luck. Who's got the keys? Good. No. Pretend they're lost. Just hold them off. I'll drop by in . . . hold on just a minute –

Now I've got it. Christ, where did she get that? It's the first time we met, when I was showing her around one of the flats. I was just trying to pull her then. I was pretending to ring the office. Now my voice has moved into the distance again. This time it's audible.

Listen, Vronky. We might have struck it lucky here. There's this property that came on just this morning, that we got as part of a multiples deal. Farquarsons, and Braxton-Halliday are marketing it too. The vendors are desperate to sell, but I know that Farquarsons had a cash buyer lined up. They've rung twice for the keys. There's just a chance that we may be able to beat them to it. But I think we'd have to go over there right now.

Veronica's voice sounded once more from the tinny speaker.

I – I can't. I've got to be back at work in half an hour.

I start to get agitated, try and grab the tape machine out of her hand. She moves it quickly out of reach.

*Come on, Vronky. That doesn't **count**. It's just the job. It's not like real lying. You can't —*

She holds up her finger to her lips, to make me listen. I close my mouth, stare angrily at the window. I hear a barking, lecherous laugh – mine – sound from the speaker of the tape recorder.

Noooo. It's not that at all. She's just a very nice young woman. Yes, that too, if you must know. Mmm-hmm. Yeah, well, believe it or not even I have a heart sometimes.

Well, says Veronica, stopping the tape. *That's nice to know.*

When I speak, the sound is of anger, carefully controlled.

Where did you get that from?

I was looking for a message a friend had left for me at your flat and I just stumbled across it.

And you kept it secret. Isn't that a form of lying too?

*Frankie, don't flatter me. I'm not in the same **league**.*

Never defend yourself. Attack. Basic rule for liars.

When did you find that tape?

Ages ago. A week or two after we met.

So you knew then that I was a liar. So why didn't you ditch me then? Why did you even say yes when I asked you to marry me?

Sometimes I wonder.

Well, why did you? Why did you say yes? Come on, tell me. I remember that day. You didn't seem

268

exactly thrilled. You didn't precisely climb the walls. Whatever possessed you to want to marry an evil wicked dissembler like me?

Fuck knows.

Swearing again. She must be upset. But I can sense she's going on the defensive. I decide to push on.

Come on. Tell me. Why did you want to marry me?

Leave it, Frankie.

Why? Why? Why?

She looks up, eyes flashing bitterly.

You really want to know?

Yeah, I really want to know.

Fine. It was because the light was broken.

What?

The light in the restaurant sign was broken.

What the fuck are you talking about?

Now I'm on the defensive. I'm bewildered, lost. Veronica looks sad now, but determined. I suddenly don't want her to speak. But she talks, in a low, clear monotone.

At that very second you asked me in the restaurant, I didn't know what to do. I thought I would almost certainly say no, actually. I thought you were too . . . young. Not in years. Just young. Hadn't seen what I've seen. At the hospital. Little kids dead on the slab. With faces that said, I'm sorry. Women strangled and raped. Men whose hearts have exploded, whose livers have rotted away. You know. All that stuff. So I was just about to say, I'm sorry, Frankie, no. But I wasn't **absolutely** *sure. There was this strange*

269

shadow of doubt. Then, I just, I just looked around the restaurant. Perhaps something would help me.

What could help you?

Veronica ignored this.

I was looking around, looking around. Then I saw it. Right in front of me, behind your head. The light was broken. The restaurant sign.

I don't understand. What are you talking about?

The restaurant. It was called Angel Eyes. Do you remember that?

Of course I remember it.

Well, the 'e' wasn't working. Do you see? Do you understand?

So the 'e' wasn't working. So what?

So it didn't say what it meant any more. It said something else.

I scratched my birthmark, hard, until it hurt.

So it said 'Angel Eyes'. So what? Then I saw, suddenly, what it was she was saying. *The sign said 'yes', didn't it?*

That's right. It said Angel: yes.

Angel: yes. And you agreed to marry me because the sign was broken.

Not only was it broken. Not only was it broken so that it said 'yes'. But it was a, literally, a **sign**.

It was a **restaurant** *sign. To let you know the name of the place.*

The fact is that the function of that arrangement of lights was to tell people something. That's what a sign is for. It gives messages. Then suddenly I knew, I knew I had to say yes. See, I believe I have a guardian

270

angel. I truly do. So Angel: yes. How could I ignore that? Someone was telling me something. The world, Frankie. It speaks to you. I can't explain it. I believe in logic. I'm good at it. I use it every day. But logic isn't everything.

I felt flabbergasted. I remember the panic in that restaurant, imagining that she was balancing the reasons – her desires, her hopes, her love for me, her fears before answering. That long, embarrassed pause.

And the only reason she really had was that the fucking restaurant sign was broken.

I think my jaw actually did, at that moment, drop, just like in the cartoons. There was a brief, neutral silence. Then I picked up the baton again.

Well, thank you for that bulletin. It's refreshing that my looks and my personality didn't enter into the equation. But what I'd like to know is, what has that got to do with anything here? We're not talking about why we agreed to get married.

That's exactly what we're talking about, said Veronica under her breath.

We're talking about why we can't spend today together. Do you understand? It's not my fault when you were born. I've known these people for more than half my life.

Veronica, with a distinct air of triumph, slowly and deliberately puts the tape recorder back in her bag.

And you've only known me six months.

Yes.

So it's simple mathematics.

271

I think to myself, *yes, it's simple mathematics.* But I say, *No. It's just that I don't believe it right to drop all your old loyalties the moment you, um . . . you . . .* I am about to say *fall in love,* then see immediately that it would make what I'm saying still more incomprehensible to Veronica. *The moment you get a new girlfriend.*

This comes out even more wrong. I try and work out a way to pull it back, but it's too late. When Veronica speaks again it comes out clenched, armoured.

You're going to be late.

The knife hits the toast again. She isn't eating it, just buttering it again and again and again. I stand where I am. She's right. I am going to be late if I don't leave soon.

I didn't mean that the way it sounded. I'm sorry. I know that sounded like I'm saying you're just a new girlfriend. And you're obviously not. You know what I feel.

Clearly not the same way you feel about your friends. You love them.

Yes, but the love you have for your friends . . . it's different.

When Veronica speaks again, her voice has changed. There's exasperation, there's bewilderment, but less anger.

I just think it's weird . . . And a bit . . . sad. You all trying to hold on to some memory. It's ludicrous, trying to re-create, or hold on to, what's gone.

We're not trying to re-create it.

272

Then what are you trying to do?

I look back at Veronica blankly, searching for the answer, surprised that I am unable to locate it.

Anyway, says Veronica, *I bet it wasn't anything like as perfect as you think it was. The further the past gets away, the more people colour it in.*

No. I hear the sound of my own voice and am amazed at the intensity of it. *It was real. We just decided that we wouldn't forget, that's all. It's a matter of –*

A matter of what? Life and death?

No. Not really. It's a matter of . . . of . . .

My voice trails away.

Veronica mutters at me scornfully, *It's habit. That's all it is. A bad habit that you can't shake off. It's obvious.*

I try not to think too clearly. This is what I do when I want to hide from my thoughts. I concentrate on the clock. Unpunctuality bothers me. My car keys hang from a hook on the wall just by the window. I unsling them and jiggle them in my hand. A series of beeps sounds. It's a device on the keyring that helps you find them when they're lost. The beeps sound when you whistle, but also for no reason at all. It gets to be annoying.

Everything's a habit. Nothing's obvious, I say.

I say it just because it sounds good, or just to say something, anything. Then I see that both statements are true, absolutely true.

I throw the bag of golf clubs over my shoulder, then jiggle the keys some more. I'm still hoping that the rift can be healed. But a charge of resentment and incomprehension still arcs invisibly between us.

I move towards the door. There are steel-corner repairs to the heels of my shoes and they make a rhythmic click as I progress towards the newly stripped paintwork of the doorway. I debate with myself whether to try to give Veronica a kiss, but the certainty that it will be shrugged off deters me. My mouth opens emptily for seconds before I finally speak. The words that come out sound ridiculous and entirely inappropriate.

Happy birthday then.

For it is indeed Veronica's thirtieth birthday today, on this, the very sacred and historic day of remembrance, 14 August. I begged and pleaded with her, tried to explain that to move her birthday celebrations forward one day wasn't the end of the world, that I'd make it up to her, that it was only minutes hours and seconds. So we celebrate tomorrow instead of today. What was the big deal? But she won't listen, she won't *see*.

Veronica doesn't move or speak. I gaze at the back of her head, the slight redness in the hair, its fullness against her small shoulders, hulked up by the padded gown. For a moment, I feel like giving it up. Putting the clubs back in the cupboard, phoning Tony with my apologies, showing her what's really important in my life. For a second, no more, I really want to do it.

You better not walk out of that door.

Why?

She pauses, gathers herself.

You walk out of that door and we're finished, says Veronica, with a voice as tight as locking pliers.

I feel a gauntlet has been thrown; now it's about power I can't back down. I feel angry at the attempt to blackmail me.

Have you had another sign then?

What?

A message from your angel.

Don't be stupid.

What's happened? Has he invisibly manifested himself to you bearing a luminous banner. 'Bugger off while you've got the chance, love.'

I turn, without another word, and walk towards the door.

As I reach it, Veronica shouts after me, *I mean it, Frankie. Don't walk out.* Then, *I don't understand. Why is it so **important**? That you would give up . . .*

I don't hear the rest. I carry on walking out of the door, into the corridor, then into the street. When I glance behind me, I see Veronica framed at the window, in precisely the same position as when I left the room. She does not look up to see me go. Her words echo in my head. Why is it so important? Because it's 14 August of course. 14 August, 14 August, the motherfucking, cunting, bollocking, 14 August.

CHAPTER 14

14 AUGUST 1984

I remember it so clearly. I don't think I remember anything so clearly as that day. Not last week, not yesterday even. 14 August 1984.

And yet, nothing much happened. Not on the *outside*.

It was half-way through the last summer we were together at school. There was a growing, inarticulate realization among us – Tony, me, Nodge and Colin – that the world, what was always described to us by knowing adults as the 'real' world, was reaching out towards us, unknown, exciting, edged with a vague threat of constriction, or potential freefall.

We had all become friends together by then. Tony had discovered that charm as a force had much more potency than threat or malice and had, in due course, charmingly apologized to Colin about what had happened. Colin had been enormously flattered that he had bothered and subsequently became something of an acolyte. The weak, even if only momentarily deferred to, always then flatter the strong. If I hadn't been so sure of his loyalty to me, I think I might have been jealous.

Colin had by this time grown out of his spots and found a certain kind of defensive confidence, enough anyway to enable him to be functional among the . . . less incomplete kids at the school. His father had stopped bothering him – having been found dead among the primulas in Ravenscourt Park, a bottle of Special Brew in his hand.

Colin, of course, was crap at sport, but he had found his own niche. This was the year of the BMX bike and Colin was brilliant at it. He could do all the manoeuvres: Cross-up, the Helicopter, the Table Top, the Aerial 360. He had all the gear: the waffle-sole shoes, the race shirts, the leather gloves, the padded shins with the gauze front for airflow. Colin was almost cool, for the first and last time. I would certainly say it was the nearest Colin had ever been to happy, at least since our brief childhood together.

Competitive sport had brought Tony, Nodge and me much closer together – running in the case of me and Nodge, football for me and Tony, cricket for Tony and Nodge (they had a highly successful batting partnership). Together with the newly cool Colin, we were the only four in the class supporting Rangers, despite the fact that it had been one of their most successful seasons – the Great Venables final one – ever. In the Canon

League Division One, as it was then, they were whupping Arsenal, Spurs, Liverpool, you name them. Big Stevie Wicks couldn't miss that netting, even if he tried. The artificial pitch we had then was coming up trumps every time, visitors skidding around on it like Torvill and Dean. Mad was it to be alive in such a season.

That 14 August was a hot, hot day. Our short-term collective memory at that point contained: Steven Waldorf perforated with unfair bullets, Zola Budd, Coe, Ovett and Cram in the '84 Olympics, Morgan Fairchild in *Flamingo Road*, Victoria Principal, Al Pacino in *Scarface*, Koo Stark, Yappies before they become Yuppies, and Chris Evert and John Lloyd. *Spitting Image* had started its first run on TV, vying with *Remington Steele*. The drug dealers were driving Beemers. Wogan, Harty, *The Tube*, Breakfast TV. Pia Zadora and her terrific baps were our chief hand-gallop fantasy, among many such fantasies, even though we thought she was a joke, although she made a prize cake of herself in *Butterfly*.

On that morning – sending up shimmering heat waves even as I woke in the three-bedroom rented council house that my parents had spent most of their life confined within – we had all agreed to spend the day together. It was to celebrate the fact that Tony had passed his driving test that week, the first of us to do so. He was going to pick us up from my house. Colin and Nodge had arrived already and we were all sitting by the bay window watching for him, pulling the nets to one side. The curtains smelt of my home, of my street – clean, neutral but with a faint, barely detectable undertow of chemicalized floral perfume. It was one of those smells you could also taste, and it tasted bitter and sickly at the same time. It was the taste of the past, of parents, of limitation.

We heard a noise from the end of the road that sounded like a powerful motorbike, a swelling, spreading growl. I looked past the rows of terraces to the intersection with the next block. Although it was only ten o'clock, heat was now distorting the air above the tarmac and making the privet hedges across the road billow and shift.

It was a car that was making the noise, a big two-litre metallic gold Cortina Ghia Mark V with tinted windows, a sunroof and the back wheels jacked up. It was growing larger at frightening speed through the heat haze down the centre of the road. Pigeons scattered. A woman pushing a cheap push-chair screwed her head round and glared angrily. Music mingled with the engine noise. I could just make out the low tattoo of drum sound, not enough to identify the track.

The Cortina drew closer. It was coming out of the east end of the road, with the glare of the sun behind it. There was a strip of green translucent plastic across the top of the windscreen. It said *Vince* on one side and *Sue* on the other. The paintwork was uneven, flaking off above one of the wheels where it had been rebuilt in fibreglass.

There were one or two patches of rust on the bonnet, but where the paint was good it had been burnished to a high sheen, and sunspots glinted and paraded on the roof where the light penetrated through the leaves of the plane trees that lined Churchill Street.

I could see Tony now, his face leaning close to the windscreen. He was wearing yellow tinted wraparound sunglasses and sounding the horn, which gave out the first eight notes of 'Colonel Bogey'. I recognized the music now as 'White Lines (Don't Do It)' by Grandmaster Flash and Melle Mel. That drastic, unstoppable bass.

Tony honked again. He had lit a cigarette, one of those long brown unfiltered Turkish Mahawatts he smoked when he could afford it. The liquorice paper always stuck to his lips and stained them brown. He held the cigarette between his fingers and waved in time to the beat of the drum that thrummed and shook the car from the speakers of the Pioneer stereo cassette player. I pulled myself up from my window seat and yanked up my white Levi's, laundered lovingly by my mother. She had also shortened the legs for me, but not quite enough, so that the backs of the trousers trailed on the ground if you didn't keep them hitched. Already white thread was showing through the cloth at the back ankle hem, which frequently caught beneath the flat heel of my black Doc Martens. My T-shirt read 'Like a Virgin' and had overlong sleeves. Cut short, it barely met the waistband of the trousers. It was inauthentic, clashed with my soul-boy wedge haircut.

I stood still for a moment, watching Tony in the car beckon to me, a grin stretching across his handsome, suntanned face. Patches of light penetrated through the trees and made puddles of shadow on the crazy-paved footpath.

At that precise moment, a feeling burst inside me like a tiny flare, something that I could not name but experienced as a kind of opening up of portals, a turning towards light. It lasted only five seconds, I suppose, but it left an afterglow that stayed with me the whole day, and that I remembered for ever, a kind of imagined awareness of freedom, of potential, of possibility. Tony is framed in this scene, this frozen tableau in his gold Cortina, intertwined for all my life with that feeling, staring out of the window with his smile, still genuine in those days, still open. Many years later I would turn this picture around in my mind like it was a photograph and ache for those few luminous moments.

The scene unfroze, became fluid, and I moved down the garden path towards the gold Cortina, the engine still revving. There was a splash of petrol under the car that spread into a series of concentric rainbows. Tony reached over and pushed the back door open, and I stepped inside. Despite all the windows being open, the plastic seat was burning. I shifted the base of my thighs, which already felt wet with perspiration.

It's my uncle's. He lent it to me for the day.

That was good of him.

He didn't have much choice. He's in the Scrubs, doing a two-stretch.

I remember Nodge did not smile or give any sign of being impressed by the car. His imperturbability, his absolute refusal to be even slightly awed, was still half-affectation then; we were all trying on personalities of one kind or another to see what fitted, and Nodge had only fairly recently begun to opt for detachment and laconic, cool amusement. He was more or less pre-political, possessing a sense of judgement but with nothing larger than his private world to exercise it on.

The detachment, in the end, would harden into what he was and become irrevocable. But a sense of choice and possibility danced around us and within us then like the sunspots that slid around the polished windscreen of the old Cortina. We did not understand then about coagulation, the irresistible solidification that would be shown one day to be life's main impulse.

Nodge very calmly walked around to the side of the car. He was wearing khaki army shorts, some mad cutting-edge trainers that he'd saved six months to buy, no socks, a plain white no-message T-shirt. His clothes carefully pressed, the shorts even having a crease in the front that looked inappropriate, prissy. Sitting down in the back seat on the passenger side, I could see his face in the side-view mirror, which Tony had not bothered

282

to twist into the correct position. Believing himself to be unobserved, his face was open, soft with anticipation and a kind of apologetic joy.

Tony revved the engine again. Only now did Nodge speak, having to shout over the sound of the engine noise and Morrissey singing 'There is a Light That Never Goes Out'. Tony had put this on specifically for Nodge's benefit. Nodge had been singing along with Morrissey's self-pitying, beautiful whine. He stopped singing and said, *Bit of a fucking rust bucket, isn't it?*

We don't compliment each other, the four of us. We never show that we're impressed or overjoyed on each other's behalf. Don't ask me why. It was the rules. There are always rules.

Colin, who was still slightly pockmarked from his acne, was wearing bad stone-washed jeans and a ripped T-shirt. He looked awkward, but Colin always looked awkward. Clothes never quite fitted, the styles were always slightly outdated. His body language, self-conscious and stiff, added to the overall effect of a misfit. He gave one of his endless slow smiles, which was like a sponge that soaked everything up. You could praise Colin or humiliate him or laugh at him and that same smile would appear, like Muttley in *Wacky Racers*.

Tony kicked the car into gear and let out the clutch, too fast. The car stalled and threw us forward. Tony started laughing like a maniac. His laugh was the same then as it is now, high, loud, slightly hysterical. His hair was spiky, sticking up

283

on top, but soft, not too punky, after the style of Nik Kershaw or Howard Jones. Tony revved the engine, then shouted above the roar.

I've got something, he said, grinning, showing his big teeth like mosaic tiles.

What, I said, *is it that you have?*

You'll see, said Tony, theatrically fingering something in his pocket.

The Cortina bucked forward. Now 'Eliminator' by ZZ Top was playing, presumably for Colin's benefit, blasting out of the speakers. The tyres made a terrified sound as Tony took a corner.

None of us knew where we were going, and it didn't seem to matter. All the windows were open and a hot breeze pushed through the inside of the car. The endless terraces arranged around the main road fell past us, seemed to part for us. The sun beat down on the gold roof.

I felt in my bag, took out some cans of Hofmeister beer and passed them around.

Follow the Bear! said Colin, unamusingly and unsuccessfully trying to ape the TV ad.

Mine sprayed wildly when I opened it, soaking Colin next to me, who whooped with the shock of the cold liquid soaking into his T-shirt. Tony and Nodge in front laughed, and Tony revved the car harder. Although we were on side streets now, it felt like we were going fifty miles an hour. The beer smelt of promise. I heard Nodge shout from the front.

Where are we going?

Tony's reply was lost in the sound of rushing air, but soon enough we found ourselves pulling into a small crescent half-way down the Harrow Road.

It's a cemetery, said Colin.

Not a cemetery. Not just any boneyard. It's a necropolis. A city of the dead, said Tony.

Tony slammed on the brakes, sending me and Colin piling forward into the front seats. We flipped back as the car came to a halt. My head banged against an exposed piece of chassis at the back of my seat.

Ow.

You're going to forgive me, said Tony.

Now that we had stopped, the heat suddenly began to build again. Tony had reached into his pocket and brought out a small white-paper folded envelope, about an inch long and half an inch square. He waved it in front of his face as if fanning himself.

Sulphate? said Nodge, looking mildly pleased.

Tony shook his head and took a single-sided razor blade out of his top pocket.

We can do better than bathtub speed today. This is the Moment of Freedom. This is the Declaration of Independence. The Magna fucking wossname. We have a Cortina Ghia Mark V. We have Hofmeister beer. Many cans. We have a big fat sun. We have each other. And furthermore and to boot and to wit, we have two grams of A-grade toot.

What's that? said Colin. There was a large dark

285

patch down the front of his shirt where the beer stain was still drying out.

Coke. It's coke, said Nodge. For one of the very few times in his life, I could tell he was truly impressed.

Colin immediately looked nervous. He rarely did drugs, except blow, which even then made him paranoid and restless.

We all got out of the car and trooped in a line into the vast deserted cemetery. The air was absolutely still. Tony knelt down by a gravestone with the name worn away. He surveyed the scene around him.

Stiff city. It's what we've all got coming. Forty, maybe fifty years. You can't waste it. It's not a rehearsal.

Underneath, cool black marble. He began carefully levering out some of the white powder in the envelope on to the gravestone, making small shovelling motions with the edge of the blade. All of us fell into silence. Coke then wasn't like it is now, cheap, plentiful, about as rebellious as a large advocaat. It was still a bit unusual, expensive, rock-star speed. We were a little in awe, a little nervous. Somewhere in the distance a police siren sounded. Colin started, but the rest of us ignored it, hypnotized by the forbidden ritual that was taking place, made more religious still by the presence of the dead all around us.

Tony made little chopping movements until the powder was separated into four lines. One of the monuments threw a shadow, cooling us. There was a sense of time suspended. I watched an ant scramble over the marble until it disappeared into the earth.

Tony had rolled a ten-pound note into a cylinder. Then he was leaning over, bending right in half from the waist. There was an inhalation of breath and he straightened up, sniffing loudly. He wet a finger, cleared up what was left of the powder on his line and rubbed it on his gums.

Colin look perplexed.

What are you doing that for?

You just do it. Something you do. Deadens the gums.

What do you want to deaden your gums for?

The question, unanswerable then as it is today, was left to hang. Nodge was repeating Tony's movements now, bending down and sniffing. He tossed his head back as if it would help the powder reach his lungs.

I took the rolled-up note and ingested the line of powder. It burned my nostril and I immediately felt an infuriating itch develop. I rubbed hard at the bridge of my nose to try and rid myself of the sensation. Tony was smoking the Mahawatts non stop now, sending out an odour of liquorice and tobacco.

Then Colin was fumbling with the rolled-up banknote. He was clearly nervous; I sensed he didn't want to do it, but that he didn't want to lose face in front of everyone. He began to bend, then dropped the banknote, reached for it on the floor and rerolled it imperfectly so that it coiled outwards at one end, like the point of an outsize crayon. He rammed this up his right nostril and bent suddenly down towards the last line of cocaine, and immediately exhaled. The fine powder dissipated into the air in a tiny cloud, catching Colin in the face. When he came up, a screen of white powder covered his already pale face. Tony and I started laughing, while Nodge, trying as ever to keep control, dampened himself down to a broad smile.

Sorry . . . I . . . I'm not used to . . .

Colin was blushing and gasping slightly. The banknote was still thrust up his nose, looking like a proboscis.

After the gale of laughter blew out, Tony cut Colin another line, and this time he managed to take it in, although with much subsequent hawking and throat clearing.

After a while, we headed back to the car. Tony revved it, cranking up the Pioneer to maximum volume; this time Frankie Goes to Hollywood and 'Two Tribes'. The car seemed to rock at the power of the bass line. Tony reversed out of the driveway. We laughed as the car rocked.

It was still only around noon and the sun was directly overhead. I could feel the effects of the cocaine now, pumping my heart, lifting my mood still further. We were all singing along with the tape.

288

The Cortina skidded round the corner, throwing us against the sides of the car. Colin was giggling as he fell across my lap, and I pushed him back upright.

Tony screamed to a halt by the side of a patch of empty playing field, on which were erected two unnetted goals at either end of a poorly marked football pitch. He switched off the engine, reached into the glove compartment, pulled out another can of beer and yelled, *Chelsea vs. QPR! The Hofmeister Bush League, Division One.*

He slid out of the car, opened the boot and took out a small camera and threw it towards me. I caught it with one hand. He struck a he-man pose and I took a shot, then pocketed the camera. He brought out a black and white vinyl football from the boot and took a kick at it, sending it flying into the centre of the field. Nodge leapt from the other side and chased it. The cocaine had given him an extra thrust so that he seemed to cover the ground like lightning. Colin, me and Tony followed, each holding a can of Hofmeister. We tossed to see who was going to be stuck with being Chelsea.

It was odd that day – wherever we went, we seemed to see no one else, as if we were living in a private sealed off universe. The streets were deserted, and this park, which was backed on to by several large housing estates, was quite empty, apart from a runty dog that ran back and forth at the end of the pitch, as if maddened by the heat.

I felt omnipotent, invulnerable as we squared

up to each other, me and Colin as QPR, Tony and Nodge as Chelsea. The drug and the sunshine surged through me like wild electricity, and I looked at the laughing faces of my friends and I felt a secret adoration; it was as if we had known each other for ever and would know each other for ever. The dog barked in the distance. Somewhere the clack of train wheels could be heard.

When we played it seemed impossible to get tired, despite the heat and the fact that it was only two on two on a full-sized football pitch. We'd all taken our shirts off, Colin pocked and pale, Nodge stocky and red, Tony tall, olive and muscled, me medium height, average build, but my infirmity, my birthmark, now glowing red and luminous in the sun, as if to compensate for all the awesomely median aspects of the rest of me.

Normally when we play games an intensity of competition falls among us, but this time it all seemed glorious, soft, generous. We played well, despite the drink and cocaine; the pitch seemed to shrink, the goals expanded. It was just us four in this wide-open green space, and the dog prowling the perimeter. At one point, when the score was squared, Nodge took a long shot and headed for the goal right from the half-way line. It landed, was trickling away past the left hand post, when the dog suddenly rushed on to the field and butted it right into the middle of the goal. Classic Nodge luck. Tony and Nodge collapsed on to their backs, felled by their own laughter, while Colin chased after the dog, loudly claiming a foul. It didn't matter. Nothing mattered that day. The present opened up from a spotlight into a floodlight, and we were in the centre of it, moving like happy, gloriously stupid ghosts.

After forty minutes in the hot sun, we finally began to flag, and sat down together in the centre circle. Hair matted, all gasping for breath, we stretched out under the sun. I turned my head to level with the playing field and watched the distortions in the air that the heat caused, bending the white light. Far in the distance, I saw a patch of deep blue on the extreme edge of the park.

I think there's a pool up there, I said in a voice hardly above a whisper. The words drifted into the air between us like vapour.

Impossible, said Nodge.

Why? said Tony, still short of breath. A slight peeling of skin had developed around his neck. Tomorrow he would suffer.

It would be too perfect, said Nodge.

Nodge, then as now, believed all events slanted towards misfortune, despite his personal flair for small lucky accidents.

Let's take a gander anyway, I said.

Each of us hauled himself upright and began trudging to where the patch of blue appeared to be. As we got closer, it became clear that what I had seen was indeed a pool, a children's paddling pool. At one end, a mock waterfall, spuming white water. Surrounded by melting tarmac, it was perfectly blue. Incredibly, it was also completely deserted.

Tony was first through the open gate, ripping off what remained of his clothes as he went. His cock and balls threw themselves up and down pneumatically as he ran. He took off at a flying leap, into the deep end, which still came only up to his knees. Immediately he fell on his back and went under, then came up spouting a jet of water from his mouth and singing the Eurythmics' 'Sweet Dreams are Made of This'.

Each of us by now had also taken his clothes off completely. Colin was last to do it, and turned his back slightly as he stripped. We all fell into the pool, silently now. An almost reverent mood had fallen upon us. We stretched our bodies out under the water. White patches marked out the areas left by swimming trunks. The water was cool but not cold. The sound of the waterfall dashed against our ears.

I don't know how long we sat in that city pool, unmoving apart from a slight sway with the water, not speaking apart from the occasional punctuation of a long satisfied sigh. Light reflected off the surface of the pool and on to our faces, creating liquid patterns on the skin. Occasionally a jet liner would pass overhead. The dog in the distance still barked, but these seemed to be the only sounds.

At one point I took out a camera from somewhere and told everyone to pose, naked. We all held up our beer cans under the sun, we all laughed with real laughter. The football floated in the pool.

I set the camera to automatic and it made a click that echoed around the park.

Then, out of nowhere, sitting in that pool, I was filled with a sudden gasp of sadness. It lasted only a second, like a miniature imitation of the earlier ecstasy, but seemed to hit with enough force to knock the air out of me. It was some mixed-up sense that I was at a strange fulcrum in my life. Nothing could ever be this perfect again, I knew, and this moment would slide away into other moments, moments full of imperfection and indifference and low boredom. The sensation of loss pierced me like a slaughterhouse bolt; suddenly I could see myself years in the future, looking back on this day, wondering what had happened to this shining moment and why it had never happened again. Then, as suddenly as it came, the sadness passed. The bubble of our mood was broken anyway by a shout.

What do you think you're doing? This is for kids. And put your bloody clothes on.

Unseen by us, the park keeper had come from behind the rhododendron bushes that flanked the pool. He had a pointed stick for picking up litter that he was waving generally in our direction. Despite the heat, his uniform and shirt were fully buttoned and he was wearing a tie. A good old-fashioned parkie. I had thought they were extinct.

Christ, it's the filth, said Tony, mock-terrified.

Best do a runner, said Nodge, continuing what was a well-rehearsed joke.

293

It's a fair cop. But society's to blame, I added, finishing the performance.

We all started laughing again, but obediently left the pool nevertheless and, shaking and rubbing ourselves dry with our T-shirts, we got dressed. The park keeper watched us resentfully. I watched back; he was in his fifties, bald, full of fury and disappointment. I wondered what life did to people. I wondered how it soured them. Suddenly I felt pity for the parkie, all stuffed into his shirt and suit. Somehow I felt his envy at us, and our opportunities yet to be wasted. Dressed now, I wandered over to him.

Sorry, mate. We didn't know it wasn't allowed.

I looked into his eyes, which were yellowing around the cornea. They seemed glacial, empty, sorrowful. He was filling up with something, some emotion he didn't want to acknowledge. He took his eyes away from mine and glanced in the general direction of the pool.

Just go home.

But when he spoke this time, it was with a weary, defeated tone, all the anger bled out of it. I felt the strangest desire to put my hand on his shoulder, but then he turned and walked away from the pool.

In formation, this time spread out and parallel with the horizon, like a chorus line, we began walking back across the park towards Tony's Cortina. The chlorine was stinging my eyes, but I still felt refreshed, glowing. We murmured rather than talked on the way back, kicking at dandelions

294

and idly casting stick balls at each other. Although we were nearly adults, there were melting centres within us that were still possessed of the qualities and knowledge of children. But that childhood somehow within us I knew was ebbing, on the cusp of being lost.

We went to the pub after that, a big old barn of a place ten miles out into the deep suburbs – somewhere like Uxbridge or Pinner. Again, it was more or less empty, and we drank ice-cold beer under parasols in the garden and ate Ploughman's Lunches with piccalilli and onions. By the time three o'clock and closing time came around, we were beginning to feel sleepy; the running, the sun and the aftermath of the cocaine had given us a kind of perfect languor.

We climbed into the Cortina, uncertain what to do next, but not much minding. Tony started the engine and eased the car into gear. There was a friendly, pre-season QPR match that evening. That was four hours away. We decided to head back to Tony's, drink some more beer and finish up the remainder of the cocaine.

I noticed that Tony's lids were becoming heavy as we headed back towards Shepherd's Bush. In the distance, the floodlights of Loftus Road could be seen, towering over the White City Estate. A gentle snoring came from Colin's direction; he was slumped down into the seat. Nodge too had his eyes closed. The underpass at Hanger Lane was closed, so we headed up the slip road towards the roundabout with the North Circular. I vaguely sensed that Tony seemed to approach the red lights rather fast.

Out of nowhere, there was the sound of breaking glass. Tony, not far from a condition of stupor, looked up. He had clipped the taillight of a black taxi cab waiting at the stop line. The driver's face was set in a rictus of fury. He was beginning to get out of the cab.

It was Nodge who reacted first. He had, then, a reckless streak that could surface and surprise everybody with his lack of concern for consequences.

Motor it! he screamed, as Tony fumbled for the gear stick.

I sat bolt upright, looking confused. Colin slept on, a slight smile playing about his lips. Tony revved the big motor on the Cortina, swung past the turning cab, through the red lights and into the roundabout system. I was aware of Hanger Lane Central Line station like a flying saucer made by Trabant, a circle of glass atop a wider circle of plain concrete.

I turned round to look at the cab, which was coming behind us. I could see the driver speaking into a microphone.

He's radioing his mates, I shouted.

Tony was cackling like a maniac now and pulling round the curve of the roundabout. The Cortina, despite its beaten-up bodywork, was tuned up and powerful.

As we turned the curve rightward coming towards the eastbound exit for the A40, I saw another black cab going in the opposite direction down one of the slip roads off the roundabout. As I watched it, I became aware of a faint squeal of brakes. I screamed at Tony, who had turned Heaven 17's 'Temptation' up full blast on the Pioneer.

Fucking hell. He's doing a U-ey.

Tony turned in his seat, and we could now see this other, second taxi driver also talking into his radio. He was close enough for me to make him out through the windscreen – big, meaty, with a cropped head. All sense of tiredness had left us now.

Colin had woken up and was craning his neck to see what was happening. He started saying, quietly, afraid, *Don't you think we ought to pull over?*

But Tony was flushed with excitement; it was clear he had no intention of stopping.

We made it on to the A40 and motored down towards Gypsy Corner. There was a press of traffic at the lights, and we were forced to slow down and stop. Ten or fifteen vehicles behind us there was not one or two, but now four black taxi cabs. The nearest two to us were stopped in the traffic twenty yards back. I could see both of the drivers leaving the cabs and beginning to walk quickly towards us. They didn't run. Somehow this fact was very threatening. Nodge pointed to a sign on our left that had an arrow indicating the Central Middlesex Hospital.

That's handy, he said, absolutely deadpan.

Fuck! They're coming, I shouted, now genuinely frightened.

Drivers in other cars were turning towards us to see what was happening.

Tony revved the engine pointlessly. The cabbies were closing in; in ten, twenty seconds they would be upon us.

Lock your doors! he shouted, as the first one made the rear of the car. He was big, tattooed on both arms, with a face like raw meat. We could see him, but, because of the tinted glass, he couldn't see us. He gave an almighty yank at the rear door, but we had managed to get the locks down. He began hammering on the roof. Ten yards behind, the second taxi driver was approaching with a crowbar in his hand.

Please please please please please please, I muttered, staring intently at the traffic lights ahead of us.

I was stiff with apprehension now. Colin had gone into a foetal position. Even Tony was crouched over his steering wheel, as if the weight of his body would propel the car through the jam in front of us. Only Nodge seemed unafraid, solid.

The lights had changed now and the three cars in the line ahead began to move. The car was already in gear; a gap appeared between our lane and the inside one. Tony flung the car forward, swerving the wheel to the left. Panicking, he let the clutch out too fast and stalled the car.

Fucking ADA!

Desperately he began to turn the key in the ignition again. There was a crash as the crowbar made contact with the boot of the car. The first taxi driver was now trying to force down the back window, pushing his fingers through a tiny gap at the top. His face was framed in the square of the reinforced glass, like a Gorgon, full of hate and anger. I felt my fear turning into terror; then the engine caught, and Tony sent the car hurtling forward past the lights. He swung it to the left. The taxi driver went flying on to his back behind us. A surge of relief as the car sped into the empty road ahead.

The joy of escape possessed us now, stronger than any cocaine. We headed through the industrial estates that backed on to the A40, driving towards the shit capital of west London, Harlesden. Tony weaving at terrible speed round blind corners and through red lights to get away. Now he seemed exhilarated again.

Is it going to be OK? said Colin, like a child to his father.

As he spoke, another black cab came past us in the opposite direction. Again, he began to perform a U-turn.

Jesus! said Tony.

I stared at the cab, eyes widened.

Nightmare. Every cab driver in London is out for our blood.

It's too late to give ourselves up now, said Nodge insouciantly, as if he was idly enjoying the whole performance. Then he said with a grin, *They'll murder us.*

Thanks for the pep talk, Nodge. We're going to have to ditch the car, I said.

Tony nodded in agreement, muttering at the same time, *Uncle Vince is not going to be very happy.*

Nodge carried on smiling.

It was probably half-inched anyway.

We continued travelling towards Harlesden. It was uglier than the Goldhawk Road on a wet afternoon. There was warehouse after warehouse, lonely petrol stations, a railway bridge with one single slogan, 'Support the Miners', tragic pubs, a bargain basement of light industrial furniture. Tony turned sharply into a maze of back streets, twisting and turning the car round from one terrace to the next. After a while, the black cab seemed to disappear and Tony headed in the general direction of the High Road. We could see Harlesden Town Clock in front of us, a church to the right with a poster of a hang-gliding Christian in front of it. As we headed towards the main road again, a terrible vista unfolded before us. At least ten black cabs filled the one-way system around the clock, their engines idling, the drivers checking around them.

We were all totally silent, even Nodge. Tony immediately swung the car round to the right into a small alleyway, a little cobbled almost-street. It was just wide enough to get a car down. The alleyway

300

curved at the back behind a row of terraced houses, then came to a dead end, out of sight of the road. Tony pulled to a halt and we piled out into the alleyway, climbing over a wire fence. There were abandoned rubbish bags, broken prams.

Leg it! yelled Tony, and as one beast, we raced down the alleyway and out into another street, indistinguishable from the rest – terraces of six, car-ports, pitched roofs.

At the end of the street, we turned on to a pavement.

Act normal, said Colin, and suddenly we all began giggling at the ludicrousness of the situation and at the impossible effort of doing what Colin had instructed.

I noticed then that Nodge had had the self-possession to bring the football with him. He dropped it and we began kicking it to each other along the pavement.

Then there was the sound of a diesel motor behind us. I turned. It was a black cab. Suddenly we stopped giggling. We slowed and started to walk, trying to muster nonchalance. The cab began to slow as it came towards us. The window came down and the taxi pulled over to where we were walking. Inside, the half man, half monkey who had whacked the car with a crowbar at the lights. I felt the colour drain out of my face. He looked at us without hostility but an edge of obvious suspicion. On his forearms, the tattoos were now clear. One was scrawly, blue. It read, 'We are QPR'. The other was simply two letters: 'NF'.

Hello, lads. You seen a Cortina going down here anywhere?

Nodge calmly caught the football off a kick from Tony. There was a slight pause before Nodge answered the driver.

What colour?

Gold. Tinted windows.

Nodge nodded, as if considering carefully this new information.

Yeah. It came belting round that corner at about 100 miles an hour and down towards Harlesden Circus.

The taxi driver nodded, but didn't move an inch. He seemed to be making his mind up about something. We were all frozen in place, trying to act normal. Then Nodge leant against the cab and pointed at the Rangers tattoo.

You going to watch the match tonight?

The taxi driver paused, then seemed to relax slightly.

They your team?

Come on you Rs! said Nodge, pulling back his jacket to reveal a small enamel QPR badge.

He nodded gravely, as if a sergeant in the army recognizing someone of equivalent rank.

Yeah, I'm going. Should be a fucking corker.

Shame about Stainrod.

Simon Stainrod, one of the key men, had pulled a hamstring in the previous match and was rumoured to be dropped for tonight.

I heard he's going to be OK. Least that's what they said on the radio.

Excellent! We'll fucking hammer them, said Nodge, still as cool as a cucumber.

The rest of us, I felt, looked nervous and guilty. The taxi driver scrutinized us, still suspicious, and opened his mouth to speak again. His voice was as ugly as his face, ignorant, cruel, violent.

Did you see what they looked like?

Tony spoke this time, clearly shamed by Nodge's courage under fire. He had seen the NF tattoo.

There were three of them — two were niggers and one was a white girl. They were laughing their heads off.

The cab driver visibly brightened at the use of the word *nigger*.

Spades, were they? With a white girl?

Tony nodded. The taxi driver looked grim, but gave a thumbs-up and began to pull away.

Probably on drugs. Pot, innit? Black bastards. Thanks, lads. Sweet. We'll get the cunts, eh? Teach those fucking jungle bunnies a lesson. See you at the match, maybe.

Yeah. Give the coons a smack from us, said Tony, grinning that famous grin.

Nodge looked uncomfortable now. He sensed that Tony was enjoying this a bit too much. Even back in '84 and not that politically committed, he had been on marches with the Anti-Nazi League. Tony liked to wind him up even then.

But any tension between Nodge and Tony evaporated as we watched him begin speaking into his mike and then disappear around the corner. Then

303

it was as if we all breathed out at the same moment, and began whooping and slapping each other on the back. It felt great, it felt real.

We made it back on to the High Street, where a bus headed east was stuck in traffic. We pulled through the open platform and went upstairs and sat at the front. Downstairs, the street was packed with cabs, all with their lights turned off. Now we began to relax; looking down on the ranks of cabbies, we were overcome with a sense of power and triumph, of beating down the odds. We were invincible that day. We could all feel it now.

By the time we got back to the Bush, the pubs were open again and we headed into the Bush Ranger in readiness for the game. The day was cooling now, but the pub was warm and welcoming. The big windows threw shafts of light into the room; we sat in a puddle of yellow sun on the first floor. Tony was on top form, making us laugh with a string of filthy jokes. Colin wasn't saying much, but smiling, sipping at his bitter shandy. Nodge smoked and blew rings. Everything was perfect.

After a while, as the kickoff approached, a silence began to settle over us. Each of us had caught the sun, Nodge the worst. The room was filled with smoke now and the sunlight pushed through it, as if it were a projector in a pre-war cinema. There was music playing on the sound system, 'The Look of Love' by ABC, one of the greatest all-time records. I beat my fingers in time.

Nodge then gestured towards the left of the pub.

Take a butcher's at that.

At the far end of the room, sat at a small table under an old station clock, a man the same age as us, a half-finished drink in front of him. Next to him, a thin woman, her hair in bangs, wearing a tube top. She was young, but looked old. The couple were holding hands, but their faces were masks of boredom and irritation. Neither was speaking or looking at the other.

It's Pigshit! said Tony.

All of us stared in his direction, taking in the scene. Pigshit Pete had left school the year before to join his father's garage as an apprentice mechanic. His academic record was not good, hence his nickname. Thick-as-Pigshit Pete, Pigshit, also known as TAPP or Tappy. I didn't recognize the woman with him, but we'd heard that he'd got engaged to someone or other.

At that exact moment, Pigshit looked up and towards us. Something in his face registered recognition, and he gave a weak smile and raised his glass towards us. As one, we raised our glasses back. Pigshit's face did not move away from us, nor did his hand leave the hand of the woman next to him. There was a look of very palpable longing on his thin, lumpen features. It was embarrassing in its intensity, like a starving man staring through the steamed-up windows of a restaurant. We each quickly looked away, as if we had spent too long observing a road accident.

There was a long pause. Tony shook his head and drank deeply from his glass.

Poor old Pigshit.

Nodge began singing softly the Specials' record 'Too Much Too Young'.

A new crowd of Rangers supporters crushed into the bar, cutting off the sight of the couple in the corner. They were chanting, *Terry Venables's Blue and White Army!*

We joined in, banging our glasses on the table, soaking the cork mats with spilt beer. After a few seconds, the chant died away.

Tony looked around at us, his face suddenly grim. When he spoke, we could hardly hear him over the din of the pub.

It's been a great day, he said.

We all nodded solemnly.

It's not over yet, said Nodge.

No, no. But it's been a great . . . day, Tony repeated. *The sun, the pool, the parkie, the coke, the taxi cabs. Rangers. It's hard to . . .* He shook his head. *The thing is . . . we should remember this day. Somehow. I mean, old Pigshit. There but for the grace of God . . .*

It easily happens, I said. *Then you forget. You forget what things can be.*

Tony looked up again, eyes bright with intensity.

That's exactly it. That's precisely what I'm saying. We need to remember what things can be. You leave school, you get a job, you get a girlfriend. All the shit starts to hit you, all the . . . necessity. Before you know it, you're all

306

dumbed up, like poor old Tappy. Then it's the city of the dead, and . . . bing. All fucked up. Too late. The thing is to remember. To have a way of reminding yourself.

We each nodded.

You got to be Y, F and S, says Tony.

We nodded as one. It stands for young, free and single. Nodge lit a cigarette. In those days he smoked No. 6. He stared outside the window, where there was, in full sight, a war memorial. A few tattered flowers lay around the base. He waved his hand towards the monument.

We should have a commemoration. You know, like old gits do when it's Armistice Day, or VJ Day or VD Day or whatever. All get together and whoop it up once a year.

Tony slammed his fist down on the pine table, making the glasses jump.

*That's it. Let's do it. We'll have a . . . a . . . **commemoration**. On this day, every year, the four of us get together. So when we're doing our shit jobs and twisted round the fingers of some insane doris, we can meet like this and . . . and . . .*

Remind each other, I said.

Yes, said Colin. Even he seemed worked up, transfixed.

Remembering's what counts.

Nodge stood to his feet and raised his glass.

14 August, he said.

We all stood and put our glasses into the middle of the table and clinked them together. And then we sat in silence, like praying.

CHAPTER 15

14 AUGUST 1998

We met at the Bush Ranger as usual, had a few rounds. Tony was late, as usual. The three of us drank a toast anyway, with pub champagne. It was a nice day, hot and sticky like the first 14 August, all those years ago. As I sat there, wondering if I felt happy, I wondered if Veronica meant what she said about it being over between us. I had to assume that she did. Then I wondered if I *wanted* her to mean what she said.

As we sat there, me, Nodge and Colin, fumbling for words, I found myself inspecting the faces of each of them, trying to remember what they had looked like when we first did this. Tony, who still hadn't arrived, I knew was much the same – slicker, more expensively dressed, perhaps, but having lost no hair, the only signs of age being the faint imprint of crow's-feet appearing by the edges of his eyes. But looking at Nodge, I could see he was fatter, sadder, more constipated, I would say. There was something rigid and regretful in him that I knew now, that I could momentarily remember,

308

had once been absent. Colin had changed as little as Tony – he still had that defensive smile, that gathering in of himself as if preparing to defend himself from attack. Still, finally, the tortoise.

And me; I didn't know. I'd stopped being able to see myself years ago. Perhaps that's why I had hitched up with Veronica. Because she was a mirror and I had forgotten about mirrors, and where they were hidden. And perhaps now I didn't like what they showed you. What Veronica showed me.

The conversation, having run out of road, sputtered and stopped. We waited another half-hour for Tony, still drinking. Things were going out of focus already.

Tony wasn't answering his mobile. Eventually we decided that we should head off without him – each in our separate cars – to the golf course at Perivale. It had been decided that we would play nine holes, have lunch there, then go drinking together in the afternoon. We presumed Tony would turn up. He usually did in the end, breezing in with charming apologies.

Now, having had a clear run down the Uxbridge Road, I arrive at the slipway that leads to the golf course. There's an ad for a Saab 95 on the hoarding as you enter. The catchline reads, 'There Should Be No Forces Outside of Your Control'.

Nodge and Colin are already there, in the café. Still no sign of Tony. Nodge is looking at his watch. He has a can of beer in his hand, as does Colin. We're all drinking quite heavily, in order to cover up the gaps. That's what drinking's for, isn't it?

Nodge's lips, always narrow, have tightened and thinned and he is smoking at a slightly higher rate than usual – I would estimate four an hour rather than three. Craven As of course. A few minutes ago, he allowed himself an exhale of breath that was too loud to be anything other than a public protest. He is getting angry, I'm sure of it.

Why does that make me feel good, I wonder? I pick at the remnants of a toasted bacon and egg sandwich, ordered by Colin, uneaten, already gone cold. If Nodge gets angry, I will forgive Tony. I will forgive him anyway, sooner or later, but this time I will forgive him right away. Just for the pleasure of rattling Nodge's cage. I chew at the bread and bacon fat, the taste subsumed under vinegary tomato ketchup.

I notice that Colin, sat diagonally opposite Nodge, is picking his thin, angular, badly sunburnt nose. He removes something from the dark interior, then flicks it into the middle distance, where it disappears among the collection of old cigarette packets, crumbs and spilt coffee that decorates the floor. He is reading the *Daily Mirror*.

It's hot in here. There's a blankness in the air, a sense of something suspended. Dark patches of sweat are crawling out from the pits of Nodge's Gap Essentials charcoal grey three-button sports shirt. It's annoying him, but he won't complain. He'll sit there smoking and pretending he's not bothered. His ankles revealed just beneath where his black Stone River Island chinos end, are as pale as cauliflower.

They're not real, are they?

Colin is indicating, with a slight cock of his head, a colour photograph on the centre pages of the *Mirror*. A woman smiles brightly upwards, clad in a thong only. The thong is so tiny, she must be shaved. Her breasts protrude mightily from her chest, fully cantilevered. The nipples have been prepared so as to appear slightly hard. Her back is arched away from the camera; no flaws show.

It's hard to tell.

I make a play of studying the photograph, squinting as if to get the newsprint into focus.

It's not the same any more, is it? says Colin, with an air of mild regret.

Mild, Colin is so mild. A Chicken Korma of a man.

What do you mean? I say, nervous that Colin is going to own up to the discomfort between us.

I look at my watch. Tony is an hour and a half late now. About the average.

Well, if you don't know if they're real or not, it's harder to get excited. Because fake ones are . . . cheating. I mean, if you know they're fake, it's not as sexy as if they're real. Like when I found out that that . . . that girl . . . in . . . what was that film . . . you know, with Harrison Ford and . . . er. The one where the girl turns out to be a robot. She's gorgeous, but once you know she's a, she's a . . .

311

Replicant.

*Replicant, that's right. Then you think, if she's not really a **girl**, how can you . . .*

Nodge shifts on his chair. He hasn't looked at the photograph and is gazing out of the door into the sunlight with a hazy disdain at the use of 'girl' for 'woman'.

*Woman. She's a **woman**.*

That's the point, says Colin obliviously. *She's not a girl. She's an android. And once you know that, your stiffy goes. It's the same with breasts, you see. If you can't be sure –*

I don't see that it matters, I say. *Fake, real, whatever. You're still going to **respond**. Anyway, she's not a replicant.*

What? But I thought –

*She's an actress **playing** a replicant. Everything's real.*

Colin looks confused.

*Yeah, but it's diluted, somehow all the same. Because in the **film** she's not real. And that's what's real while you're watching it.*

I glance across at Nodge. He's looking pained, putting himself above the argument as usual. He's making it plain that he finds this sort of thing childish. It annoys me, not because he's not right – it *is* childish – but because he's making a virtue out of standing aloof. Whereas me, I'm trying to make Colin feel comfortable, talk his language. I'm the good guy here, not him. I'm the good guy because I don't mind seeming to be the bad guy.

Anyway, I can help you on this one. The girl from the Mirror. *They are fake. I saw her interviewed on* The Big Breakfast. *She said she was very proud of the job. She said it made her feel – what was it? Empowered.*

Colin looks a degree more crestfallen.

Really? So she's not . . . they're not . . .

They're plastic fantastics. Both of 'em. Sorry.

Colin closes the paper and picks up his mug of tea thoughtfully. He nods as if he knew all along.

It just goes to show.

Just goes to show **what**? Nodge says, with naked irritation towards Colin.

Good. A crack in that smug, fake implacability. But his face is still composed, superior. The Court of Star Chamber.

Colin looks faintly startled.

Er . . . I don't know. It just goes to show that you never can tell, I suppose.

Colin is peering through Nodge's cigarette smoke, eyes narrowed to protect against fumes. Colin is always protecting himself against something, one way or another. He gives a slight shake of the head and a pucker of the lips, then gazes at the open doorway. We fall into silence again.

Colin has not been offended by Nodge's obvious disdain. He adjusts his New York Nicks baseball cap, snapping the brim up. Nothing ever seems to offend Colin. Then he says brightly, out of the blue, *Do you think there's life after death?*

Nodge doesn't even turn around as he replies.

Have you ever wondered how Father Christmas gets down the chimney?

Nodge is a militant atheist, a relic of his distant past as a cracker-barrel Marxist. Colin smiles wider. His smile is wide, but his eyes seem colder and more and more distant every time I see them. I wonder if something is happening to him. I've heard from my mum that Olive is very bad, so I've been keeping off the subject with Colin. I don't want to upset him. Also, I don't want to be embarrassed. There's always the possibility he might blub.

Seriously, though. What do you think? I mean, we can't just disappear, can we? Then everything would be pointless.

He smiles again, as if in wonderment at some newly discovered conclusion. He picks up his cellphone and starts to play with it, flicking the aerial with his finger so it springs forward then bounces back. As if activated by this movement, it begins to trill.

I bet that's Tony.

Colin puts the receiver to his ear and presses a lit green button marked 'OK'.

Hello? Oh, hi, Tony. Oh, don't worry. No, we're fine. Yes. No. Can't be helped. Sure. See you in a minute then. Bye.

Colin switches off the phone and balances it on the cusp of his stomach. He moves small muscles so that the phone rises and falls. An inch of red flesh shows beneath his T-shirt, which has a bright picture of a beach and palm trees printed on it, and the name of a holiday destination, Cancun, Mexico, where, in fact, he has never been. He sways back and forth on the white plastic collapsible chair.

That was Tony. He'll be here in five minutes. He said he's sorry, but he's stuck in traffic on the Uxbridge Road.

I feel my irritation level rise a notch. The Uxbridge Road was clear when I drove down it. But I'm not going to show anything if Nodge isn't. And Nodge is still maintaining his stance of emotional maturity. He shrugs, gives a faint, forgiving smile.

Diamond Tony. He'll never change.

There's a short pause, as if Nodge is calculating something. Then he says, *I'm amazed he got up at all after last night.*

Colin doesn't seem to hear. The mobile phone loses balance and falls to the floor with a crack, and separates into two pieces.

Uh-oh.

He scrabbles for the phone. It has fallen into a puddle of old orangeade. He gingerly picks up both pieces and begins to wipe them with a paper towel. I have begun to strike my thumbs against each other, interlocking the fingers of my hands in front of me. Nodge clocks this and I seem to see a shadow of satisfaction pass across his face. He sits and waits for me to speak, as he knows I will.

I affect an unfelt nonchalance.

What? Did you two go out together last night then?
As if it didn't matter.

We went down the Anglesea. That place they've tarted up.

Colin is trying to piece together the two sections of his phone. His tongue protrudes slightly from his thick lips. There is a tiny fleck of spittle on his cheek.

Bare floorboards. Charcoal grill.

Oh. Right.

But it isn't right. It's wrong. It's a . . . breach of *protocol*. Tony is primarily and foremost *my* friend. I have priority access. If Tony is around, then he should call me, like he always has in the past. I was sat in last night, desperate for company if the truth be known, anticipating the fight I was going to have with Veronica today. And Tony called Nodge for a drink. No – maybe it was the other way round. Maybe Nodge called him. It won't be so bad if it was that way round.

I was quite surprised to hear from him. I thought he was still away in New York.

Nodge always knows exactly what buttons to push. I can feel a stupid little ball of pain and rage gathering force in my stomach. Colin is still fumbling with the phone, with infinite patience. I search for something to say that won't sound childish. After all, why shouldn't Tony call Nodge instead of me? But I feel betrayed, furious. It's OK to leave Colin out. But not me, not *me*. I'm not *like* him.

316

You never said at the Bush Ranger. About you going out with Tony.

Nodge shrugs, gives a particular kind of smile. This smile is really clever, because it is a reaching-out kind of smile, almost a smile of sympathy. It is an on-my-side kind of smile, which puts Nodge a moral notch up while he enjoys his triumph. It's a smile that says, *I was only trying to protect you.*

Well, I didn't think. Does it matter?

No. Of course it doesn't, you fucking *thief.*

No. Of course it doesn't. How was he?

I can feel the look on my face now, occupying the planes and curves. Sullen, sulky. I realize that I am more than mildly drunk. It suddenly occurs to me, through the slight fog of alcohol, *I want to cry.* This, I know, is meant to be a ridiculous thought for a thirty-year-old man to entertain. I want to be grown up, indifferent, big, large-hearted. But I'm not. I'm a schoolboy. We're all schoolboys, schoolboys in the playground. And Nodge has dead-legged me. But now we look like grown-ups, it's secret, it's all in secret. I take a determined pull of lager from one of the cans we've brought with us.

Oh, you know. Same old Tony.

Done it!

Colin looks delighted. His phone makes a soft bleep to announce its return to functionality. He is entirely oblivious to what has passed between Nodge and me. I notice that my fists are clenched and make a conscious effort to relax them.

317

There is a blast of music from outside in the car park, cranked up so loud it sounds like there are speakers in the café itself. It is Radiohead, *OK Computer*. Old men pulling golf trolleys with Pringle sweaters and tams on their heads turn at the sound, looking resentful.

Through the door, wedged open in an unsuccessful attempt to generate a breeze, I see his white 1965 Merc Cabriolet whack into a small parking space at a dangerously high speed. Tony's face is in profile and he is singing along to the music. Gold-rimmed Ray-Bans, shoulders protected from the sun by a white T-shirt.

Tony turns and sees us through the door. He grins and gives a big thumbs up, then revs the engine before switching it off. The music abruptly ceases. He gives an almighty whoop, *Yee ha!* and catapults himself out of the car. He is wearing beautiful cream linen shorts, Birkenstock sandals. When he walks towards us, it is as if he is still dancing to the music. He jigs into the café and immediately throws himself on to the floor in an attitude of caricatured apology.

Forgive me! Forgive me! I am guilty. I am the arse of all arseholes. I am the scum of all scumholes. I am the butt of all buttholes, the piss of all pissholes.

He is bowing up at us now, flickering his eyes as if in prayer, on his knees. There is a small Prada logo on his T-shirt, a larger Armani label on his shorts. Colin gives an amiable grin, as does Nodge, the hypocrite. I make no response.

He springs to his feet, reaches out to shake Colin's hand. Two gold and diamond rings, one on the index finger, one on the middle.

*Am I forgiven? Please say I'm forgiven. I would have worn sack-cloth, but it **does** clash with the Armani's. Anyway, sackcloth went out with the spring collection.*

He indicates the shorts, just to let us know that they aren't just any shorts. He's talking in high camp now. He gives a little flounce with his hips.

Colin doesn't know what he's talking about, but reaches his hand out and shakes it anyway. Colin's hand is white, small, and seems to completely be encompassed by the brown manicured ham of Tony's.

Forget it.

Colin means it. Unlike Nodge, who just isn't showing it.

*I knew I could rely on you, Colly-flower. You are Christ-like. No. You **are** Jesus. Nodge, what about you? You can't be angry with me. It was all your fault, man.*

He turns to me.

It was his fault, Frankie. If he hadn't plied me with vodka for three hours, I would have heard the alarm clock. He's a fucking maniac. Whoa. Are those real?

He's clocked the copy of the *Mirror*.

Colin perks up.

It's funny you should say that because we were just —

Tony ignores him and begins to talk over the top of him.

Frankie, come on. Cheer up, you miserable cunt.

I frown. He comes over and begins to tickle me under the arms like I was a big baby. At first this just fuels my anger, but I find the wherewithal to play the game.

OK. OK. Forget it.

That's my man.

I'm just in a bit of a mood today.

Tony looks uninterested. Having re-established connection, he's ready to move on to other things. He reaches for his mobile. I continue anyway.

I think me and Veronica have reached the end of the road, I say. And I want to add, *I sacrificed her. For you.*

I stare at the back of my hands, as if embarrassed to look up.

It was her birthday today. She wanted me to cancel. I said I wasn't going to do it. So she told me it was her or you lot. That I had to make a choice. So that was that. No doris is going to get in between me and my mates.

I sit and wait for the reaction. I look up in anticipation. But instead of the unbounded joy and gratitude I had imagined, there is hardly any response at all.

That's a shame, says Colin.

Too bad. Women are all mad anyway, man. Oh, hi! Polly. Darling, I'm sorry about the weekend.

Tony's talking into the cellphone again. Nodge doesn't say anything at all. He's just shaking his head. It's all very muted. It's as if . . . as if . . .

320

is this really possible? They didn't really care one way or another. That maybe it was all in my head. That there was no choice to be made.

This thought is stabbing at me. I look out of the open door. Out of nowhere, dark clouds have begun to assemble, blocking the sun. Tony finishes his conversation, gets up and goes to close the sunroof on his Merc, then takes some smart new waterproofs out of the boot, plus a grand's worth of clubs and equipment. Ping Zings, Bubble Burners, electric trolley, the whole kit and caboodle.

Nodge is hauling his clubs on to his trolley – good to medium quality, second-hand, polished and cleaned – then taking out a ball and wiping it thoughtfully. Colin has only a half-set in a bag that looks like it has come from a car boot sale – a Robin Hood quiver bag, tartan, canvas, *circa* 1975. He has a novelty Daffy Duck cover for one of the woods. He takes out a putter and swings it in an arc. I can see clearly that it is bent. He wobbles slightly when he walks, carries the bag on his back. He doesn't have a trolley. We trek as a foursome towards the first tee. Tony ahead, impatient as ever, the three of us just behind.

Anyone want a side bet?

Tony is waving a fifty-pound note in the air. No one responds.

Aaagh, you **pussies**. *Nodge, what about you? Give it some spice.*

Nodge looks doubtful. Colin is shaking his head forcefully and grinning. I look at Tony's set of clubs and electric trolley and my own second-hand set. I look at his mocking grin. I think of him and Nodge out drinking together last night.

Come on, Frankie. Be a man. Get your revenge, eh?

He laughs again. He's talking about his lateness, but I'm thinking about his betrayal. There is something unpleasant in the laugh, something that mocks the fact that I was upset by him in the first place. He's getting at me. I feel my hand tighten around my club.

Sure. Why not? If Nodge will join in too.

Nodge shakes his head.

Too rich for me. Anyway, I think we should just keep it friendly. This is meant to be fun, you know? You two are always too competitive. It spoils things.

The slight schoolmasterish tone provokes me. I become determined to engage him in the bet.

Come on, you fucking poof.

I see a flash of unconcealed anger in Nodge's eyes which takes me aback slightly. But I continue anyway.

I'll even give you two to one. What about that?

Nodge furrows his brow.

Two to one. Double your money.

Nodge tenses slightly.

What about me? says Tony.

Evens with you. But I'll give Nodge the odds. Because he's shit.

This is meant to come out more lightly than it does. But Nodge's face puckers angrily.

It's a deal.

The gamble has somewhere solidified the tension that was already hanging vaguely in the air. We all shake hands, affecting indifference but with an unmistakable solemnity.

What about you, Colin. Fancy a go?

I know Colin will refuse, but I don't want him to feel left out. I'm smiling, but I feel grim inside. Colin shakes his head softly.

No. Then he appears to think for a second and says, *This is silly. Can't we just play for the fun of it?*

This is fun. Isn't it, Nodge?

My head is still swimming from all the booze, but I try to clear it, to concentrate on the game. Nodge grunts. He's very definitely got the egg on. He's already distracted, concentrating on the game ahead.

Tony hits a good first shot straight down the fairway, Nodge hits about forty feet behind him, Colin muffs and hits into rough off to the right. Now it's my turn. Just as I'm about to hit, Nodge puts his club back in his golf bag, making a loud clunk. I let loose anyway and miss the ball almost entirely. It goes about ten feet.

*Come **on**. That's not fair.*

Nodge shrugs. Colin looks away.

Tough beans, Frankie, says Tony, offering an apologetic grin.

***No.** Hold on. Nodge made a **noise**. It put me off. Well, you shouldn't have hit the shot then,* says

323

Nodge, who has already begun moving his trolley down the fairway.

Look. Let me take a free shot as it's the first hole. Let me take a mulligan. This is meant to be friendly.

Colin shifts uncomfortably, but doesn't start moving towards the next tee. Tony has put his clubs down and is rubbing sun oil into his face. His eyes are closed.

I continue, whining, *We always do mulligans. Ever since we started playing, we've given mulligans.*

Nodge has stopped pushing his cart and turns round towards me. He's speaking with an exaggerated evenness that I know indicates absolute intransigence. He's definitely got a major strop on.

Other games were different. We weren't playing for money. Also you hadn't just called me a fucking poof.

Colin, your casting vote. Do I get a mulligan or not?

Colin averts his eyes and shifts uncomfortably. The sun passes behind a cloud. I can feel a drop of rain on my face.

I dunno.

I bite my lip, Nodge-style.

Fine. If that's the way it's going to be . . .

Now I feel angry towards Colin as well as Nodge and Tony. After all I've done, the times I've protected the little shit. I march up to my ball, stand astride and, hardly thinking, slash at it with the club. The club meets earth and sends a clod out into the air. The ball moves maybe another five feet.

The formless anger inside me begins to harden into something colder, more purposeful. I become absolutely focused on winning the game, on obliterating them all. I compose myself again over the ball and feel myself going very still inside. The club, still a three wood, swings slowly back into the air and comes down smoothly. Nodge is in line with the green, but I don't bother to call a fore. The ball whizzes within a few inches of his head and he jerks to one side in shock. Then the ball takes off into an upward trajectory, seeming to hold still at the peak of its arc, then falls perfectly just inside the edge of the green. An absolutely brilliant shot.

I hold my hand up in apology, slightly shocked at how close I came to hitting him. Nodge looks back at me, doesn't return my wave.

Fuck him.

I manage to get the ball, amazingly, down in one from the edge of the green. Colin blows the hole completely, but I don't care about Colin, because I know he isn't going to win anyway, and even if he does, it doesn't matter. I am silent and grim. One part of me is whispering that I am behaving badly, but I'm not listening.

We jockey back and forth for the next three holes. On the fifth, a short par three, me and Nodge hit mediocre shots well short of the green. Colin does an air shot, missing the ball completely, and we let him have another go for free. He's going to lose anyway. Then Tony does exactly the same thing.

One stroke, says Nodge.

Bullshit, says Tony.

You can't play one set of rules for Colin and another for me.

One stroke, I say firmly. I'm thinking of the mulligan I never got.

Tony turns on me, spreads his hands and speaks evenly as if he were patiently explaining something to an idiot child.

That's not fair, Frankie. No one ever counts air strokes. Not once – not once – since we started playing together has anyone ever counted an air stroke. And now, suddenly, air strokes count.

Big-boys rules, Tone. It's only fair, says Nodge, looking stern.

*How can it be **fair** when you give Colin a free stroke and not me?*

Nodge and I don't say anything.

Colin fidgets with his tees and says, *Look, **I'll** count my air shot. Then we –*

*That's not the **point**.*

Tony almost spits when he says this.

Nodge and I are shaking our heads with, as it happens, almost perfectly synchronized movements. Tony pulls himself up to his full height – over six foot – reaches into his pocket, takes out a wad of notes and peels off three, rolls them in a ball and throws them on to the ground. The wind begins to move them; neither of us makes a move to pick them up.

If the betting money is so fucking important to you, here it is.

326

With this, Tony shoots his club into the bag and makes as if he's going to walk off the course.

The money's got nothing to do with it, says Nodge quickly. *It's the principle of the thing.*

Look, says Colin irrelevantly, *I said I'll give up the air shot.*

No one seems to hear him. I start to plead with Tony. It's gone too far now.

Don't walk off, Tony. Finish the game.

But he grabs the handle of his trolley and begins to walk.

I feel myself beginning to crumple. Tony's gone for the nuclear option and I'm not up for it.

OK, look, take the shot.

Nodge says nothing. Tony pauses momentarily. You can tell he doesn't want to go through with the walk-out either.

For fuck's sake! shouts Colin.

We all look in amazement at him. He's gone red in the face. For one awful moment, I think he's about to cry.

Why can't we just be . . . just be mates? Why have we got to go through all this? I mean, I don't know . . . it's pointless. Can't we just stop it? Please?

The whole situation is getting out of kilter now. There's a danger, the worst of all dangers. The danger that we're going to be embarrassed.

I look towards Colin and say, *You're right. Colin's right. It's stupid. Tony, take the stroke. Come on. Take the stroke.*

Nodge also nods, albeit reluctantly. He doesn't want a scene either.

Sure. Whatever. Go ahead.

Tony's almost mollified, but not quite. It's a long way back from the place where he's ended up.

I don't want the stroke. Not if you're going to be pissy about it. Not if it's just because of . . . of . . . **crybaby** *here.*

Crybaby. The memory of Colin's debagging all those years ago comes back to me in a horrible flash. Colin recoils, like he's been slapped. But Tony has stopped moving his trolley and playing with the head of his three iron. You can see he doesn't want to go, but he doesn't want to stay if it means losing face.

Look, why don't we all start again? I say. *My shot and Nodge's were pretty crap anyway. We'll just pretend we've all arrived at the hole for the first time and we'll go from there.*

OK, says Nodge tentatively, whose shot, although crap, was better than mine.

OK then, says Tony, as if he's doing everyone a big favour.

Colin nods and immediately begins to tee up the ball again.

We each hit off from the fifth again. Tony this time hits a beautiful ball, which bounces on the green six feet from the flag. Nodge also gets on the green and even Colin makes the rough on the edge. Feeling the pressure of three good shots in front of me, I fluff completely and send the ball

328

skewing off into a patch of woodland. It's all I can do to keep from hurling my club after it.

Bad luck, says Tony.

He's embarrassed now, but pleased none the less. I make my face into a neutral mask and head towards the clump of trees. When I reach it, there's no sign of my ball. The rough is very deep, and cut grass, dead and brown, adds to the impossibility of the task. I hack about with an eight iron, trying to uncover it, but three minutes of searching yields no results.

I see Tony and Colin heading back towards me to help me look. My body is hidden by the horizontal branches of a monkey puzzle tree. Nodge calls, and Colin and Tony momentarily look back towards him. Something in me gives and I reach in my pocket and fish out my spare ball, hesitate for a second, then let it drop. I tell myself this isn't cheating, just levelling the pitch. Tony shouldn't have got the free shot. When I look up again, Tony still has his head turned away from me, but Colin has resumed walking in my direction. I gesture with a thumbs up.

It's OK. I've found it.

Tony turns and raises his hand in acknowledgement. Colin doesn't move and holds himself towards where I'm standing. He stands like this for several seconds, then slowly turns and makes his way back towards the green.

I look down. I pick up the eight iron that I've been using to search for the first ball, stand to one side and take a slow swing backwards. The down stroke connects beautifully. The ball loops up into the air, hangs for a second, then drops on to the green. A single bounce takes it past the hole six inches for what should be an easy uphill putt.

Tony and Nodge putt out, Nodge jammily sinking an improbable twenty-footer after his ball is diverted towards the centre of the hole by a stray twig on the green. Colin goes down in two and I sink mine. I'm standing level with Tony now and two behind Nodge, with four holes to play. The atmosphere between us is tense and hostile.

For the next hole, you have to drive over a small stream. Me, Colin and Tony all clear it easily, but Nodge mishits and drops the ball straight into the middle. Above, the sky is getting darker and darker. There is a distant rumble of thunder.

We walk down to the bank of the stream. Incredibly, the ball has skimmed off the water and is resting on a hollow in a flat rock. The stream is only one or two feet deep, but if flows fast and the ball is clearly unplayable.

You'd better drop one, I say, in a tone that I calculate to be sympathetic but which comes across as mocking.

I don't think so, says Nodge.

He bends over and begins taking off his shoes.

What are you doing?

Playing the ball.

You can't play the ball. It's in the middle of the fucking river.

So?

The shoes are off now. He's hitching up his trousers to knee level and reaching for what looks like a high iron. Silver fish dart past the rock where the ball balances. Droplets of water fill the dimples that punctuate the sphere of the white globe.

We watch Nodge lower himself over the bank into the shallow stream. Tony and me exchange disbelieving glances.

You two are always too competitive. It spoils things, says Tony sarcastically, parodying Nodge's complaint at the first tee.

Nodge doesn't answer. He hasn't rolled his trousers up far enough and the stream is catching the gathered material just below his knees, turning the pale thread dark. The floor of the river is uneven and he's finding it hard to keep upright. He makes it as far as the rock where the ball is, then tries to straddle either side of it. He half falls in the manoeuvre and, struggling to keep balance, drops his club, which sinks immediately.

The outline of the club can be seen clearly on the bottom, shifting slightly in the movement of the water in a soft bed of mud. He bends down and fishes it out, and begins wiping it on his shirt to dry the handle. Great brown streaks appear on the material as the mud comes away. Nodge's face remains composed in a rictus of concentration and intense determination. None of us speaks for fear of provoking him.

Again he straddles the rock, this time finding

331

what appears to be firm footing. He tries to line up the club head with the ball, taking short, awkward strokes that stop a couple of inches short of contact. I feel suddenly in my bones that he's actually going to pull it off, that famous luck of his coming like the cavalry to save him once more.

He goes for the real swing. There's mud on his shirt and his trousers are soaked. The motion of the stream is rocking him back and forth on his heels slightly. The club goes back slowly, for no more than a half-swing. Nodge has his eyes fixed on the ball, which shivers in the slight breeze.

He takes the club back to the end of the arc, then begins to swing it down in a sudden rush. His head comes up, eyes leave the ball. The counter-motion of the club pushes him backwards, and the club head misses the ball almost completely, just catching it with enough of a whisper to send it dribbling off the rock and into the water. Very slowly, Nodge's body collapses backwards. Trying desperately to balance himself, he waves the club in the air, but to no avail. Top-heavy, he goes over in an almost perfect reverse head-over-heels and collapses into the water. Immediately his head surfaces, spitting out scraps of moss and pond life.

There is a moment's hiatus, then Tony's laugh begins to catch, then ignite. Lower than usual, since it is unusually spontaneous, it still sends birds flying from the trees. It starts me off in a gasping counterpoint, and Colin chimes in with that silly, girlish giggle, and it builds as a trio until we are all incapable of speech. I am doubled over and clutching myself. Tony has sat on the grass for relief, and Colin's giggles have opened out into something full-throated and almost hysterical.

When I finally manage to bring my eyes into focus, Nodge's face seems at first to be composed into a kind of visible crucible of feeling. It is almost as if, in sequence, frame by frame, I can see the possibilities advertise themselves across the small muscles of his face, then sink back into the milky distance out of which they have floated. At first there is shock at the recent impact of the cold water, which recedes, as if in a lick of transparent flame, to be replaced by something like morbid humiliation. Droplets of water and dilute mud trace paths down the features of his face as they undergo these transformations.

The look of humiliation, which is the most fleeting, is overcast by something approaching naked, unbridled rage. His chest begins to heave up and down, his fists tighten on the club, the skin rouges. The face goes tight, as if something is going to actually burst through the skin and obliterate us all. This lasts very visibly for some seconds, but I see that it is not an emotion Nodge can allow himself because it does not sit with his image of who he is; mature, wise, supremely sensible. With great difficulty, he fights it back down, then there is a moment of neutrality.

Finally, a smile appears on his face. It is a

convincing smile, wide and even, which seems to announce that this moment of farce has wiped out all wrongs. With poetic symbolism, the sun appears from behind a cloud and makes Nodge squint. This throws the accomplished smile out of joint slightly, and I see the effort that is going into maintaining it. But I say nothing, as Nodge apparently recovers himself and his composure. He makes a stab at laughing at himself.

Wrong club, he says drily.

Colin and Tony laugh again, and Tony reaches out a hand to help him out of the river. I smile cautiously. I know Nodge better than Colin or Tony, and I think Nodge is still furious. What's more, he's furious at me in particular, though I can't say exactly why. I think it is something to do with the fact that he suspects that . . . not that I can see through him, but that I *think* I can see through him. He hates that about me more than anything.

Nodge blows the hole completely, while Tony and I both make par. Now we're joint leaders, one point ahead of Nodge, with three holes to go. Tony and me bogey the next two, while Nodge makes par on the eighth, so at the tee for the ninth and last we're all even.

Superficially, since Nodge's dousing in the stream, the atmosphere has improved. We're all talking to each other again at a low level, about the hazards, the wind, which clubs to use. But it's smokescreen. The weight of the bet presses down harder than ever and bad blood still pumps just below the skin. The three of us look tense, but Colin looks simply miserable, although he has nothing more to lose and has given up the game. A childhood spent with parents screaming at each other has left him paralysed by any display of conflict.

Colin goes to tee off first. It is against etiquette – leader tees off – but since he's dropped out of the real game, he's outside the rules. He spends a long time addressing the ball, as if he can't concentrate, then looks up with a pleading face at the three of us standing to the side of the tee and says, *Can't you just call it a draw?*

No one answers.

Then he says it, his last hopeless attempt to rescue the situation, *It's only a game, after all.*

I feel like groaning. Tony and Nodge shuffle their feet and look away.

Colin, I say, reaching for my three wood from the bag. *Who on earth ever told you that?*

Well, it's true, he says desperately, as if wishing made it so.

Nothing, I say, *is ever only anything.*

The ninth is the longest hole on the course, a good 400 yards, trapped with bunkers down the middle and woodland to the right and left. It's a par five, and I've only ever made par on it once. If Tony's long swing catches the ball right, it will give him a big advantage, but there's a lot of luck on this hole; and that's Nodge's speciality.

I'm relying on staying steady, staying calm under pressure. At this moment, losing the game seems simply unacceptable. Tony and Nodge have both stuffed me, and I'm going to stuff them right back. That's the *real* game. It's called friendship. The continuation of table football, of Go! and Risk and Monopoly and Snakes and Ladders by other means.

I tee off and rush the shot. The ball skews off hopelessly to the left fifty feet, then stutters to a stop an inch past a gaping rabbit hole.

Shit!

I throw my club to one side, where it buries itself vertically in the earth. I can see quite clearly that Tony is fighting down a smile, while Nodge is keeping a stern straight face. Colin is twenty yards away, picking slivers of the bark of a dead oak tree.

Tony goes next and hits a perfect drive, three foot beyond a range of fairway bunkers. Nodge also hits well but falls short of the bunkers by fifteen yards. Colin has lost heart and given up.

I hit my second shot cleanly to take it parallel with Nodge's ball, twenty feet to the left. When I arrive at the spot where my ball is, Nodge is dithering over which club to choose. He goes for a safe iron instead of the more difficult wood, but intimidated by the proximity of the bunkers, his shot hits the ground in front of the ball and sends it trickling into the sand. He grunts in frustration.

Twenty yards ahead, Tony hits another big one,

but the wind catches it and veers it wildly off to the right and into the trees that flank the fairway. His head goes down. Anyone's game now.

My next shot is straight and true, down the centre of the fairway, in front of a second and final set of bunkers. Nodge hits out of his bunker remarkably well and lands about twenty feet away from me, maybe 200 yards from the edge of the green. I can tell from a scream of frustration to the right that Tony has muffed again. That means he's out of it.

I take my fourth shot, with a four iron, my favourite club. I catch it absolutely beautifully. I clear the bunkers, sail right up into the air and plop on to the edge of the green, twenty yards from the flag. Nodge grunts again. With hardly any hesitation, he hits too. His ball lands three feet from mine. We both have one very difficult putt to make par.

We walk solemnly towards the green. Tony has picked up now. Apparently he hit it twice against a tree. Tony and Colin stand either side of our two balls on the green. I am slightly closer, which means that Nodge goes first.

The thunderclouds have gathered together again. I look up and notice that the sky has turned black. I can actually see sheet lightning on the horizon. Suddenly, in the blink of an eye, and torrentially, it begins to rain – a driving, massive, drenching rain that almost blocks out vision entirely, that stings the skin like maddened, tiny wasps.

None of us speaks or changes expression. Nodge, already drenched and soggy from his fall in the river, addresses the ball. Droplets of water fall from the edge of his nose as he bends over to strike, legs slightly apart, wrists locked. Colin is attending the flag with the formality of an undertaker. We all stand perfectly still in the rain, blurred, pale, as if in a Polaroid photograph before the colours have fully developed.

Then, finally, Nodge takes a backswing and strikes the ball. It would have been perfect a minute ago, but the drenching has softened the ground and the ball, right on line, runs out of steam and halts a foot from the hole. A gimme, pretty much unmissable.

I am also soaked through, but am barely aware of the cold driving rain. Everything is focused on getting it right: not too tense, not too relaxed, not too fast, not too slow, not too hard, not too soft. Everything's balance. Don't wait too long to hit it. Don't hit it too quickly. I stand over the ball, stare at it as if asking it to reveal to me what stroke to take. I inspect the ground a last time, try to take into account Nodge's last shot and give it a bit of extra welly. I wait a second, take a soft, even backswing, rivet my eyes to the ball and make sure that my head stays still, then let it go.

The ball leaves the club, travels past sodden daisies, a small unnoticed sweet wrapper. It goes past where Nodge's ball was, travels directly towards the hole. I hold my breath. It is going fast, too fast. I see that I have overcompensated, that it is going to swing wildly past the hole, leaving me maybe ten feet past. It's not on line. It's going to miss, then take me far out of range.

Then suddenly the ball swerves with a slight rise in the ground, pulls to the left, and, still travelling too fast, it swings round and whacks the rim of the hole right dead centre. For a moment it looks like it's certain to bounce over, but instead it skips, loses velocity to the rim and begins to revolve at what looks like immense speed. Once, then twice, then three times. Finally it gives up the fight and falls into the now rain-filled hole with a plop.

I immediately fall to my knees, throw my club in the air and give a whoop.

*Fuck you all! You fucking pussies you **losers**. I did it! I am the champion. Wooo-hoooo!*

Nodge sags very slightly and idly hits his own, futile ball towards the hole. It drops, but it's too late now. Then moves morosely towards the hole to pick the balls out.

Well done, he manages to mutter.

Good putt, you jammy cunt, says Tony, only half jokingly.

Colin doesn't say anything. I look at him and he is wearing a fiercely pained expression, which I can't fathom. Why does he care?

Nodge picks my ball out of the hole along with his own. He goes to shake my hand, and I take it and shake it back. He's just about to hand me back my ball, when he checks himself.

339

Hold on. Last time I looked you were using a Dunlop 1. This is a Titleist 3.

I nervously wipe my drenched face with my left hand.

I changed balls. I thought I was getting spooked. I'm superstitious.

So where's the Dunlop now?

I feel a faint panic welling up. I say, *I threw it away. It was damaged anyway.*

Well, which was it? Was it damaged or were you superstitious?

Now Tony has moved over to where we are both standing. Colin keeps his distance. The rain is still coming down. All the other golfers have either fled back to the clubhouse or are standing under umbrellas. The storm is truly appalling, but none of us moves.

Are you calling me a cheat?

No, says Nodge coldly, carefully. *I just want to know where the Dunlop is.*

I told you, I threw it away. You're just getting the hump because you fucked up on the bet.

At least I've only fucked up a game of golf, says Nodge, half audibly.

What?

Nothing. What's the point?

No. Not nothing. What did you say?

I said, At least I've only fucked up a game of golf.

*No, you didn't. You said at least **I've** only fucked up a game of golf. Like you emphasized **I've**. Implying*

*that someone **else** here has fucked up something else,*
something much more important.

Nodge shrugs.

If you say so.

I do say so. Come on. Spit it out, if you've got
something to say.

I've got nothing to say that you want to hear.

We're eyeballing each other like boxers now
before a fight. It's Colin who tries to defuse the
moment. His face is soaking wet, droplets falling
from everywhere. Claps of thunder practically
drown out his words.

Come on. How about a cup of coffee?

We both see a way out, show a slight muscle
relaxation. The half of me that wants to avoid
the confrontation, that does not want to taste the
truth, moves towards that exit. But the half of me
that wants to club Nodge to death with a sand iron
kicks in its heels. Then, after a long moment, we
both, as if synchronized, move slowly towards the
café behind Colin, but way out of each other's body
space. Tony lags behind slightly.

We reach the entrance to the café. Nodge and I
sit opposite each other, as if accuser and accused
in a police cell. Tony is to my left and Colin is
buying the coffees. Nodge reaches into his pocket
and hands me a soaked fifty-pound note, and I take
it silently. Tony gives me two twenties and a ten.
As I go to put the money in my pocket, an impulse
strikes me to hand all the notes back. Winning is
feeling less and less good with every moment. The

cost in bad blood is so high. My head beats with a hangover, a shooting pain in my skull.

Tony has begun a post-mortem, in the way that he invariably does after a golf game – rerunning each shot, trying to work out where precisely it was that he lost the game. He breaks it down into shots, but golf isn't like that. It's all of a piece, like everything else.

See, it all came down to that easy putt on the seventh. If I hadn't missed that – and if you hadn't sunk that lucky ten-footer . . .

Yes, but if I hadn't muffed my swing on the fifth or if Nodge hadn't gone in the river . . . you can go on like that for ever, I say.

Although I'm saying the words, in my mind I'm still having an imaginary conversation with Nodge about what it is I've fucked up. He's lit a cigarette now and he gives me a little smile. Not a nice smile, but one that mocks me, that takes my willingness to walk out of the confrontation on the ninth as fear. It stings me immediately and as Colin delivers my coffee and sits down, I take a purposeful sip, take a glance at Nodge and say, *So what is it that I've fucked up?*

Tony groans, but Nodge answers immediately, like he was expecting the question and had this time decided to answer it.

You know what you've fucked up. You've fucked up your relationship with the only half-decent woman you've ever been out with. Your first non-bim. You've dumped Veronica, who was more than you ever deserved. And for what? For a game of golf.

Nodge smirks again. It's driving me crazy. I dumped Veronica for *him*, for all of them. And he talks to me like this. The hangover aches. I'm soaked and cold. The victory tastes like ashes. Nodge puffs on that fucking Craven A cigarette. Puff puff puff. Fifteen years of puffing.

*I don't what I've fucked **up**, but I'll tell you what I've **fucked**.*

Nodge gives a little upturn of the side of his mouth that means, *Who gives a shit?* This pushes me over. I feel the words sliding round my tongue like venom. I try to keep them in, but it's too late, they dribble out of the edge of my mouth.

*Ruth. That's what I've **fucked**.*

Nodge sits still for a moment, then, to my amazement, begins to laugh.

That's meant to hurt me? Do you think I didn't know? Do you think I could care less? How little you know me, Frankie. How little you choose to know me.

There's a silence. Colin and Tony are hardly breathing. I never told them that I fucked Ruth.

Ruth was just a friend. That's all, says Nodge.

*Come **off** it. Then why have you told us all these years that she was the one, the so-called love of your so-called life?*

*That's for you to work out. But you're so fucking **thick** you never will.*

The silence that follows no one seems to have a

343

clue how to finish, and it seems to stretch on and on. Tony finally makes an attempt.

Anyone fancy a drink?

He holds up a four-pack of lagers.

Nodge, without turning towards him, says, *I'll just have a Coke please. Something soft.*

And Tony says, *What are you, a fucking pansy?*

And now Nodge does turn, right towards Tony, and his self-control, the first time I've ever seen it, goes completely and he shouts, not speaks, or reasons, but shouts, so that everyone in the café can hear.

That's right! says Nodge. *I **am** a fucking pansy. I've been a fucking pansy for fifteen years. I'm as camp as a row of tents, as bent as a nine-bob note. I'm a fudge-packer, a chocolate-stabber, a nance, a poo-jabber. I like it right up the Gary Glitter. I'm a big fucking girl. I've liked it ever since Frankie did it to me, on 14 May 1982. Remember **that**, Frankie? Frankie, I don't think he was so keen. Certainly hasn't shown much interest since. And now you'll never get the chance, will you, Frankie? Because I am oh you tee, out of here. For keeps.*

And with that Nodge leaves his seat and walks out of the door, every eye in the café trained on him. He turns as he goes.

What a total fucking farce!

There is a terrible, seemingly endless silence that spreads to the corners of the room. Nearby, I hear the faint clatter of saucers, a car engine revving in the distance, a train passing.

The silence is finally broken when Tony says, in a voice so quiet you can hardly hear it, *He wasn't **serious**?* He's completely glazed over. As if the parameters of his world-view have completely evaporated. He stares at me and says pleadingly, *Was he, Frankie?*

I look at the empty doorway where Nodge has just exited. I look back at Tony's awestruck face.

*I **know** he was serious*, I say drily.

And I do. I know. For the first time, I know what I've *always* known but haven't been able to quite grasp hold of with the little bit of my mind which is conscious.

Tony is stricken, twitching almost.

Are you saying you . . . him . . .

I examine my fingernails indifferently.

So what?

*What? You're **both** fucking poofs?*

I don't say anything.

Are you? Is that what you're saying?

His eyes are wide, blazing at the impossibility of it all. I feel the dull beat beat beat of the hangover pain in my head.

Sure, Tony. We're poofs. Happy now? And you are a bigoted, selfish, vain, untrustworthy scumbag.

I don't know what I'm saying any more. The rain has started again, my head is pounding, my stomach feels sick. Now it's Tony who's up on his feet.

*You're mad. You're **both** fucking mad.*

He reaches for the horns and the hand around his neck.

345

Vanvanculo! Tilodio! Tu Sei un grande finocchio! Mi vieme da vomitare! Sie discussoso! Sono molto imbarazzato!

The Calabrian guttural comes out like spit. I didn't even know he could *speak* Italian. He looks at Colin, blinks.

And you're mad too.

And he walks out too. I wait, and hear the engine of his Merc rev up. This time Radiohead, for once, aren't playing. I hear his brakes screech as he pulls out of the car park. I look at Colin from the dim reaches of my trance.

Just you and me now, Col, I murmur and think to myself, rubbing my birthmark, *Yeah. Just you and me. The tortoise and the hare. The spakker twins.*

Colin's staring into the middle distance, as if nothing much has happened. He takes a sip of coffee and says to me, *Why did you cheat, Frankie?*

I look at him, totally bewildered.

*What the **fuck** are you talking about?*

I really have no idea what he means. My two best friends have just gone, I've given up the woman I love for no reason at all, and I have absolutely no idea what Colin is going on about.

The ball. I saw you.

*You saw me do **what**?*

*I saw you drop a new ball. Back on the fifth. You cheated. Nodge really won, not you. And you took his money. I knew were a liar. But to do that to a **mate** . . .*

346

I've lost it now completely. I'm cold, wet, embarrassed, lost, angry and bewildered. I look at Colin's accusing, angry little face and suddenly I'm back in the classroom, the day he was debagged, thinking how I want to put myself as far away from him as possible and join the big boys.

What's it to you, you **saddo**. *You fucking* **crybaby**. *You do what you have to do. You learn you have to survive. You draw your own lines. You make your own rules. There aren't any* **other** *rules than the ones you make up. So you* **saw** *me. So big fat deal. What the fuck? What the* **fucking** *fuck? You. Total. Fucking. Mummy's boy. Loser.*

And then Colin sits there like stone, and I know I've lost him too. And I'm sitting in the Perivale golf course café with a cold cup of coffee and fifteen sixty-five-year-old men in tams and tartan golf trousers staring at me like I was from Venus.

That must be it. I'm from *Venus*. And my parents forgot to tell me. That's why I don't understand this. Any of it.

Not a fucking thing.

CHAPTER 16

WHEN HARRY MET FRANKIE

It's not so bad being on your own. I kind of like it.

It does take some getting used to, I won't say that it doesn't. At first it's a kind of cold, dry feeling in the centre of your chest at three in the morning. I've had that feeling before, but worse, after dad died. It's like a wind. It's like the shackles that hold you are tugging at their moorings.

So far, that feeling hasn't disappeared, but it's not such a surprise any more, and that makes it bearable. And it's not as if I am entirely disconnected. There's Mum, God bless her, worrying and dithering and making a fuss. I'm glad she's there, in her British Home Stores separates. After years of hating it, I like, I *need*, her total, lump-like unchangeability.

Then there are my other friends. Nodge, Tony and Colin are gone, but they weren't the only ones. Of course not. They were just the ones I was most used to, I cleaved to from habit. I have a good few others. I've been round their couply, or childy, or couply-childy houses, where they invite me for dinner with a few on-the-turn women who seem nice enough, but with that tinge of lurking fear that acts as a natural libido extinguisher. It's OK. Nothing much is demanded, nothing much is offered.

Then there's work. Since 14 August I've just thrown myself into it like a maniac. I turned up that next Monday morning half an hour early, determined to break every sales record held at Farley, Ratchett & Gwynne. And I'm doing pretty good. I'm hard-selling, soft-selling, opening and closing, hustling and bustling and tussling. Ten-hour days, then back home for a Tesco Microwaveable Chip-topped Curry, a few cans of beer and then stunned, subterranean sleep. Then it all starts again. We open on Saturdays now too, so it leaves me only Sundays to deal with.

No, it really is OK. People say that people are all you've got, that without them you've got nothing. But I don't know that that's true. Yes, there's a certain . . . numbness to being on your own. Although I prefer the word neutrality. Then, what's the alternative? All that messy human thing. All the misunderstandings, hatreds, resentments, slights, envies, all the negative parts of connection. And somehow *that* stuff is so much easier, so much more readily accessible than that other stuff that you see on the lying greetings cards – the hearts, the fluffed clouds, the grinning cartoon characters. Love. What the *fuck* is that all about? Show me it.

349

Draw it for me. Two children on a beach with sky the colour of a Zoom ice lolly in golden sands. Romeo and fucking Juliet. Ren and fucking Stimpy, Beavis and Butthead, Tom and Jerry. It's all, it's all – I don't know.

Sundays. They're hard to fill. I spend a lot of Sundays watching cartoons, stuff I've taped in the week, or archive material. I usually start out with a *Duckman* fest, then move on to *Beavis and Butthead* and *King of the Hill*, then *Rocko's Modern Life*, and finish up with a Klasky Csupo Medley, *Aaagh Real Monsters!* being my personal favourite. Though it has to be admitted, the cartoons just aren't as funny when you watch them by yourself.

I go and have Sunday lunch with Mum now. It's kind of comfortable. Sometimes I can see why Colin goes for that whole Oedipus thing. Not that I want to bang old Flossie, but it's nice to have her looking after me again. Laying out that meat and three veg at one-thirty, picking fluff from my sweater. Football afterwards, though having Mum snoring in the next armchair isn't quite the same as Tony, Nodge and Colin heckling and belching. A lot more peaceful, though.

Now it's Monday morning and I've made it through another weekend. Really quite a pleasant one, if quiet. Amazing how much you can sleep when you don't care that much about being awake.

The office is surprisingly calm today. Rupert and Giles are out on house calls and I'm holding the fort, but the phone is barely ringing. I'm running through my bank statements to fill in the time. It's building up nicely, very nicely indeed. Now I haven't got Veronica to subsidize – and she would have got half all my cash if we had hitched up, which, I'm sorry, is simply taking the *cake* – I reckon in six months I'll be able to move up another notch. I've got my eye on a one-bedroom top floor in Notting Hill, a penthouse. When I get interested in women again – it *has* to happen soon – it'll be a perfect shagpad. And I'm going to be *so* cashed. After the one-bed, I can get a two-bed, then a house, then a house in Kensington, then . . . Well, that's the beauty of it. It goes on for ever. Acquisition is so beautifully open-ended, so unfinishable.

I stare out of the window. A man and a woman are staring in at the sales sheets pasted all over the walls. They're both in their mid-twenties, arms round each other. She reaches up and gives him a little kiss. See how long *that* lasts.

The day wears on. The light goes on well into the evening here in the fading of the summer. Six o'clock. Seven o'clock. I get up to lock the front door of the office. I have closed two sales today, which nets me a commission of close on two grand. Not bad for a Monday. I pull at my tie and look in the mirror. My birthmark looks raw. My face looks raw too, as if it stepped too close to life and didn't withdraw in time. I quickly look away and turn towards the window. I focus past the glass. There is an old man, dapper, kind-looking, dignified, something of the Burt Lancaster, coming towards the door with one of our catalogues in his hand. My immediate instinct to lock the door before he gets there momentarily recedes in the face of the fact that I have a faint shiver of recognition, the vaguest idea that I have seen this man before. Then I dismiss the thought and point at my watch and mouth through the window. *We're closed.*

But he makes a gesture like a key turning in the lock. Clearly he wants me to let him in. He puts his hands together, as if in prayer, I hesitate, then wave him into the office. He enters briskly, closing the door carefully behind him.

Sorry. I know I'm a bit late. I got held up. Busy day. Busy day.

I nod, arrange my face into the efficient sincerity that the job demands.

Well, never mind. You're the last one. Have a seat. What can I do for you?

I lock the door after the man to stop any more punters coming in, then I sit down behind my desk. The man slowly, puffing slightly, sits heavily down on the other side. He takes out a notepad and clumsily flicks through it.

Yes, yes. Here we are. Well, I want a little flat. A one-bedder. Something that's easy to look after.

I see. And what kind of price range were you looking at?

I . . . I'm not really sure. Mr . . . Mr . . .

Blue. Francis Blue. Here's my card.

The man takes my card, inspects it for what

seems a long time, then looks up suddenly and blinks nineteen to the dozen, as if trying to remember something. There is something wrong about this gesture, something not quite right. I can't put my finger on it. Then he lets out a little grunt and a light seems to go on behind his eyes.

Frankie **Blue**. *Of course. I knew I recognized you. How are you, son?*

I'm sorry, I don't –

Harry. Harry Butson.

I still can't get it.

You showed us around 27 Brook Green. Start of this year. Maud Coldstream and I. A lovely house, but the roof turned out to be in need of replacing. We pulled out in the end. Reluctantly, very reluctantly.

Now it hits me. The snogging geriatrics. Just after I hitched up with Veronica. Harry and Maud. Darby and Joan in person.

Mr Butson, I say levelly. *Of course. How are you?*

He smiles eagerly.

Fine, I suppose. Not too bad at all, considering. Yourself? You've lost a bit of weight. You're looking a bit under the weather.

No, no Mr Butson. I'm doing good.

Are you sure now?

Oh yes. Business is excellent. Booming.

It is? Well, that's terrific. Just fantastic.

He nods, not taking his eyes off my face, as if he were chewing me over in his mind. I don't say it, but he's lost weight too. He looks frailer, paler, although still elegant, still tough, strangely

353

gentle in his body language. I stare past him out of the window. The young couple are back again, studying the window display. This time they're arguing loudly. I allow myself a grim little smile.

Have you had the big day yet?

What big day is that, Mr Butson?

Call me Harry. Weren't you thinking of making the leap? You know. Getting spliced and so forth. Tying the old knot.

Was I? Anyway, it never happened.

What a pity. Still. Plenty of fish in the sea. Plenty of seas, for that matter.

He wrings his hands and looks past me at nothing in particular. I suddenly feel myself irritated, can't work out what I'm doing here, when I could be at home, watching the . . . doing the . . . having a . . .

Yes. Well. I hear a slight edge of impatience creep into my voice. *Mr Butson. Women, you know. Who can fathom them? Anyway. What kind of price range were you looking at?*

Harry.

Harry. What can I do for you?

Do for me?

Yes. What kind of property are you interested in exactly?

He shakes his head, as if waking from some kind of daydream.

Yes, of course. A little flat. A one-bedder. Something that's easy to look after.

So you said. Can you tell me a little more perhaps?

Something . . . something nice and clean, near a bit of greenery. I was hoping to get within walking distance of a park.

Which park?

Butson seems bewildered again.

It doesn't matter. Holland Park. That would be nice.

I barely suppress a groan. Then I tighten myself up, ready to make the pitch. I'm pretty sure he's a flake . . . Last time him and Maud just disappeared, wasting everybody's time.

Right . . . You won't get much for your money around there, I'm afraid. A one-bed is going to cost you not far off 200 grand. And that's not going to be big enough for you and your wife. You're going to need something a bit more spacious.

He nods, as if that won't be too much of a problem. Fucking flake. My head begins to ache. I rub my birthmark with the pad of my index finger, then look theatrically at my watch. I want to get out, go home, fall asleep in front of the telly. The telephone rings. I ignore it. Butson seems in no hurry. A silence falls, forcing me into a bit of small talk.

So how is Maud?

Maud? What do you mean?

He suddenly seems close to some kind of panic.

Maud. Your . . . your wife.

Now he relaxes and his face fogs over slightly.

Oh, of course. How could you know? She's passed on, I'm sorry to say.

He's looking me right in the face with those old watery eyes, the grief suddenly showing like two blinding flashlights.

Oh, I'm sorry.

I feel embarrassed, but also obscurely manipulated. I have the strangest feeling that there is some kind of . . . calculation going on here.

No need to be sorry. No need.

I look at my watch again, more pointedly this time. But I feel I can't just leave the subject in the air.

How did it . . . did she . . .

Well, it's hard to talk about.

Of course. I understand.

He sits still for a few more seconds, then pulls at his collar as if adjusting it. Then he begins to speak again.

She had a heart attack. While we were having sex.

He says this with absolute gravity, as if he were a coroner delivering his report before the court. The effect is overwhelming, and horribly comic, coming from this sad, strange old man. Despite every effort I make to suppress it, I bark out a sudden, short, but obvious laugh.

Oh, God. I'm so sorry. I didn't mean . . .

Oh no, no. I suppose it is quite funny. Not a bad way to go, I should say.

Harry Butson seems unoffended. I regard him carefully. He remains centred, solid, unfragile, just as I remember him, despite his obvious physical decline. Yet I can see now that there is something

356

different about him. What Veronica would have called his aura, something in the lines of his face. Then I see suddenly what it is, and it is what I saw in my mother's face all those years ago, the same intensity, blindingly clear. *Loneliness*, like a cold blue light seeping out of his eyes, coming towards me like mustard gas. This makes me panic, makes me want to get out of the office even more. But now I feel duty-bound to continue. I am hooked into a situation that I have no place in, no responsibility for . . . And I also realize that this was his intent all along. To have a conversation. Any conversation. To stop him being alone, if only for a few minutes. My voice is softer when I speak again.

And you, Mr Butson. How are you then?

Oh, you know. I can't complain. Maud and I, we had some wonderful times. As most lives go, ours was . . . well, it would be hard to beat. Of course, I miss her. Every day, I do. Every single day. Like a bruise, it is, an awful bruise. He pauses and catches his breath. *But I get by. I get by. Life's still worth having, I should say. Of course, I'm alone a lot of the time. But you get used to it.*

Like you get used to the plague, I think to myself, then say, *You have kids, I suppose?* making my voice light, falsely optimistic.

Butson smiles.

Kids. Yes, they're fine. But they go their own way. Long gone now. About your age, they are. As a matter of fact you look a bit like my youngest. Peter. He's out in Saudi now. Don't see him much.

I feel the intimacy now like a sucking of air out of the room. I feel an urgent need to push the conversation along, get it out of the way.

But you must have friends? I say, pointedly putting away my papers, tidying up my desk, rattling the door keys softly.

Oh. Maud and I didn't have much time for that sort of thing. It was just me and her, and the family. You know, I wish now . . . of course . . .

Then he looks up at me beseechingly, and I suddenly know what he's going to say next, and I know for certain that he hasn't come in here to buy a flat at all, but because he recognized me all along, because he saw me as a potential *target*, an aspirin for his tremendous hurt.

Per . . . Perhaps we could go and have a drink sometime. I'm always passing this way.

His old watery eyes fix me with what I think for a moment is a stare of mad intensity. I suddenly see his desperation and am terrified by it. I realize now that I've seen him walk past the office on several occasions, presumably trying to work up the courage to come in. I take a deep breath. By now I feel genuinely sorry for him and I wish I could do something to repair his life, but I can't. My own life is trouble enough, scorched enough. And Butson, sitting there, suddenly seems like my future, or one of my futures, come to warn me, or mock me. In a faint panic now, I get up from my chair.

Well, Mr Butson, that's a very nice idea. But I'm afraid I'm extremely . . .

He blinks, holds his hand as if silencing me.

Of course, of course. I mean, it was just a thought.

Too quickly, he gets up and reaches over with an open palm. I take his hand and shake it. His hand is firm and dry. I can see the agony of this dignified, grave man, the shame he feels at being reduced to trawling for company like a rich man turned suddenly into a beggar. I am ashamed that I cannot – that I will not – help him. But he is a vortex into which I am not prepared to fall.

I'll let myself out. Good luck then, Frankie.

You too, Mr Butson.

Harry.

Harry.

And with that he is up from his chair, out of the door and gone into the late summer dusk. He leaves the catalogue behind him on the chair. I stare at it. His fingerprint still shows on the gloss.

And then, after sitting there not moving for about five minutes, I reach for my phone and begin to dial.

CHAPTER 17

WWJD?

It was Colin I called first. I've been worried about Colin. I know his mother is very ill because my mum told me. And if Olive Burden relies on Colin, it's impossible to guess how much Colin relies on her. What's more, I called him twice, left messages, but he didn't call me back. I couldn't believe that he had *that* much of the egg on. Up until the fight at the golf game he would always return my calls, gratefully, within minutes.

This morning he *did* finally call me, but something was wrong. It wasn't that he was still angry – quite the reverse. He seemed high, airy.

Hi, Frankie!

Colin. How are you, mate?

Fine. Fine.

Listen I'm sorry what I . . . I didn't mean to . . . at the golf course.

Forget it, Frankie. It doesn't matter. Really.

I felt a wash of relief.

No, Colin. I want to see you. To explain. That I never meant it.

The phone went quiet.

Colin? Are you still there?

Yes. Of course.

Have you seen Nodge? Or Tony?

No. *I've not seen much of anyone really.*

No one at all?

Not really. Just this other mate. You don't know him.

Good. Terrific, I sputtered, wanting to get past the small talk.

Silence again. I've met some of Colin's friends before. There's quite a high turnover. He has these little crushes. They're all nerds, losers, computer dinks. I'm hoping he's not going to try and introduce us. I've had enough conversations about gigabytes, ram and fuzzy logic to last me a lifetime already with Colin.

Listen. Can we meet? Just the two of us, I mean.

Yes, said Colin simply.

I took out my diary and began to check. The week was very full. I was still working myself half to death. Then I saw that I had a gap this morning, when I'd got to go and see the vicar of the Church of the Holy Innocents, where Veronica and I were going to get married. He had been pretty put out that we were cancelling at such late notice, and I'd made a note to go down and see him and give him a bung of some kind. For the church spire, or new cushions, or orphans, or a dozen angels, whatever the fuck they spend the cash on in churches. He was a nice bloke, and you don't want to get on the

361

wrong side of any of the prominent locals when you're an estate agent. So I'd pencilled him in between midday and one o'clock. It was only a quarter of a mile from Colin's place.

There's no way you can make today, is there?

Sure.

I've got to go and meet a vicar down by Ravenscourt Park. Twelve o'clock.

Yet another long pause.

A what?

A vicar. You know. The cunts with the dog collars. Hymnbooks, funerals, all that toss. Weddings.

Oh.

Shall I meet you then? In the park, say, quarter to twelve?

Great.

Later, Col.

Bye, Frankie.

That was three hours ago. So now I'm driving down the road at the perimeter of the park. I pull up the Beemer, park it and step out on to the pavement. In the distance, on a park bench, I can see Colin throwing breadcrumbs at the pigeons. He is alone.

It's a chilly day and the park is more or less empty. Colin cuts a solitary figure sitting there. He is dressed worse than ever – his clothes are dirty and unironed, and his hair is not combed. Although it is cold today, he is wearing only a thin, short-sleeved shirt. There is a shadow of stubble around his chin.

362

He sees me and his face lights up. He immediately gets up and moves towards me. To my amazement, he reaches his arms out and gives me an enormous hug. More. He kisses me on the cheek. Then he steps back and regards me as if I was fresh out of the packet. I feel the need to say something.

Hello, Colin. You look well made up. Won the lottery?

Still Colin doesn't say anything. He just nods his head. My sense of awkwardness grows and I reach out for some small talk.

What you been up to then?

Oh. This and that.

I sit down on the wooden bench, but Colin remains standing.

So you haven't seen Tony or Nodge?

Nah. Just this other bloke.

I'm already struggling for things to say. I vaguely sense that there is a new impenetrability about Colin and it makes me nervous. I find myself picking at a bit of old paint from the wood. It comes off in my hand and I start to tear it into small pieces.

That was a funny old do, wasn't it?

What?

The golf game.

I suppose it was, yeah.

This is getting a bit torturous. I'm beginning to regret phoning Colin in the first place.

How's your mum? All right, is she?

Colin's smile widens very slightly.

Fine.
Good.
Very well.
Excellent.
*Though . . . Not all **that** well, I suppose.*
No?
No.
He blinks at me. His eyes are slightly sunken. He looks much older than thirty, but then he has for the past five years.
Actually, they took her away.
Who took her away?
The hospital.
Why?
Because she went a bit funny.
Well, she's been a bit . . . you know . . . for a long time.
*No, but she **really** went . . . funny. Didn't know who I was any more. Didn't have the faintest idea.*
Oh.
And she started wetting herself and everything, and doing her, you know, stuff in the bed. Shit and that. Then she got violent.
Violent?
*She punched the social worker. Right in the face. She bit the postman's hand when he tried to get her signature for a letter. She even tried to attack **me**. With one of her knitting needles . . .*
He held his right arm up. There was a raw, freshly stitched scar there just above the elbow.
So they had to take her away.

364

Oh, I . . . that's —
I'm living by myself in the flat now.

I dry up. There is a very long silence. I become aware of the sounds of the park. Ducks are fighting at the pond. Children at the playground are screaming at each other. The thwack of tennis balls on the tarmac courts. The wind in my ears.

Do you go and see her?

Sometimes. But she just sits there, staring out of the window. Doesn't know me from Adam.

Will she . . . can she get better?

No. She'll be dead soon.

He says this in a tone no different from if he had been ordering a pint. Flat, polite. I feel a small shock inside me.

Colin, I'm so very sorry. I really . . . I wish you'd called me. I didn't know. I feel awful.

Colin shakes his head.

*It's OK, Frankie. I'm fine. It's been coming a long time. I think I needed to be alone anyway to sort myself out. I see things much more clearly now. You know, sometimes I think poor old Mum relied on me too much. I'm sure of it. I wonder if I didn't feel too sorry for her sometimes. Or if somehow she . . . she made **sure** I felt sorry. Do you get what I mean?*

Fucking A, Col, I think, but I say gravely, *Yes. I know. I know exactly what you mean. Poor old Olive, though. Was it . . . is she in pain?*

For a moment he looks sad, before his face recomposes into a mask of rigid tranquillity.

Oh yes. A great deal, I think. She's scared. Terri-fied. I told her there was no need to be. But it went in one ear and out the other.

I nod and wring my hands. I want to throw my arms round Colin, but something is stopping me. It's the same thing that stops silences, that makes us compete, that causes us to punish each other instead of comfort each other. I can think of very little that I'm prepared to say. The wind is making Colin's unwashed hair stand on end, so he looks even more eccentric. A tiny, carefully polished QPR enamel badge sits on the lapel of his dirty shirt. I notice that next to it he is wearing another, slightly larger badge with the inscription 'WWJD?'.

What's that stand for?

Nothing. It's a kind of joke.

Oh. Pretty funny. You seem OK, though, I lied.

I'm fine. In a strange kind of way, I've never been better.

Well, it's an ill wind . . .

That's true.

A stray dog runs up to us and jumps at Colin's leg. Colin has always been nervous of dogs and this is a big one, some kind of Alsatian crossbreed. But he just leans over and pats it on the head.

Good boy.

I look at my watch. I'm going to be late for the vicar.

Colin, I have to go to the church and see the vicar. It's about the wedding.

Oh.

366

Why don't you walk along with me?
If you like.
Colin leaves the dog alone and begins walking towards the exit of the park. I fall in behind him. His pace is steady, slow. As he walks, he suddenly begins to talk in a low monotone, like he was hypnotized. He does not look at me.

You know, you've always been a good friend to me, Frankie. I know you don't think you have but you have. Of course it's been annoying for me. That you've always been stronger, more successful and so on. It's kind of humiliating in a way. I suppose it's been a bit like . . . drug addiction. Something you need but . . . hate at the same time.

He stops walking, looks up at me. I stop too.

But it's not your fault, Frankie. Although you must have got something out of it, I suppose. A feeling of power? I suppose there must have been an element of that. I don't think you see me as a friend really. More a disciple, or maybe a pet. Yes, that's it. A pet. Loyal little Colin. Woof woof. Woof woof.

He's really starting to bark like a dog now, and laughing at the same time. I start to protest, but Colin holds his hand up to stop me. He has begun walking again and I'm following half a pace behind. His voice has gone flat.

*It doesn't **matter**. It doesn't matter whether you agree or not. Not any more. Our relationship is different now. I see things more clearly, since they took Mum away. And before that, the thing at the golf course. That was weird – all your friends disappearing*

367

in one go, in an instant. It's so strange – like you've been walking around with big black sunglasses on, so you can only see the shapes or shadows of things, but not the detail. Mum going, you all going, was like me taking the sunglasses off. I saw that you looked down on me. I saw that you thought you were better than me. I saw that you pitied me, and that that was a kind of . . . contempt.

*This is **crap**, Colin. You don't know what you're –*

*But I don't **mind**, he says brightly. It's OK. Really it is. Is this the place?*

We're standing at the big gates to an Anglican church which abuts the park. There is a board outside with its name – the Church of the Holy Innocents. Above this a mosaic in gold, blue and green showing a dove and what are presumably saints. The door is half open, and Colin begins to walk through. Above the interior entrance, two baby angels stick out, as if escaping from the woodwork.

What's the difference between a cherub and a seraph? says Colin.

I think I've heard this one, I say.

*No. It's not a **joke**. I just wanted to know.*

I nod, staring into the musty interior of the church. These places always depress me, with their air of lost, closed-in, finishing lives. I look in the vicar's office. No one there. Then a little bun-haired secretary peers out.

I'm sorry. Mr Blue?

Yes.

The Reverend had to pop out on an emergency for

ten minutes. He'll be right back. Would you mind waiting?

No. Fine, I mutter, annoyed.

What kind of emergency? What kind of emergency could a vicar possibly have, other than the big JC making a comeback? I just want to give the cunt some money.

Colin has already gone into the church proper and I follow him, my voice already echoing around the high stone walls. We walk further into the church. I idly pick up the parish magazine and read the doggerel on the back cover:

> *'Circle me Lord,*
> *keep protection near*
> *and danger afar.*
>
> *Circle me Lord,*
> *keep hope within*
> *keep doubt without.*
>
> *Circle me Lord,*
> *keep light near*
> *and darkness far.'*

I sling the pamphlet at Colin.

Fucking profound that, eh, Col?

Colin tries to catch it, but drops it.

Inside, the church appears deserted. There's an altar table with candles, a nave, parallel benches. It has that eerie, dead feeling that most churches have, at least the ones in Shepherd's Bush. The sun

369

has come out now and speckles of coloured light are forcing their way through the dirty windows. Some of it falls on to Colin's face, making him appear a kind of ghostly yellow.

There's the usual church stuff – an altar, stained glass showing incomprehensible scenes from the Bible, uncomfortable seats. A small blue poster announces that £238.70 has been raised for the daffodil campaign. Terrific. There's a picture of an old bloke in a caftan of some sort. I read the inscription underneath: 'St Matthew. Patron Saint of Tax Collectors, Accountants and Security Guards'. I wonder if this is a joke, but decide that it can't be, because it's in proper golden italic script.

I'm still feeling irritated by Colin's speech, most particularly because I know it's more than partly true. About my disdain for him. I want to get away now.

I look for Colin and see that he has a match out and is lighting a votive candle, presumably for poor old Olive. I inspect the cushions on the long wooden benches. They are embroidered with slogans about peace and pictures of angels with harps, lutes and flutes. I notice the one nearest me.

Fuck me. There's a sheep with wings and a halo on this one.

It's the holy lamb of god, Frankie, says Colin quietly.

Oh. Right, I grunt impatiently, then wait for something else to happen.

I'm beginning to hope that the vicar will arrive soon. Anyone's better company than this.

Would you like to meet my new mate? says Colin.

Sure. Next week maybe, I say, not meaning it.

What about now? says Colin.

His face is still caught in the light. He turns and takes a step towards me. That faint smile is back again, as if he's in on a private joke.

Now?

Yes.

What are you talking about? Is he here?

Of course he's here. He's everywhere. My new friend is Jesus.

I start to laugh, then stop dead when I look at Colin's face. There is a horrible expression of rapture, of phoney contentment. I've seen it a dozen times when I've accidentally switched on *Songs of Praise,* watching amazed at the poor, dumb faces grinning absurdly, self-consciously, for the camera. Colin has that exact same expression, a dreadful mixture of piety, self-satisfaction and fear.

You are taking the piss, I hope, I say desperately.

Colin nods, acknowledging that this is exactly the reaction he has expected.

*I know it's hard for you to understand. But you don't know what it means to have a friend like Him. It's like every day, someone you can rely on absolutely. Someone you can tell all your troubles to, someone who is always there for you. Someone who loves you. It's a wonderful thing, Frankie. I know it's going to be difficult for you to accept. I know it must be strange. But I **know** it's the truth, I know God is guiding me. I know even more now, after you phoned and said*

371

you wanted to meet at the church. What else could **that** *mean? The church, Frankie, the church. Are you saying that's . . . what? A* **coincidence?**

I stand gawping at him. Colin is sat in one of the pews now, looking towards me, but not quite at me. Pointlessly, I answer him.

Sure. A coincidence. Why not?

But he's still talking in this stupid, dim monotone, ignoring me.

You know, Frankie, I've always felt . . . unhappy. Shy, I suppose. A misfit. I've never been able to tell you that. That's the sort of stuff you can't talk to your friends about. Anything real, I mean. That's why I didn't call anybody after Mum got taken away from me. Because I know it would just have embarrassed you. It's not part of the game, is it? It's not something you can have a beer over. Mum dying, slowly, going mad, losing everything. Your so-called friends are nowhere to be seen. And even if you had been there, you'd have just talked about the football results, or the latest gash, and how many orgasms you'd given them.

I shuddered. The church was cold. All churches are cold, all year round. I wondered, stupidly, if they had air conditioning. I could still hear Colin talking. His voice was no longer flat but lilting now, suddenly as light as a chemical air freshener.

But it's OK. I love you all – Nodge, Tony, even you. I love you all, because someone loves me for the first time. And that makes it easy.

I suddenly feel I'm in the middle of Colin's favourite film, *Invasion of the Body Snatchers*. As if one of my closest friends has been taken over by aliens, as if he simply appears to be the same person.

And lo, I say, you shall be changed in the twinkling of an eye.

Colin is looking at the stained-glass windows in what I take to be an attempt to mimic awe and wonder. I suddenly feel sick – sick with shame, sick with having let Colin down, sick with the sight of his Pope-with-acne-scars act. I feel the church walls are closing in, that the high windows are sickening the light, that I have to get out of there as quickly as I can.

I turn to Colin. I'm still trying to believe that this is a joke, that he hasn't gone completely radio rental. I stare at Colin, noticing his little badge again. He doesn't seem to be aware of me. I suddenly remember what that badge he's wearing, 'WWJD?', means. I saw it in a feature in a magazine about American evangelists.

It stands for 'What Would Jesus Do?' Somehow, this brings it home to me at last that this is absolutely not a wind-up, not a sick schoolboy joke. With that realization, it is as if I can feel all air leave me, so I am small, deflated. I sit down next to Colin, pat him gently on the back.

Colin, if this is what you want, I'm . . . I've . . . I'm very happy for you.

Colin, to my shock and surprise, turns fiercely to me.

Your sins catch up with you. Do you know that?

Your cheating and lies, your indifference, your selfishness, your hatred of women, your love of money. I'm saying this to you because I'm your friend, Frankie. He seizes my hand. *The world is rotten. We're all just filth.*

I try to pull my hand away but he's holding it too tight.

I hope you'll be able to come towards the light one day, Frankie. I don't want your sins to condemn you. I want you to be able to share this with me.

I nod.

Terrific, yeah, Colin. Maybe. We'll talk about it. Jesus and that. I can see what you're saying. It's not really my . . . But you know. Whatever gets you through the night. We'll have to have that beer, eh? Soon.

Colin suddenly lets go of my hand, looks back at me dolefully, as if I were an errant schoolboy and he a wise and knowing headmaster. He doesn't speak though. I keep gabbling.

Look, mind how you go. I'll give you a call, eh? This is great, Colin. I'm very happy for you, though. Later, eh? Later.

But of course there will be no later, I think to myself as the daylight hits me from the portico of the church. Now I know I've lost Colin more completely than I ever could have before. Beyond argument, beyond apology, beyond a couple of beers. I practically run back to my car, the sound of insane seagulls screeching in my ears.

CHAPTER 18

DIAMOND GEEZERS

I've just turned up at Tony's shop in North Kensington. It's a men's haircutters called Diamond Geezers. He's got another one, for women, in Islington called Girls Best Friend – as in Diamonds Are A.

Me and Tony have *got* to make it up, because I don't hold out much hope for Nodge. Tony's well known as an arsehole, but he's a good guy underneath. He's just a wind-up merchant. If he wasn't OK, why would we have stayed friends this long?

I have rarely visited either of Tony's shops. He likes to fence off areas of his life – work, women, friends, family. They're all compartmentalized, carefully sectioned. It enables him to keep control, I suppose. I don't think he'll much like me turning up unannounced, but I don't want to phone him in case he simply hangs up on me. It's been known.

It's Friday afternoon. The shop looks good – a mosaic floor with an arrangement of glass tiles in the middle depicting a giant diamond, original

Belmont Apollo chairs, with the black leather trim and polished chrome tail end. A few paintings by local artists, some good, most not. And a lot of mirrors, even for a hairdresser's. Tony has loved mirrors ever since he was a teenager. He used to keep a mirror compact in his back pocket at school, which would have had the rest of the kids taking the mick out of him, had they not been scared of him.

There are four cutters in the room, all male, all white. A young, shy Mediterranean looking girl is sweeping the floor vigorously. Behind the cash till, there is a large, studio-shot, extremely flattering picture of Tony. On a pinboard nearby, there are informal snapshots of him with minor celebs at anonymous parties – B-list singers, up-and-coming actors, fly-on-the-wall documentary makers.

One of the cutters – a rather overweight and surly-looking man wearing a white T-shirt with the word FUCT printed on it – ambles over to me. The shop is empty of customers, despite the fact that Tony always used tell me how you had to book a week in advance to get an appointment. I feel my wallet bulked in my pocket and wonder if maybe the competition from Tony wasn't actually nearly as tough as I'd always imagined it to be.

The fat man musters a professional smile and a rather curt *Yeah?*

He looks at me like he was doing me a big favour being prepared to cut my hair. No wonder the shop is deserted. I attempt a return smile, equally fake.

Is Tony here?

Who?

Tony. Diamond Tony.

Oh. Did you want an appointment?

He's moving his frame slowly to the loud beat of some anonymously horrible Speed Garage record. His whole demeanour is one of boredom. I answer patiently, as if speaking to a moron.

No, I don't want an appointment. I've come to see Tony. He's a personal friend of mine.

Mmm-hmmm. Tony has a lot of friends.

Apparently, I say, looking around the empty shop. The music is giving me a headache. *Is it all right if I wait?*

The man shrugs. The little Mediterranean girls shuffles past his planted feet, but he doesn't move to accommodate her. She seems flushed and bothered and obscurely worried. The noise from the sound system suddenly rises another few notches.

Mind if I wait somewhere a bit quieter?

The fat man looks surprised, but squints at me with studied indifference.

You're a mate of his then?

That's right. Frankie Blue.

Frankie Blue.

The man looks puzzled, then his face lights up slightly. He shouts across to another of the cutters, who is sitting with his head back in one of the chairs, eyes closed, nodding to the music.

Hey, Donny! Guess who this is.

The man called Donny turns round slowly in the swivelling chair and opens his eyes very gradually. He raises an eyebrow.

This is Frank the Fib! I am right, aren't I? Frankie Blue. Frank the Fib.

Donny nods slightly and raises a hand in acknowledgement, then closes his eyes again and resumes the slow movement of his body.

So, says the fat man, scrutinizing me in a new, not altogether pleasant fashion, *you're Frank the Fib. Tony's told us all about you.*

Only nice stuff, I hope.

The man doesn't respond at all. Instead he indicates a small single door to the rear of the shop.

You can wait in the staff room if you like. There's a TV in there. Tony should be here any time now. He's usually late, though. I expect you know that.

Yeah, I know that.

I walk through a small anteroom where there's a sink and a tiny cupboard with a toilet in it, then through to a room about 10 by 10 covered in large floor cushions. There's damp pushing up from the bottoms of the walls. On the back wall, there's an emergency fire exit with a push bar. Against one wall, there's a desk and a chair. The desk is covered with a mess of papers.

I sit down and try to watch TV for a while, but it's the usual daytime cack. After a while, I check my watch. I've been here twenty minutes. No one has offered me a coffee, no one has come into the room. I switch the TV off. The hideous beat is still penetrating through from the front of the shop. I can see that the shop is still empty.

I wander over to the desk and begin fiddling with the papers, just for something to do. There are brochures for hair products, a page-a-day diary, a copy of *FHM*, a few utility bills. There's a small hand-mirror. I notice a few grains of white powder on it. I rub the powder on to my fingers, then my fingers on to my gums. After a few minutes they begin to go numb.

There's a half-drunk cup of coffee, three pens, Post-it notes, a full packet of cigarettes and an empty ashtray, a few letters. One is from a local pizza delivery firm, another a flyer from someone who calls himself the Loft Ladder King.

I have always had a weakness for snooping. Doubtless it's one of the reasons I ended up as an estate agent, spending my working life digging around in other people's homes and lives. I've lost about three girlfriends so far by reading their diaries. Believe me, I don't recommend it. The things they write are *terrible*. Like I say, the truth is overrated.

Bored with the surface of the desk, I start to idly pull at the drawers. Mostly they are full of junk – Sellotape, loose paper, drawing pins – but the bottom one has a lock on it. I pull on it. To my surprise, it opens. Inside, there are two plain buff envelopes.

I glance through to the shop. Now one of the cutters is actually cutting hair, though I notice that it is actually the hair of another stylist, the fat man with the FUCT T-shirt. The girl, amazingly, is still sweeping the floor. She must have been at it for nearly three-quarters of an hour.

I take out one of the envelopes. Inside, there is a small plastic bag filled with what looks like about a heaped tablespoon of rocky yellowy-white powder. I pull open the bag and again touch a dusting of powder to my gums. Sure enough, it's coke – about five grand's worth, I would guess. I hurriedly put it back in the envelope, trying to arrange it as carefully as I can to be where it was before.

I look in the other envelope. It is simply a letter, clearly an official one. I think for a moment that it is a parking ticket, but then I see that the headed notepaper is from a County Court. Then I read the first line of the text.

INSOLVENCY PROCEEDINGS IN THE CASE OF ANTHONY DIAMONTE, TRADING AS DIAMOND GEEZERS, AND ANTHONY DIAMONTE LTD, TRADING AS GIRLS BEST FRIEND.

CASE SET FOR 17 SEPTEMBER 1998

Suddenly I hear the music cut off and a voice boom out from the shop. Panicking, I shove the letter back in the envelope, the envelope back in the drawer, and close it. The voice is bellowing. I recognize it now as Tony's. I peer through into the shop. Tony, at his full height, is standing above

380

the shop junior, the little Mediterranean girl, who is gripping her broom so tight the knuckles show white. She is about fifteen. She is clearly terrified.

*You're FUCKING USELESS. Do me a favour next time. DON'T TRY AND THINK. Just do what you're fucking well told. If I ask you to get some **Paul Mitchell** Aloe and the supplies shop haven't got any, then FUCKING come and tell someone who's got a brain. What the fuck am I going to do with twenty-five bottles of FUCKING Acme ALOE SHIT from the fucking Paki shop. And I need Paul Mitchell stuff NOW, not in ten minutes, not in half an hour. NOW. Now fuck off back to the Handy Gandhi, and get them to give you your money back, not that they **will**, since they are fucking **Pakis**. Not a fucking credit note, the MONEY. And if they won't, it can come out of your fucking wages, you useless little Dago cunt.*

The girl has started to cry.

And don't start with the fucking waterworks. If you don't want this job, I know about fifty people who do. Now get out of here.

The girl picks up the box of shampoo bottles and staggers towards the door, still weeping. Tony shakes his head as if in disgust. Then snorts loudly, several times, a noise I know well. I can see his nostrils red and inflamed. It's no excuse.

I see his face from this hiding place, clearly, as if for the first time. I see that it is, in fact, not good-looking at all. It is violent, and ugly and stupid. I see that Tony is not a wind-up merchant, an expert at irony, the player of a game. Tony is nothing, a vacuum that has acquired a series of useful gestures.

I turn away from the doorway and move back into the room. Stepping over the cushions, I hit the push bar on the emergency exit and go out into the street, where it is warm and still. A drunk wrapped in filthy rags sitting on the pavement lets out an enormous belch, then looks up at me and says, with perfect poise and politeness, *I **do** beg your pardon.*

CHAPTER 19

TAXI DRIVER

Only the other evening, I picked up Bertrand Russell and I said to him, 'Well, Lord Russell, what's it all about?' And do you know, he couldn't tell me.

TAXI DRIVER TO T. S. ELIOT

I'm heading over to Nodge's flat. If I phone, he *definitely* won't speak to me. And Nodge is my last chance of taking something away from this mess.

I've got a vague memory that he starts his taxi run out of Shepherd's Bush at about ten a.m. It's nine-thirty now, so I should be able to catch him. I'm walking along the Goldhawk Road, trying to steel myself. The fumes from the traffic smell like cigarette ash, sulphur, used fireworks.

Then I see coming towards me a black cab with the light on. It's one of those new, fancy ones. It has been painted with an ad for Neutrogena. I can just make out Nodge's face behind the windscreen. He's travelling fast, beyond the speed limit. It's a shock to see him there. Oddly enough, I've hardly ever seen him in his cab. Off duty he always drives a Ford Escort. The cab changes his context, makes him seem smaller, sadder.

I put two fingers in my mouth and give a loud whistle. At first I think he's going to drive past, but he pulls over from the central stream of traffic and comes to a halt just in front of me. His light switches off. I walk up to the open front window. When he looks up, from his startled expression it was clear that he didn't see my face. He doesn't say anything. Neither do I. Then he turns and switches his light back on, and goes to drive off.

Nodge!

His hand hovers over the gear stick. When he speaks, it is very quietly and coldly.

I've got to get over to the West End. I'm on a radio call. You want a ride, take a bus.

But he doesn't move his hand to meet the gear stick.

Mind if I ride with you? I've got to go over there myself to see a property. It's near Centre Point.

This is a lie and Nodge knows it. Still he doesn't move, so I go to open the front door.

Can't travel up front. I'm not insured for it, he says in the icy tone. Still he doesn't look at me.

Fine. I'll just be a punter.

I reach for the back door, but I hear a click as I touch the handle. It's just been locked.

Come on, Nodge. Please.

Nodge sighs for a long moment. The moment hangs. Then he makes to drive off.

I'm just a fare. You don't have to switch on the intercom if you don't want to talk to me. Anyway, if you turn me down, I'll report you to the Hackney Carriage office. I know the form. You can't refuse a legitimate fare. You could have your licence revoked.

Nodge shakes his head, apparently with a mixture of disgust and resignation. Then there is a soft clunk as the door unbolts. I reach out and open the door and climb inside. There is a sign saying, 'Thank you for not smoking' and a small green fir tree air freshener. In the front, three empty packets of Craven A.

The cab pulls out into traffic. The atmosphere is freezing.

I shout into the intercom, *Tottenham Court Road station please.*

There's the faintest of nods but no reply.

I shout again, *Did you ever see that cartoon in Private Eye? The back of a taxi cab. It shows the driver turned round, giving it some mouth. And there's a sign up in the back saying. 'Thank you for not disagreeing.'*

Again Nodge shows no sign whatsoever of having heard me. I notice that the meter is running. Nodge is sitting firmly facing the traffic. All I can see are his eyes in the mirror which seem to hardly blink. I notice their colour, a solid chocolate brown. Oddly, I don't think I could have told you what colour his eyes were until this moment.

I lean over to open the glass panel that separates us, but it won't budge. I knock on the glass with the tip of my door key. At first he ignores me, but eventually I make the noise irritating enough for him to have to respond.

I hear an intercom crackle.

It's staying locked. I can hear you through the intercom if you've got something to say.

Nodge is still looking right ahead at the road as he talks. He is driving fast. He's already made Lancaster Gate in five minutes flat. I estimate that I've got about fifteen minutes to salvage something from this.

I try to look and see where the intercom pick-up is so that I can make sure Nodge hears me, but can't see anything. So I speak as loudly and plainly as I can over the engine noise.

Do you remember that chase we had with the taxis? The first 14 August. Back in '84.

No answer.

*Weird that you should end up being a taxi driver. I would never have believed what happened to us all. I mean, me, an estate agent. I never **wanted** to be an estate agent. Yeah, 14 August 1984. Now that was a time, eh? That was a year.*

Nodge says something, barely above a mumble. It comes out in a distorted, solemn crackle. It takes me a moment to work out what the two words are.

Things change.

We cut in front of a silver Merc. The driver screams at us and shakes his fist. Nodge doesn't respond. He keeps a steady pace. The meter ticks. I take a gulp of air, feel increasingly nervous.

Wisely and slow. They stumble that run fast.

I have no idea where that came from. Nodge seems to tighten in his seat slightly.

I give a shit-eating grin and shout, *It's from* Romeo and Juliet.

I realize immediately that this is the wrong thing to say. Nodge will take it as intellectual one-upmanship. The grin on my face seems cemented there. I see Nodge's eyes blazing in the mirror. Then I hear his voice, loud and clear now.

*Shakespeare, eh? Here's a bit of Shakespeare for you then, Frankie. Hamlet, Act IV, Scene I. 'A man may smile and smile and be a **cunt**.'* Now he turns in his seat, his face a stiff mask. *I'm paraphrasing slightly, of course.*

I see him reaching to switch off the intercom. I answer back quickly, before his finger makes contact with the button.

Was it true what you said at the golf game?

I watch the back of Nodge's head, which doesn't move at all.

About being, you know. Gay.

I wonder after a while if the intercom somehow has been switched off, then I see him give a single but distinct nod. Although I know that this is the truth, even before I ask, I still feel vaguely shocked. I've got nothing against fruits, mind you. It's none of my business where you put your todger. I just never thought Nodge . . .

I stare intently at the back of his head as if I could, by concentrating, penetrate his thoughts. It's Nodge who speaks first.

*Was it true what **you** said?*

What?

About you and Veronica splitting up.

Yeah.

You're an idiot. She was great.

Yeah, I know.

But I'm not really listening. I'm rerunning Nodge's single nod, the amazing affirmation of the answer to my question, over and over in my mind.

Why didn't you say anything before? About being. You know.

He turns a corner round the back of the Bayswater Road, where he has navigated to avoid traffic. The taxi straightens up and I hear him say bitterly, *A poo-jabber? A fairy?*

*Yes. **No**. About being homosexual.*

The word sounds all wrong, too clinical, like I was a social worker or a slightly embarrassed policeman. I hear Nodge talking again.

I'm the same as you, Frankie. I just want to fit in. Be liked.

His voice through the intercom sounds thin, robotic. Despite the volume of the thing, I have to strain to hear him.

Suddenly, he makes a sharp left turn that slams me against the side of the cab.

Hoi! Careful.

He doesn't acknowledge me. Then he starts speaking again.

Also, it's against the rules. There's rules, aren't there? Big boys' rules.

I straighten myself up in my seat and wonder whether I should strap myself in.

But, Nodge. I always thought you of all people believed in telling the truth. It's what you always said anyway . . .

Nodge throws us around another corner, this time in the opposite direction. Again, I go tumbling, this time catching my head on the empty ashtray that someone has left open on one of the doors. I think it has actually cut me, but I hardly notice the pain.

What you say and what you think are different things. You should know that, Frankie.

There is silence for a while. I feel a thin trickle of blood coming down the side of my face. We are heading down beyond the perimeter of Hyde Park now, running parallel to Oxford Street. I can see to the right Marble Arch blocked in by a sea of grunting, panting traffic. Nodge starts speaking again. I look in his rear-view mirror. This time, I notice that his eyes are almost, not quite, looking at me. It's as if he's trying, but he just can't do it. Anyway, I can see now that instead of angry he seems misted up, far away.

*Anyway, it would have meant the end of everything. It **did** mean the end of everything. You, me, Colin, Tony, 14 August, everything. And pink ain't the Rangers colours. No. I couldn't tell anyone. Particularly not **you**.*

Why particularly not me?

Taking another tiny back street to avoid the crush, Nodge throws the cab to the left, with even greater violence than before. This time, I hold on tight to the handle. I feel gravity pulling at me like a flying fist. Nodge is talking again. Static interferes with his voice, but I can make out, too clearly, what he is saying.

*You know when you slept with Ruth? She told me right away, you know. That's why we split up. It wasn't me that was dumped. I dumped **her**. I was so hurt. Frankie, you wouldn't believe it. I trusted you. To do that to a friend.*

I feel a gobbet of shame, as real and actual as an ulcer, gather acidically in my stomach. I can't think what to say. Lies are so fine, so lovely and harmless, until you get caught out. Then they transform into tiny, vicious, vengeful dragons.

Nodge continues in the same brittle voice.

*But it's not quite what you think it was. You see, it wasn't that I was angry with you for sleeping with **Ruth**. Ruth and I were only ever friends, although she wanted much more. I couldn't blame her really. Our sex life was pretty disastrous. I was just impressed by how grown up she seemed. I loved her sense of . . . certainty. And I've always been so uncertain, Frankie.*

I feel myself blink. There is blood in my eye. I've found the intercom now and speak right into it, but in a low, sorry voice.

But I thought you . . . of all of us, you seemed to

*know exactly what you thought . . . I wanted to **be**
like that . . .*

I don't think the mike picks it up, though, because
Nodge simply continues with hardly a pause.

*But the thing is, I was angry with Ruth for sleeping
with you. Do you see what I'm getting at, Frankie?*

I look in the mirror. For the first time, the
reflected chocolate brown eyes are looking right
at the reflection of my eyes. We hold our one-step-
removed gazes. I shake my head, bewildered.

*I wasn't jealous for Ruth. I was jealous for **you**.
I've wanted to . . . be more than your friend, ever
since that night at your house. You remember. The
Morning Glory.*

A large articulated lorry sounds an ear-splitting
horn, then passes by. Nodge is saying, almost
desperately, *Say you remember, Frankie.*

It begins to dawn on me what Nodge is trying to
say. Now I feel the sting of the cut on my forehead.
There is a little bloodstain on my chest where it has
dripped. Nodge's eyes now seem to be desperate,
pleading.

I remember, I barely whisper.

Nodge nods.

*And that's the way it's been. You think we've been
close. We've always been close. But I've been much
closer than you think.*

We are moving down past Great Portland Street
now and join a short jam of traffic before the stop
light. The halting of the cab draws everything in,
makes it more intimate, like being trapped in a lift.

But I know that that night didn't mean to you what it meant to me. Did it, Frankie? Did it?

He has actually turned to me now. I can hardly bear the look of faint, fading hope in his eyes. I suddenly recognize that look, recognize that it has always been there. Something in me hardens, toughens. When I speak, my voice is firm and decisive.

No, Nodge. It didn't. I remember it, but it wasn't for me. I don't . . . I'm not like that. It's cool. But it's not me. That was just a kids' game to me. You understand what I'm saying?

Nodge is nodding, fiercely. I catch his eye again. The glimmer has gone. His eyes look flat, unreflective. I look up and see that we're at Tottenham Court Road station. Centre Point looms above us. Suddenly he pulls the cab over, with the roar of New Oxford Street traffic outside.

We're here. That'll be nine pounds fifty, he says briskly.

I don't move. Neither does Nodge. Then he turns round and there is a click. He pulls the glass screen back. His face is framed in the window, round, older than I thought it was. He looks at me for a moment, searches my face, then smiles, a kind, open smile that I remember so clearly from all those days at school, a smile I thought he had lost altogether.

Then he says softly, *Still friends, Frankie?*

I smile back and reach to open the door of the cab. *Still friends, Jon.*

I get out and stand next to the now open window

392

of the front door. He puts his hand through the window and I hold it, first with one hand, then with both of them. We stay like that for what seems a long time. Then Nodge lets go, pulls back and rearranges himself briskly behind the wheel. I automatically reach for my wallet.

This one's on me, he says.

Not hearing him through the intercom makes his voice sound very different. It's richer, fuller. It's like hearing the real Nodge, for the first time.

Thanks, I say.

There is a long pause.

You going to the game on Saturday? he says.

I don't know.

I scratch my birthmark, feel its slight contour.

I've got a spare ticket anyway, if you want to . . .

I smile.

Great. Come on you Rs, eh?

Yeah. Superhoooops.

A mobile cement mixer has pulled up opposite us and traffic has slowed to one stream. Now Nodge's cab is blocking the road. The car behind us is honking loudly. Nodge turns around and out of his window.

All right, for Christ's sake! Give me a moment! He turns back to me, and goes to switch his yellow light on. *Mind how you go, Frankie.*

*Mind how **you** go, Jon.*

Nodge drives off into the almost stationary traffic, his yellow light gleaming in the half-darkness of the overcast day.

393

CHAPTER 20

FRANKIE'S NEW GAME:
14 AUGUST 1999

I'm sitting, alone, naked, on my bed. It is seven a.m. I am staring at the backs of my hands. I can see the blue of the veins like still snakes beneath the skin. There are nests of wrinkles and whorls.

Outside my window, the sky is absolutely blue, fading at the horizon to milk, and the street is quiet apart from the soft buzz of a single, bothering wasp. I put a hand up and feel the friction of stubble on my face.

I rise and walk to the mirror. It is freestanding, full-length, placed so that the daylight is behind it. I find this the most flattering. Sometimes I will tour every mirror in the house until I find the one that gives the best impression.

I stretch myself and stare at my reflection. My body is still good, compact, a V tapering from shoulders to waist, but around my hips there are the beginnings of small pads of fat. There is the start of a varicose vein knotting at the back of one of my calf muscles.

My uncircumcised cock hangs in front of a medium-sized pair of balls. It seems self-pitying, grief-stricken.

A bush of pale hair shoots out from the stem of the cock like a small, harmless explosion. My legs fork out at either side, stocky, a little too stout. I balance on the arch of my feet, shift the weight about so that I sway slightly, as if propelled by the breeze.

A packet of muscle, fat, bone, water, memory, shit, hair, feeling, loss, rage, hope. Sometimes I think I'm Superman, sometimes I think I'm nothing. But I'm neither. I'm just a bloke, among millions of other blokes. Not more, not less.

I'm stupid, I'm clever, I try, I fail, I succeed, I stumble, I'm pushed and teased by luck. I'm meat, I'm a ghost.

I stare and stare. My face stares back. Watery eyes, blue on the outside, flecked with a halo of broken brown on the inside. Pale skin inter-rupted by tiny rogue blood vessels, filament fine. Nose slightly skewed to the right, a small mole rising on the bridge. Full lips, the mouth a little too narrow. Heavy lids. I look tired. My hair, just cut, stands on end like a coxcomb. Terrifyingly, from my ears, more new and tiny tufts of wild bristle that make me think of my father.

Will I be the same person after today? Are you ever the same person after today? I'm scared. The future scares me. The past is so much safer, worn

out though it is. I wish I could stay there. I can't.
I mustn't.

Strange thoughts. I walk over to the CD tower
and put one on. Something old, reassuring – Tom
Waits's *Frank's Wild Years*. It's melancholy. His
voice is like a struggling earth mover.

One by one, I lay out my clothes. Everything
is brand new. This is about rebirth, like all true
ceremonies. To be reborn you have to die.

A wedding is also a funeral.

The last part of me that is hanging on will go today.
If I have the courage to finish what I have begun.
After all, it's not too late. All I have to do is pick
up the phone. The thing could be done in a matter
of seconds. Of course, it would be embarrassing and
awkward. A lot of people would be disappointed. My
mother, it would break her heart.

But it will sink into nothing in months and years.
Everything fades to nothing in time.

I move towards the telephone, but do not
pick it up. Film/life. Right answer/true answer.
Past/future. All these choices. I wish there weren't
all these choices. Life would be so much easier if
everything just happened. Perhaps it does, more or
less. The wind of circumstance so strong against
the flickering of your will.

A car drives past, the stereo blasting, some anonymous contemporary soul about love and strength
and sexual conquest. I wait until it passes. I stare
at my clothes on the bed. They are all wrapped in
dry-cleaner's plastic, or shop packets, and a slight

breeze makes the cellophane crackle. Tom Waits's moan is audible in the room once more.

Left to right. One pair of Calvin Klein briefs, charcoal grey, thirty-inch waist. They're one size too small, but I can't bring myself to face the fact that I've expanded a couple of inches. One Giorgio Armani white poplin shirt, double fronted, sharp, stiff collar, single pocket. Brand new black Gucci shoes. Plain black Muji socks.

The suit. Off the peg from Prada. Single-breasted, three-button, narrow-cut, black cashmere, high-waisted, zip fly, no turn-ups, single vent at the back. Secured at the waist with a Mulberry crocodile-skin belt. A single white carnation in a vase stands by the bedroom table ready for cutting, to wear in the lapel. A plain, shot silk dark green tie, the only touch of colour.

The wedding is at midday. I have a sudden picture of the person I am marrying turning in small circles, like a figure in a musical box, in white in front of the mirror. I wonder what it is they are thinking. I wonder if they have doubts. I wonder what they will be wearing under the dress. I think of crimson, moistened lips under the cool white material.

I move to the bathroom, where I draw a bath, hot to the point of pain. The room fills with steam until the mirrors are misted and the furniture is a blur through fog. Then I sink into the bath, wincing as the sharp heat gnaws at me. I sit absolutely motionless for a long time. The phone rings once, twice, but I do not go to answer it.

I fill my palm with shaving gel the colour of emeralds, spread it on to my face and adjust my face in front of the mirror. I've put too much on. Gobbets fall from my chin into the bath. Gradually I whittle away at the foam with my razor until my face is clean. There is a small nick showing blood on the left side of my neck. Tiny bubbles adhere to the side of the bath. The plughole is distorted and enlarged by the lens of the water.

I leave the bath, dry myself and put a scrap of toilet tissue on the cut. I take a deep breath, then go into the bedroom and dress. The cashmere of the suit feels like perfect felt, contrasts with the collar of the shirt, which is stiff and constricting.

Fully dressed now, I inspect myself. I look grave, composed rather than handsome. I am falling into the film of my life again, that same sense of absence, of disinterested amazement. Everything slowed up and deliberate. An exaggerated pulse of calm beats through the room.

I am not sure what to do next. I walk around the room as if testing myself for presence. I feel my own weight pushing down from my shoulders.

I stop at the wall where my friends are displayed. They stare down at me, most of them smiling for the camera. Lost smiles from my past.

A photograph catches my eye. It is a paddling pool. Me, Colin, Tony and Nodge naked, grinning at the automatic camera. We are all slightly out of focus, as if the subjects of an Impressionist painting. Only the pool in the foreground has developed clear and sharp, sun spots decorating the surface. We are so young.

We all have our arms around each other and are swaying slightly off balance. We are all holding up beer cans. You can even see the label – Hofmeister. I notice for the first time that Colin's hand, to the left corner of the picture, is clenched tight against my shoulder as if holding on for dear life. The knuckles are white. The muscles in his thighs are knotted as if struggling to stand upright. There is a football floating in the pool. I've never noticed that before. It's funny how that can happen. How you can see something a thousand times, then suddenly see something entirely new in it.

There is a loud buzz from the front door that makes me buck. I smooth my hair nervously. My shoes click on the wooden flooring, seem to echo. I open the door. It's Nodge. Jon.

He is shaved – not only his face, but his head, which has been subjected to a full number-one cut. He is wearing a beautiful sky-blue suit, a crisp white shirt, a plain dark tie. There is a white carnation in the lapel. He is tanned, and is a stone lighter than he was. Instead of the once-Plasticine frame of this face, there are the outlines of hard cheekbones. He is smoking a cigarette – a Gitanes – with perfect grace. His unibrow is carefully trimmed and plucked.

He steps forward and he wraps his arms around me in a hug, holds and doesn't let go for about five seconds. I smell some faint, delicate citrussy aftershave. Then he stands back a few feet and inspects me.

The bee's fucking knees, Frankie.

You too, Jon. The bee's fucking knees.

Outside, his Metrocab with two lines of bunting on the bonnet, polished up and gleaming like new. He surveys it proudly, then says, screwing up his eyes against the cigarette smoke and the bright sunshine, *How are you feeling?*

I consider this carefully, retreating back into my house. He follows me, hands now thrust into pockets.

I'm not feeling anything in particular. I don't think I've felt so absolutely neutral in my life. It's like an . . . out of body experience.

Don't worry, he says with a warm smile. *It'll be fine.*

He says this with absolute conviction. It makes me feel better. Not so long ago he would have just grunted or left a long condemnatory silence. But it is clear to me now that he is completely on my side. I feel an enormous gratitude well up inside me.

I pull at my cuffs, adjust my tie. I am a real fuck-off groom, I decide. Full on.

I sit down on the settee, no, the sofa, to compose myself for a few minutes. No. I sit down on the fucking settee. That's what it is. That's who I am. I go to the toilet. I sit in the lounge, I have dinner at lunch-time and I have tea at dinner-time.

Shall we go? says Nodge.

Have you got the ring?

400

He takes a small plain gold hoop out of his pocket and holds it up to the light. A shackle, a halo.

Too early yet.

We both sit down in comfortable silence.

After a while, Nodge says, *I've booked a holiday.*

I knew it, I say. *You're going to Fiji, aren't you? After all these years.*

Nodge looks puzzled.

No, he says. *Pevensey Bay. In Sussex.*

I start to laugh and he joins in.

Way to go, Jon.

I check the clock. I feel preternaturally centred, shocked before the event. I rise, take a last look at myself, then we walk out of the house, Nodge first, and I climb in the back of his cab and he takes the wheel. It's an hour to go until the wedding, but I want to be on the steps to greet everybody. My mum's bought a new video camera especially for the day and she's eager to use it.

It's five minutes to the church. Nodge and I don't speak. I stare out of the window. On the corner at Shepherd's Bush Green, a clutch of young, ill-looking, hair-gelled men stand on the corner, holding cans of beer. One is wearing a QPR shirt. They see the cab approach, clock the bunting and the QPR sticker on Nodge's windscreen and begin shouting and applauding, and waving hello. I wave too, but I, unlike them, am waving goodbye.

We pull up at the church. There is a single figure, my mum, waiting on the steps. She's nearly seventy now, and she's absolutely done up to the nines. Her grey hair has been teased into an elegant bob, her dress is covered with some orange flower I can't name. She is wearing a large maroon hat.

To my right, coming up the road, I see some of the bride's relatives, dressed in high style, all little black dresses and £300 shoes. My mum looks like a dumpy housewife from Shepherd's Bush, which is what she is. She shifts nervously.

Then she looks at me, and the pride and happiness in her face beam out at me like headlights on a Series 5 Beemer. Her shy, apologetic self has been wiped out for this day and replaced with some strange incandescence. I have never seen her so happy. I walk up to her and throw my arms around her, and think how much I love her, and how glad I am she is a dumpy suburban housewife and not someone else. She stands back and surveys me and says only this.

Frankie.

But there is a birth, a childhood, a whole life buried in the word. Her eyes are rimmed with balancing tears. We hold the moment. Then she looks away, as if embarrassed, and starts dithering and fussing and fumbling with the video camera. I feel a strange expansion inside myself, start to laugh idiotically.

The bride's relatives arrive, and I muster myself into some kind of gravitas and greet them with a polite, *All right?*

I kiss their cheeks, although I do not know them.

They are composed, self-possessed, elegant.

Even their handshakes are elegant. Once, they would have made me feel small.

This is all so nice, I think to myself, as I await the guests. Perhaps it really is happening. Perhaps I really will be able to go through with it.

One by one they arrive, friends and strangers both. It is as if the past is washing over me, suddenly renewed. Faces from the board on my wall brought to life again, sometimes after years' absence. They are all bright with proffered happiness. I find it incredible, surprising. Each of them, one by one or in couples, files past me, shaking hands, hugging, grinning, wishing me well. Nodge leads them to their place in the aisles.

The last remnants of the guests are straggling into the church now. A breeze is freshening and I worry that my hair is being forced into uncomplimentary angles. I push it down with the palms of my hands. Then I cover my face with the balls of my palms and push against my eyes and rub, as if to wake myself up. When I remove them, a figure is standing there, in a cheap, badly fitting dark blue suit. He seems fragile, lost, and is blinking too rapidly.

Colin.

Colin doesn't say anything, but just nods and blinks some more and tugs furiously at the left lapel of his suit with thumb and forefinger.

I'm . . . so pleased you could come.

I feel ridiculously formal, a petty officiator. My voice sounds robotic. I didn't expect him to be here, although I sent the invite. I haven't seen him since the day in the park. Then suddenly Colin falls forward into my arms, and I hug him stiffly. Almost immediately he pulls back as if he has shocked himself. When he speaks, finally, it is in a firm, solid voice that sounds too evenly spaced, as if rehearsed.

Frankie, I'm very happy for you. Congratulations, and I hope . . . I hope . . .

Suddenly the words dry, as if he has forgotten some carefully prepared script. He stands silent for a moment, his mouth working as if trying to chew juice out of tobacco. Then he speaks again, forlornly, in almost a whisper.

I brought this for you.

He is holding a small, badly wrapped package. He turns the package around and around in his hands. The gaily coloured paper rustles. It is secured with brown gaffer tape rather than clear tape.

What's in the parcel?

It's a wedding present.

I take the scruffy package. It's small enough to fold and put in my pocket.

Thanks, Colin.

Yeah. Like I said.

He begins to retreat slightly, slowly, then a little faster, down one step then another.

Congratulations . . .

Then, without another word, he bolts. He walks not into the church, but away, round the corner and out of view, at a fast, almost desperate pace.

I feel a hand on my shoulder, turn and see that it

404

is Nodge standing there. He seems fatherly, grave. Behind him, the vicar, professionally smiling while looking at his watch. He looks up and beckons. I feel a tightening in my stomach, turn and begin to walk towards the church doors. I feel suspended, weightless, as if I am treading water.

Heads turn towards me as I make my way down the aisle. My eye focuses on a large stained-glass window to my right showing unrecognizable saints prostrating themselves before Jesus. Looking away, I see the heads continuing to turn. I am a wind parting corn. I am aware of a slight tremble being set up within me, like there was a pager vibrating next to my heart.

I come to the altar, where the vicar stands in his cassock. I rock back and forward in my shoes, giving out a slight, repetitive squeak. We wait. There is an epidemic of muffled coughing and whispers drifting towards me from behind. Then the wedding march strikes up and the congregation rustles like a warehouse full of cellophane.

The bride is approaching down the aisle, absurdly, fluorescently white. She seems stern, wreathed in concentration. I try to take the sight of her within me, to absorb and incorporate it, but somehow it bounces off. She is a woman in a white dress. Who I barely know, who I've spent less time with than half the people in this room. Who is a mystery, an enigma, a lottery ticket, a wild guess. She sweeps towards me, but I cannot give way. Then she is beside me, and I feel a sheen of sweat break out on my brow. The irrevocability of the moment hits me like a mortar. The vicar is smiling. Nodge stands firm to my right like a tree.

Now the vicar has started speaking, beginning the seal on our partnership as it was begun, with a volley of cliché, rendered both more and less real by its familiarity.

Dearly beloved, we are gathered here today . . .

Dearly beloved. Who's he referring to? To us? To the congregation? Is he saying he is in love with the congregation? That's stupid. Or is he saying that they are *our* dearly beloved? Why am I thinking about this now? It's a mere ritual. My wife to be is looking at me through her veil. Her briskness has departed and I see something I haven't seen in her before, a deep nervousness, a fear that bleeds out of her like mist. I see that she is trembling, and I put my hand out to steady her. She vibrates softly, as if fending off cold. Some kind of blackness envelops me.

Vaguely, through the blackness, I hear the vicar's voice, and he is asking if anybody present knows any reason why the couple here should not be duly joined in matrimony, and I hear my own voice, and I am astonished at the voice which is saying, *I have a reason.*

— I have a reason, because marriage is a leap in the dark against the odds.

— I have a reason, because there are other women I could have as easily married and there are dozens more who I could yet marry, and this meeting here today is a

406

product of circumstance and panic and a kind of long stretched out accident of sleepwalking.

– I have a reason, because the woman standing next to me is not something sheathed in white and incorruptible, but is something as frightened and lost and stumbling as everybody else, and we are both just whistling in the dark.

– I have a reason, because I don't want my freedom to do what I wish blotted out by another's purposes.

– I have a reason, because I want things to stay the same for ever and ever, because I want my past like a blanket over me, because I don't want to be someone else.

– I have a reason, because I am stupid and have no idea how to make myself happy, let alone anyone else.

– I have a reason, because this piece of theatre was just meant to be an excuse for a party, a bit of a lark, and it's all gone too far, it all sounds too serious, too transformative, too real.

– I have a reason, because I want to be left alone, to stay in the playground, to be with my boyfriends, to laugh at women and keep life where it deserves to be, as a joke, a game, a giggle, an endless jockeying for position.

– I have a reason, because I'm scared.

And I hear the voice, all in these few seconds, and I say nothing, because the voice is inside me, because the tide of events is too strong now, and because, and because, and because . . .

I want it to be over.

I want it all to change, whatever the result.

The vicar smiles at me and asks, *Do you take this woman?*

And without any hesitation and in a voice which amazes me in its strength and certainty, I say, *I do.*

And then he says, *Do you, Veronica Tree, take this man to be your lawful wedded husband?*

Veronica says the same, and the vicar says stuff about pronouncing us man and wife, and we kiss, and at that moment – as advertised – I am changed, in the twinkling of an eye.

The reception is a happy, drunken affair at a large room above the Bush Ranger, in which I dance with my mum, and I dance with Veronica's dad, and everyone laughs and shouts and falls over and makes stupid speeches.

Now we are driving to my house to get changed for the honeymoon, with Veronica by my side. We are both a little bit drunk and laughing at anything at all. We stagger up the stairs together, and I find myself ridiculously carrying her over the threshold. I look in her face and somehow I know that I would not have loved her as much, no, not that, would have loved her *differently*, if we had not been through what today we shared.

Is my freedom gone? What the fuck is that? A little drop of life between childhood and marriage. It's not all it's cracked up to be. Marriage is what happens when you learn that life is bigger than you.

Is it me who's thinking this? Or is it something I'm just meant to think?

I am waiting for Veronica, who is in the bathroom, making final preparations for our trip to some obscure island in Greece. I feel light-headed and giddy, but the suspension that held me apart from my life has gone, and I am connected to the present and the future instead of just the past. I know there will be endless problems and failures in the future, just as there have been in the past, but it will be a different kind of problem, a new kind, a whole new vista of mistakes, cruelties, reconciliations, of as yet unknown love.

I hear Veronica moving about in the bathroom and find myself distracted, impatient. I thrust my hand in my pocket. Something rustles there, smooth against my hand.

It's the gift Colin gave me on the church steps. Idly, I tear off the shiny paper, which is undecorated, a solid block of red. I imagine the gift to be some kind of half-mad fragment of scripture, or perhaps a biblical calendar. It is certainly simply made of paper, but it seems old, worn out, ripped at the edges. It is folded into four segments and tied with a piece of simple string.

I cannot undo the knot on the string, so I find a knife from the kitchen and cut it open. Then slowly, so delicate does the paper seem, I unfold it, and blink at what is revealed. I cannot at first say what it is, a mess of flaking colours and uncertain shapes. Then at once it comes to me. I see the yellow sun, the sky the colour of a Zoom ice lolly, I see the two figures on the empty beach, the rolling dunes, the concentration of love at the centre of it. I stare at Colin and me, our lost childhood selves.

Then Veronica walks in the room, in a simple black dress, no make-up, a faint, vulnerable smile, and I glance back at the picture and think that I understand, for the first time, the power of the feeling that went into the making of it. For the first time, I understand the picture. It makes me want to weep.

I slowly fold it up again and put it carefully to one side. I lean over to give Veronica a kiss. She kisses back quickly, briskly, has returned slightly to her old efficiency, but she too has changed. She is dreamy, softened. Maybe, like me, on this day, at this time, she thinks it will last. And who am I to say that it won't? Nothing's certain. Everything that marriage is there to deny is what, in the end, gives it hope.

Looking forward to the honeymoon? she says.

Christ, yes. I want it to go on for ever. Already, I'm dreading having to go back to the office. And we haven't even started yet.

She smiles. I turn to her with a sudden burst of earnestness.

You know . . . maybe . . . just maybe . . . I'll give up this estate agent lark. All this lying, finagling, dodgy dealing. Maybe I'll go back to university – a proper university, Oxford or Cambridge, not Staines Tech. Maybe I'll study a proper subject. After all, I am clever. More clever than that job deserves. Do a degree in literature, or history.

Veronica looks at me cautiously. She gives me a look which says, *What?!*

I start to laugh, right deep in the belly.

*Vronky, you're bang on. I **like** being an estate agent. It's my . . . it's my **destiny**. It's great. I like lying. I'm good at it. Who wants to study for three years and come out with a headache, and knowing less than you did before? Stuff that for a game of soldiers. I am . . . I am **Frank the Fib**, the legendary Frank the Fib, of Farley, Ratchett & Gwynne.*

She throws her arms around me.

Frank the Fib, she says, her eyes shining, just like in the movies. Then she says, *Tell me a lie.*

I'm hardly listening. I look down at her big face, her smudgy nose, her wonderful glowing eyes, and a wave of emotion sweeps over me. I grab both her hands, bring my face close, and I say, *I love you, Vronky.*

And she takes a step away, brings back her arm and her hand flies towards me. I catch her wrist just before it lands on my cheek, bewilderment flexing a thousand small muscles on my face. As I catch it, I feel her relaxing from her momentary fury. Relaxing, as she sees, as she sees, as she understands, that for once, and at last, I was *doing* it, against my nature, my principles and my habit and my life. I was *doing* it and I couldn't help myself, I was out of control. So her slap turns into an embrace, as she realizes, and as she knows, that for once, that for once, that for once, I am telling The Truth . . .

CHAPTER 21

PUNCHLINE

. . . I *think*.